Through Magic and Mayhem

The Adventures of Eka and Christelle

Book One

S.D. PIXLEY

Published by *Dreaming of Dancing Bubbles*

An imprint of Shelrie Dawn's Desk, LLC
Florida, USA

Copyright © 2021 Shelrie Dawn Houlton

www.DreamingOfDancingBubbles.com

Front cover image by Casey Gerber.
Book design by Lorna Reid.
Story Edit by Claire Baldwin
Copyedit by Nick Hodgson

Graphics from the following sources:
freepgnimg.com
openclipart.org
Vector-Images.com
BuySellGraphic.com

ISBN (Paperback): 978-0-9992608-4-5
ISBN (Epub): 978-0-9992608-5-2

Part One

Eka Breaks Down

Eka brought her left foot up on the cab seat next to her and rested her arm on her knee against the window, the road smooth ahead. Finally, she'd be on time for a job, maybe even early.

"This is the life." She sighed contentedly, tapping on the steering wheel to a song on the oldies station. Suddenly, bright, rainbow-hued light erupted inside the truck's cab, blinding Eka and upending her usually innate sense of direction. She swerved right across the rural road, her cheek slamming her knee, and onto what felt like the most uneven bit of grass shoulder in existence.

"Whattt tthhee…" Her rattling voice cut off as her phone flashed a blinding rainbow light again, just as she was starting to make sense of the line between grass and asphalt. She instinctively threw her arm over her eyes and flipped down the visor, which, of course, did nothing to block the blinding light. It did, however, aid in the escape of a box of Tic-Tacs, which bounced off her forehead, followed by a few maps and a butt-load of bills, all of which managed to cartwheel off her face.

"Hey!"

Eka finally managed to pull off the road completely, slamming her truck into park on the grass between the narrow lane and the ditch. Rubbing her forehead, she tentatively reached for her phone on the passenger seat. Just as she made contact, the sneaky little bastard buzzed to life, startling her head into the window with a third burst of color.

"Ow!"

Then, the phone lay suspiciously quiet.

"Are you trying to kill me?"

Still no movement, the screen lit only by icons. Taking a deep breath, Eka closed her eyes and snatched the phone, tensing for fireworks. Nothing. She slid one eyelid open. Still nothing. Then her second eyelid inched warily open, but the phone just lay there, in her palm, innocent and quiet. For now.

"Don't think I trust you."

Sighing, she blinked away splotches of rainbow colors floating in her vision blocking parts of the wooded, nondescript, lacking-in-signs area surrounding her.

Shit, I'm lost.

She tossed the paper map of Florida off the passenger seat and onto the floorboard trashpile of empty water and soda bottles. She really needed to figure out where she was, which meant using the phone. Another breath, tension gripping her body, she tapped on a mapping app and…it opened. Without the multi-colored blitz of light.

After a moment of shock she relaxed. Until she saw the screen with a ton of waiting, unread texts. All from the same person.

"It's so time for a new number," she muttered as she pulled back onto the road. "Seriously, how many times can she text?"

Her truck creaked and she eyed the dashboard. "What?"

Years of driving alone left her talking to the truck and now she found it to be a better listener than most. Almost as if she were talking to herself. Almost. Because admitting to constant conversations with yourself was definitely that one step too close to the cliffs of crazy.

Just then the truck creaked and she shrugged. "I had to sneak out. I mean she was getting clingy." Without waiting for another creak, because when would that happen, she switched to talking to the quiet dashboard. "A bedroom window is, too, an exit. Besides, she didn't have any sense of humor. What?" As if she needed a prompt to continue this very one-sided tale. "It was funny. And, it's not like I meant for her tires to fall in the molasses when we hid them." Her right hand came off the stick shift as she animated her story with gestures. "I mean, we got her car off the tracks with almost no damage. You know," she shook her head, "some people can't take a joke."

The next creak seemed to mock her and she narrowed her eyes at the dashboard. "Like you know anything about humor. Or dating."

Just then, a memory resurfaced, of a midnight swim, clothes left on the shore, skin pressed against skin. Eka smiled. "She had her moments, though."

She caught the steering wheel with her knee and entered her destination into the map app, blinking at the ETA.

"Eight frickin' hours? That can't be right."

Eka lunged for the fallen map, toppling bottles and swerving along the road. She finally managed to grab the grubby, folded paper and, by some fortune, stay in her lane. Mostly. When she finally checked her route on paper against the app, it showed the same thing. She'd missed her exit by forty-five miles. Tracing and retracing the route ended at the same spot. "Ninety miles of gas and time gone." And late for her gig.

"Ahhhh!" She threw up her hands, just to slam them back on the wheel as her rig swerved across the road. "Jees!" Eka eyed the dashboard. "What's your issue?"

Without waiting for an answer, she shifted down and started to maneuver into a U-turn. Just then she caught a glimpse, in the rear-view mirror, of familiar rainbow colors dancing across the sky behind her. She spun around in her seat just in time to watch a palm tree fall across the road. And block her way back to her missed exit.

Eka blinked at the tree spanning the road, then slowly sat forward.

"Great." Outside, blue skies stretched as far as forever, cloud-free.

She glared at her phone. Had that lightning really been the same color as the weird flash from her phone? Outside, no other rainbow flashes marred the clear sky. What the hell was going on? It was like something was playing with her.

"I'm not a toy!" she yelled at the sky.

Who am I yelling at?

"Get it together. Probably some weird local weather thingy."

Probably.

"And a phone glitch. With similar color bursts as the weather."

Right.

Eka stared at the sky, then back at her phone, and finally shook her head to clear out all the weirdness. "Focus on getting to that freakin' job."

She inhaled deeply, the air distracting her enough to focus, then blew out and scanned the fold-out map. After a few moments, a long, winding, maze-like route took shape. "Okay." Leaning out the window, she took a last look at the suddenly inconvenient palm, then the road ahead. "Guess I'm going forward."

Driving a few uneventful miles relaxed her shoulders, then her back, and finally her mind. The radio came on and 'That's Life' blared in the cab, her voice challenging Frank's for volume, if not pitch. As she sang along, swaying to the beat, her left hand undulated in the gusty breeze, moving to the rhythm. As the song ended, lightning, this time the standard bright-white variety, flashed across the sky to frame dark clouds rolling towards her from the left.

"A storm? Are you kidding me?"

She eyed the folded map again, which only highlighted the miles of roads before she was back on track, and slumped down the bucket seat. "I'm never gonna make that gig tomorrow."

Overdue bills, now strewn across the cab, almost shouted their demands at her, while outside, thunder grumbled closer and a few raindrops hit her windshield. Squeezing the steering wheel, she glanced between the clouds and the bills.

"Ugh. Fine, I'll stop until it passes."

Deep breath.

Eka sat up, raising her eyebrows at all of it. "I could really use a nap and shower anyway. And Ron will totally see that, late or not, his aerial show can't live without me, rigger extraordinaire."

This time, the creak was right on time, a perfect segue.

"Exactly. I'll just turn on the charm. Always worked before." She winked at the dashboard then glanced back at the phone. "If I'm gonna find a proper camping spot, I need your help. But if you so much as flash a rainbow emoji, I swear I'll throw you out the window." She brought the phone close to her face. "One piece at a time."

The mapping app continued to move the little car on the original route she'd typed in, no strange flashes lighting up the truck's cab. Satisfied, she searched for an RV park nearby and hoped there was time to hook up the camper before the storm caught up. "Focus, Eka. Do not get distract—?" A worn wooden sign flashed by, hanging at an angle with the words

'Hapton's Place' painted on it in sun-worn blue.

"Hapton. Huh."

The name had a faintly, familiar feel. A faded, hazy agitation, swirling in darkness and fear, caught her breath, crawled across her skin, and set off a wave of goosebumps. Before she could suck in any air, a rapid fire of sensations drowned out the fear; a long-ago flash of rainbow light, a memory of trees, the smell of earth and heavy humidity, her grandmother hugging her, a sense of love and connection, belonging.

Belonging.

She shook her head and cracked the memory's hold on her. "Home is where the heart is, right?" She patted the dashboard. "And my family is with me wherever I go."

No creak always meant it was implied, because a conversation needs two. So off she went in answer to the unspoken creak.

"Yes, Sema and Win are family too. Speaking of which." The sensation of her grandmother's hug, from her memory, flitted back. "Maybe Sema knows something about Hapton's Place."

She smiled and tapped her grandmother's icon on the phone, listening to the few rings.

"Hello Little Bird." The familiar voice danced out of the phone.

"Hey Sema." Eka smiled. "How's Bali?"

"Oh, I left there weeks ago. Win and I are off to New Zealand. How's your travels?"

"Of course you already left." Sema could never sit still. "I'm driving down the coast of Florida right now. Hopefully to a gig. Listen, I saw a sign that seemed familiar. You know a Hapton's Place?"

"Oh." Sema sucked in a breath. "Are you there at Hapton's?"

"You know it?"

"Um, yes. It's a great place. Wonderful people."

Eka squinted as more rain drops hit the windshield. "Did we go there once? The name seems…familiar."

The line went quiet and Eka frowned. "You okay?"

"What? Oh, I'm fine. Just memories. Anyway, we went there, right after…" Sema coughed. "Um, when you came to live with us. There's a farm and a preserve. And the Haptons are wonderful people. You should stop by; maybe you'll remember more."

At the mention of that time period, Eka's chest tightened. She grabbed the twisted vines of her childhood bracelet, turning it around her left wrist to the smooth surface of a lone shell. Rubbing the shell with her thumb, breath expanded and contracted her chest until her heart slowed, and pushed thoughts of her parents and Ke from her mind.

"Eka, I didn't mean to bring them up."

"No, no I'm fine. Just distracted by the weird weather. I'm stopping soon at an RV park. Probably should go."

"I could call Shirley Hapton. She's an old friend," Sema almost whispered. "I'm sure you could stay there."

"Um, the weather just turned. Gotta go!" Eka heard 'love you' as she hung up.

Don't think about them. Focus on the road.

A few, slow heartbeats later she sighed and threw the phone on the seat. Her truck purred down the quiet road and Eka turned up the radio even more, joining back in and drowning out any lingering memories. A few miles farther, the road angled up onto a causeway, a large river flowing languidly below.

Eka gazed across water, sparkling in the few rays of sunlight fighting their way through heavy, dark clouds while pelicans glided inches over the surface. Despite the strangling thoughts of a few moments ago, a laugh bubbled out of her as a dolphin broke the surface of the water and undulated in and out of the waves. A second dolphin jumped straight up, a few rays of sun glinting off its back before it splashed back down. The shimmer off the dolphin's skin reminded her of something. Another dolphin, a beach, her parents. Images flashed through her thoughts and Eka's temples erupted in pain as a strange memory played in her mind.

"Mama, dolphins!"

Eka pointed to movement in the water as her small legs pulled her to the edge of the ocean. Without a single hesitant step, she plunged into the waves, the sound of her parents' voices fading as water flowed around her and wrapped her in a liquid blanket. Beneath the surface, the ocean opened up to her and she lost herself in an unending playground. Darting through bluish-green water, Eka searched for the dolphins as warmth rolled in her chest, morphing to heat as it spread out to her finger tips. A giggle of bubbles escaped her at the glowing violet shimmer of her skin and the suddenly swirling water. Her violet light mixed with the pale, greenish-blue glow of the ocean and she was gently pulled forward by a watery caress. Just then a rough surface brushed against her leg. She instinctively grabbed at the dolphin's fin, which turned and dragged her up, up, up until they broke the surface. She sucked in air as the creature pulled her along, giggles eventually tumbling out of her and mixing together with the dolphin's chatter as they cut through the waves, then jumping high above the water. A tickle suddenly danced across the back of her neck as the warmth of her mother flowed over her.

Eka, come home! Her mother's silent call went through her.

She let go of the dolphin with a hug, then relaxed on the ocean's surface as it glided her to the beach, rolling her ashore. She giggled as she tumbled onto the sand, only stopping when she bumped into her mother's feet.

"Ekanam Rahasia, what did you think you were doing?" Her mother frowned down at her.

Eka wiped sand from her eyes and smiled up. "I was playing." She pointed to a disappearing fin and rolling waves.

Her mother helped her up and took her hand, leading her back to their blanket. "You haven't started your training. You're not ready to do these things alone."

"But she is already in tune with water, dolphins, air. Amazing," her father said, popping up from the sand Ke had buried him under.

"I'm amazing too!" Ke stomped his foot and glared at Eka.

"Of course you are." Their mother swept him up in a hug and he wrapped his arms around her neck.

"Really?" Ke asked.

"Of course!" Their father laughed as he broke free of the sand, shaking his body and sending sand spraying every where. He picked up Eka, then stumbled into the others and they all fell to the blanket, giggling and hugging.

"See," Ke stuck his tongue out at Eka, "I'm amazing."

"I know." Eka smiled at Ke and squeezed his hand.

The four of them lay on the blanket until the sun started to appear. The pinks and blues of sunrise outlined the few clouds floating by and reflected off the water.

"Look how late it's getting." Their father sat up. "We've got to get you two home and in bed." He tousled Ke's hair. "Don't want to be tired for the first night of training."

Her mother ran a hand through Eka's hair. "I can't believe my babies are seven already."

Her father grinned and pulled a bundle from his pocket, untying the cloth to reveal a small, brown clump that crumbled to pieces. Eka squinted closer and touched the pile, dirt moving around under her fingers. From his other pocket, he pulled out a seed and pushed it into the dirt. His body glowed a bright orange that flowed from his hands to the earth and a moment later an a'ali'i sprout popped up from the soil in his hand, exploding in growth. Tiny banches pushed out of the sapling and leaves emerged along with buds that opened into bright red flowers. Eka and Ke watched with wide eyes as the plant slowed it's growth to about the size of Eka's arm.

"This a'ali'i plant marks an incredible family moment." He stood up and spread his arms, as if announcing to a crowd. "The time Eka and Ke started training and changed the world."

His voice seemed sillier today and Eka giggled but Ke crossed his arms.

"Dad, this is important." Ke actually stomped his foot and their father put on his more serious face.

"Of course. This is serious for all of us." He nodded and Ke seemed to relax a bit.

Their mother, smiling slightly, gently took the plant and held it between them. "We'll plant it at home and it'll grow with you both. You'll always remember your first step as a Waker."

Their father, grinning again, pulled them all, even the plant, into a giant hug. "Okay, first step, training. But then, the world!"

A pothole jerked Eka back to the present. She'd barely noticed the road, only vaguely aware of leaving the causeway and river behind. Dense stands of trees now whizzed by on either side, the hint of water sparkling through the trees on her left.

"What the hell?" She shook her head trying to clear out the weird memories. "I am not going crazy."

Even though there wasn't even a hint of a creak, she really needed to talk to someone, or something.

"No, I'm not. Just because I remember communing with the ocean and dolphins? Or dad growing a plant in his hand in seconds. Or my family…" Her suddenly shaky hand touched the picture taped to the dashboard, an image of her parents smiling, their arms wrapped around her and Ke. Eka slapped her face. "I'm just tired."

Yet the memory kept replaying. She could almost feel the cool, fluid blanket of the ocean and the rough skin of the dolphin as it pulled her through the water. Another pothole woke her from this second, shorter trance, but the thought of her family lingered as her chest squeezed the breath out of her. They were gone, lost long ago and a few memories were all she had now.

But she knew for a fact, the movie that had just played in her mind wasn't one of those memories. Frantically spinning her childhood bracelet, she twisted it until her wobbly fingers found the smoothness of the shell. Her tension eased and Eka scratched at a wet tickle on her cheek, smearing a tear across her face.

"No, no, no. Not going there. No looking back, only forward." She rubbed at her eyelids, eyeballs flashing light from the assault. "Nothing there but pain and dead-ends." She patted the dashboard again. "In other words, Crazy Town. So, just you and me, and adventures ahead."

A dimmer flash of colorful light erupted from within the cab and she looked down to find her phone's screen pulsing with those frickin rainbow hues. Eka's brow creased and she shook the phone, then banged it on the dashboard. The pulsing light faded and the map popped back up.

"What is going on with this thing?"

"Turn right in point-five miles." She jumped at the app's robotic voice.

"I really need to pick a better voice." Setting the phone back down, she readjusted in the seat and looked for the turn.

The turn was quick and she eased her truck and camper onto a two-lane road already showing signs of civilization. Old buildings replaced dense woods along the river's edge. A few men with cold beers sat outside one of the buildings, a small, blue shack with a sign that sighed, more than stated, that this was Salty's Bait and Beer. Tom's Orchid and Bonsai sign was much more dignified, and maybe a bit judgmental of Salty's sign, as it sat on a large plot across the road from the bait and beer. Tom's plot had an old seafoam green cottage out back, and on the front lawn a large group of people gathered up stuff from picnic benches ahead of the impending storm. Despite these signs of a community, Eka passed nothing that even remotely resembled an RV park or campground. After a few miles, the community ended and the sides of the road became densely wooded again.

Nothing? Not even a rest area?

She flipped the headlights on just past the last street lamp's fading light in the darkening afternoon. The glowing map display hinted at a route that would take her into a large patch of undeveloped land, not towards an RV park. Apparently the map had been reset.

"Hapton's Place in two miles." The robot voice echoed through the cab.

"What?" Eka pulled over onto the grassy shoulder. "Hapton's Place again?" The strange memories, her family by the ocean and her grandmother hugging her, returned along with the tightness in her chest.

"I'm not going to Hapton's Place," she growled at the phone.

She scanned the narrow road and the ditches to the sides, estimating her turning radius, then glared at the map display. Was she being herded to Hapton's? Her forehead scrunched at that weird possibility. "Ha!" She shook her head. "That would just be crazy."

Eka grabbed the paper map and traced a route back to a main road through the town she'd just passed.

"Okay, that's doable." Thunder grumbled. "Hopefully." She scanned right and left then pulled forward in a turn, using the entire road. "Just as long as no cars show up in the next twenty minutes."

Her turn didn't clear the opposite ditch so she put the truck in reverse just as a flash of colorful light ran across the sky, striking the base of a palm tree just ahead and to her left. The tree wobbled and, in slow motion, toppled across the road, blocking her return route. Her mouth dropped open and she stared at the palm.

"Did I piss off a unicorn?" She looked around for the source of the strange, colorful lightning. "Maybe a leprechaun?"

After moment followed moment without a real answer (seriously, had she expected one?), Eka pushed open the door and got out of the truck. She crept over to the felled palm and lightly tapped it once then jerked back her hand. Nothing happened. "Normal tree."

For now.

There seemed to be two options. Continue on or move the tree. "Okay, I can move this. No problem." She arched her back and touched her toes, then grabbed a palm frond and pulled, straining against the truck-sized tree laying casually across her escape.

"I. Am. Not. Going. To. Hapton's. Place," she grunted at the immobile hunk of tree. The frond slipped, getting in a few slaps to her face before she tumbled back.

"Oh, you want to make this personal." She glared at the tree then strode back to the truck. "There's still a turnoff at the end of the road. Ha!" she yelled.

Eka jumped in the truck and slammed into gear. Singing 'My Way', her voice drowned the radio as adrenaline pushed her faster down the road. "I'll be at an RV park before the rain starts." She looked at the blackened sky, the few drops not yet turning into rain. "What's it waiting for? Is luck finally smiling at me?"

She grinned at the strange but hopeful weather, then another multi-colored flash ripped through the sky. Illumination spread across the landscape, a tight curve appearing ahead as a crack exploded beyond the turn.

Her face dropped. "Oh no."

She held the wheel tight as the truck and camper rushed into the turn and slid around the curve, barely gripping the asphalt. The whole shebang almost two-wheeled it around the curve.

When the road straightened, and her truck finishing bouncing, she exhaled and glanced back.

The vardo's still attached and in one piece!

But, when she turned forward, the source of the crashing sound lay in front of her. A massive oak branch blocked the road ahead. She gripped the steering wheel for, like, the hundredth time, and swerved left to avoid it. A front tire bounced off the limb and the steering wheel ripped from her hands and spun right. She grabbed it and pulled with everything she had to the left but the back right tire hit the branch and lifted briefly, jolting the cab like a shaking roller coaster. Her phone flew off the passenger seat and out the window.

"Damn, damn, and double damn!" Eka eased up on the brakes and hung on to the steering wheel, managing to pull off to the side of the branch and stop without jackknifing the trailer. When the world, thankfully, stopped moving, Eka finally exhaled and looked out the window.

And sucked in another lungful of air as she stared at a canal that dropped off just inches from her front bumper. Moments later, her lungs screamed for fresh air. She finally exhaled and breathed, then slid out of the cab and walked around to the back of the truck. The thumping in her chest drowned out the sounds around her, even the thunder.

"Crap."

The camper, still hooked to the truck, sat at a strange angle. Her wobbly legs finally gave way; she fell against the little vardo and slid to the ground.

What was she going to do?

She absently reached up, gently running her fingers across the intricate wood carvings attached to the outside of the wooden camper. Another memory, a familiar one of the smell of used oil and rusty metal, drifted into her mind. That wonderful day, in an Oregon junkyard, she'd nearly stumbled over the broken wheels of the discarded vardo. She'd stood there, falling in love as the minutes went by. Her grandfather just shook his head when she'd dragged it home, later laughing at her plan to bring it back to life. She ran her hands over the decorative white shells and dolphins she and her bemused grandfather had carved, carefully attaching each one to the exterior over a seafoam green coat of paint.

"And he thought I wouldn't stick around to finish." She smiled, then sighed. "But now look at you."

Patting the camper's jacked-up wheel, she assessed the damage. "What to do, what to do?" Another deep breath, then she hopped up and kissed the camper. "Nothing to do but get help. Now, where is that phone?" She patted her pockets.

"Oh, yeah." Yet another sigh as the image of her phone flying out the window and disappearing into the dark, flitted through her mind's eye. "But it has to be here somewhere."

With no other option, she scanned the ground, crawled under the truck, waded through brush and tall grass. But despite an epic search, the phone remained elusive. After a third pass underneath the truck, she lay on the ground with her legs poking out from under the pickup bed. She stared along the ground, gravel pressing into her cheek as her mind stalled.

Fortunately, the weather jump-started her motivation as raindrops hit her legs and the wind picked up, running across her back.

"Eka, get a hold of yourself." Crawling out from under the truck was trickier, and less graceful, than getting under it, but she squirmed out and brushed off the dirt and pebbles, then eyed the sky. "Okay Universe, now what?"

As if on cue, colorful light flashed above a house sitting back from the road. Around her the sky dimmed further and the rain fell like little pellets against her skin. The wind blew colder, rushing over her face and yanking her hair straight back.

"Weeellll." She slowly scanned her surroundings. Her broken truck and camper, the giant branch that blocked her way, her missing psychotic phone. Then there was the stalkery rainbow lightening. "Maybe I'll take a quick break." She backed away from the destruction on the road, closed up the truck, and power-walked towards the house. "Yeah, can't hurt to stop for a minute." Another flash crossed the sky. "Or longer." She broke into a run, heading straight for the house, and wondered just what flavor of crazy was taking over her life.

Christelle Sees the Light

Christelle dropped the book, again, and stared at the kitchen walls. When had the paint gotten so dingy? And her grandmother's bright, colorful clothing clashed hard with the dull, brown-mottled counter tops and nothing-but-scratched stainless-steel sink. Her brain actually hurt taking in the two extremes.

"What happened to the kitchen, Grams?"

Shirley glanced up from the runes on the table.

"Looks the same to me."

Christelle shook her head. "Didn't it used to be bright yellow?" She looked quickly around. "And bigger?"

Shirley chuckled. "You're just growing up, kiddo. Always been blah in here."

"I guess." Then Christelle inhaled salty air from the open window, the smell as comforting now as when she was little. It was good to be back here. Still, the kitchen could use some help. "Didn't you guys ever want to change it?"

Shirley shrugged and pushed the runes around into a seven-stone spread. "Better things to do. Like see what the future has in store."

Christelle leaned toward the runic spread, forgetting the kitchen for a moment. "What do they say?"

Shirley raised an eyebrow then tilted her head and slowly ran her fingers over the surface of the runes. Her hand stopped and hovered over the stones' pattern, then she inhaled sharply.

"What is it, Grams?" Christelle asked, moving behind Shirley.

"I think…wait."

Christelle leaned further over her shoulder.

"There's something coming." Her voice just a whisper. "A darkness."

A chill went through Christelle as she focused on the runes. Christelle hadn't seen a lot of her grandmother's readings, but what she had seen was often uncannily spot on, and this time her grandmother looked seriously troubled. "Really? Can you see what it is?"

Shirley sat and stared at nothing for a minute, then looked sideways at Christelle. She waved her hand as if shooing flies. "Don't worry, I think I just read it wrong."

Christelle frowned. "Grams, what's going on?"

At that moment thunder rumbled in a darkening sky.

"Oh, must mean the storm." Shirley frowned briefly as she glanced out the window, mumbling. "Yep, there it is. Reading's never wrong."

"Really?" Christelle sat back across the table from her grandmother. "You seemed so worried just now."

Shirley turned back from the window, then blinked a few times.

"What's going on?" Christelle asked again, narrowing her eyes at Shirley.

Shirley shook her head, then absently patted Christelle's hand. "Nothin, kiddo; you're reading too much into this."

Christelle jerked her hand away. "Fine, don't tell me."

Why did I even come here, I could be back with Dad, working on my aerials. Appreciated.

Her hands started tingling, a tingling that'd been bothering her since she'd arrived here a week ago. What was up with her skin? And her sudden irritability? Staying here was supposed to be a nice break. Like when she was young and she'd come her with Dad. But it wasn't the same without him this time.

I've got to get out of this slump.

A bolt of lightning shot across the sky in front of the window and Christelle jumped at the thunderous crack.

Shirley, without a flinch, pushed the runes around some more. "Relax, honey."

Christelle sighed and rubbed her tingling hands. "Sorry. Guess I'm not settled in. And it's kinda strange being here without Dad. I worry about him." A rogue tear made a break for it, but she quickly crushed it. "What if he doesn't understand the accounting software? Or doesn't remember the show schedule..."

Shirley slapped the table and Christelle jumped, again. "Slow down there. You need to take a breath. Your father can handle all that; he's a grown adult."

"I guess," she nodded. "It's just...I've been doing all that for him for a while."

Shirley scooped up the runes and dropped them in a bag. "You've done an amazing job taking care of your father. And you've become a standout performer in those traveling shows. But that's the life your father chose. You, kiddo, are supposed to be taking a break." Shirley raised an eyebrow at her. "And trying something new. Figuring yourself out." She slapped the table again and hopped up. "Now, how about some tea? Good for what ails ya."

And with that, Shirley sauntered over to the stove and put the kettle on.

"I just..." Christelle sighed, "don't know what to do? What I want."

Shirley leaned against the stove and narrowed her gaze at Christelle. "Give yourself some time. Doesn't happen over night. Look at me." Shirley raised her arms. "I still don't know what I'm doing."

Christelle's grin escaped her struggle against it and spread across her face. "You're a bad role model."

Just then, the kitchen door swung open and a tall woman strode in. "Your grandmother *is* a horrible role model." Anise's arms wrapped around Christelle and she sunk into her aunt's warm hug.

"Hey, I'm your mother." Shirley crossed her arms, starring at Anise. But her pursed lips twitched, hinting at the grin waiting to explode.

"Uh huh. Ben still doesn't know how you got his truck hanging in the tree like that."

"What?" Christelle stared at Shirley. "You put a truck in a tree?"

Shirley turned toward the kettle. "Just practicing driving. Going for my test next week."

Anise dropped her arms and stared. "Your what?"

"What is all the noise in here?"

Her uncle Ben stood in the doorway. Anise strode toward him and he absently wrapped his arms around her waist. Christelle noticed, for the millionth time, the contrast between her aunt and uncle; Anise's dark skin against Ben's pale skin, her short, tight hair against his red, unruly mop, and her need of solitude pushing up against his love of people. Yet the balance was inescapable. They worked and Christelle loved the energy from their connection.

"Mom wants a driver's license." Anise turned from Ben, his arms still around her, narrowed eyes on Shirley. "You are not ready."

"She really wants to?" Ben whispered.

"I'm doing it," Shirley stated from the stove.

"Uh huh," Anise responded, crossing her arms.

"Who's hungry?" Ben piped up, squeezing Anise around the waist.

"Me!" Christelle jumped in. Grams and Aunt Anise seemed to be fighting more this visit, or maybe she hadn't noticed before. Why did everything seem so tense and…off?

Ben sighed and grabbed Anise's hand. "We'll get some stuff from the garden."

Anise held her ground, silently, for a moment, then mirrored Ben's sigh. "Should we have a picnic?"

"In the storm?" Christelle frowned. Why did Aunt Anise always wanted to eat outside? Or hang out outside? Or everything outside?

"No," Anise shook her head, then smiled at Christelle. "Of course not. Would you mind setting the table?"

Christelle nodded as Ben pulled Anise outside. Christelle crossed to the cabinets, taking the dishes down then stacking them on the counter. "Grams, could you help with…" she turned around to find a missing Grams just as the kitchen door opened and a tall, familiar man walked in.

"Hey, Gramps. Hungry?" Christelle held up a dish.

"Absolutely. Seen Shirley?"

"She was here a minute ago."

He eyed the dishes and nodded slightly. "I see. Like some help?"

"That'd be great."

Bu grabbed some plates from the counter and joined her at the table.

She loved her grandfather's smooth way of moving. Almost as if every movement was part of a dance, graceful and quiet. She rarely got time alone with him, though. "Do you ever miss home?"

He frowned, setting a plate down. "I am home."

She shook her head. "No. I mean China, when you were a kid. All the things you did there, grew up with, your family."

He set down the rest of the dishes and patted a seat. "What is going on? I know that look. You aren't just curious about my childhood."

Christelle shrugged. "I don't know, maybe missing Dad."

"Ahhh." He patted her hand. "Sometimes leaving what we know is hard. Especially if there isn't a clear way forward." He leaned in. "We're all just making it up as we go. You can change your mind anytime."

Her heart did ache for her father and their familiar life, but she had agreed to come here. To try something new. Even if it had taken her dad months to convince her to. "I know."

"And I'm happy you came."

His smile was contagious and she grinned back at him.

"How about going out on the boat with me tomorrow? Thought I'd get out before the sun came up. Maybe lunch on one of the islands?"

"Before the sun?" She grimaced. "Maybe."

"Adventure awaits for no one," he chuckled. "At least that's the magic words Shirley used to lure me away from home and travel the world with her. Didn't know her home town was smaller than mine until I got here. The way she talked about Manatee Isles, I thought it was a bustling city."

"She does tell good stories."

"The best."

Anise and Ben walked in with baskets of food.

"Mom disappeared, huh?" Anise asked, to no one really, and Christelle and Bu exchanged glances, laughing.

Soon the meal was ready. Salty air mixed with the scent of Anise's freshly baked bread. Of course, Shirley popped in just as the work finished and she was the first to dig in, before the rest of the group had even sat down. These were the moments Christelle loved, when everyone gathered around and chatted. She sank deeper into her chair as the sounds of her family washed over her. Ben whispered in Anise's ear and her face broke into a big grin. Shirley and Bu kept poking each other and stealing food off each other's plates. The kitchen's beauty may have been a childhood illusion, but this room still held some magic. The chatter drifted off as everyone finished their meal and sat back.

"Thanks for that food you two." Bu smiled at Anise and Ben as he patted his stomach.

Shirley nodded. "Agreed! And Christelle and I will clean up."

"Are you volunteering?" Bu's eyes twinkled. "I think I've witnessed a miracle."

Shirley swatted him and he leaned over and tickled her knee. Squirming, she tipped sideways off her chair and rolled away from them all.

"So, the gardens are doing nicely this year." Anise ignored the ruckus as if it happened every night and turned to Christelle. "You ready to start working?" She hadn't said it, but Christelle heard the words between those lines. Learn how to run this place.

Christelle opened her mouth but Shirley, with lightening speed, pulled herself up off the floor and jumped into the conversation.

"Oh pish. She's not interested in farming. She's got art, her performance stuff, maybe classes to teach." Shirley motioned to Christelle. "Did you get your web-thingy up?"

Christelle froze as she glanced at Anise. "I put a few things up. Nothing big yet. But I can still help here."

"I thought we had agreed that you would wait until later for that online stuff," Anise said through pursed lips.

A hush fell over the room. Christelle looked between Anise and Shirley, then pleaded silently with Bu for help. But Bu pushed his chair back and rushed to the door. "Better tie things down; storm might get worse."

Christelle glanced at Ben with the same desperate look, but Ben hopped up and went after Bu. "You need help?"

"Sure," Bu replied without looking back. Ben grabbed his hat off a hook on the wall and they both ran out the door as Anise's glare fell on Christelle.

"I...I thought I could just get started." Christelle worked to disappear into her chair as she rubbed her clammy hands on her shorts. "It takes a while to get noticed."

"You have no idea how long it could take to get noticed." Anise shifted her glare briefly to Shirley, then back to Christelle. "You promised you'd be careful. Not expose yourself."

"Sorry. I really didn't think anyone would see it yet."

Shirley sat back at the table then folded her legs under her and pinched Christelle. "No need to apologize."

"Ow." Christelle rubbed her arm, frowning at Shirley. Why did Grams have to pinch so much?

Anise narrowed her eyes on Shirley. "Shirley…Mom, we talked…"

"Shhh," Shirley's voice rose. "Not every way is a straight path. She needs to get out, explore the world. Grow a bit."

Anise rolled her eyes, clearly not buying Shirley's philosophy.

Christelle opened her mouth to plead for group sanity but decided against it, shrinking frustratedly back from their glares instead. Anise finally looked away from Shirley and sighed. "Honey, you know that we love you. But ever since your mom disappeared," Anise dragged in a long breath at that moment, as Christelle's body tightened, but kept going, "we've worried about you. Especially your dad."

Christelle stopped moving. Her fists balled up and her heart beat ramped up.

"The world is a dangerous place and putting yourself out there is risky." Anise bulldozed onward. "You have to be careful."

A fuzzy memory surfaced in Christelle's mind. A memory of her mom and dad running with her, both yelling, acrid smells all around her, blasts as her own screaming engulfed her. "Stop!"

Anise and Shirley froze and the kitchen went silent. Christelle desperately focused on her panting, slowing down the rhythm of her breathing and calming her heart. After a few minutes, the movie in her mind faded. Heat spread from her cheeks and crossed her face as her eyes misted up. "Sorry I yelled."

Shirley narrowed her eyes at Anise as she patted Christelle's arm. "Again, no need to apologize, kiddo."

Anise nearly ran around the table to wrap her arms around Christelle. "I'm so sorry, honey. Really, I'm just worried about your safety. I should never have brought up your mother. I love you."

Christelle nodded and smeared a tear across her chin, body still tense. "I love you too."

Anise squeezed Christelle harder, seeming afraid to let her niece go.

"Really, everything's alright, Aunt Anise."

"Alright." Anise straightened up, seeming to hesitate.

"You go on." Shirley shooed Anise toward the kitchen door then grabbed some plates and dumped them in the sink. "We've got this."

Anise raised her eyebrows at Shirley's suggestion, but Christelle nodded and, after a moment, Anise left.

Christelle turned and grabbed another stack of dishes. The two of them danced around each other silently as Christelle put the dishes in the sink and turned on the water, while Shirley grabbed a rag and cleaned the table.

Christelle stared out at storm clouds darkening the sky, lightning zipping through them. A few flashes lit up the windowsill and the flowers on it. As she zoned out to the pulses dancing in the clouds, her arms grew warm in the water. Soon the rhythmic motion of washing the dishes soothed the last bit of tension in her body.

"Electrifying, huh?" Shirley's soft voice broke the silence.

Christelle blinked. "What?"

"The storm. All that energy and potential."

Christelle's skin prickled with goosebumps as another flash streaked by. "Does seem like there's electricity in the air." She smiled at a memory. "Dad and I used to sit on the stoop of the camper and watch storms roll through. The lightning in the clouds seemed almost magical."

Shirley finished wiping the table and leaned against the counter near Christelle. "Change is difficult, but I'm glad you're here."

"I love you all, just…" She stopped washing and looked at Shirley. "I was putting together a new aerial act and I had finally got the accounting right. And we had finally stayed with a show for longer than a month." She sighed, her chest tight. "I don't know why he he thought I needed to leave. Why I agreed."

Shirley wrapped her arms around Christelle and gave her a squeeze. "Kiddo, it's way past the time for you to strike out into the world. Even if that world is living with others in your family."

Christelle shook her head. "Well I've done a great job so far, causing everyone to fight."

Shirley ruffled Christelle's hair, a bit too much as Christelle flattened it quickly. "You didn't cause anything. Listen to me. We all want the best for you, we just don't always agree on what that is. And Anise worries more than the rest of us. Likes things to follow rules." Shirley glanced out the window, the shadow of a smile on her face. "I remember when we adopted her and went out to Texas to pick her up. She was just a tiny thing, a baby, yet she had the most serious look. Like she was deciding if we were up to her standards." Shirley chuckled. "She did used to have more fun, but it's like pulling teeth getting her to relax these days. To stop taking care of everyone and worrying. Probably why everyone here comes to her for guidance and healing. She even manages to sort out community disputes. They all look up to her." Shirley suddenly sighed, shaking her head. "So don't be too troubled by her grumbling; she just has a lot of people depending on her. Can make anyone grumpy."

"Wait, she's like the local wise woman?"

"Yep. A lot of people 'round here look to her for advice. Anise is a smart one and has a great instinct for choosing the best course for many things."

"I had no idea."

"Of course not." Shirley raised her eyebrows and smiled. "You haven't really been part of this community, even when you visited." She elbowed Christelle. "Here's your chance now, to learn about your family. And maybe meet some other people who are starting out like yourself."

Christelle shrugged and refocused on the dishes. Maybe Grams was right. She could stay a while, try selling some of her art or teach some aerial classes. It would be nice to meet some people her age. And what did she really know about her family? Anise a kind of community leader. Wow. And Grams. She looked at her grandmother, a woman who, like the rest of her family, seemed weirdly young yet insightful.

"Grams, what's up with you and our family looking…so young? I mean, Gramps looks like he could be Dad and Uncle Ben's brother."

Shirley shimmied and spun. "We're young at heart."

Christelle shook her head and struggled to frown at Shirley's awkward hip shakes, but a smile escaped and soon they were both giggling and shimmying.

"Well maybe I'll get your genes," Christelle giggled.

"No doubt," Shirley winked. "Can you finish up here? I've got somethin' to check on." She turned and left the room before Christelle could reply.

She shook her head and yelled at the door. "Okay, Grams. No problem, as usual."

After a few minutes, an electrical pop went off in the distance and all the lights went out.

What happened?

Christelle fumbled around the darkened kitchen, trying to find a flashlight, candles, anything for a light source. After the fifth empty drawer, she wondered if they ever prepared for anything. Just then more lightning zipped across the window, catching her attention, but she soon forgot it as she noticed another light coming from inside the window.

What is that?

She leaned closer to the windowsill planter and squinted. The surface of the leaves and flowers seemed to be emitting a green, shimmering glow. Mesmerized, she did something she would never, ever do in her cautious, every-day life. Instead of evaluating what a glowing flower could mean before she even thought of a plan of action, she reached slowly over the sink, toward the glowing flower. Somehow, that seemed like the right thing to do. And, as her hand grew close, there seemed to be movement.

Were the petals reaching out to her fingers?

A green light streaked out of the flower and across her hand, igniting a familiar tingling that continued across her body, chased by a surge of green light.

"I'm glowing!" Her own voice seemed so far away.

Then a wave of heat swept over her and a bright flash of lavender light spun out of her skin. It twirled around the green light, flowed across to the plants, and sank into the foliage.

For a moment, the whole world seemed to hold its breath. Then, as the lavender faded, the plants exploded in a burst of growth, twining up and around the entire sill.

A moment later, her skin and the plants went dim in the darkness of the kitchen. Weak and shaking, she fell forward against the sink, her hands barely catching her.

"What the heck? Did those plants just grow?" Plants always grew, but the way they grew seemed…crazy. Christelle's brain grasped at words and concepts but nothing stuck as she slowly sunk to the floor.

When the kitchen lights came back on a few minutes later, she craned up at the windowsill. The plants were now twice their size, covering the entire window and muting the flashes behind them.

"Christelle?" Anise rushed in. "Honey, are you okay?"

Christelle lifted her hand towards the plants. "The…plants. Big."

Anise frowned at the window then turned back to Christelle. "Let's get you to the couch."

Anise helped her out of the kitchen and to the sofa, then brought some water from the kitchen. She sat down next to Christelle and put her hand on her niece's forehead. "I think you had a shock."

Christelle stared toward the kitchen door. "Lightning. Flash. Plants," she mumbled.

Anise briefly eyed the direction of the kitchen. "The plants are fine."

"I saw…they were different. Bigger." She struggled up and pulled herself off the couch, stumbling to the kitchen and pushing open the door. And just stared. All the plants were their normal size. "But…how?"

Anise put her hand on Christelle's shoulder and guided her back to the sofa. "You've had a rough day. Please rest. You're going to need your strength."

Christelle's exhausted brain slowly processed the words. "Need my strength?" Why would she need strength?

Anise shook her head and her mouth seemed to relax. "Just rest. You need a lot of rest."

Rain started to hit the glass windows just as Christelle's eyelids closed in exhaustion. She drifted off to images of giant, glowing plants.

AbbracaBam

Rapping twice on the front door, Eka looked back at the road and pulled her jacket tighter. How was she ever going to get the truck and camper fixed?

A loud 'Hello!' had her spinning around to face a tall, pale, colorful woman in the doorway. Her scarlet hair tried to escape a lime-green fedora and a vest, covered with embroidered astrological symbols, fought against her lavender capris. "Need some help?"

Eka pulled her gaze up from the outfit.

"Uh, um…hi! I'm Eka." She threw on a smile through the flash flood running across her face. "I had some trouble with my ride." She nodded towards the darkened road. "And I can't find my phone. Wondering if I could use yours?"

"Of course, come in. You must be Eka." The woman's green eyes smiled, almost too friendly.

"Wait, what?" Eka took a step back. "How do you know me?"

"Oh, Sema called and said you'd be by. Come in before you drown. Besides, I remember you when you were just a little thing." She lowered her hand to her knees then cocked her head. "No, maybe here." She raised her hand to her shoulders. "I'm Shirley Hapton, by the way."

Eka glanced up at the sky. "Of course, Hapton's. Where else would I be," she mumbled to herself, then stepped slowly inside. "Why'd Sema call?"

Shirley waved off the question. "All worked out." She gestured Eka along as she walked down the hall. "Come on in to the living room."

What was Sema up too and how did she always seem to know where Eka would be?

She watched Shirley's form disappear, sauntering down the hallway like a college girl.

"Fine, I need help," Eka mumbled again, following Shirley down the hallway, "but I'm using the phone and that's it."

But the moment she walked into the living room, Eka's thoughts of Sema vanished. Lightning illuminated the room through walls of glass that rose from the floor and arched into a curved glass ceiling. Sheets of rain flowed down the dome and walls, blurring the light and dark clouds gathering outside.

What is this place?

A prick on her arm jerked her attention down to the spine of a bush pressing into her skin. "Ow." Eka rubbed her arm absently as she traced the bush into a mix of small trees and shrubs jostling for space. What kind of living room was this?

Ahead, small lights lined a narrow walking path that disappeared into more greenery, dotted with flowers and fruit. Faint illumination came from within the plants, the only other lighting on this dreary day.

"Would you like a towel?"

Eka, startled, bumped into Shirley. "Where'd you come from?" Eka could've sworn she'd been out of sight.

"Just know my way around."

"Uh huh." Strange place, strange people. "So, you live in a giant greenhouse?"

Shirley shrugged. "Well, it is a 'living room'."

Really? A bad pun?

Shirley spun and strode down the path, Eka trying to match her pace and keep her in sight. As they walked, a small alcove emerged from the dense foliage. A young woman, with pale blue eyes and a shock of white hair, lay on a couch within it, another woman next to her in a white and aqua dress, bright against her brown skin that mirrored Eka's.

Shirley gestured at the blonde. "This is my niece, Christelle. And that's my daughter Anise."

Shirley raised her eyebrows at Anise, in what felt like a challenge to

Eka. "You remember my friend Sema. This is her granddaughter, Eka."

Anise's blank face dropped into a frown, her gaze narrowed on Eka, and her hand moved to Christelle's shoulder.

Okay, what did Sema tell these people?

Shirley, seemingly ignorant of Anise's reaction, gestured to a hanging chair. "Eka, relax, and I'll be back with that towel." Then she trotted off, leaving Eka to fend for herself.

Anise clearly hoped to expel Eka with a truly impressive glare.

Eka shook her head.

This should be fun.

Eka, ignoring the glare, gracefully walked to the hanging chair and plopped effortlessly down. Just to have it swing back, with her shuffling feet chasing its trajectory as her hands hung on, keeping her somewhat upright. Across from her, Christelle giggle. Eka smiled back at her. At least someone had a sense of humor.

"So great of Shirley to open our home to you," Anise continued glaring at Eka and her smile sulked away.

Christelle's giggle morphed to a quick inhale as red spread across her face and she bolted up. "Aunt Anise, maybe you could help Grams."

Anise sat still for a long moment, still glaring that obvious glare, then finally stood. "I think I'd like to have a word with her."

Eka pasted on a smile, waving. "Nice to meet you."

There's always one.

She steadied herself on the swinging chair and scooted all the way up on it, finally settling in. Across, Christelle just stared at her, but in a this-is-something-new-and-interesting kind of way. As Eka met the woman's gaze, a dizzying sense of something lost hit her. Something about this space, these people, seemed uncomfortably familiar and she rolled her bracelet back and forth. At the same moment, Christelle frowned at Eka, her blue eyes briefly unfocused. "Do I know you?"

"Maybe," Eka shrugged. "Apparently I was here once when I was young."

"Huh. You just…seem super familiar."

Eka shook her head, wondering what she had stumbled into. Was getting help from old friends the only reason Sema had suggested Eka stop here? And why did she feel as though some forgotten door in her mind was being cracked open? She rubbed her arms.

"So, did you miss your turn, back in Manatee Isles?" Christelle asked.

"What?" Eka refocused on Christelle.

"Not many people make it out to our farm. Our motto is 'try and find us'."

Eka laughed despite her discomfort. "Yeah, I wasn't aiming for here, but the weather seemed to have other ideas."

Her laugh petered out and silence settled in the space, scratching at her nerves. She pushed the chair in a circle and pulled at her wet, clingy shirt.

Where's that towel?

After an eternity of increasing silence, she hoped up and started checking out the foliage.

"So, uh, weather suggested you stop here?" Christelle broke the smothering quiet.

"Huh?" Eka asked absently as she caught sight of a tiny streak of blue light zipping in and out of the foliage, forgetting Christelle's question. She darted after the curious light, absently pushing aside branches and leaves in the chase.

"Are you okay?" Christelle called out.

Eka hopped across some short flowers. "Not sure. Maybe shock from the accident!" she shouted back.

"Accident?"

Eka stopped abruptly as tiny eyes hovered right in front of her face. "Do you guys have glowing insects in here?"

"Glowing insects?" Christelle's voice seemed confused. "Uh, just some wasps and bees, but they don't glow."

The light suddenly dissipated and a red and black body launched itself at her, followed by a few more. She stumbled backwards, swatting at the buzzing around her face, then tripped back into a fern. The buzzing hovered just above the bushes, so she rolled onto her stomach and low-crawled back through the brush to the alcove.

"What is wrong with her?" Christelle mumbled, probably not meant for Eka.

Eka crawled out from the brush and looked around. No buzzing followed, so she stood and headed back to the swing.

On the couch, Christelle's deep frown started to morph. "You have some…" Christelle's face contorted into a grin that she seemed to fight, "twigs in your clothes. And hair." She burst out laughing.

Eka looked down, a tiny smile working its way out. She never could leave the outdoors without trekking something back on her clothes. She brushed off some leaves, and a lot of dirt, then hopped back in the swinging chair. As she swung, she pulled out twigs and leaves, letting her long, dark hair work itself back to straight, then pulled her legs up and crossed them, waggling her eyebrows. "Good as new."

Christelle coughed. "So you, uh, said you were in an accident."

"Yeah, nearly put my truck and camper in the ditch." Eka smiled at the last-minute avoidance of that catastrophe.

Christelle's eye's widened. "Wow. Are you hurt?"

"Well, let me think." Eka tapped her lip. "I nearly trashed my truck and camper in a crazy storm and am stuck forty-five miles out of my way with no transportation. But I did walk away, so…there's that."

"Oh." Christelle seemed to take a moment to process that image. "Don't worry. Aunt Anise will get you out somehow. She's great at getting things done."

"Right." Eka leaned back in the chair and looked out the roof. "She seemed super helpful."

"She's just worried about me." Christelle crossed her arms and frowned. "She's really a good person."

Eka held up her hands. "Sorry, just a little worried myself."

The stifling quiet popped up again and Eka scanned around. Where was that towel and phone?

"Aunt Anise is just a bit serious, that's all." Christelle continued to defend her aunt.

"Sure."

"So." Christelle took a left turn. "You mentioned a Sema."

"Yeah. That's my grandma."

"Has she been here?"

Eka shrugged. "Apparently, she met Shirley a while ago. Kinda fuzzy on the details."

Shirley walked in then and handed Eka a towel. "Sema's been here a couple of times." Shirley's eyes twinkled as she sat on a green lounge chair next to Eka. "In fact, I remember when you two met." Then she just started playing with her sleeve.

A cliff-hanger? Really?

Just when Eka thought Shirley had some explanation to why a strange, familiar feeling overwhelmed her when she realized she'd passed through here as a child, Shirley wants to practice storytelling technics?

Before Eka could express those thoughts, lightning lit up the room and they all jumped.

"Well, this storm came from nowhere," Shirley stated.

Distracted, as usual, Eka agreed. "Is this normal? I was driving in clear skies and then, boom, the clouds rolled in. I swear, in less than five minutes, the sky went from clear to dark."

"We get storms in August, but we usually have a bit more warnin'," Shirley confirmed. "Oh, I almost forgot. I called a friend of ours, a mechanic. He's coming out as soon as the storm quiets to look at your truck."

Eka stared at the friendly woman. "You didn't have to go to so much trouble."

"Don't worry about it," Shirley waved off her response. "And I called Sema. She's happy you made it."

"Thanks, I'll have to call her."

To find out what the hell was going on.

Eka leaned closer to Shirley. "So, you mentioned I'd been her before."

"Yeah, Grams, what about that?" Christelle perked up again.

Shirley stood. "Anise has some cookies she's been saving in the freezer. How about I get them?"

Before either could press the question, Shirley literally raced out of the room.

So weird here.

"Sema, you better have some answers," Eka mumbled.

"What was that?" Christelle asked.

Eka shook her head.

I need to stop talking to myself.

Yeah, like that's gonna happen.

Exactly.

"Well, that was weird," Christelle leaned back, glancing at Eka, voicing Eka's thoughts on Shirley's departure. "I guess...we kinda know each other."

"Seems like it."

Christelle coughed. "So, do you remember anything?"

Eka shook her head and twisted the seat back and forth. She really needed to get moving. Even if her truck and camper needed repair, maybe it would drive. And she wasn't staying here.

"I could show you around. Maybe it'll jog your memory or something."

"Maybe." Eka gazed out the glass ceiling, letting the invitation sit unanswered.

Just get help and get out of here. Get to the gig.

A chill went through her as the door in her mind creaked open just a bit more. Eka frowned, scanning the room. Was there something important about this place? These people?

Thunder shook the glass over her and the thoughts out of her head.

Probably just some commune Sema and Win stayed at and dragged me into.

"Sooo," Christelle said after a few minutes, "Where were you headed?"

Eka relaxed. Finally a topic she could get into. "Down to the Keys. I do rigging for traveling performers and there's a show setting up in a week that needs a rigger."

"Really?" Christelle leaned closer. "My dad and I work the circuit. We have a couple of acts."

The feeling of the past and present colliding crept into Eka's awareness. "A lot of coincidences popping up."

Christelle's open face closed off and she leaned back, frowning. She pulled her knees up to her chest and wrapped her arms around them. "I guess."

Eka sighed. This whole situation seemed off, but, since she was stuck here for now, maybe Christelle had some answers or at least some clues to this weird feeling she had about this place, because, frankly, no one else was helping. Sema was obviously avoiding the topic when they had talked, and Shirley, while friendly, sure wasn't giving any straight answers. And Anise, well, friendly wasn't the word Eka would use. So, she smiled at Christelle. "I mean, cool coincidence. What acts do you do?"

Christelle slowly unwrapped herself. "Well," she started slowly, "our latest act has some silks and a static trapeze and a slack wire routine. Dad does the slack wire and I'm mainly in the air."

At the mention of familiar territory, traveling performers and shows, Eka's tension eased more. "Sounds awesome. Maybe I did some rigging for one of the shows."

"Maybe," Christelle shrugged. "You seem kinda familiar."

"Maybe we could compare notes some time. I've gotta get on the road soon but I could swing back by and you could show me around. Why don't you give me your number?"

"That would be great." Christelle pulled out her phone. "What's yours and I'll call."

"Oh. Lost it in the accident."

No phone and no truck. Crap.

"No problem." Christelle took a napkin and pen from the small table by the sofa and wrote down her number. As Eka reached for it, the strange, skin-crawling feeling roared back. Her own movements seemed to slow as Christelle's hand came at her in slow motion. Christelle frowned as she put the napkin in Eka's hand and, as Christelle's fingers touched Eka's palm, lightning raced across the sky overhead. Energy seemed to surge through Eka's body and an image of Ke and her parents flashed through her mind. A moment later, her body stiffened and the room faded.

"Eka, wake up."

Eka's mind swirled. She slowly opened her eyes to Shirley's fuzzy form leaning over her in candle-light. "Are you okay, Kiddo?"

Eka blinked and looked around the darkened room, candles flickering everywhere. "What…what happened?" She struggled to sit up but nausea kept her down.

"Slow down there tiger! You had quite a shock ta the system." Shirley reached behind her and adjusted a pillow under Eka's head. "We aren't sure what happened. We heard thunder, saw a flash and the lights went out. When I got here, both you and Christelle were passed out."

"Odd how you showed up just before all this happened," Anise said from her seat by Christelle.

"Odd things happen," Shirley replied, not looking Anise's way.

Eka frowned.

Is Anise blaming me for this?

"Last thing I remember, I was talking with Christelle and then," she shook her head, hoping to jog her memory, but her stomach took to somersaulting so she stopped moving. "There was lightning and everything went blank. I probably just need to eat."

Two strangers with low blood sugar, at the same time, in the same room, that pass out at the same time. Right.

"Anyway, as soon as I can get someone out to help with the truck, I'll be on my way."

"I'm sure we can make that happen. Quickly." Anise almost growled.

"You are in no condition to travel. Sema would kill me if I let you drive after passing out." Shirley shook her head. "Besides, fate seems to be pointing you in our direction." Shirley picked up Eka's hand and ran her finger over the palm. "Yep, says here you should stay here."

"Mom, this is no time for reading palms. I'm going to get some water for these two. Why don't you help me?"

Shirley stared at Eka's hand for a few moments longer before putting it down. She dug in a small bag hanging from her waist and pulled out a rune, tossing it to Eka.

"I think this message is for you." She winked, then turned and followed Anise through the thick plants.

It's like she's trying to win an award for being enigmatic.

Eka picked up the little stone off her stomach and studied it, turning it over in her hand. The shape of a sideways table had been carved on one side, while the other side was smooth and blank. She had no clue what this meant. Would Christelle? Across from her Christelle lay back on the sofa, pale and disheveled.

"Does Shirley always come in sideways?"

Christelle frowned and focused on Eka. "What?"

"Does she ever give a straight answer?"

"Huh," Christelle frowned. "I can't remember her ever really answering a question."

Eka held up the rune. "Well, she said this was some kind of message for me."

"Wow." She raised her eyebrows. "Grams read for you."

Eka studied the rune again. "Okay. Does she usually give any information to go along with these? What does this even mean?"

"What does it look like?"

Eka tossed it to Christelle, missing her by a foot.

The woman picked it up off the floor and squinted at the marking. "I think this one is about secrets or initiation or maybe hidden stuff. Not really sure." Christelle dropped her hand with the rune and sighed. "I tried learning to read the runes so I could see what Grams' readings really meant, but the symbols never made much sense to me." Christelle shrugged. "That's all I've got on this stone. Maybe you could get a full reading later. Grams loves to give readings for the people in town." She paused briefly, then smiled. Lowering her voice, she continued. "But between you and me, I think she really likes to hear the gossip."

"A flighty fortune-teller, a giant greenhouse home, and a mysterious storm that maybe knocks people out. I think this is one crazy place."

"Hey, Grams and Aunt Anise are great and this is their—I mean our—home." From Christelle's face Eka realized she had crossed a line.

Don't burn bridges.

"No, no. I mean it all seems so colorful. Alive." Eka quickly backpedaled and Christelle seemed to relax "Seems like Shirley was also reading my palm."

Christelle relaxed a little more.

Good.

"Yeah, she does like to take readings without people knowing." A hint of a smile snuck onto Christelle's face.

"Oh really. A ninja fortune-teller, huh?" Eka laughed at the image of a ninja-clad woman throwing tarot cards down as she back-flipped over a client. "Can you picture that?"

Christelle giggled. "And watch your tea; she'll probably try to read the leaves."

Just then, Anise and Shirley returned with water and tea, and Eka and Christelle broke into laughter. Shirley raised an eyebrow at them. "Conspiring already?"

"Just thinking how exciting this introduction has been," Eka laughed.

Shirley handed Eka a cup of tea, staring at the swirling liquid as she passed it. Eka reached for it, covering the cup with her hand and her laugh with a cough.

"So you're staying tonight," Shirley stated.

What?

"No, no. I really need to get on the road."

"Mom, if she doesn't want to stay…" Anise stood stiffly near Christelle, her go to spot apparently, staring Shirley down.

"But Aunt Anise, she's just had a shock. You've never thrown out someone who needed help."

Anise glared at Shirley then shook her head and bent down to Christelle with a kiss on her head. Without another sound, she left the room.

"Grams, what's up with her?"

Shirley waved away the question, straining to look in Eka's tea. "We have a guest cottage out back." Shirley offered a hand up to Eka.

Exhaustion hit and her eyelids drooped.

"I guess one night couldn't hurt."

"Great!" Christelle seemed bubbly for someone who had recently passed out. "See you in the morning."

"Right." Eka stumbled tiredly after Shirley, out of the living room and down a path that ended in a small cottage. She tried to take in more of her surroundings, get her bearings and even planned to text Sema when she was alone, on some borrowed phone. But exhaustion hit and, before she could even ask if Shirley had a phone on her, she collapsed on the bed of the cottage before Shirley had shut the door.

Isn't the Coffee to Die For?

Eka woke up in a large room, one too large to be her vardo. Her head throbbed and she couldn't remember anything.

Maybe she'd gone to some crazy party.

She reached under the covers of the massive bed, but no one else was there; at least she wouldn't have to sneak out of here. She examined herself to check she was in one piece.

Where'd these clothes come from?

Pale linen shorts and a tank top lay airily against her skin. They were more comfortable than anything she had, but why was she wearing them? Before she could begin to answer that, her stomach grumbled and, without a pause, she swung out of bed to search for food. And nearly fell as her jelly legs crumpled under her, temporarily incapacitated and sprawled out on her back. She blinked, trying to focus on the cloud and sky painting spanning the domed ceiling. Then squinted and cocked her head.

That's not a painting.

Above a crystalline dome opened up to a pale blue sky as a single cloud puffed gently across the view. "What a cool roof."

"Yes, it is."

Eka instinctively rolled toward the the voice, knocking her shins into the bedpost. "Ow!"

Shirley lounged against the door, a tray in her hands. Then, with her brows furrowed, she strode over Eka's body to the bed. "Is there something wrong with the bed?"

The events of last night flooded back into Eka's memory. The storm, the glass-domed living room and the Haptons. Eka rubbed her shins then climbed, with noodle legs, back up on the bed. "No, just checking out the room."

Shirley shrugged, then set the tray down on the bedside table and flopped down on a chair. "You and Christelle seem better this morning. A friend of ours stopped by to check on you both. Thought rest was the best action."

"A *doctor* friend?"

"No." Shirley pointed at the try. "I brought some breakfast."

Eka frowned at Shirley then at the tray. "Uhhh, thanks. So these clothes, and this friend…"

Shirley waved off Eka's half-formed questions. "Tea?"

Just one straight answer.

"Tea's fine." Shirley poured a cup and passed it over, eyeing the contents as Eka took it. Eka slid her hand over the top. "So, I appreciate everything you guys've done for me, thanks for letting me stay. I really can't believe I passed out. I was fine yesterday."

"Yesterday!" Shirley burst out laughing. "You've been out a week."

"What?" Eka jerked straight up. Tea sloshed and rolled over the cup's rim and down her shirt, then onto the sheets. "Crap." She grabbed the napkin off the tray and blotted tea spillage. "How could…a week? What?"

"Whatever it was, must have hit you hard. Wasn't sure when you or Christelle were gonna come out of the delirium, but the worst seems ta have passed."

"What do you mean, 'delirium'?"

Shirley shrugged as she stood back up. Staying still didn't seem to be in her skill set. "You were talking a lot." She frowned at Eka. "You never really made any sense. Who's Brandy and why did you climb out of her window? Did you really hide her tires in molasses barrels?"

Tea sprayed out of Eka's mouth, spreading the liquid further onto the sheets. "Great tea! And breakfast, thanks!"

Shirley paused, as if she were waiting for more of an answer, but Eka busied herself wiping up tea.

"Well, anyway. I thought you might be as hungry as Christelle. Eat something, relax. I'll be back in a while to check in. Oh, your suitcase and clothes are in the closet."

Eka spotted the closet then turned back. "Who put…" But Shirley was gone.

How did she move so fast?

At that moment, a familiar tune played on the night stand next to her and she caught the screen light dimming on her phone.

"They found my phone?" she mumbled absently as she picked it up and read the texts. "Oh crap."

All of the texts were about the gig she was supposed to start last week.

"How am I gonna explain this?" she asked the room. "Oh, I know I was supposed to be there but I seemed to have passed out for a week. Still need me? How about a recommendation?"

She sank back under the covers.

How am I gonna pay to fix the truck and vardo? Where will I stay?

The phone played the ominous tune again but this time Sema's name popped up. Sema's 'Good Morning' seemed so mundane in the middle of this weird, surreal place. But maybe mundane was just what she needed. So despite her grandmother's questionable choice of destinations for her, Eka called.

"Hello?"

Eka's back and shoulders relaxed at the voice. "Hey Sema."

"Eka, my little bird! How are you?"

"You can probably tell me. You seem to know every move I make. Sometimes I think you're psychic."

There was a pause on the other end. "You still have such an imagination."

"Yeah. Well, I'm here at Hapton's. And I've been asleep for a week, as your friend probably told you."

"Shirley has kept me in the loop."

Eka pushed back the covers and wiggled up to sitting. "Sema, I'm happy you have these interesting friends, but I needed to be some where. And now, because of some weird…I don't know, virus at this place, I've missed a job and maybe screwed up any chance of a reference."

"Oh honey. I'm sure it will all work out. Maybe this is just a sign you need a vacation. A change of scenery. And Hapton's is so relaxing."

Eka huffed and muted the phone, inhaling deeply.

One. Two. Three. Relax.

"Hello? Eka?"

Eka unmuted the phone and exhaled. "Just dropped the phone. Anyways, I've got a lot of phone calls to make to try to fix this. I really need to go. Just wanted to say hey."

"Eka, Shirley thought you were mumbling about your parents and Ke. Something about a beach and dolphins."

Eka touched her bracelet. "I…I was probably just sick with whatever this was."

"Little bird, it's okay to think of them. We all miss them."

Eka spun the bracelet. "Really, it was just some silly memory of the beach. It wasn't even a real one. I mean, I must've been hallucinating. How could Dad grow a seed into a plant, in his hand? And I was communicating with the ocean and swam with dolphins. Crazy, huh?"

Eka pulled her ear away at the sharp intake of breath. "Sema?"

After a pause, Sema answered. "Nothing, just dropped the phone myself."

"Are you okay?"

"Yes, yes. Just distracted. Those are strange dreams but I'm sure you're alright. You should rest a while."

"I really need to get to work," Eka protested.

"Well, I have a friend with a burlesque cirque show somewhere near you. I'll talk with him about some work if you want."

Eka perked up. This might be worth hanging out for. "That would be awesome, Sema! That might help save my career."

"Okay, well, try to take a little time to recover. And you never know, you might like it there. Maybe find a whole new world you missed."

"I'll tell you what, I'll wait a week. I'm gonna need to find some work after that if nothing happens with your friend."

"Deal. And Eka, be gentle with yourself."

That was a weird thing to say.

"Uh, okay."

"Okay. I have to go catch up with the surfing group. The waves here in Bundoran are good but cold. You take care of yourself. And be respectful."

"I'm nothing but respectful."

"Eka, Shirley's a good friend. No messes left behind. You're getting a bit old for that."

"Hey, I don't leave messes!" She could hear the slight exasperation in Sema's breathing. "Okay, but they're all in good fun."

Sema sighed. "Alright little bird. Love you."

"You too." Eka exhaled as she hung up. Surfing with Sema was one of the things she missed most about her life with her grandparents. She hadn't really surfed since; never seemed to make it to the ocean.

Before surfing visions sucked away her time, an intense earthy smell invaded her awareness and overrode her nostalgic thoughts.

Coffee!

Her legs seemed to have recovered from their jelliness and she hopped off the bed and out the door. The smell led right to the main house, then into the kitchen, as a jolt of energy ran through her. She exploded into the room, sliding across the tile and slamming into a counter.

"Slow down there!" Shirley caught Eka before she fell back. "You just were in bed for a week. No need for Olympic training."

"I smelled coffee…" Eka's nostrils flared as coffee overwhelmed her senses. She spun in search of the source, catching a foot on the cabinet. "Ow!"

Stumbling back, she flailed at the counter top, just brushing the edge with her fingertips. Hands went wide and she grabbed Shirley's arm on the way to a very up-close and personal meeting with the floor, a wide-eyed Shirley following behind. They both lay on the tile for a moment, before Shirley rolled away. "I'm not sure you should be out of bed." Shirley shook her head and crawled up.

"But don't you smell that?" Eka asked from her sprawled position on the floor.

"Smell what?" Anise appeared in the far entrance, frowning. Eka ignored Anise's snippy tone, crawling up to rest against the cabinets in a coffee-scented haze. "Um, the coffee. What kind is it? I feel like I've had three cups just from the smell!"

Shirley and Anise looked at each other, then back at the heap that was Eka.

"Maybe you should get back to bed," Anise shook her head at the heap.

"No, seriously. The smell is incredible."

Christelle burst into the room. "What is that smell?"

"Right?" Eka grinned. "I could almost taste it from the guest house."

"I need some right now." Christelle leapt onto the counter and grabbed the coffee pot.

"Don't burn yourself!" Anise started towards Christelle.

Christelle poured the liquid down her throat. "Not." Gulp. "Hot."

"Hey, save some for me!" Eka demanded.

Christelle slide the pot across the counter to the edge where it tipped over. Eka caught it just before it hit the floor, warm coffee sloshing all over her hands. Liquid dripped down her hands and chin as she poured the coffee in her mouth, a nut and chocolate flavor bursting onto her tongue and warming her entire body, the spills forgotten. When the coffee stopped flowing, she opened her eyes to an empty pot and Christelle splayed on her back, across the counter. Anise and Shirley stood at the kitchen table wide-eyed, shifting their gazes between the two laying haphazardly across the kitchen.

"Um…" Eka gently hoisted herself up and set the pot on the counter-top. "It's really good," was all she managed.

"Good to hear," Shirley laughed.

Eka's coffee stupor finally dissipated and she scanned her surroundings. Beside the four of them, two men sat at the table, staring at her.

"This is my son-in-law, Ben." Shirley nodded to the red-headed man. "And this is my husband Buwei." She patted the man's hand.

"Just call me Bu," he laughed, glancing at her clothes. "Glad to see you're out of bed."

Eka looked down at herself. She was covered in coffee.

"Quite a show you two just put on." Bu's eyes seemed to twinkle along with his laugh.

"Yes, an impressive display of coordination," Ben added.

"Um, thanks. Always try to make an impression." Eka smiled more brightly, her legs less wobbly.

Shirley stepped over Eka and next to Christelle. "Kiddo, you need to get up." Christelle opened her eyes, looked at Eka for a moment, then glanced down at her own coffee-stained shirt. Her giggling started subtly but grew into a full-on laughing fit, pulling in the rest of the room, even Anise.

Maybe this place wasn't so bad.

After a few moments, Eka caught her breath. Her coffee craving had vanished but she had definitely ruined this unexplained outfit and needed a shower. She took a step away from the counter to discovered puddles of coffee around her feet.

Don't leave messes, Eka. Sema's words flitted through her mind.

"Sorry about all this. Do you have some towels?"

"Oh, don't worry about that." Shirley caught her own breath as her laughter receded. "I'm just glad the two of you are feeling better."

Eka's energy level was high and so was the familiar itch to move, to escape. "I think I'll take a walk."

"I'll join you," Christelle chimed in.

Eka tensed, the walls and people suddenly too close. "Um." She twisted her bracelet as she moved to the door. "I've got to make a call to Sema. Rain check?"

"Oh. Sure." Christelle's voice was just a whisper now.

Shirley called after Eka. "Are you sure you're up for a walk? I mean, you were out for a week, then practically doing acrobatics in the kitchen."

"Yeah, I'm fine. I think I slept too much." She waved behind her. "I just need to get outside."

As Eka stepped out the door, she smelled the coffee lingering on her clothes on top of the grungy feeling from sleeping for a week. She took a wiff under her arm.

"Ugh!" She needed a shower yesterday.

The guest cottage she was staying in was just behind the house and soon water washed away a week's worth of living while she wondered what was happening to her. Bizarre memories popping up, a week-long illness, overly friendly strangers from Sema's past and now going crazy over coffee.

"I'm probably losing what's left of my mind," she laughed as the water slowly rejuvenated her. "Or still sick. All of this is probably just a really crazy hallucination."

Finally dressed in familiar, yet miraculously clean, clothes, she stepped out of the cottage to overwhelming brightness. Her arm reflexively went up to shield her eyes. In the blinding light, she stumbled off the steps and down a path, ending up in an area dense with flowers.

Floral aromas suddenly overwhelmed her, like the coffee had. A honey scent mixed in with the flowery fragrance, then flowed through her nose and throat, startling her taste buds. She grinned as the smells awoke a memory of the honey and peanut butter sandwiches she used to eat with her dad. Abruptly the aroma of honey subsided and a cotton candy smell took over. She gagged at the sticky sweetness. Smell after smell invaded her nose, eventually roiling her stomach until she heaved up the morning coffee. But still, scent after taste after scent of flowers, wood, lemon, pepper, and smoke fought to grab her olfactory attention.

"Stop!"

She stood up and slowed her breath in an attempt to control the scents. And just as her stomach started to calm, the colors of the landscape intensified, pushing all smells to the background. Yellows, reds, blues, purples, and hundreds of shades of greens from the field grew brighter, as if she were staring at the sun through a prism. Eka struggled to focus on one color, but failed as she collapsed to the ground, her head level with a single flower. The small purple flower filled her vision and narrowed her focus. And with that narrowing, she seemed to be able to tune the brightness down to something bearable. Up close, she could see tiny flecks of yellow mixed with the purple on the petals. The flower swayed gently, then bent toward her hand that lay next to it, and made contact. At their connection, the sensations of Eka's body distorted. The pressure of grass on the skin of her feet morphed into a warm, sweet sensation of earth. Her body seemed to lose fullness, now just a swaying stalk. She couldn't seem to lift her head easily and instead of seeing, her skin vibrated with heat and pressure. And dozens of 'voices' came from the connections of her skin with the earth.

What's happening? I was touching a flower then—am I a flower?

She blinked and was back to staring at the little purple and yellow petals. Her hand lay on the ground, disconnected from the plant.

"Whoa."

But the weird sensations had a familiar feel, stirring up more strange pieces of memory, of the vast ocean and of becoming water. She lost herself in the perceptions that were as real as any she'd ever had.

Maybe not an hallucination after all but the promise of an adventure like no other.

Christelle's Got It Going On

Christelle slumped backwards on the counter-top as Eka bolted out the door. Again she asked herself what she was even doing here? She should be back home working, not playing around and wasting time. And what was going on with her, and Eka, getting sick for a week and freaking out about coffee? It was like she was suddenly in a parallel world, where nothing made sense, instead of her family's farm. And things just kept getting weirder.

"I don't even like coffee," she mumbled.

"What's that, honey?" Anise turned from hugging Ben as he left the kitchen with Bu.

"Nothing," Christelle sighed. "I think I'll head back to my room."

"Why don't you join me in the garden this morning?" Anise yawned. "I think it's time I set you up with a job on the farm."

"Anise!" Shirley nearly shouted and then coughed. "Sorry. Just remembered. There's some problem with the plants down in the south field."

Anise spun toward Shirley. "What's wrong? When did this happen?"

Shirley shrugged and shook her head. "One of the gals down there said something earlier, but with all the excitement…"

Anise hurried toward the door. "I told them to go easy on the ener…on the fertilizer."

"I guess this could be interesting." Christelle slid off the counter.

Anise grimaced then held up her hand, stopping Christelle. "I better handle this solo; I won't have time to show you anything." The smile that started on Anise's face met her grimace and retreated. "Sorry, but I'll come get you later."

"Okay," Christelle sighed, her default expression this morning, as her aunt hurried out the door.

Okay, Dad, I gave this a try but it sucks. I'm coming home.

She stuck her hands in her pockets and sulked toward the back of the house but, Shirley cut off her very slow escape just before the door.

"Could you let Eka know I've got a quote for her camper and truck?"

Christelle frowned. "I think she wants to be alone. Besides, I'm feeling light-headed. I thought I'd lie down for a while."

"Nonsense!" Shirley slapped her back and she lurched forward. "You just need some fresh air. Besides, I'm sure Eka'll want to know what's going on with her stuff." She grinned a little too much while shooing Christelle out the side door.

"Okaaaay," Christelle managed as Shirley shut the door in her face.

Suddenly outside, sunlight hit Christelle's eyes like a spotlight at midnight and she staggered down the path toward the cottage.

What is going on? I mean, I wasn't inside a cave for a year, why is the sun so bright?

Ignoring her weird sunlight sensitivity, she blindly felt her way to the door and pounded on the entrance. Or maybe it was a wall, she couldn't be sure. Either way there was no answer.

Swinging around, she headed back in the general direction of the house, covering her eyes with her forearm. "She could've at least answered the door." As she staggered back toward the house, her flip-flop slipped on the gravel, then flew off, and her bare foot hit brittle rock bits.

"Darnit!"

Glaring colors flooded her vision with watercolor rainbows, throwing off her bearings. She staggered around, completely lost in the visual sensations, until she tripped and fell over something.

Crap!

She patted the object next to her, then held both her arms up to block the sun. Eka lay there like a lump, staring at a flower as if it held the answers to the universe. Before Christelle could even think about that scene, intense floral smells hit her and she covered her mouth and nose.

Why did these sensations seem familiar? Something about last week's storm, the plants in the window. Christelle reached out and touched the petal of a red and yellow flower that glowed, even in the flood of sunlight. As her fingers brushed the silky petal, Shirley's message for Eka faded as another, far-off field flooded her memory.

Her hand was small. Like a child's hand. Her small fingers disappeared into the long slender fingers of a tall, blonde woman. The woman walked next to her, dwarfing Christelle as they passed through towering flowers.

"Regarde cette fleur," the woman said as she pointed.

French?

Christelle's gaze followed the woman's finger to a particular plant with a red and yellow flower.

"See the energy from the flower, my love?"

Her brain was translating French. How?

Christelle squinted and moved closer. "The colors, mama?"

Her mother smiled and squeezed Christelle's hand. "Yes, that's it. Now, picture the flower taller, reaching for the sky." She raised her hand above her head. "And dance with the flower."

Christelle swayed as she reached for the plant, her stomach warming. The heat crawled along her limbs as a faint, pulsing lavender glow emanated from her hand. The flower's head bent toward her and a pink, glow burst out of it, dancing towards her and into the lavender shimmer before haloing her hand. The pink energy tickled its way up her arm and she squealed, grabbing at the plant, but her mother caught her hand before she caught the flower head.

"Gently my dear. Ask it to dance with you."

"Ask?"

Her mother nodded. "May we dance?" Her mother held out a palm and the flower swayed atop it.

Christelle hopped up and down and held out her arms. Pink energy swirled with lavender and the plant shot briefly up, growing taller than her mother. As the plant slowed, then stopped growing, Christelle's stomach cooled and her lavender shimmer faded, lights drifting away from her like the seeds of a dandelion in a breeze.

Then she fell on her butt. "I'm tired, mama."

Her mother picked her up and swung her around, kissing Christelle's face all over. "You did wonderful, my brave girl!"

A man popped his head up through the flowers, yawing.

"Poppop!" Christelle grinned. "I danced with a flower and it got bigger than mama." She pointed at the giant flower.

He grinned at the two, then stood up and wrapped them both in a hug.

"Of course you did it. You made your own magic with your gifts!"

"Hey?"

A muffled voice penetrated Christelle's thoughts. She frowned, pink and yellow petals raining off her face. Eka lay next to her, rubbing her eyes.

"What?" Christelle asked her.

"Are you two okay?"

Startled, Christelle rolled over to stare up at a young couple, both wearing overalls and blue T-shirts. She vaguely remembered them from the farm.

"My friend loves flowers," Eka mumbled.

Christelle's mushy brain searched for something to add. "Uh, yeah."

The woman cocked her head. "Aren't you Anise's niece?"

Christelle kinda nodded. She had an Aunt Anise, right?

"Um, do you need help with anything?"

"No, we're fine," Eka squeaked.

The two hesitated a moment longer, then shook their heads and moved on. Barely noticing they'd left, Christelle examined the strange flowers.

Was I really in a field with Dad? My mom?

She'd never remembered that before. She brushed a petal with her fingers again, but nothing happened. Sighing, she searched the area with the hope of spotting bright, colorful lights. Anything to prove that whatever she'd experienced was real. But…nothing. Beside her, Eka struggled up into a sit, brushing grass off her face and clothes.

"What…did you see…?" Christelle stammered.

"That was freakin' amazing!"

Christelle frowned. "Amazing?" Were they even talking about the same thing? She had no idea.

Eka seemed oblivious to Christelle's confusion as she prodded some flowers. "Hello?"

Christelle squinted at Eka.

Why is she playing with the flowers?

Christelle leaned forward and examined the plants. Still no bright colors, lights, overwhelming smells. Maybe she'd hallucinated everything.

"Come on, flower, stop being normal." Eka leaned over the little flower and poked until some petals fell off. She jerked her hand back. "Sorry."

"Eka, did you notice something, uh, strange about those plants?"

Eka cocked her head, then stood up and started toward the cottage, still ignoring Christelle.

"Hey! Did you feel something weird?"

Eka spun toward her. "You too, huh? Bright lights. Crazy smells." She threw out her hands. "Incredible!"

Christelle stopped. "I'm…not sure."

Eka narrowed her eyes and looked Christelle up and down. "Huh." She shrugged then spun around and continued up the path.

What is her problem? Why is she always leaving?

Christelle stumbled to catch up again. "Hey! I don't know what I saw, or smelled. Maybe it's a hallucination." Which seemed the most likely; they'd been sick, after all. But…her mother. Could she have really remembered that? Seen all that other stuff?

No. It must be the sickness.

Eka shook her head, still walking. "Both of us hallucinating?"

"Maybe we're still sick."

Eka stopped in front of the cottage then spun toward Christelle. "It could be us both hallucinating at the same time." A grin peeked out of her face, raising her eyebrows. "But what if it's something more?" Eka paused just a moment before striding the last bit to the cabin. "I don't blame you if you're a bit freaked out. Take your time." She smiled behind her as she walked in the door. "But I just had a crazy experience and I'm gonna figure out what really happened."

Christelle stood, confused. "I'm not freaked out." Okay maybe a little but still, she was curious. A flame went off inside her. Who was Eka to dismiss her? "Hey! I wanna know what's going on too!" Christelle shouted to an empty porch. She stomped up to the door and pounded, then jumped back as it swung open.

"What?" Eka stood tapping her hand against the door frame.

"I…this was…how…" What was she even trying to say?

Eka sighed. "Mind-blowing things just happened and I wanna know what it means. If you want to believe it's all some crazy hallucination, to each their own, but that's not gonna work for me."

Christelle fumed. "You don't know what happened, so you can't rule it out!"

Eka raised an eyebrow, grinned slightly, and leaned against the door frame. "No, but being wishy-washy isn't gonna get me anywhere. This is a jump-on-board-or-you-miss-it, moment."

Christelle dropped her shoulders as her anger drained away. This was useless. She was sick, not having some kind of extra-sensory experience. She wanted to see her parents and her mind had created a memory for her. That was all. But Eka obviously wanted to believe the crazy explanation. She should just go home.

"Fine." Christelle turned and walked off the porch, the door closing behind her. She'd come here to find a solid life and didn't need this kind of drama right now.

As she stomped into the main house, her stomach roared and she wondered when she'd eaten last. Just then her legs weakened and exhaustion overwhelmed her. She hobbled into her room and onto the bed, barely registering her stomach's protest as she fell instantly asleep.

Magical Hangovers Are Killer

S unshine tickled Christelle awake and she rolled over, burying her head in a pillow.

"Ugh."

What had she done to her body? Every joint and muscle ached, her head thumped, and had she tried to eat a bag of cotton balls?

But before the hint of an answer could form, stomach grumblings overrode her body's moaning.

When was the last time she ate? Memory failed as her head shut down any attempt to think.

Fine.

Crawling to the edge of her hanging bed and away from the sun, she kept her eyes shut tight, refusing to acknowledge the bright rays. She hung her head off the side of the bed, cracked open her eyes, and stared at the door. Was it always so far?

I'll never make it to the kitchen.

Contemplating a next move, she poured herself off the bed as it swayed with her movements and onto the numbingly cold tile, aches and hunger fading briefly away.

Yeah.

Laying in the sweet embrace of the cold, she squinted at the door. Did she really need to leave?

Faint grumblings argued for food and eventually won as she glared at her stomach.

Okay, okay. The tile's getting warm anyway.

Huffing and dragging her body upright, this time the bright sun tried to slap her fully awake the moment her head crested the top of the bed into the direct light. She blocked its aggression by throwing her face in her hands, but, in her shaded palms, instead of relief she found colorful images and intense smells that drifted through her awareness, reminding her of the strange encounter in the field. Irritated, she struggled up to a sit, then slouched over her knees with her head buried in bent arms.

"What happened to me?" she asked the room.

"Who're you talking to?"

She jerked up as Eka jumped on the bed behind her and swung it gently next to her.

"Nice bed." Eka pushed off the tile and swung higher. "This is awesome."

The bed swung back with more speed, coming back and knocking into Christelle's head. "Hey!"

"Sorry." Eka shoved her feet against the floor and skidded to a halt. "Feeling hungover, huh?"

Christelle buried her head back in her arms and shrugged. "Maybe."

"Try this."

Something cold pressed into Christelle's leg. Christelle reached down and grabbed a bottle of some orange stuff that sat next to her.

"Juice seems to help. I guess all that craziness has a kickback."

Christelle looked up and, of course her stomach lurched and the throbbing in her neck grew. "Why are you here?"

"Shirley offered me a side job so, voila." Eka spread her arms wide. "Besides, something happened yesterday that made us both face-plant in a field, then pass out for the rest of the day. Thought I'd check on any new theories you might have. Maybe we're still sick, crazy or maybe," Eka winked "your aunt or grandma slipped something in that coffee."

Christelle's head jerked toward Eka. "They'd never do that." Pain screamed through her neck and grated on her nerves. "Ow."

Eka grinned. "Okay. So how about," she leaned over and wiggled her fingers in front of Christelle's face, "magic. This is my personal favorite."

Christelle sucked in a breath. "Magic?"

"Why not? I mean, I saw flowers grow when you touched them. Everything was glowing and the smells were intense. I swear I thought those plants were gonna say something." Eka shrugged. "Why not magic?"

"It's just," Christelle whispered, "I heard that word in, I don't know, a memory." She looked directly at Eka. "But not something I remembered before now. Like a new memory, with my parents." Christelle's body tightened and she briefly squeezed her eyes shut then took a deep breath and stared out the window. "My parents were there and I was little and weird things were happening and…my mom. I saw her, really saw her." She looked down and mumbled. "Probably just a hallucination."

Why am I sharing? With her?

Eka stopped fidgeting next to Christelle. And Eka never seemed to stop moving.

"What?" Christelle asked.

"I…I don't know." Eka slid off the bed and sat next to her. "Just, I had a weird memory too. About my family. And it was like what you're describing, a new memory."

"Did it feel like you were there, living it, right then?"

Eka nodded slowly.

Christelle sat in silence for a few moments. They couldn't both have strange new family memories, could they? And what about the magic? A rumbling snapped Christelle out of her rememberances, the smell of bread and fruit overwhelming her. She crawled to the bedside table and grabbed a piece of sourdough and a slice of pineapple off a plate.

"Want some?"

Eka nodded and took some sourdough, sinking her teeth in. "'Is whol fing akes e ungry."

"What?"

Eka pointed at the bread then her stomach. "Ungry!"

"Grams must have left this. Sometimes she knows just the right thing to do."

Eka nodded.

"Can't believe this smell didn't wake me up. I'm starving." Christelle attempted to appease her angry stomach with large amounts of bread and fruit offerings.

"Probably slept right through it," Eka said clearly between bites. "I know I could have slept through a hurricane last night."

This time Christelle nodded, gulping down the rest of the pineapple.

"Look," Eka blurted between bites. "I get all this seems freaky. Strange memories popping up, the world feeling like a kaleidoscope of colors and smells, becoming a plant." Eka paused. "Did that happen to you?"

Christelle closed her eyes. The rooted and connected awareness of the flowers, mixing with her solitary experience, again flooded her senses for a brief moment. She scrunched up her face, cocked her head and nodded slowly. "Yeeeaaahhh?"

Eka raised an eyebrow. "Okay, I'll take that as a yes. So the next question is, what to do about it? We can sit around wondering forever; maybe pretend it never happened."

Would that work? Maybe all this craziness was a result of being sick. Some kind of weird virus and it's over … yeah, right.

"Eka to Christelle!" Eka snapped her fingers in Christelle's face.

"Hey!" She pushed Eka's hand away.

"So I was saying, we can pretend this was a one-time experience or we can run with it. Figure out what happened. I mean, what if we can really make things grow? Maybe we could do other tricks. This has got to be the most exciting thing in forever."

What if that flower had actually grown at her touch? What if she did have a new memory of her parents together with her. Christelle smiled.

"Okay. Maybe this is something…positive?." She sat up straighter. "Grams might be able to help. I mean, she likes all that weird stuff."

Eka shrugged and stood up, brushing crumbs off her capri's. "Might be hard to explain to her, but good luck. Let me know what she says. Right now I have a job to do." She pulled out a map and laid it out on the bed. "Do you know where the Fenwrought Woods are? I couldn't get it on the GPS."

Christelle stood up and scanned the map, finally pointing to a densely wooded spot. "Yeah. We go there every time I visit. Aunt Anise likes to search for some medicinal herbs there and it's a great place to picnic." She stabbed at a spot further down. "We're here. You just go out left on Hapton Drive for about a mile, turn off on the dirt road after that really big boulder on the right. Drive about three and a half miles…"

Eka held up her hand. "What is this, Green Acres? Don't they have street signs?"

Christelle laughed. "Took me three summers to learn how to get there and it's definitely not on any GPS app I've used. I can't even find the dirt roads on the aerial pics."

"So." Eka ran her fingers over the map. "Where are we again?"

Christelle studied the map. Only some of the roads appeared on the map; a lot were missing. She leaned closer to the part of the map with Hapton's Farm. Only one of the roads from the farm to Fenwrought showed up. "You're not going to get there with this map. Want a guide?"

Eka crumpled up the map and shoved it into a tiny backpack. "Sounds perfect." She spun and headed to the door. "You coming?"

"I need a few minutes to change." Christelle looked down at her pajamas. "Hey what did Grams want you to do, anyways?" When she looked back up Eka was gone.

Can't she ever pause? I'm the one helping her.

But Christelle threw on some shorts and a T-shirt at breakneck speed, then ran toward the front door as a surge of energy flowed through her. Maybe this past week made no sense and was scrambling her brains and emotions, but right now she had something to focus on. Lead Eka to Fenwrought Woods. Hopefully it'd be enough to ignore the weird sensations, her sickness, the plants growing at her touch, new memories popping up, and abandoning her responsibilities to her dad.

Take Eka to the woods and forget everything else, no problem. Just help Eka...

What was she helping with, though?

"Ugh. Eka never explains anything." She ran out the front and slid to a halt next to Eka's slowly moving truck. "Can you stop?"

Eka stopped and popped her head out. "Just keeping things rolling," she winked.

Christelle huffed, rolled her eyes, and shook her head. Quite an impressive display of exasperation, really.

"The joke wasn't that bad." Eka grinned.

"Yeah." Christelle took a deep breath. Eka was as secretive as Grams, but if Eka needed her this damn early, she better start talking. Christelle couldn't think of any kind of work Grams would need, especially nothing worth the cost of truck and trailer repairs. And why in Fenwrought? "Look, either tell me what Grams wants you to do or I'm going back to bed?"

"Hey, don't get all wound up. It's just some repairs on a few lookout towers in the woods. Said my rigging equipment would be perfect."

"But, there's no towers out there." Wait, how would Eka find them anyway? She narrowed her eyes on Eka. "How were you going to find them? You can't even find the right woods?"

Eka shrugged and smiled a bit too much. "She said you might help. And it'd be good for you to get out of the house."

"Are you kidding me?" Why was everyone trying to control her? She spun around and stomped back to the house to find Shirley.

"Hey! I thought you were helping me find those towers!" Eka's truck door slammed behind Christelle.

"There are no towers!" Christelle didn't look back as Eka's footsteps headed toward her.

"What?"

But Eka's question was lost as she headed through the front door and down the hall to the living room. She scanned the greenery and saw a colorful flash in the bushes.

Eka stopped beside her. "What do you mean there's no towers?"

"Ask Grams." And Christelle headed into the bushes.

The Local Sites are a Blast

I can't believe I trusted Shirley. But why would she even send me on that goose chase?

There was only one way to find out. Eka ran after Christelle as she pursued Shirley.

"Grams, stop trying to hide! I saw you duck down! Grams!"

Eka glanced left as she caught the movement of bright fabric through the foliage and slammed into Christelle, who had stopped in front of her, both of them tumbling to the ground. Eka quickly rolled away from Christelle and onto a pathway that branched left, then lay there staring out the glass dome of the living room into the afternoon sky. "This place is really amazing."

"Yeah." Christelle scrambled to her feet and stuck her head into the bushes on her left. "Grams, I saw you go by." She pulled her head out of the branches and tried to look over the top of the leaves, then headed down the left path. "We need to talk!"

A small branch broke to Eka's right.

How'd she get over there?

Eka sat up and glanced to the left were she'd seen Shirley pass by earlier, then back to the right.

You are one sneaky lady.

Eka strained to hear any more noises that might give away Shirley's hiding spot. A faint rustle came from behind her, just to the right and off the path. She pushed into a crouch then waddled next to a bushy cycad, long stalks of dense leaves concealing anything behind it. A moment later a few of the long leaves wiggled. Waiting for that signal, she sprang around the cycad and into the middle of the foliage, crashing into a familiar someone and rolling with them through the plants and out to the mulched walkway on the backside. Eka hopped up and stood over Shirley's splayed-out form. "Hey, Shirley."

Shirley sat up and brushed foliage off her pink and neon green T-shirt and shorts, frowning. "Eka, do you usually fly through shrubbery to tackle people?"

Just then, Christelle rounded the brush from the far left and skidded to a stop. "Grams? Why are you on the ground?"

Shirley hooked her thumb at Eka. "She thinks she's a flying squirrel and I'm some giant nut."

Eka glanced at Christelle. "That last part's right."

Christelle walked over, biting her lip, as Shirley crawled up to her feet. "I know you heard me, Grams. I've been shouting at you for, like, ten minutes."

"Sorry dear." Shirley coughed and picked at her sleeve. "Just lost in my own world. Didn't notice."

Christelle thrust Shirley's hat and coat at her. "Then why did I find these hanging on plants, looking just like a decoy person from behind?"

"Oh." Shirley looked around, anywhere but at Christelle. "Um, just got hot. I took them off and hung them on whatever was around." She smiled up at her granddaughter. "I must have a natural artistic flare."

Christelle narrowed her gaze on her grandmother. "Uh-huh."

Shirley seemed to ignore the look while collecting her stuff from Christelle. She patted her hat on without comment and speed-walked up the path.

"Grams, we're not done!"

"What's that, dear?" Shirley stopped and turned back.

"Why'd you tell Eka there were towers out in the woods?" Christelle practically growled. "And tell her I would help her?"

Eka raised her eyebrows at Shirley, whose eyes crinkled briefly.

Did she just smile?

The look disappeared so quickly, Eka couldn't be sure.

"No towers?" Shirley regarded them both, then she nodded. "Oh, that's right. I forgot. They never put them up. My bad." She blinked at them both. With a straight face.

"What are you up to Grams?" Christelle glared.

"Nothing. Sema said Eka could use some work while she was here and I thought I could send her to fix up the towers, to help out Anise in exchange for repairing her camper and truck. That's more than fair, I think."

"A pretty generous offer," Eka admitted.

"Sure. If it were a real offer," Christelle finished.

"I can't believe you two are so inconsiderate. Anise is working her butt off, trying to take care of this community and the farm. She's worn out and I thought I'd help her by taking care of this for her. And, after chatting with Sema, I thought I'd help Eka by giving her some work. And get you," Shirley looked directly at Christelle, "out of the house by suggesting you help her. I was just trying to help everyone. I forgot about the towers; I can't help my memory issues." Shirley's lip trembled. Suspiciously.

Anger seem to dissipate from Christelle, replaced by…was that sympathy? No way.

"Grams, I'm so sorry. It just seemed weird, that's all. I'm really tired but I believe you wanted to help." Christelle ran over and gave her grandmother a hug.

Apparently it was sympathy. Eka shook her head at Christelle, but couldn't help grinning. Guess they weren't getting anything out of her today.

You are good Shirley.

"Well." Eka patted Shirley on the back. "I guess we were wrong. You're a great Samaritan and I'm happy for the opportunity. Thanks for taking care of my truck and camper."

Shirley lifted her head from Christelle's shoulder. "I'll be happy to pay when we find a real job for ya."

Eka frowned. "What exactly do you mean, 'real job'?"

Shirley stepped away from Christelle. "Well, you really didn't do anything."

"You knew very well there was no tower and I stayed an extra day to do this. Besides, I helped get her," Eka pointed at Christelle, "out of the house." Eka then tried to stare Shirley down. "That's at least part of what you wanted."

"What? That's just helping a friend, not a job. Why would you want to take advantage of an old lady like that?" Shirley blinked at Eka, lip trembling again.

"Grams," Christelle grabbed Shirley's hand. "She's not trying to take advantage." Christelle glared at Eka. "We all just got our wires crossed."

Eka sighed then mumbled. "I think I did everything you asked; that was possible."

"Anyway." Shirley suddenly perked up, ignoring the mumble, and headed out of the living room and toward the kitchen. "Glad we straightened that out. And Eka, I'm sure I'll find a job that'll work out. If you stick around."

Eka stared after Shirley as she left. "She's up to something."

Christelle spun towards Eka. "Why would you say that? You saw how hurt she was."

Eka raised her brow. "Really?"

"I'm sure this is all innocent." Christelle crossed her arms.

Eka rolled her eyes. "Look, I don't know her, obviously. But I'd say she's holding something back. I mean, she was acting sneaky, don't you think?"

Christelle's face turned red. "Grams isn't sneaky!"

Eka threw up her hands. "I'm sure she's a wonderful person, I just mean she wasn't telling you everything. Just because she's family doesn't mean she can't hide something."

"Well." Christelle uncrossed her arms and clenched her fists. "Some of us have families we actually care about, not run from."

Eka froze.

In that split second, Christelle's anger seemed to abandon her and her eyes grew wide. "Eka, I'm sorry." Christelle reached out, but Eka flinched away as she bolted.

"No worries." Eka spun away and headed for the back of the atrium.

Christelle's apologies faded as Eka slammed the back door. Jumping in her truck, she turned over the motor and shoved it in gear. The truck fishtailed briefly, then peeled out of the driveway. As she cranked the window down, her heart slammed her chest over and over and she dug her hands into the steering wheel while the wind whipped through the cab.

"What the hell is wrong with me!" She slammed a palm against the steering wheel. "I know better than to trust anyone!" Her breath caught as her truck pulled left. "But Shirley had to offer to cover the repairs. Damn it!" She hit the steering wheel repeatedly, yelling at the roof, until her raging heart went quiet.

"Screw this magic stuff. It's not like anything's happening to me except a few weird, disturbing memories." She sighed and patted the dashboard. "Besides, I can cover the bills. I don't need the Haptons. Just need another gig soon."

A glimmer of colorful light flashed to her right.

Rainbow light?

"No way. Been to the Haptons and I'm done with it!"

She glimpsed right, to check for any fallen palms, but saw nothing weird.

"I'm probably losing my mind." She shook her head.

Just then, a brown sign flashed by, with a canoe and a swimmer painted on it in white outline.

A bit of canoeing, and swimming, could be fun, though.

She followed the signs, pulling off the road into a small gravel parking lot, surrounded by a few tourist shops. Kids ran by with bathing suits and beach wear, headed down a trail toward the river.

"Now, where's that suit?"

She climbed into the back of the cab and scrounge around for the bathing suit she kept in her truck for swimming emergencies.

"Aha!" Pulling the suit out from inside a cooler filled with empty water bottles and a discarded sandwich wrap, she tentatively smelled it. Not too musty. After shaking out the suit, she half-crawled, half-tumbled behind the front seats and wriggled out of her clothes, feet catching discarded papers and more food wrappers, as the not-so-musty suit and cut-offs slid on. Then, shoving a towel, filled water bottle, and sunscreen in a backpack, Eka hoofed it down the same trail the kids had taken, winding past three shops then passing through a lightly wooded area before reaching a river.

Water, sparkling and bright, spread out before her and some of the tension slipped away.

This is so what I needed.

On the riverbank to her left sat a rack of kayaks, all flipped over. A sign on the rack pretty much yelled 'rent me'.

"Totally am," she mumbled her answer, as her hand slid over the hulls of the kayaks. Small dents and repaired cracks were a testimony to their well-used and river-tested status.

"Do you need some help?"

Eka spun around to face a shirt-free chest leaning up against a kayak paddle in front of her. Swim trunks sat well below the chest, on a well-defined set of exposed abs.

"You know," a soft voice stated, "I'm up here."

She looked up into crystal green eyes and a crooked smile and she found herself grinning back, stretching out her hand.

"Nice to meet the rest of you," she winked. "I'm Eka."

He held her hand and gaze for a long moment. "I'm Devlon."

Now that's...wow.

After a moment, she managed to gather her thoughts and focus. "So, who owns that shack?" She nodded towards the open building behind him.

"Shack?" His hand flew to his chest and he stepped back, still grinning. "I'll have you know that this is the finest rental place on the river."

Still examining his body, she nodded. "I can see some possibilities here."

This time, he seemed to take a moment to compose a response. "What exactly are you looking for?"

She slowly turned back to the kayaks. "I was thinking of exploring some of the river, maybe a few islands."

"We have plenty of kayaks and maps." He crossed his arms over the paddle and leaned into it again. "Even personal guides."

A warm flush went through her at the prospect of exploring more than just the body of water, and she stepped closer, almost close enough to feel his breath. "I think I'll explore alone, this time. But," she brought her hand up slowly, brushing his leg with her fingertips on the way to move some hair out of her face, "I'd love a rain check."

His breath caught and his eyes widened.

"Devlon?"

Eka spun toward the voice to find a short woman with frizzy black hair staring at her as she made her way past the rental shack. She clutched two coffees tightly, to the point where one was caving in.

Eka stepped away from Devlon as he turned toward the woman.

"Hey, Janice."

Janice scuttled over next to Devlon. Really close. "Did you forget our coffee date?"

Eka stepped back farther. "Hey, Abs, don't let me keep you from your date."

Janice scowled at Eka, then turned and looked up at Devlon with a wide-eyed, toothy smile. "Oh, Devlon loves coffee as much as I do."

Devlon's body seemed to tense, a not unattractive look. "Not a date," he frowned at Janice, "just coffee. Friends."

Janice's eyes narrowed at Eka as she handed Devlon a coffee. "Close friends," Janice said loudly and attempted to put her arm through his.

Devlon slowly extracted himself from her grabby hands.

"Janice, this is Eka."

Eka put out her hand, but Janice just glared.

"Well," Devlon nodded toward Eka. "She's looking for a kayak and I need to get back to work."

Janice made no motion to leave, just stared quietly in the awkward silence. After a long, actually excruciatingly long, moment, Devlon finally motioned Eka toward the other side of the kayaks.

"I'll see you later, Janice." Devlon lifted his cup. "And thanks for the coffee."

Janice shoulders hunched over. "I'll call you later, Devlon," She said before skulking away.

"Okay," he waved.

She seemed to take forever to leave, her slow movements mesmerizing. When Janice was finally out of sight, Devlon held up his hands as he blew out a breath. "I'd apologize, but that would be awkward."

She looked him up and down.

This one could be complicated.

"Fan or 'very' understanding girlfriend?" Eka asked.

He glanced over at the dirt path leading back to the shops. Eka followed his gaze over to the trees Janice had disappeared into. Devlon shrugged. "We hang out sometimes. Although she might have different ideas about what that means."

Eka whistled. "Fan then."

He blinked and turned back to Eka. "Sorry?"

Eka let it go and looked back at the kayaks. "I'd still like to take a kayak out. What's your rate?"

"Tell you what. This is on the house. For all the awkwardness."

Eka raised an eyebrow.

"And I'll throw in a dinner."

"Very tempting, but not sure I'm into a potential stalker complication." She nodded back at the trail.

"I promise no problems with Janice. And, if she's hiding in the plants at the restaurant, you can walk. No questions asked."

She glanced at his abs and inviting smile. Maybe she'd hang around a little longer. "Alright. But I'm checking the plants."

His face lit up and he helped her with a kayak. As they lifted it off the rack, his body brushed up against her and the warm flush was back.

Twenty-five minutes later, Eka dropped her paddle between her feet in exhaustion and relaxed into the kayak, drifting past a few islands. Boats and jet skis sped down the river channel in the distance, probably too busy to notice the river itself. The kayak lolled back and forth when the wake from the speeders finally hit the hull and she lay back on her pack, the August sun warming her skin. Any lingering thoughts of magic, and Christelle, disappeared as she drifted off to sleep.

Eka.

She stirred from her sleep and blinked. The sky above was dark now and stars blazed out of a moonless night.

How long was I asleep?

She sat up and rubbed her eyes. On all sides of her, a dark mist hung over the river. Then a voice, like wind blowing through glass chimes, echoed in her mind.

Not long now.

"Hello?"

She searched around her for the voice, but there didn't seem to be anyone else here.

Not long for what?

Out in the river she suddenly saw colorful lights pulsing around in the mist.

"Okay. I'm sleeping." Maybe everything looked very real, but it couldn't be. So, she pinched herself. "Ow."

What the...

Rubbing her arm, she leaned over the side of the kayak just as the lights began to swirl in the mist, mesmerizing her and spinning faster and faster, until her stomach roiled. But, she still couldn't look away. Suddenly, the lights slammed to a stop and all the tiny pinpoints imploded down to two glowing spheres.

Eka, released from the spinning light trance, fell back into the kayak, holding her stomach.

The spheres began to bob up and down in the mist.

Ominously dark mist and two dancing, glowing spheres. Totally normal.

As if hearing her, the globes rose out of the mist and seemed to float toward her. Eka crab-walked back across the hull until her back was pressed against the wedged bow and her heart beat like it was a drummer in a speed metal band. When the two bright orbs finally floated across the kayak, she almost flipped it over trying to scramble past the bow.

She threw her hands up in front of her and the globes stopped inches from her face. Balancing on the edge of the kayak for what felt like an eternity, she watched the spheres from between her fingers. But they just hovered.

Hesitantly, Eka lowered her arms, finally face to…uh…face with the swirling orbs. A subtle warmth emanating from them. Impulsively, she reached toward an orb, but before contact, the lights shimmer-pulsed, and she jerked back, almost flipping off the bow. Again.

"Really?" she whispered, before a warm tickling in her stomach distracted her. Heat exploded out, spreading across her torso and down her limbs, her skin abruptly glowing in rainbow hues like the orbs in front of her.

She held up her hands and stared at the tiny rainbow lights moving just under her skin, the same lights moving in the orbs.

Holy crap. I can see through my skin!

Then, the orbs blinked and the swirling lights inside became eyes.

Eyes. They're eyes!

Eka yanked her hands in as a wind-chime voice spoke.

Eka, do you have your pendant?

Her hand went instinctively to her neckline.

"Who…what are you? What pendant? What's going on?"

You need to remember. It's not long now, so wear the pendant. Always. He's coming. See what he is.

Before she could reply, a coldness crept down her back and she turned around. Across the water, the mist swirled apart like curtains opening and something crawled across the water's surface. At least that's what it seemed like to her eyes that hurt trying to focus on the spot. She squinted and the shadow crawler suddenly seemed less like darkness and more like the absence of light. A Nothing. Even in the minimal glow of the night sky she could see the color drain from the river as the Nothing passed over it. Draining it of light, of life. And then there was the coldness that spread across her. All of her heat was sucked away as that encroaching, life-sucking Nothing honed in on her. Trapped on the edge of her kayak, she spun her bracelet, trying to focus on an escape plan.

Eka turned back to the floating eyes and they were gone. She grabbed the paddle, slid onto a bench and paddled desperately away. When she finally turned to check her progress, the Nothing seemed to be gone, just like the eyes. Only mist remained.

"What the hell is going on?" Eka whispered, trembling.

Eka. The voice, a faint tinkling, responded. **Time to wake up. And remember the pendant. And him.**

Intense heat rolled across Eka and she jerked upright, blinking at sun glinting off water. Her desert-of-a-mouth ached and she shook, freezing despite the heat. Shakily, she grabbed the bottle from her bag and gulped water, trying to wash away any lingering fear.

"What the hell was that?" she finally croaked, to no one.

Fragments of glowing eyes, a Nothing eating the river and her bright, colorful skin, played through her mind.

Maybe the pinch test was bullshit and it was a dream.

But it all felt real. Her hands clenched and unclenched, the ache of frantically paddling away from that Nothing still throbbing in them. And a hint lingered, of strange warmth from her glowing skin. How it had pushed out a bit of the cold from that Nothing.

"It seemed so freakin' real."

The sinking sun only warmed her so much until the cooling evening finally fragged her out of her circling thoughts. She wasn't going to learn anything sitting in a stationary kayak, in the middle of a river. She scanned the area to get her bearings, comparing it to the map Devlon had given her. Dozens of crowded mangrove islands surrounded her; they matched up on the map with a clump of islands about a mile from where she'd fallen asleep.

If *I was asleep.*

The map indicated a narrow waterway through two islands to the northeast. As she turned for the paddle lying in the stern, a gray shape on the river grabbed her attention and she spun around. A dull, gray island sat apart from the other little islands around it. All the others were bright with the greens of plant life, and the tans and browns of sand and dirt, and every one of them seemed to shrink from the mute and colorless surface of the gray mass that lay between them. As her kayak drifted towards it, a sense of despair settled over Eka. Dead, gray trees sat back from a gray beach. No sound came from the shadowed center and Eka's still chilled body shook more violently with each moment. She grabbed the paddle and backed away from the island, her tired arms struggling to move the kayak. She kept paddling for what seemed like hours, through the small channels before she was far enough away to stop shivering.

"Okay, get a grip. What am I so wigged out about? A nightmare?"

She lay back and tried to focus on the drifting clouds, to let go of the dream, but the colorful voice echoed in her head.

Something about a pendant.

She touched her neck, remembering an i'iwi bird pendant she'd had as a child.

"When did I stop wearing that?"

Was this another part of her past surfacing?

"Why does all this have to be so freaky?" she yelled. "I mean, floating rainbow eyes." She lowered her voice and breathed deeply. "That's really out there. Kinda cool, but out there." She shook her head. "But that darkness thing was not okay. And what is up with that island?"

She looked back toward the cluster of islands hiding the creepy, dead mass within them.

"Probably heat stroke mixed with this magic crap."

She shook her head again, then paddled back to the rental dock. With her body and head aching, she was glad no one was around. Flirting was the last thing she could handle, so she left a note with the kayak before taking off to her truck.

Should she go back to the Haptons' cottage after storming away from Christelle? She'd have to at least get her stuff. Then she could go to a campsite and figure out what was happening to her.

Pulling up to the cottage, she hopped out of the truck and ran inside, tearing through her room until she finally found the old memento box in her messenger bag. The smooth driftwood pulled at her fingers, tugging old, shuttered memories of Hawaii closer to her awareness.

Gently, she lifted the lid. At the bottom, her parents' wedding rings lay tied together with a strand of hair. Her brother's first haircut. These mementos were all that was left of them. As she stroked the cold metal and soft strands, her breathing shallowed and her chest tightened, until her hand jerked back.

It's just stuff. I can do this.

Wiping her watery eyes, she dug back into the box. An old lei took up most of the space and her fingers caressed the seeds and shells that sang of her birth, lifting her heart a bit. She'd heard the story so many times that she could picture Sema and Win as they gathered the materials and strung them together on the day she was born.

She finally found the small object of colorful stones and gold in the corner, almost forgotten. Her fingers brushed the metal, touched its realness, brushing out doubts over hallucinations and nightmares. Lifting the pendant, she examined the small i'iwi bird of stones set in gold. The bird dangled from a braided vine, poised in mid-flight and ready to flit over anything. A brief memory of her grandmother, Haipo, taking it from her after her parents' death, flashed through her thoughts but she still had it. Haipo was always hard on Eka but why would she take a necklace from he, especially at that time? And where had it come from?

Why can't I remember getting this?

At its touch, bright, colorful light and warmth seemed to flow through her. Without a plan, she untied the vine and lifted it to her neck. But, as she tried to tie the vine behind her, a coldness enveloped her and the necklace fell, landing back in the box.

So close to ready. A faint, frigid voice flowed through her like a subzero wind and a needle-like pain shot into her head, as an image of Ke and her parents, devoured by the cold Nothing, overwhelmed her.

"No!"

The cold voice swirled frigidly inside her and she pulled all the blankets around her.

"Gr-great. G-g-gonna freeze to death in the F-florida heat."

At that moment, tiny colored lights appeared and floated onto the i'iwi pendant. She reached again for the bird but another vision of Ke falling into a Nothing pit flashed through her mind and this time, the vision pulled Eka into the same pit. Her body went rigid and hit the box, sending the flying as she collapsed.

Foot-in-Mouth Syndrome

I *totally made a mess of this.*

Christelle paced around her hanging bed, morning sun shining through the picture window.

Why did I say that?

Should she call Eka? Go over to the cottage? Christelle paced a few more steps and stopped.

I'll just talk with her. Apologize.

Before she could change her mind, she rushed out of her room. But, as she turned toward the back door, whispered arguing from behind a closed door stopped her. She tip-toed over and leaned her head against the door, trying to catch what was going on.

She hated spying, almost as much as lying, but her world seemed upside down now and she couldn't get a handle on it. Besides, everyone was acting weird and evasive. She needed answers, so she pressed her ear against the door.

"It's time you told her."

"You know I'm trying, but I don't know how. What if she can't forgive me?" Soft crying followed.

"Keeping her in the dark any longer is dangerous. And it isn't going to help her understand why you made this choice for her."

A sniffle. "Maybe Jake could tell her?"

Dad's keeping stuff from someone? What stuff? From who?

Christelle peeked under the door and recognized Grams's yellow sandals by the window. Aunt Anise's blue flats paced the room.

"It's best it came from you. And you need to tell both of them." That was definitely Grams's voice

The crying ceased and the flats halted in mid-stride.

"She's not one of us, Mom."

"Yes, she is. I know this is hard and things are…uncertain but…"

"The danger is back, we can feel it. Like the last time she showed up."

What danger? Who showed up?

"The last time they both showed up. Anise, listen, she was a victim too."

"No, Mom, it's settled. I don't want to talk about this anymore."

Blue flats beat toward the door and Christelle just managed to scramble around a corner and into a small alcove, cowering behind a large fern as the door flew open. She guessed the footsteps stomping down the hallway to the front door were Aunt Anise's.

Slam!

What were they arguing about? Aunt Anise could get angry once in a while, but Christelle had never heard her slam doors.

Other footsteps seemed to sashay into the hall then yellow sandals suddenly stopped just in front of the fern. Christelle shrank back into the corner, breath held. If she held it in, could she disappear? Maybe that was another magical ability.

Shirley looked directly in Christelle's direction and Christelle's eyes shut.

I am the wall. I am the wall.

After a moment, as Christelle's lungs screamed they were ready to explode, footsteps receded down the hall. Then the front door opened and closed, quietly this time. Christelle snapped open her eyes and finally exhaled, nearly hyperventilating, trying to satisfy her throbbing lungs as her heart pounded away in her chest. When her body finally quieted, she seemed to be alone. Well, not completely alone. Questions, left behind in the wake of that weird conversation, swam around her mind, softly whispered suspicions tugging at her from the same place all these new memories were coming from. And now there was one more thing she couldn't talk to with her family.

They wouldn't hide something big from me? Especially if we're in danger. They would tell me. And who isn't part of the group.

Another whisper.

Eka.

"This is silly. They're probably talking about some farm thing." She knew nothing about the farm. Maybe that's it.

But what about the magic? Should she bring it up to them? Would they understand?

Whispers again in the background of her thoughts, then doubt.

"Maybe this isn't the best time, with all this farm stuff." But she couldn't shake the feeling it wasn't about the farm.

Her thoughts went round and round, to no where but the beginning. She really needed a confidant, but the only person she could possibly confide in, was angry at her.

Well, what did she have to lose?

"Damn it, Eka. Please still be here. And please listen," she whispered.

She crawled from behind the fern and ran towards the back door, away from the lingering argument and the whispers.

Christelle ran up the two steps and into the cottage door, raising her hand. Then, stopped.

What if she hates me? But I didn't do anything, irreversible. Did I?

"Just knock!" The sudden sound of her voice, outside her head, made her jump. "Fine."

She tapped, the sound barely audible against the wooden door. Nothing happened.

She probably didn't hear it. Or doesn't want to see me.

She rubbed her fidgeting hands against her pants and knocked harder, the sound reverberating inside as the door creaked open. Blinking in the darkness, she realized no one stood on the other side.

"Eka?"

An achy groan floated out and Christelle instinctively pushed the door open all the way and stepped inside as heat hit her.

Why's the heat on?

A box and travel bag lay discarded on the floor, while sheets and a blanket seemed to wrap around themselves like an octopus tangled in itself. Another moan escaped the tangle and the blanket shifted. She rushed over and touched the blanket, the cloth shifting under her hand.

"Eka?"

The lumpy blanket mumbled something and Christelle pulled back the cover, discovering Eka, damp hair stuck to her head, clothes soaked.

"Okay. Remember that class on first aid." She paced for an itchy, uncomfortable moment trying to remember anything, then slapped her palm against her thigh. "Get a temperature!"

Christelle lightly tapped Eka's forehead. It was freezing. "Is that right?"

She laid her palm on Eka's forehead, then jerked back, her hand cold and burning from the contact. A faint hand print of lavender lingered briefly on Eka's forehead before disappearing. Christelle leaned closer and touched the same spot. The skin seemed warmer now, less sticky than before.

"Did I do that?"

She stared at her hand, the same lavender color as the hand print on Eka's forehead. The same as that stormy night in the kitchen, when the plants in the window box seemed to insta-grow crazy amounts. Or when she touched the flowers alongside Eka in the field. She refocused on Eka, noticing a gray light coming from her skin that seemed faint and still, except in the spot where her lavender hand print glowed. There the energy seemed to pulse.

Eka's eyes flew open, locking on to Christelle.

"So cold," she whispered, then her eyes rolled back.

"Eka!"

Christelle's breath shortened and she grabbed Eka, shaking her. She called Eka's name over and over, the name becoming a mantra. Everything else faded; her whole focus on her friend. At some point she noticed that as she shook Eka, limp and unresponsive, lavender light radiate from Christelle's skin and hands and spiraled into the gray, barely flowing, light within her friend. Christelle squinted and leaned closer to Eka's face. As the lavender mixed with the gray, it brightened and began to move and pulse. Christelle exhaled a breath she didn't realize she'd held. Something felt right about this movement and glow.

At that moment, a shadow flickered within the gray and Christelle froze, goosebumps racing across her skin. As the shadow slithered in and out of the gray and lavender light, a cold prickling crawled across her, like the pinpricks when her numb hand woke up. The shadow's edges expanded with every slow beat of pulsing light and the gray in Eka slowed to a stop while the lavender disappeared into it. Christelle shivered as cold spread across her skin then sank inside. All around her, the room became a runny watercolor painting.

"No, this isn't happening." Her words sounded muffled and her mouth seemed miles away. Reaching up, she touched her lips but nothing seemed there. Her senses seemed to be disappearing.

Then, at the edge of her collapsing perception, a tickle ran across her arm. In slow motion, she glanced down at her forearm as a rainbow of melted colors flowed across her skin and towards the shadow in the stagnant, gray energy. Christelle's skin prickled to life along the rainbow trail and a burst of warmth flowed through her, chasing out the cold. Within the gray, colorful light spun around the shadow, squeezing it into a tighter and tighter ball that finally collapsed into itself. The lights then flowed into the room and out the ceiling, disappearing with the warmth. Christelle jerked her still cold hands away and dropped to the floor, as her vision darkened.

Christelle's eyelids fluttered open, an expanse of sky visible through the dome of glass overhead. She was stretching her neck up off a pillow, examining the narrow floor space she lay on when a cup popped in front of her face. Eka's outstretched hand held it.

"Cocoa?"

Christelle nodded and wiggled up on the pillow, taking the cocoa. The warm, chocolaty concoction ran down her throat, heat spreading everywhere, reminding her of cold, shadows, Eka's gray energy, and rainbow lights.

A coughing fit ensued.

"Whoa, slow down." Eka plopped down on the bed.

Christelle downed another gulp of hot chocolate.

"You left and I went looking for you and, oh!" Her stomach tightened and she drew her eyebrows together, voice less scratchy but less confident. "I'm so sorry about what I said. Really, I don't know why..."

Eka waved away her words. "Don't worry. People say things all the time."

Christelle shook her head. "No, really. I just overreacted. I *do* need to figure things out on my own sometimes."

Eka waved off her words again. "It's whatever."

"Okay. Well, I really am sorry." Christelle frowned. "Anyway. I came by to talk to you and your door was open and I found you bundled up with the heat on and ... "

"Hey," Eka butted in, "take a breath."

Christelle breathed deeply then jumped back in. "You were cold. I mean, it's hot out and you were bundled up, but you were freezing." She looked straight into Eka's eyes. "I mean like Arctic-cold freezingn."

Eka frowned and stared out the window. "I remember the darkness and cold. Like something, or a Nothing, breathing me in." She shivered, her gaze unfocused and far away. After a moment, her body shook and she seemed to refocus on the cottage. "And I had some weird dream, before, while I was out in a kayak. With a dark island and weird voices."

"You went kayaking?"

Eka nodded. "Sure. Nothing rids my head of unwanted stuff like physical activity."

Christelle sank into the pillow. "I didn't know there was kayaking around here." She'd been worried that Eka was mad at her. But no, she was off kayaking. Enjoying herself.

"Yeah. So you said something about darkness and lights?"

Christelle sighed. "I saw those lavender lights from my hands again. Like with the plants." She examined her hands. "And you had gray light coming from...like, from under your skin. It was so weird. And the lavender, kinda, I don't know, mixed with the gray."

"What?"

"Yeah, the colors were mixing. And I think I got excited and more lavender light flew out of my hands." Christelle sat straighter. "I think my energy helped warm you up."

"You brought me back?"

"Maybe." She shrugged then shivered, remembering the slinking dark in their combined light. "There was a dark thing, moving in your gray light." She found herself whispering this last part.

Eka's brows furrowed and she shivered then slid off the bed to the floor next to Christelle. "Thanks."

"For what?"

"For trying to help me."

"Of course. And I'm so sorry, again."

Eka shook her head, then nudged Christelle with her shoulder. "It's all good."

These words, acceptance, seemed real, even genuine. Not sure where the quick turn around came from, but she'd take it. Christelle smiled at this new…friend, and finally relaxed. A glint of brightness from Eka's neck caught Christelle's attention. A small pendant hung there. Was that new?

"That's weird. Just before I passed out, rainbow lights swirled around something on the floor." Christelle squinted at the necklace. "It was glowing and kind of looked like that pendant."

Eka brushed the pendant with her fingers. "It was glowing when I woke up too; kinda called to me." Eka glanced at the necklace and ran her fingers along the edges of it. "I know it's not talking, but I felt the need to put it on, like it's keeping me safe or something." She looked back at Christelle. "I started to put this on before everything went cold and dark. Right before I had a weird vision."

"A vision?"

Eka nodded, rolling the pendant on the chain.

"Ever since I got here, I've been experiencing memories of my family. And then this dark…" Eka paused, brow knit. "Presence, I guess is the word."

"Do you think it's the same thing that sucked up all the heat?"

Eka shrugged. "Seems like I saw those colorful lights when my truck broke down. Of course I told myself I was just tired." She attempted to grin.

Christelle sighed. "Guess this is all hard to take in."

Eka stood up and slowly paced the room. "Since we're talking about the weird stuff…I saw those lights out in the kayak. Well." Her pace quickened and she crossed back and forth, opening her mouth as if to speak then shutting it.

Christelle dug her fingernails into her palms. "Just spit it out!"

Eka stopped pacing. "Maybe I was dreaming, but it seemed so real." Eka stood in front of Christelle, her leg jiggling. "I think I fell asleep in the afternoon but I woke up at night. And there was mist everywhere."

"Mist? On the river? That's not normal."

"Right!" Eka paced in front of her again, arms swinging in her description of colorful lights, giant eyes, a voice she'd heard saying 'he is coming', another voice telling her she should wear the pendant, and a dark thing attacking out of the fog.

Christelle shivered. "Weird."

"Yeah." Eka's animated hands fell to her side. "The really weird thing was, when I woke up, there was this creepy dead island that felt like that shadow thing."

Images of it all danced across Christelle's mind.

Eka slumped next to Christelle. "I don't understand what's going on." She pulled her legs into a hug. "And I keep having visions of my family. Why would I have visions of them now? And what could they possibly have to do with any of this…magic? I mean, they've all been gone for so long." Eka's head dropped on her knees.

Christelle gasped. "Eka. I didn't know you lost them." She threw her hands over her mouth, which was becoming a habit. After a moment, she touched Eka's shoulder. "I never meant that you would run from your family."

Eka shook off her hand. "It doesn't matter. The one thing that keeps nagging me is that all of this seemed to start the night I stopped here, the night we got sick. And Shirley seems to know something. I mean, I get that she's your grandmother and all…"

Christelle crossed her arms. "No, you were right, she did avoid our questions. And … "

"And what?"

She stared at her hands. "I heard Grams and Aunt Anise talking about revealing a secret to someone, but Aunt Anise didn't want to. And she got mad when Grams mentioned a second person that needs to know the secret."

"What secret?"

Christelle shook her head. "I don't know what they were talking about, they didn't mention names, but I felt, maybe, for some reason…it was us." She took a deep breath. "And they mentioned a danger returning when that someone showed up here again."

Eka stared back. "Why would that mean us?"

Christelle shrugged. "I don't know. But Aunt Anise thinks that some person, who recently showed up, is dangerous." Christelle rubbed her hands on her pants and turned away from Eka's gaze. "I think, maybe, you."

"Me?"

Eka hopped up and put Christelle's cup on the bedside table. She frowned, then raised her eyebrows, as if having some internal dialogue. She finally fell back on the bed. "Why would I be dangerous?"

"You're not." Christelle shook her head. "Whatever is going on, Aunt Anise is just over reacting. We'll figure out what's happening to us, if it has anything to do with that conversation, and what Grams knows."

"Not a tall order at all." Eka blew hair out of her face.

"Nope."

"All the clues have been more confusing than enlightening," Eka continued. "You might be right about needing help." Eka sat up. "But who? Obviously your family doesn't feel like explaining."

"What about your extended family? You mentioned a grandmother."

Eka shook her head. "No. Sema and Win, my grandparents, are great. They love me in their way. And they've always been there for me. But Sema's been…weird since this started. I think she actually tried to trick me into coming here and meeting Shirley." Eka twisted her bracelet. "I think her and Shirley might be up to something together."

"What is going on with everyone?" Christelle huffed then sagged further down. "I can't really think of anyone else." She thought back to the vision of her parents. "It's weird, both of us having new memories of our families. Until the other day, I didn't have any of my mother. But I saw her in this new one. She held my hand." Christelle held up the hand; the sensation was back, of her mother's skin pressed into it. "It was like I was there at that moment, experiencing it for the first time. And I magically grew a plant." She closed her eyes and was back in the field, the sun's heat warming her skin as she stood next to her mother, the flower growing in front of her. After another moment, the sensations faded and she opened her eyes. Her mother was gone.

She breathed in, trying to inflate her heavy chest.

Eka tapped her shoulder. "You okay?"

Christelle nodded and quickly rubbed a tear away. "So, um, how could it have happened? Did I forget, until now? And why now?"

Eka shrugged. "Honestly, I have no idea. And I don't even know how we could explain it to anyone without sounding like we're fifty-one cards short of a full deck?"

"Right?" Christelle laughed, a tiny bit lighter. "Hey, Aunt Anise, let me help you on the farm. And by the way, I see colorful lights flowing in everything, Eka hears voices, and I can grow plants with magic. Great, huh?"

"Well, if that didn't work out," Eka's smile grew, "you could take the plant-growing thing on the road as a new show."

Christelle threw a pillow at her. "Sure, and pretty soon, I'm the main act at a lab somewhere."

"Now that's something." Eka threw the pillow beside Christelle and sat on it, leaning against the bed. "I kinda thought that was a movie thing, but…well, I hope it's a movie thing."

Could there be a lab that studied magical people? Christelle shivered.

"Do you think there's others like us?" she asked.

Eka shrugged. "Not sure what 'like us' is. Maybe. Add it to all the other questions."

What if there was a whole world of people like her; people who knew what was going on and could help them? Could explain all the craziness?

"Well." Eka broke into her thoughts. "I guess it's just you and me for now."

Christelle nodded. "I think, at some point, we've got to talk to someone, even if all this magic stuff sounds crazy. Even if Aunt Anise wants to hide something. But maybe we should be more careful for now?"

"I am careful."

Christelle frowned and crossed her arms.

"Fine," Eka sighed. "More careful. For now I've got to go to Silasville tomorrow. Check out a job."

Christelle's heart sped up. "You're leaving, in the middle of all this?"

"I've got to," Eka shrugged. "I missed the Keys job and Sema called in a favor and set it up. I've gotta earn a living, right?"

Christelle couldn't help deflating like an old balloon. "Okay."

"Hey, why don't you come along?"

"Really?" Christelle sat up, reinflated. "I mean, that'd be awesome!"

"Yeah, it'll be fun. Be ready around five. That's a.m."

"What?" Christelle sighed and leaned back against the bed next to Eka, air gone again. "I hope you're good at waking the dead."

The Amazing Wobblinas

"Thirty minutes to destination."

Christelle rolled over and fell on the floor.

"You okay back there?"

She sat up on the backseat and peered through the windshield as trees and the road speed by. "Where are we?"

Eka glanced at her phone's map. "Almost to Silasville. Maybe another forty-five minutes."

Christelle bounced around as they hit potholes. Behind them, the vardo hit a bump and jostled the truck some more. "Hey, you brought your camper. I didn't even notice it this morning."

"Yeah, zombie girl. You were seriously like the walking dead when we left. Hope you're okay with staying overnight. I don't feel like making the drive back today."

"That's fine." Christelle climbed over the seat back and plopped down on the passenger seat, still in her pajamas. She yawned and stretched her arms out and her hands hit the window and roof. "Darn it." She shook out her hand, still yawning. "Why am I so tired? What time is it?"

"Ten."

"Ugh." Christelle slumped in the seat. "Can't believe I'm up."

Eka grinned at her. "I can't believe you slept through this road trip."

Christelle yawned again. "How can you be up so early?" She leaned her head against the window, watching the landscape drift past. A few houses were partially hidden among the trees, tiny dots of reds and blues in the greenery. Who lived there? Maybe a family that just sat down for Sunday breakfast. Kids who scarf down their food so they can go hang with the friends they've known forever. A place they all knew inside and out.

"Hey, sleepy, you're fogging up the window."

Christelle's head rolled front and she pulled up her legs. "Do you ever wonder what it's like to live in those houses?"

"What houses?"

"You know, the ones in all the places you pass through. Toys and cars out front. Swing sets in back. Houses with families that have lived there forever."

"Uh, no. Stuck in the same place, with the same people forever. Kill me first."

"I guess."

"Hey," Eka pushed her shoulder, "you okay?"

Christelle rested her chin on her knees. "Yeah. Guess I'm just tired."

Eka nudged her shoulder again. "You've had a good time traveling, right? Seeing the world?"

"Well, some of this country. But yeah." She half-smiled, focusing on a memory instead of the road. "Out in Utah, near Moab, Dad and I went hiking. We saw this amazing sunset that filled the whole sky." The sunset was still vibrant in her mind. "We just sat together, watching the moment, the changing sky, and the whole world seemed perfect."

Eka nodded. "Yeah. That's exactly what I mean. You would have missed that sunset if you'd lived there all your life. Most people don't notice the beauty around them, just pass it by."

"I guess." She remembered leaning against her father as the last rays hit and the stars grew brighter. His arm wrapped around her shoulders, giving her a comforting squeeze. "But it was special, you know, because my dad was there. I thought, when I came here to the farm, that maybe I could find that connection with the rest of my family too."

Eka laughed. "With that crazy crew! They're hardly…"

"Forget it." Christelle stared out the window again. "It's a stupid fantasy."

Eka's laugh died. "Sorry. It's not stupid. I'm sure they'll be great."

Christelle nodded.

"Listen. I'm the worst person to give advice, especially about family stuff."

Christelle shook her head and sighed. "Whatever."

"No, seriously. I pretty much raised myself, like those stories where kids are found and raised by wolves. Except, it was just me."

"Oh come on, you had your grandparents."

"Technically, yes. They're awesome, and they really loved me, but they believed in self-sufficiency. Anyways, you should try and connect with your family if it's important."

Christelle leaned against the window and sighed again. "I'm not going to have any kind of real relationship with them if I don't figure out what's been happening to me. I mean, how can I be part of a family if I have to hide all this crazy magic stuff?"

"What exactly do you think a family looks like? Again, I'm no expert but I'm pretty sure crazy stuff is the foundation of most families. Magic or no."

Christelle rolled her eyes. "Never mind."

"No, seriously. People spend years in therapy because of their families and their crazy stuff."

Christelle turned on the radio and leaned her seat back. "You're right. You're horrible at giving advice. Just wake me up when we get there."

Christelle spun around on one leg, her other one missing the pants, as Eka pounded on the vardo's door, and she finally fell on the bed.

"Christelle, we've been here for thirty minutes. What's taking so long?"

"It's not like I knew what I was grabbing this morning!" She finally pulled on the bright purple yoga pants and held up the yellow tank top. "I wasn't even awake."

"My meeting is in like ten minutes. I'm going ahead. I'll meet you at the office."

"No, wait! I'm almost done. Promise!" She hoped out off the bed, threw off her pajama top and squirmed into a bra and the tank top, then slammed the door open and stumbled out of the vardo. "Sorry."

"Holy crap." Eka shielded her eyes. "Are you color blind? Wait." She felt Christelle's forehead with the back of her hand. "Maybe it's some kind of magic side effect. Crap. You think it's catching?" She looked down at herself. "How's my clothes? Oh, never mind. You wouldn't know."

"Ha ha." Christelle scowled and pulled down on the tank top, futilely trying to hide her pants. "I told you I was still sleeping when I grabbed these."

Eka cocked her head, trying to keep her face straight. And failing. "It's okay. I'll still hang out with you. Sometimes."

"Oh come on. You've seen me dress, I know how…"

"Wait!" Eka held up a hand then pulled her chiming phone out of her back pocket. "Great." She glanced at Christelle then turned towards the parking lot exit. "Well, magical malady or dysfunctional dress sense, Sam's waiting. Come on. I can't blow this job." She nearly sprinted out of the parking lot and toward a sea of tents across the road. Christelle ran after her, stumbling as she tried to hide her outfit.

She followed Eka under a huge metal archway decorated with metal letters, painted in teal, white, and violet, announcing the traveling show 'Folly or Farce'. The archway opened onto a clearing in a wooded area, dense with tents. In front of her, a strip of dark blue carpet divided a row of teal tents on the left from a row of violet tents on the right. Christelle slowed down to read the signs posted by the arch, on either side of the carpet. On the left, two white signs on a pole, painted with teal letters, had 'Folly' painted across the top sign and 'Your Choice Awaits' painted on the sign below. Similar white signs on the right read 'Farce' on top and 'Choose Your Disgrace' on the bottom in violet letters.

"This is amazing!" Christelle turned and realized Eka was gone. Rotating full circle to search for anyone that worked here, she found the walkway empty.

A huff later, Christelle headed down the carpet in hopes of finding Eka. Open tents lined both sides of the carpet and she peeked inside each one, but found their shells empty of life. It did seem a little early for performers to set up.

At the end of the row, Christelle caught a small office sign pointing off to the right and quickly made her way to the only structure in the area, a large travel trailer sitting at the edge of the woods behind the tents. All offices she'd ever seen at these types of shows seemed to look like this, bland and functional.

Guessing Eka's in here.

Managers were usually early risers, so she didn't feel too intrusive tapping on the door. It swung open almost instantly, revealing a tall, gray-bearded man who over-filled the door frame. Christelle stumbled back at the looming figure.

"You must be Christelle." He looked her outfit over then shook his head and gestured inside. "Your friend's here, so come on in." He turned and disappeared inside, leaving her standing on the steps.

"Okaaayyyy." She recovered quick and stepped in, bending over in expectation of a tight space, after Eka's vardo and her father's trailer. But instead, the space was almost cavernous. A bathroom door stood open to her right and a cavernous living space spread before her. Framed pictures were strapped to the walls and dishes piled up in the kitchen area. A desk, littered with papers, took up a back corner, sitting completely inside the slide-out. And there Eka stood, by the desk, as the man joined her.

"Christelle," Eka waved her over, "this is Sam."

He nodded at Christelle. "Sam Bright."

She walked over and shook Sam's hand. An eruption of pale red, pinpoint lights flowed over his skin and she immediately dropped their connection.

He frowned at her. "Are you okay?"

"Yeah, uh, nice to meet you." Christelle smiled, tearing her eyes from the red light.

That looked like the light in my skin. Except red.

She glanced at her own hand, hints of lavender bubbling up, then shook it out.

This is so weird.

Sam sat his massive form at the desk and turned his attention to Eka. "So," he gestured towards a stool, "Sema says you need a job."

Eka sat, attempting to balance on the wobbly seat. "Yes."

Sam's eyebrows went up. "There's a rumor going around that you never showed up at your last job."

Christelle clenched her fists when she noticed Eka slump slightly. "She couldn't help it, she…"

Eka straightened her back and shook her head subtly at Christelle. "I was really sick, but I'm good as gold and ready to go. Definitely a one-off. And I have some excellent references and carry my own equipment."

"Well, Sema's been a friend for a while, and our regular guy has a family emergency. I'll give you a go but I'll need you to start on Tuesday."

"Sounds perfect." Eka grinned wide, showing a bit too much tooth.

Oh, like that smile is less annoying than a friend defending you in an interview.

Christelle heard the words in her head and deflated. A fake smile probably was more helpful.

Sam leaned across the desk, inches from Eka. "Don't flake out."

"Absolutely not."

"Okay." He nodded. "Now, where are those work forms?"

He dug around his desk while Eka waited, nearly crawling over it to help him. But, probably best she didn't. Christelle slinked away from them and the discussion of work details, drifting around the room filled mostly with paperwork and props. Against a wall, near the door, a miniature circus display sat on a table. Tents, equipment, and figurines were set up as if a performance were about to start. The display didn't seem to be 'Folly or Farce'—there were fewer tents—but those few were definitely larger than what she'd seen here. And they were a midnight blue with bright white stars or white swirls in a deep red color. Outside the circle of tents, something hovered that looked like a dirigible.

That's something different.

Above the display, several old, sepia-toned photos hung on the wall. The images seemed to depict a real-life version of the miniature circus. In the first photo a tall man, bearing a striking resemblance to Sam, appeared to direct a crew in erecting the tents. In the next photo, the Sam look-a-like stood next to a man and a woman, engaged in conversation. The clothes the pair wore hinted at the 1920s. The woman, in particular, caught Christelle's attention. She leaned in for a closer look.

Something about her. She looks like…

Christelle spun around and stared at Eka, then turned back to the image just as chairs scraped the floor.

"So, bring those forms back on Tuesday. Meanwhile, take a look around. This afternoon I'll have one of the ground crew show you the setup."

They walked past Christelle on their way to the door.

"Eka look." Christelle pointed at the picture. Eka glanced at it, then stopped and leaned closer. "Sam, who are these people?"

Sam slowly joined the picture admiration society. "Just some old family photos. I'm running Folly or Farce for a friend until the end of the week. That's my home show." His chest stuck out further. "*Fantasmes d'âme*. And that's me…my great grandfather back in our heyday." A smile spread across his face. "He was quite the showman."

"Great. But those two." Eka pointed at the man and woman talking to the showman. "They look like my grandparents."

His grin dropped and he put his hands in his pockets. "Oh, those are just some people I…he was friends with."

Eka touched the picture then dropped her hand. "But they look exactly like Sema and Win."

"Probably just the camera angle. A different view and they'd look completely different. Photos can be strange like that," Sam babbled as he opened the trailer door wide. "Well, thanks for stopping by. Make sure you meet up with that crew member this afternoon."

Christelle stared at Sam. What was up with him? She cocked her head back at the picture. Could there be something about the man and woman?

"Okay, thanks." Sam pointed out the door.

Eka wasn't moving from the picture, so Christelle grabbed her arm and pulled her out the door. Sam was obviously done with the discussion and them. As soon as they stepped outside, the door slammed behind them.

"That was weird," Christelle said as she dropped Eka's arm.

"I could swear that was Sema and Win."

Eka seemed confused as she spun her bracelet and paced around Christelle. "How could they not be Sema and Win? The people in the photo look exactly like my grandparents."

"And that really looked like Sam."

"Exactly!" Eka spun to face Christelle. "But that would make them all like a hundred or something." She paced again. "No, that can't be right."

Christelle threw up her hands. "I have no idea."

Eka seemed to continue a conversation with herself, not hearing Christelle. "Why so many secrets? Everywhere we go. I've had it!" She darted off through the grounds.

"Eka, wait!" Christelle jogged after her, following past the violet tents, across the blue carpet. When she caught up with Eka, they were in a storage area between the backside of the teal tents and the woods, discarded props littering the area. Eka paced between them, finally stopping next to a slack-wire hung between trees.

"Hey, what's going on with you?" Christelle asked.

Eka pulled the wire down and sat on it, rocking back and forth, then lifted her foot up onto it and held out her arms as she tried to sit up. The wire bent almost to the ground.

"Have you ever tried the slack-wire?"

Christelle shook her head.

"Tricky stuff." Eka managed to stand up on her right foot, wobbling. She gently placed the left in front, and when she leaned her weight forward the wire swung out to the left. Eka's feet arched out with the wire and out from under her, her body tumbling to the ground and rolling a few feet.

"Eka!" Christelle ran over to her.

Eka hopped up, apparently unhurt.

Christelle rolled her eyes. "Of course you're okay."

Eka didn't respond, but resumed pacing as she brushed herself off. Her wild gestures matched the gray energy popping inside her. "No matter what that picture really was, Sam seemed to be lying. Maybe it was taken recently and Sam just told us that story. But why? If that really was taken during his great-grandfather's day then there is something really weird going on here, on top of everything else." She halted abruptly in front of a short blue and yellow tube about half the length of a person, mounted vertically on a platform. Eka climbed up the platform and stuck her head inside the tube.

"Hey, it's hollow!" Eka's voice echoed from inside the tube.

Christelle crossed her arms, huffing. "Can you please focus."

Eka jerked her head out. "Okay. The strangeness of my time at your family's farm is off the charts. I mean, I'm practically forced to your house by some strange, colorful weather, then we both pass out for a week."

"Okay," Christelle nodded, rubbing her right palm with her left thumb.

"Then our senses blow up and it's like we're on an acid trip. Without the acid."

"An acid trip?"

"Trust me on this one. Then those weird, lost memories of magic. And our families."

My mom.

Christelle's eyes watered and she turned her head to wipe away a few tears. All the strange events suddenly seemed to be too much. Her insides felt like a million hands were scratching, trying to get out. She began pacing as well, too much energy to stand still. A unicycle leaned against a tent and she grabbed it. The balance of it was familiar and she realized it was just like the one she had trained on with her dad. She put it in front of her and set her foot on a pedal, rolling up to a rocking balance. As she focused on staying upright, the scratching subsided and her mind cleared. After a few laps around the area and a successful attempt at traversing a teeter totter, a stray laugh escaped her. When had she last laughed? Like, really laughed?

"That's awesome." Eka watched her. "Where'd you learn to ride a unicycle?"

"I did this in a routine with dad, when I was little. This and some aerials." Christelle rolled around a few more laps, the unicycle becoming an extension of her body. Like when she was a child.

"You're really good."

Christelle giggled as she rolled and twisted through the props. "So…now…you…saw…whoa!" The wheel bumped a rock and she tipped forward then jerked back, arms flying to catch her balance, but she managed to stay on it.

"Nicely done." Eka clapped.

She bowed and continued through the obstacles. "You're right about all the things that have happened. I can't seem to put them all together but I feel like there's a connection."

"Yeah. Do you ever get the feeling too, that everyone around us knows what's going on? That we're being set up?"

Christelle rolled past Eka. Things she'd overheard seemed to point that way but why would her family hide something from her? Especially something this big. That would be…cruel. She shook her head. "I don't know. Maybe."

"Maybe." Eka climbed inside the tube then bent over the edge. "But remember that rune Shirley showed me? Didn't you say it meant initiation, or secrets?"

Christelle struggled to remember the rune. "I think so."

"Sounds like a hint to me. Maybe she was trying to tell us about the initiation into magic. Or, from what you said about the argument the other day, Anise keeping secrets."

Christelle stopped moving forward. "Maybe something's going on with the farm or Manatee Isles and that's what the argument was about. But you can't believe…"

"Hey," Eka interrupted. "Did you notice anything else weird about Sam? I mean, besides avoiding the picture topic."

"Can't you ever focus?" Christelle mumbled.

"What?"

"Nothing." Christelle rolled around, ignoring her irritation. "I did see flashes of red lights around Sam's hand. Like the lavender around me, or the gray light around you."

Eka sat up. "You think he's like us?"

"How would I know?"

Eka threw up her hands. "Ahhhh! This is so frustrating!"

Irritation bubbled up in Christelle too and she cycled faster. What was going on with everyone? Why did her family seem so evasive?

But, I trust them. I mean why wouldn't I?

She was losing her mind going round in circles on this.

"I think we should just forget all this drama and start our own show," Eka interrupted her thoughts.

"Yeah, right," Christelle fumed, holding onto the drama.

"Oh, come on." Eka pointed at the tube. "You know this is a human canon."

"Really?" Christelle, slightly distracted; couldn't remember seeing one in any of the shows she'd worked. "It seems shorter than I thought they were."

Eka pointed to another yellow and blue tube lying on the ground. "That's the rest. Guess they aren't using this right now. You know," Eka raised an eyebrow and smirked, "I've always wanted to be a human cannonball."

Christelle's shoulders finally relaxed, despite herself. "You definitely are flighty enough for that job."

"Right!" Eka spun around in the tube. "I could be Eka, the human cannonball! Sailing through the air without a care. And you could be Christelle, the one-wheeled wonder."

"I guess I could see that," Christelle smiled. "But maybe we should work on the names."

Eka leaned her elbows on the tube and cupped her chin in her palms.

"We could travel around the world. I could shoot out of the cannon and land on your shoulders while you ride the unicycle."

Christelle opened her arms. "You could do a flip first and I'd be blindfolded!"

They giggled as Eka spread her arms. "The Amazing Wobblinas on a fifty-city tour. Around the world in eighty days!"

Memories of traveling ran through her mind. City after city, everything a blur, only ever really knowing her dad. "Did you enjoy growing up traveling?"

Eka nodded and smiled. "I saw so many places. Met so many people. Did you know there's a place right here in Florida that has a mermaid show?"

Christelle shook her head and tried to picture women and men swimming with tails.

"How do they breathe?"

"A pump would send air down through small tubes in the tank and when anyone needed air, they'd just take a breath."

"Pretty cool." Christelle smiled absently.

"During the show they'd turn a soda upside down and drink it underwater."

"How do you know all this?"

"I substituted for a mermaid who was out sick." Eka grinned.

"Of course you did."

"I'll admit, my performance was a little shaky. But what a trip! I don't get to perform much but it's a blast. You perform a lot, right?"

"Yeah."

"Do you miss it?"

Christelle nodded. "I loved performing. There was so much excitement from the crowds and the other performers. But I don't miss the other stuff."

"Other stuff?"

"I was in charge of the schedule and finding our next gig. Dad was never good at the admin part of working the traveling show circuit. I spent most days working on schedules and finances and taking care of Dad."

"Didn't you explore the places where you were performing? Meet the locals?"

"Not really."

Eka stared at her. "Then we'll definitely start our own traveling show. And we'll take a month at every stop to explore the nooks and crannies of the place. Meet everyone!"

Christelle laughed. A whole life traveling around, deciding where to go and what to do. And not stay so isolated.

"Sounds perfect. Maybe we could even add a little magic in the performance."

"Now that's thinking outside the box. We could…" Eka threw back her hands and hit a lever. Metal creaked then a click rang out and Eka, suddenly in slow motion, hurled out of the cannon and into the air. She arced up, her trajectory ending in the woods.

"Eka!"

Christelle instinctively reached for Eka, trying to grab her out of the air. A gust of wind, filled with swirling lavender lights, lifted Christelle slightly off the unicycle then blew forward, the lighted air wrapping around Eka and stopping her in mid-flight.

"Holy crap!" Eka shouted as she floated above a lightly wooded field that separated the circus area from the dense woods. She hovered for another moment before her body dropped to the ground in a dusty cloud.

Christelle ran over to the settling dust, trying to find her friend. "Eka?"

A muffled sound came from under a pile of leaves and twigs.

"Is that you? Are you okay?"

Christelle dropped down next to the pile and dug around in it, eventually contacting skin. Eka bolted upright, coughing out dust as she brushed leaves and clods of dirt off herself. After her cleanse, Eka took a moment to touch the ground. A smile spread across her dirty face. "I was flying."

Christelle shook her head and plopped down. "How are you okay?"

"I saw lights." Was all Eka got out.

"How did you see anything, you shot off so fast?" Christelle scanned Eka.

"But something stopped me and pulled me out of the sky. Like a blast of air. And there were lights."

Christelle glanced up then back at Eka.

"Wait." Eka scanned Christelle's hands. "Lavender, like when you grew those plants. You did this?"

Christelle frowned. "I guess so. I mean, I reached for you, wanted to stop you."

Christelle looked at her hands.

Could I really have done that?

They sat quietly for a few minutes, then Eka looked back at the prop area. It was still empty of people. "Glad no one else was around."

"I don't think anyone noticed."

"Okay. Maybe we should exit, stage left, before someone checks that out." Eka pointed to the tube, now hanging from a large spring and swaying above the ground.

"Yeah." Christelle stood and offered Eka a hand up, leaves and twigs poking out of her hair and clothes. Christelle pulled out a twig and grinned. "Looks like I'm not the only one with a warped sense of fashion. Maybe it' s catching."

Eka laughed and put her arm around Christelle's shoulders. "I think we make a great team."

"Yeah. And maybe this team can figure out what's going on."

"Definitely. Right after this gig." Then Eka took off towards the vardo.

"Can't you ever walk anywhere?" Christelle yelled as she ran after Eka.

Exploration Galore

Eka rested her legs on the fire pit and sipped grigio wine. Across the fire orange, red, and purple clouds drifted over the vardo in a darkening sky. She sighed in the stillness. Maybe she didn't know any more about this magical mystery, but for one week there'd been no dark dreams of her family or of threatening shadows. And the nonmagical week at the Silasville gig had definitely lifted her bank account. Now that she was back camping on Hapton land, thanks to Christelle, she wasn't sure this magic stuff was the right journey for her.

"Eka!"

She jumped as Christelle barreled into the campsite and wrapped her in a hug.

"Hey!" She laughed, holding the glass away from her blouse.

"I'm so glad you're back!" Christelle dropped down on the edge of the fire pit barely missing Eka's feet.

"Wine here." Eka yanked her feet away, sloshing wine on the dirt. Luckily.

"Oh, sorry." Christelle's grin just kept going.

"No worries." Eka took a sip, the infectious grin spreading to her face. "And thanks for setting me up in this campsite."

"Of course. No one comes out to this part of the farm. Besides," Christelle hopped up again, "the place we're going to is just through the brush."

"The place we're going?"

Christelle jiggled her foot. "I texted you everything but you're awful at texting back!"

"I was only gone a week. Not a year."

"Well, I've got so much to show you. Come on!" She grabbed Eka's hand and pulled her up.

"Whoa, wait a minute." Eka set the glass down on the fire pit. "What's the rush?"

Christelle hopped in place, wound up like a coil ready to spring. "Just follow me okay? You won't be sorry."

Eka jogged out of the campsite after Christelle, who was usually so subdued. What had her wound up?

Christelle hooked a right and disappeared into the undergrowth at the edge of the camp. Eka followed, zigzagging through pines and cabbage palms. As she pushed through the foliage, fronds slapped her hands and face, slowing her down. For a moment, she thought she'd lost Christelle, but some tall bushes ahead weaved back and forth and she headed towards the movement. Just past the firebushes, the brush ended and she walked out on to the bank of a river. Christelle sat on the water's edge, leaning against a pine.

"Okay, I'm here. What am I looking at?"

"Just wait," Christelle beamed. She closed her eyes, took a deep breath, and held her hands out over the water. Dim lavender started to light her skin from within, growing brighter until she seemed to be nothing but thousands of pinpricks of light. Then the lights started moving, slowly swirling around within Christelle, until they shout out of her and into the river. Incredibly, the river remained clear and smooth wherever the lavender hit it, but a moment later, a splash of bright teal radiated along the surface in response, like phosphorescent ripples. The teal response grew brighter with each splash of lavender and goosebumps raced down Eka's back as a nervous energy seemed to fill the air around her. Suddenly, water funneled up out of the teal lights, hopping across Christelle's palms like a slinky. She moved her hands back and forth as the water jumped between them, teal and lavender lighting both the water and Christelle. She finally dropped her hands and the water did a loop before splashing back in the river.

Eka stared at Christelle's grinning face as she danced over to Eka. "Woot woot!"

Eka's stare went to Christelle's hands, but she still couldn't get her brain to work. "Whoa."

"I did that." Christelle held her hands up, turning them back and forth in front of her face. "I still can't believe it."

Eka just shook her head. "How?"

"I don't know. I remember trying to save you in the air. I wanted to help so much and, I don't know, I just tried to feel that way again. And that happened."

"That's amazing!" Her brain kicked in and the whole lights and water thing started to sink in.

"I know, right?" Christelle sat back on the river bank. "How about you? Did you figure anything out? Get Sam to tell you anything?"

Eka shook her head. "Sam had already gone back to his show when I started and no one else seemed…aware of magic or have lighted skin or anything. As far as powers, nothing."

"Oh. Sorry."

"Don't be." Eka nudged her. "Honestly, I started with freaky visions and hallucinations. Not sure I wanted those to go anywhere. Besides, I was working most of the time. Too busy to try anything."

"Nothing at all?" Christelle frowned. "Don't you want to do magic? Understand what all this is about?"

Do I want to know what those visions meant? I mean, life has been pretty good, with no dark visions of Mom or Dad or Ke.

"Maybe this doesn't have anything to do with me." Eka held up her hand as Christelle tried to speak. "Listen. It's true that I experienced all those extra sensations, the lights and smells and colors. But I haven't been able to make anything grow, or get wind to pick people up or create water slinkies. Nothing. Maybe you're the only one able to do magical tricks."

"Not a trick," Christelle huffed.

"Sorry, magic." Eka placed her hand on Christelle's shoulder. "And I don't seem to have that gift. You keep telling me you want to bond with your family. I think you're right and you should talk to them about all this."

"But, I thought we were doing this together." Christelle leaned away from Eka, scooting back against the pine and crossing her arms. "That you wanted answers. You told me I was wrong for not wanting to understand all this."

Why'd I come back? I should have just kept going. She'd be okay, she has her family.

Eka sighed. "It's really great that you set me up in this camp, but I can't just keep living off goodwill. And there's another job coming up. One that might be permanent."

"You're leaving? Again?"

Eka stood. "I don't have magic like you. And I can't see…" Something flashed across her eyes and she swatted at it. "I can't see why you…" Another flash and another swat.

"What are you doing?" Christelle grumped.

Flash. Swat. Flash. Swat.

"Nothing, just these gnats."

Suddenly, a hundred bits of light zoomed between Eka and Christelle, coalescing into a swirling mass of rainbow lights. The glowing mass shot up above them then dropped down and around, flowing through the air like a flock of sparrows.

"Do you see that?" Eka asked mesmerized.

Christelle's head followed the lights. "Uh huh."

A faint buzzing started, a rhythmic pattern that sounded something like words. The sound rose and fell with the undulating pattern of the lights. Eka stood still, following their every movement. She seemed to float out of her body and up, to join the lights as they danced. She flowed into the glowing mass and lost sense of her body below. She was light and color and brightness.

Belonging.

The thought shocked her back to her body.

"No!"

"Eka?" Christelle started to touch Eka's shoulder but drew her hand back. "What are you shouting for?"

Eka shook her head and turned away from the lights and toward Christelle. "Nothing." She blinked and the lights swarmed down in front of her and abruptly collapsed into two rainbow orbs. That blinked.

Hello Eka.

Eka sucked in air and stared at the floating eyes before her.

"Eyes…rainbow eyes." Eka pointed.

"What eyes?"

The eyes hovered inches from her face.

You need to understand now. And I can show you some answers.

"Need me to understand what?"

"What are you talking about?" Christelle shook Eka's shoulder and Eka jumped. The eyes exploded back into tiny lights that swarmed up and hovered over the woods.

"Your eyes." Christelle froze. "They're…like rainbows." She leaned in, squinting. "All swirling around."

Eka touched the corner of her eye and blinked. "They don't feel different."

"Are you okay?"

Images of a cold shadow engulfing her family popped into her head.

No, I don't need answers. Not if I can't stop those visions.

Eka turned away from the lights that seemed to wait for her. "I'm fine. Everything's fine."

"Okaaaay. Everything's fine. But why do those lights seem to be interested in you?" Christelle cocked her head. "Yes, I said lights were interested in you. Why not?" Christelle mumbled and her body sagged.

"Look, this past month has been nice. Whatever this magic is, it's been great for you. Getting plants to grow and water to jump around. But all I've gotten are weird hovering eyes and dark dreams. Even when I'm awake, I see dead islands. I think I'm not the right partner for this."

"Eka, please. I can feel something in those lights, something alive. And they don't seem dark or scary. This could be your chance for better magic. And a chance for some answers," Christelle pleaded.

"I'm not sure I want the answers."

"Please. I saw my mom." Christelle's eyes watered. "I thought she was dead but I don't know anymore. What if she's out there? I need to know."

What would she do if any of her family were still alive. Her parents or Ke?

Eka exhaled and nodded. "Fine. I'll check it out but I can't promise anything after this."

Christelle half-smiled while she wiped away tears. "Thanks."

Eka turned to the lights. "Okay, now what?" She shouted at them.

The lights spun and then danced into the woods and away from her campsite.

This way.

"Eka, what's happening?"

"I don't know, but if you want answers then follow the lights." She took off in the direction of the colorful swarm as they flowed along the river's bank, through thick brush and trees. As she ran after the lights, bushes and branches seemed to move on their own, bending away from her and opening a path. Captivated by the moving foliage she missed the giant hedge that loomed in front of her when she finally looked around for the lights.

"What the hell?" She tried to skid to the side, but tripped on roots and tumbled to the ground. Pine needles pressed into her back as she slid into the well-manicured wall of bushes, her legs resting up at an angle. Finally stopped, she had a great view of the hedge as it seemed to disappear into the clouds and stretch as far as she could see on either side. And, for a moment, the sound of cicadas was the only sensation in the quiet, wooded space. No lights, no voices in her head, no creepy darkness.

"Hello? Lights?" She frowned. "Eyeballs?"

A few cicadas hummed but that probably wasn't an answer. Not sure what the next move was, she just lay staring up at the greenery and clouds.

"Eka? Where are you?"

The calm spell broken, Eka rolled up. "Over here."

Crunching and stomping, echoed through the woods and grew closer, until Christelle stumbled out of the thick brush. She stopped and bent over to catch her breath. "You…are… fast."

Eka rolled off the wall then walked over and patted her back. "I think you did great."

"Are…you kidding?" Christelle's head lifted. "I…"

Eka grabbed her by the shoulders and directed her gaze to the hedge. "What do you think that is?"

Christelle's head fell back as she viewed the wall of vegetation. "Whoa."

"Yeah, that's what I thought."

They stood for a moment as the cicadas carried on singing a background tune.

"So what now?" Christelle turned to Eka.

"Why're you asking me?"

"I thought maybe you got something from those lights. An idea? Or maybe a plan." Christelle almost looked hopeful.

"Plan? No, I don't do plans. But don't worry." Eka waved her off while studying the wall. "I'm sure something'll turn up. Those lights have to be somewhere." She tried to sound confident but Christelle's hope seemed to run off her sagging shoulders.

A familiar gleam of color came from the left and Eka turned to see the hovering, rainbow eyes. Energy shot through her as the eyes first blinked, then shattered into a thousand bits of light that sank into the foliage.

"What the..." She ran to the spot and dug into the hedge for any sign of the colorful lights. "Hello?" She crawled along the hedge, searching for any place the lights might have gone. A few feet along, she discovered a tunnel through the branches and peered down it to see a pair of legs passing across the far end. She waited, but nothing else passed by the opening. Sitting back on her heels, she waved Christelle over. "Hey, I think I found something."

Christelle sighed and walked over to Eka.

"Look." Eka pointed through the hedge.

"A hole?"

"A tunnel. And I saw someone walk past. Do you know what's on the other side?"

"No." Christelle shook her head. "I've never seen this hedge anywhere on the farm."

"I guess we should check it out, then." Eka got up on her hands and knees and headed in, excitement building in her. "Who knows what we'll find." She winked back as Christelle scrambled after her. The small rocks and branches that dug into her skin barely registered as she crawled toward the opening. The flutter in her stomach became a cave of butterflies frantically flying as more excitement built for...what, exactly? She wasn't sure what was on the other side but *was* sure she needed to see past this hedge. She could feel energy drawing her over. Her hands moved quickly and she caught a glimmer from them. She glanced down; her whole body was glowing in a swirling pattern of rainbow hues.

What the hell?

But even that weirdness couldn't seem to stop her momentum. She continued to push on until she finally broke through the far opening. And rammed into someone's legs. Before she could look up to apologize, Christelle pushed her from behind and sent her crashing into the person.

"Eka?" A deep voice inquired.

Beside her, Devlon smiled. "Fancy meeting you here."

She inhaled his air, the smell of river and sun. His chest rose and fell beneath her, his rhythm changing to adjust to her breath. He reached over and brushed a strand of hair behind her ear. Her hand touched his for a moment and she took another deep breath. And they stared at one another, until…Christelle's cough broke the trance.

Eka quickly pushed herself up and helped Devlon to his feet. She noticed her hands no longer glowed and the urgent feeling inside her was gone.

"So." Christelle looked at Devlon. "You know each other?"

Eka nodded as Devlon stared quietly at them. "I guess the real question is where are we?"

Eka took in their surroundings. Towering oak trees grew as far as she could see in all directions and a small group of people surrounded the nearest one. The women and men there chatted around its base as if they had gathered for something normal, like a picnic or a hiking trip. But what they were doing was anything but normal. One of the men touched the tree and a ripple flowed across the bark. A second ripple followed and the bark at the base morphed into a step, then two steps, and then a circular staircase twisting around and up the tree. Next to him, a woman pressed her hand against the tree and high above her, branches exploded out of the trunk, winding up into a solid wall at the top of the tree.

Eka looked over at Christelle. "They're doing that thing you do."

Without glancing away from the tree, Christelle nodded silently.

Standing a few feet from the trunk, another man held his hand above a pile of sand. A slight breeze ruffled his clothes and hair, then a gust blew around him and into the sand. Instead of blowing the sand in all directions, the grains spiraled up into a funnel that swirled and danced to the top of the tree. On the ground a woman touched the base of the rising trail; a moment later, near the top of the funnel, the sand began to lose its granularity, compressing together into a transparent glass sheet. Another woman rested on a branch near the crown of the tree, wind whipping through her hair as she reached close to the sheet. She motioned toward the wall of branches and the glass flew toward it. Eka clenched her shoulders, expecting a collision, but a second before the glass impacted, branches parted and the glass settled between them. The wall had a window.

Eka jumped at a tap on her shoulder and found Devlon next to her. "Are you alright?"

Unable to form words, she just stared at him. Christelle stood on his other side, her mouth hanging open again. Eka reached across Devlon and closed it.

"I think, no, not alright. What's going on here?"

Before he could answer, Christelle gasped and pointed at the group of people at the base of the tree. "It can't be."

Eka squinted at them, then recognized two particular women before they had even turned around.

"Grams? Aunt Anise?"

Pull Back the Curtain, Please

The whole group at the tree turned towards Eka and Christelle; Anise and Shirley stood in the middle of them. Anise froze, wide-eyed. Beside her Shirley coughed and Eka swore she saw a brief smile before Shirley started moving behind the tree. Anise's arm whipped out from her side and caught Shirley, rooting her in place.

"Um, think my break is up."

Eka turned towards a forgotten Devlon.

He stood with his hands in his pockets. His gaze shifted between his feet and Eka. "Call me. We could talk over dinner, if you're still interested?"

She raised her eyebrows in response. "Oh, I'm definitely interested in *this* story."

He nodded then walked past the group working on the tree. Just before he disappeared down a path through the trees, he stole a glance back at Eka.

Him? He *was part of this secret?*

Eka examined the people under the tree.

Whatever this secret is.

Anise dragged Shirley towards them and stopped in front of Christelle, their faces inches from one another. She crossed her arms and focused on her niece as anger and sadness seemed to battle for control of her face. Under her skin, a dark green energy pulsated; Eka could almost feel it repelling her. Christelle's energy seemed to respond, pulsing brighter and outshining Anise's green shield.

Eka stepped back and waved to Shirley who stood on the other side of the standoff. Of course, Shirley didn't respond. Instead, she was glued to the exchange, her head swiveling between Anise and Christelle, the hint of yet another grin ghosting her face.

"Figures she's no help," Eka mumbled to herself, then nudged Christelle's shoulder as her friend's energy grew even brighter. "Christelle?"

Lavender burst from Christelle and the force from the energy pushed Anise and Shirley back a step. The energy quickly receded into Christelle and a quiet settled over the clearing. Everyone, including the group near the tree, fixated on the four of them.

Tendrils of green energy crept from Anise towards Christelle, but were torn apart by a lavender tsunami. Each time Anise's energy attempted to connect with Christelle's, Eka's skin prickled like a balloon had rubbed against it. After a number of these attempts, Anise gave up and the balloon feeling morphed into a grater scrapping down her arms and legs. Eka stepped between them then grabbed Shirley and yanked her in the middle with her. "Uh, yeah. What is happening here?"

Shirley opened her mouth to speak, but Anise cut her off, her eyes narrowing on Eka. "Why are you here?"

"Okay, not an answer." Eka met her gaze.

"Aunt Anise." Christelle stepped from behind Eka and Shirley while her voice grabbed everyone's attention. Not really for how loud it was, but for its ability to smack your attention upside the head, like a bugle playing taps. Right in your ear. "Answer the question."

Anise's energy quieted and her hard edges seemed to melt. "Christelle, I didn't expect you yet. I…"

"Yet?" She pointed at the tree and the fidgeting group near it's base.

Anise reached for Christelle's hand but Christelle stepped back. "Sweetheart, I wanted to help. Every time you made progress, I wanted to tell you, to help you but…"

"Wait. You were watching me? Knew what was happening to me and didn't explain?"

Anise nodded and pulled at the hem of her sleeve.

Christelle stepped forward, stopping inches from Anise. "Why?"

Shirley, the magical workers, and even the clearing itself, seemed to hold a breath. Eka loudly sucked in air and stepped a few feet away from Christelle, Shirley shadowing her.

She's still smiling? What does she know?

"We had to do something," Anise finally explained. "Your parents just showed up with you. No one knew what had happened. They were hurt and you were just a baby." Anise wiped her suddenly wet cheeks and eyes. "Something attacked them. And, she showed up too." Anise pointed at Eka. "Just appeared. The same moment your family was attacked. In a flash of lights. How did she survive her own family's attack? And how did all of you get here?" Anise's body emitted light and her arms gestured wildly with her rapid speech. "We had to protect you. What if he, it, whatever attacked you, came back? Killed you? What if she was part of it?"

Anise pointed at Eka again, her words stirring Eka's memories.

"My family was attacked?" Eka shook her head, mumbling. "But they died in an earthquake. They…" Flashes of memory ran through her mind, of darkness and screaming. Her breathing increased and spots danced around her in a dizzying pattern. She clutched her pendant and the necklace started to shake, the metal and stone bird growing warm in her hand. Then, before she could even breath, light exploded from between her fingers. Her hand flew open as a bright, multihued bird of light, within the pendant, fluttered its wings and flew up and around Eka, leaving a rainbow trail of light in it's wake.

"How?" Eka whispered as she watched it fly.

As the rainbow energy settled over Eka, a calmness flowed through her. The dizziness subsided and the spots vanished. Eka's eyes closed and she breathed deeply, each breath bringing down her heart rate. As the tension drained from her, a smile crept across her face and she finally opened her eyes. To find Shirley staring at her. Everyone else seemed to still be focused on Christelle and Anise's standoff. Apparently her necklace's magical flight had gone unnoticed. Except…Shirley was wiggling her eyebrows.

Did Shirley see it?

"…so we decided that you were both better off in hiding. Away from all this." Anise's voice drifted back into her awareness.

In hiding?

"What are they talking about?" Eka whispered and leaned close to

Shirley, but she was now focused on Anise and Christelle and ignored the question.

"You and this Gaia person decided? Who gave either of you the right?" Christelle asked through gritted teeth.

"Gaia's not a person," Anise said softly, almost reverently. "She's the mother of us all. She's the spirit of this planet, guiding us through difficult times, providing for us. We owe her everything and humbly serve her needs."

"Did I miss something?" Eka blurted out. "Is this a cult?"

Shirley looked between Anise and Eka then slapped her own knee. Her laughter rang out across the quiet clearing.

"A cult! Hah!" Shirley pointed at Anise, wiping a tear away.

"Mom! This is serious!" Anise shook her head. Green energy thrashed within her. "We are not a cult!"

Shirley shrugged and laughed harder. Anise just glared.

"I'm leaving!" Christelle turned away from her aunt, but Anise ran around in front of her.

"Christelle, you have to understand. We had no idea what the nature of the danger was or if it would come back." Anise reached out to Christelle, but she flinched away. Anise sagged, as if the weight of a million people sat on her; her normally strong voice barely audible. "So I consulted with others who understand Gaia's needs. We decided it was best to hide you. Repress your memories. And your gifts."

Christelle stepped forward, lavender radiating from her. "You took my memories because a bunch of crazy…cult people thought this was best? This is insane!"

Anise coughed again. "Gaia communicates through some of us. In this community, it's me." Anise's voice somehow grew even quieter. "And I carry out what needs to be done."

Christelle's face turned bright red and her fists tightened. "A bunch of you think a spirit, *of a planet*, wanted me to forget this world and my family! What kind of bullshit is that? How could you do this to me?" She stepped closer to Anise, a sliver of space left between them. Christelle lowered her voice; Eka strained to hear her. "Was my dad in on this?"

"Christelle, honey. Please." Anise reached for her once more but she jerked away. "This was out of anyone's hands. Your mother and father came here, scared and confused. Everyone was scared. There was no other choice."

"You always have a choice! And now you're blaming a...a planet," Christelle laughed in that crazy scientist sort of way, "for *your* choice. A choice that stole my true self. No wonder Dad took me out of here!" She ran towards the bystanders, who nervously glanced away from her, then she made a lap around the tree. Christelle pivoted right and ran to the treeline. She scanned left and right then turned around, facing them all.

"How do I get out of here?" she shouted.

Shirley pointed past the people at the tree to a small path in the distance.

"Thanks!" she shouted and ran forward, then turned. "No, I take my thanks back!" Then she disappeared into the woods.

Anise brushed a tear off her cheek and took a step to follow Christelle. Shirley laid a hand on her arm. "Let her be a while. She'll call Jake. He'll talk to her."

Anise pushed Shirley's arm away and took off after Christelle.

And left Eka with Shirley.

Eka stared at the path for a while as her brain spun with everything she'd just witnessed. "Wow. That was a great reveal. Maybe you guys could kill some puppies and set some unicorns on fire for your next act."

"Unicorns don't exist," Shirley shook her head.

"That's...helpful?"

Okay. Just breath.

Her necklace fluttered briefly and she wrapped her hand around it. The calm sensation flowed into her again and her thoughts stilled. "Shirley, what just happened? Seriously, was there really an attack on my family?"

Before she could answer, a short, pale, older man waved and approached them from the group.

"Wallace," Shirley nodded at him.

"Good morning, Shirley. "

Eka blinked. Did Shirley just scowl at Wallace?

"Eka, there's coffee. Want some?" Shirley asked and Eka nodded.

"Why not?" Eka shrugged, feeling kinda surreal.

"Never do coffee, thanks." Wallace smiled brightly.

"Good thing, cause I wasn't askin' you." Shirley spun on her heel and walked over to a small table with coffee and cups.

"Hi, I'm Wallace." He formally introduced himself as if nothing awkward had just happened.

"Uh, hi." Eka caught a glimpse of grayness in his hands, energy that reminded her of the gray light flowing in her.

"I hope you're okay after all that drama."

Eka nodded. "Yeah. I'm fine."

They stood in silence a moment then Wallace pointed at her bracelet. "That's beautiful. I bet that's from your grandmother."

"Yeeeaaah." Eka's eyes narrowed on Wallace. "You know my grandmother?"

Wallace nodded. "I met her when she visited here years ago. Wonderful woman. She sure made an impression." He attempted a weak smile.

Shirley walked up with coffee. "Yes, she did. Wallace had a crush on her."

Wallace blushed. "Well. Just wanted to say hi. If you ever want a tour. Or have questions," he glanced at Shirley and she narrowed her eyes at him, "I'll be around." He hurried back to the group, now mulling awkwardly around the tree.

"What's up with him?" Eka asked Shirley. "You seemed kinda hostile."

"Psht." Shirley waved away the suggestion. "Just don't trust him. You should definitely watch out for that one."

Eka tilted her head as she examined Wallace from a distance. "Interesting."

"Yeah." Shirley stirred her coffee. They both watched the workers begin to adjust the tree again, using magic to morph the trunk and branches into what looked like a treehouse.

"So. Do you trust me or are you in Anise's camp on that matter? Lump me with Wallace?"

Shirley stirred the coffee for a long while. Eka didn't expect anything from Shirley. Seemed no one here liked to answer questions. Except Wallace. Maybe.

"I don't think you're anything like him. I can't put my finger on it, but there's something not okay with him. Hasn't been for a while, but especially since he got his gifts."

"His gifts?"

What is she talking about?

"Yeah. He didn't have any until a few months ago. Now he's a whiz with the electrical stuff and…"

At that moment, another man walked by and Shirley grabbed his arm and pulled him into a hug. He wiggled out of her arms and straightened his shirt.

"Jon, you ornery luv!" Shirley beamed at Jon and he cracked a small smile. Well, he could have had constipation, but she was going with smile.

"Jon, this is Eka, a new member of the group. Eka, this is Jon, our local lighter."

Jon's tiny smile morphed at lightning speed into a scowl aimed right at Eka. "I know who you are. And once a dok always a dok."

"Jon!" Shirley replied tersely.

Jon stepped closer to Eka and glared down. "Don't know why Gaia brought you both back. If it were up to me, things would be different." He turned and stomped off to join the others at the tree.

"Wow, everyone's so friendly around here." Eka spun towards Shirley. "So what's a dok?"

"Oh, just an insult to the Asleep. Which was you and Christelle, until you got your gifts back." Shirley then pointed at herself and wiggled her eyebrows. "I'm a Waker, one of the special ones."

"Wakers? Asleep? Who picked those? Could they be less obvious?"

"And dok," she pointed at Eka, her eyebrows furrowed, "means a brain-dead, garbage-crawling, waste of life."

"Hey, what'd I do to him?" Eka looked back in Jon's direction.

"His family died because of some Asleep." Shirley sighed. Then changed gears so fast, even Eka had emotional whiplash. "So, how did that feel, to be an Asleep? Was it like being in a coma? Feeling numb in a world full of sensations?" She wiggled her eyebrows again and elbowed Eka.

Eka shoved her.

"Hey," Shirley frowned as she stumbled.

"You're wordsmithing is pretty impressive, but I have no idea what you're talking about." Eka shook her head. "And just throwing random sentences and strange lingo at me isn't working. Try storytelling, and pretend I'm new to the language."

"Fine." Shirley huffed then pointed at the group working on the tree.

"You see all that color? The lights dancing around?"

Pulsing hues of red, blue, green, purple, and every other color imaginable flowed and danced through everything. New bark grew, glass formed out of sand, and vegetation sprouted all under the glowing lights.

"Yeah. I've been seeing it since that weird storm."

"Well that, kiddo, is our energy. It's in everything, all around. Only those of us who are Awake can see it, work with it. And now, you and Christelle are Awake again. Back home, where you should be."

Eka looked at her hands. A slow-moving, murky gray trudged under her skin. "Mine is kind of muddy." Like Wallace's.

Shirley wrapped her hands around Eka's. "You and Christelle were born Wakers. And now you're back. Give your body time to adjust."

"What happened to my family?" She jumped right to the questions burning in her heart.

Shirley exhaled and dropped her hands. "I don't know. I wish I did. You disappeared and showed up right when Christelle's family was attacked. You never could remember anything. The attack, the disappearance. I think you were shellshocked." She looked across the clearing. "Christelle's family couldn't remember much about the attack on them either. So many questions." She took a long gulp of coffee then looked in her cup. "Coffee." She nodded to the coffee table and Eka followed her over.

They didn't die in an accident. They were attacked. And my memories of it are all gone.

Still. How they died didn't change the fact that they were dead. And did she really want those memories if they included the nightmares? But a different desire warred with her fear of knowing, and that was knowing why. Who attacked them and why? Why was she the only one to live? How did she lose her memories and how did she…

"Shirley. How did we Wake up?"

"Ahhhh. I guess Gaia thought it was time," Shirley winked. "Remember that storm? The one that sent a shock through you and Christelle? Well, it kinda jolted everything back into place for you both. Brought back the memories and connections that were suppressed."

Eka dropped to the ground. "How could this all be hidden? I mean, I never noticed anything…off. How could I have missed a whole world of magic?" Was that really true? Maybe something was missing, maybe she just didn't know what. Maybe that's why she…ran.

"We call 'em gifts."

"What?" Eka refocused on Shirley.

"You said 'magic'. We call 'um gifts."

Eka cocked her head. "Gifts. Magic. Kinda just words. Anyway. I don't seem to have it. I mean, I'm experiencing everything Christelle is but I just don't seem to have any active magic. Maybe Anise is right and I don't belong."

Shirley stood over Eka shaking her head. "Stop groaning. Anise's got a good heart but a hard head. Sometimes she can't see the cake for the sprinkles."

Eka frowned. "The cake for the sprinkles?"

"We had two recent deaths in the community, Wallace's parents. These deaths were very much like your family's, and that's got people on edge. With you showing up right around the same time, well…people are jumpin' to conclusions. Even Anise believes whatever was out there before, killing Wakers, is back." Shirley sighed. "Anise might be the spiritual center of this group, but she's a person with her hopes and fears and not always reasonable about 'em. She was hoping you'd leave and she could help Christelle ease back into our world. But, despite the monumental efforts of some misguided souls to keep you out, you're back. Seems Gaia wanted you back, along with a colorful accomplice."

Eka hopped up and grabbed Shirley by the shoulders. "You've seen the lights, the eyes?"

"Whoa there." Shirley stepped back. "I saw something, flashes of lights, when you got here. Both times you've shown up. Another mystery in a twisty tale, don't you think?"

"I really don't, can't…" Eka stammered.

"Okay, why don't you head back to your camper. Take some time, digest it all. Talk to a friend."

Eka nodded and allowed Shirley to head her down the path Christelle had taken, her thoughts on anything but the walk.

Eka sat on the bed and looked around the vardo. She felt completely untethered. An amazing, magical world had opened to her and then knocked her on her butt. Someone had to have more answers about the night her family died. Sema and Win must know more than Shirley. She picked up her phone and dialed.

"Eka, honey. I'm sorry, we never wanted to lie to you." Her body tensed at the sound of Sema's voice. She might have answers, but Eka kept wondering, did she want them?

"How did you know what I was calling about? Magic?"

"I talked with Shirley just now."

"Oh." Eka tapped her foot in frustration. "Sema, how could you hide this from me? I believed they died in an earthquake. All those nightmares."

Sema breathed quietly on the line for a few moments. "I'm sorry."

"Sema." Eka inhaled deeply, calming her heartbeat. "I know that you and Win did your best for me. But I just want to understand why. What happened to them?"

"We don't know." Sema's voice trembled. "No one else was there. A few Wakers were nearby but they couldn't explain what had happened, as if it didn't make sense. We went back to Laupahoehoe as fast as we could but it was all over. And your memories were taken by then. We couldn't even mourn properly as a family because we had to lie to you. Haipo," Sema growled, "claimed that this was what Gaia wanted. As if Haipo had a connection with Gaia anymore. I didn't know what to do. Ses. My beautiful daughter…"

Eka heard crying on the other end as a tear ran down her own cheek.

"Ses was gone." Sema finally cleared her throat and continued. "Lani was gone. Ke was gone. And there were no answers. Just a giant emptiness except for you. You were all we had left."

"I didn't remember anything about that night?"

"No, little bird, they said you couldn't remember anything when they found you at the Haptons'. Win and I searched for clues at your home but only found the…" Sema went quiet and Eka thought she wouldn't finish. After a few minutes, her grandmother breathed deeply. "We found Ses and Lani, all their energy drained and their bodies mostly ash along with the trees." Her voice became a whisper. "We never found Ke's body."

"Ke wasn't found?" Eka grabbed onto something she could process.

"Eka." Sema's voice gained strength. "We looked everywhere for him. Every Waker community searched. If he was anywhere on the planet, we would know."

"But…"

"I know this is all new. Just know we looked everywhere. When we were in Hawaii, we saw how fearful everyone in the community was. And we knew that Haipo wanted to stick you with non-Wakers and forget you. So Win and I decided you'd come with us. We tried our best to give you a good life. And we are so happy you are Awake. That this stupid secret is over."

Eka sat in the silent vardo. Her world had changed. "In the blink of an eye. Isn't that what they always say?"

"Eka?" Sema asked.

"I miss them," Eka whispered.

"I miss them too."

They sat in a comfortable, familiar silence for a few moments.

"I need to go." If there weren't any more answers, she didn't know what to say anymore.

"Be safe, my little bird. We're so happy you've come all the way back to us. And if you need to talk, I'll answer anything more I can."

"Thanks."

"Love you."

"Love you too."

"Eka?"

Christelle stood in the doorway of the vardo. "Can I come in?"

"Sure." Eka waved her over to the flip-down table where she sat checking her work tools. She tested the locking gate on the same carabiner for the tenth time. She finally gave up the attempt to focus and pushed it off to the side. "Needed a break anyway."

Christelle rubbed her red eyes and sat across the table from Eka. "I don't know what to think anymore. Anise couldn't stop apologizing but she still thinks she was right." Christelle slammed her hand down on the table. "How dare she! I never had a home, never knew my mother."

"But didn't your mother, uh, die?" Eka scrunched her face up at the uncomfortable question.

"Oh, this gets better." Christelle stood straight up, lavender crackling from her body. "Seems my mom is alive but everyone thought I'd be better off if I thought she was dead. I called Dad yesterday when I finally got out of those stupid woods."

"Right? Took me forever to find my way back here." Eka shook her head.

"I know. I ended up back at that spot by the river twice. Had to let Anise show me out." Christelle scowled. "Anyway, Dad said he didn't have a choice about the decision. That him and my mom were angry so they took me out of here. But I guess my mother left to find whatever this mysterious," she threw up her hands, "danger was and they didn't want me trying to find her. So Dad stayed with me to protect me."

Christelle fell back on the chair and Eka let out a low whistle.

"Wow."

"I don't know what to do. All these lies. And not just from Anise but from Dad too. And everyone just went along. All these years I was supposed to be in danger. But nothing bad has happened, except I feel empty and alone because of what they took without my consent." She shook her head, a tear flying off her face. "How could she just leave and never check up on me?"

"Yeah."

Christelle brushed off more tears, stood up and paced the tiny space. "You know, they keep blaming a planet."

"Technically, the spirit of a planet."

Christelle glared at Eka.

"Just keeping the magic clear to everyone."

Christelle rolled her eyes. "Whatever. Everything we've seen is," she looked at her hands for a moment, "beyond amazing. I mean, I wouldn't have believed any of this before I came here. It's all…world shattering."

"Yeah." Eka sighed. "A lot to digest." Words really seemed so hollow right now.

"But people following the spirit of a planet. Deciding things for us because they think a planet wants it?"

Eka shrugged.

"It's like they all have this weird faith and they want me to buy into it. Even if it were true, why would I trust something that took everything away from me?" Christelle slammed a wall.

"Hey!" Eka jumped up and examined the wall. "Careful with my home."

Christelle deflated. "Sorry. I'm just so angry."

"I think their answers suck too." Eka rubbed the place Christelle had punched, then sat back down. "Besides, who cares if there really is a Gaia thing? We need to find out what the attack was all about. Why us?"

"So, you're staying?" Christelle asked.

"Yeah. I may not have magical powers, but now my whole life's meaning is up for grabs. Sema told me as much as she knew, but it wasn't really anything. I feel like there's still more to discover here, so I guess I need to stay and find out."

"Well, whatever happens, no one, not even a planet, is going to take anything from us again. Right?" Christelle held up her fist.

Eka bumped fists. "Right. So, I'm thinking there might be a silver lining to all these lies."

"A silver lining to lies?"

"Just hear me out." She pointed at Christelle's abandoned chair. "And sit down. All your fidgeting is grating on me."

"*My* fidgeting?" Christelle sat. "You're the queen of I-can't-sit-still-or-stay-focused."

"Well, that was a mouthful." Eka started opening and closing the gate on the carabiner and Christelle pointed.

"See!"

"Anyway. I bet they all feel guilty about these lies. So we can use the guilt to our advantage and get someone to crack while their defenses are down. I mean, if we're really going to find out if they're still hiding things, now's the time."

Christelle shifted in her chair. "Why would there be more? Dad said he didn't remember the attack. And no one has heard from my mom since she left."

Eka raised her eyebrow. "Uh-huh. Convenient."

Christelle crossed her arms. "Maybe this is true."

"Gullible," Eka coughed.

"Hey, I…"

"Anyway," Eka interrupted. "Shirley said that people are worried about two recent deaths in the community."

"What? You mean whatever attacked us is back?"

Christelle sat unmoving. "What if they try to make me hide again," She whispered. "I can't lose who I am a second time."

"Well then, I suggest we figure out what's going on and uncover what it was that attacked us."

Christelle leaned across the table and whispered. "What *do* you think it was?"

"Why are you whispering?" Eka whispered back.

"I don't know. Just a creepy feeling about all of it."

A chill suddenly shot down Eka's spine. She cleared her throat and spoke in a normal tone. "This could be dangerous, I guess. If it's the same attacker and they're magic and they know we're here…"

"Yeah."

Would she be safer not knowing? Maybe leaving, like she always did? Could she even hide from magical attackers?

They sat quietly; Christelle seemed lost in her own thoughts.

"Well." Christelle jumped at Eka's voice, loud in the quietness of the vardo. "I'm doing this. You in?"

Christelle nodded.

"So your family is the most accessible."

Christelle groaned.

"Oh, come on. They are so tied up in guilty knots they don't know what to hide."

"Anise won't crack and Grams is a bit dodgy," Christelle stated.

"Literally," Eka agreed. "Maybe Ben? He seemed softer."

"He's not soft." Christelle's shoulders tightened. "He's kind. He was always the one to sneak me sweets and he even took me to a local carnival one year when no one else would let me go." She sighed. "Guess I know why now."

"Ben sounds like he cares about you. I bet if we got him alone, he might tell you something."

"I guess."

"Perfect. I think this calls for a drink," Eka grabbed some rose and a couple of mason jars, then poured. "Tonight we celebrate."

Christelle sighed and tapped her glass to Eka's. "And tomorrow we ambush Uncle Ben."

Part Two

Ben Shows the Way

"Christelle!"

Ben waved at Christelle as she got out of Eka's truck. She took a deep breath and lifted her hand slightly, then waved. At her half-hearted gesture he strode over to the passenger's side of the truck and swept her up in a hug.

"Uncle Ben," She squeaked.

He chuckled and pushed her out to arms length. "Sorry. I'm just so happy to have you at home now."

She smiled briefly.

Christelle waved Eka over and Ben's smile faded as he watched Eka get out of the cab and walk around the front of the truck toward them.

"So, Uncle Ben." Christelle dragged him towards the house and away from Eka. "I was thinking you could show us around. Introduce us to the Waker community."

He looked back at Eka and frowned, then tilted his head closer to Christelle and whispered. "I thought today was about family."

Christelle looked behind her, Ben following her gaze. Eka walked a few paces back and waved enthusiastically at that moment, a Cheshire Cat grin directed at Ben. Ben took a very deep breath and counted softly, which sent Christelle's heart racing and her shoulders tightening.

This will be fine.

Christelle channeled some of her tension into her hand, squeezing hard. Ben jerked his hand out of hers. "Ow."

"Sorry." Christelle forced a large smile. "But this would mean a lot to me. I don't know anything about my world. What with losing my memory and all." She looked up at Ben with what she hoped were sad, wide eyes. "I thought maybe you could help us get acclimatized."

Ben stopped and pulled her into a hug again. "Of course I will."

Tension drained out of her as Eka caught up to them. "Uncle Ben agreed to show us around."

"Awesome! Our own personal Waker tour guide," Eka beamed. "So, why're we meeting so late? Is it a special Waker thing?"

Ben looked between the two of them, then sighed as he turned and walked to his truck, Christelle and Eka following.

"A bit." He glanced at Christelle. "Wakers aren't day people. We do most things during the night. Keeps us away from Asleep."

Great. Another lie. Pretending to be normal while I was around.

Christelle made her way into the truck, somehow keeping her fists clenched the whole time. Eka climbed over her and into the back, bouncing on the bench seat until Christelle turned around and glared.

'Calm down,' Christelle mouthed to Eka.

Silence settled in as Ben started the truck and pulled out of the drive. As they headed left down a small road, toward the main part of the farm, restlessness crept into Christelle. She absently bounced her leg, side-eying Ben.

What do I say? Hey Uncle Ben, why'd everyone lie to me? Do you really not know where my mom is? Thanks for helping ruin my life.

She glanced back at Eka and mouthed 'What do I do?' Eka shook her head, shrugging. She bounced on the back seat again, throwing up her arms in various poses as she came off her seat. Christelle fought a grin until she let out a large snort and spun around to face forward.

"Everything okay?" Ben asked, frowning.

"I told her all this snorting wasn't normal," Eka jumped in, "especially when that sparkly blue stuff came out, but she wouldn't listen. Says she's all magical now and can handle it."

Christelle spun toward Eka, grabbing the back of the passenger seat. "There's no blue stuff!"

"Christelle." Ben laid a hand on her shoulder. "All of this is serious. Your body could be having issues adjusting. Anise should check you out. And," he glanced back at Eka, "we have gifts, not magic."

"Exactly!" Eka bounced around as Christelle glared at her.

"I'm fine." Chriselle turned back and stared out the window. "Must be my allergies, because there's something really irritating in here."

"Okay." Ben didn't seem convinced as he noticed her vigorously bouncing leg. "But don't let symptoms creep up on you."

"Okay, okay," she exhaled loudly.

After a few miles, they pulled over on the wrong side of the road, next to a thin line of slash pines. Climbing out of the truck, Christelle looked around for any signs of humans. There didn't seem to be anything but the road and trees.

"Are those secret tree houses?" Eka asked.

Christelle remembered the people transforming an oak into a house.

Ben shook his head. "No, these trees are way too small for something like that." He walked toward the tree line. "We're headed to a garden, a bit past the trees."

"Too small, huh." Eka bumped Christelle with her hip. "I guess magic can't work miracles."

"What's wrong with you?" Christelle whispered.

"Nothing, just, the anticipation of all these mysteries finally being revealed is exciting." Eka almost danced around.

Christelle shook her head and followed Ben.

"Gifts, not magic!" Ben yelled back.

"Exactly, Ben!" Eka answered enthusiastically from the back.

Ben led them through a dense area of pines then onto a narrow path and into a meadow. Christelle wound through hip-high plants, brushing her hand across silky stalks and small red flowers sitting like miniature trumpets atop rigid stems. The physical sensation felt like an anchor in her topsy-turvy world. Something to ground her for the moment. Lavender wound out of her fingers and mixed with the sparkling pink energy of the trumpets. Faint sensations of cool earth and warm sun flowed through her as their energies danced together, the tiny trumpets bending on their stems, reaching for her hand, as they followed her movements across the meadow. All around her, colors flowed in and out of the physical world, dissolving familiar objects and her momentary sense of groundedness. Flowers and plants, and even the space above the field, no longer seemed to have hard boundaries that defined where one thing ended and another began.

Like everything she believed, the edges were running together into a muddled mess. What was left to hold on to?

"Hey, space cadet," Eka said, bumping into her.

Christelle snapped out of her thoughts to find Ben way ahead of them on the path. "Sorry."

She finally caught up to him just where the meadow seemed to make way for a garden of sorts. A few trees stood in the clearing. Below them, beans, melons, and tomatoes grew alongside red, purple, and yellow flowers. None of the plants seemed organized, as if the seeds had haphazardly made their way to the spot, and bees hummed loudly as they darted in and out of the plants.

A small grassy area seemed plopped down right in the middle of the field and Ben stopped to chat with a group of people sitting in a circle within it. He waved her over and, after a deep breath, she made her way to the circle, wondering who these people were and how much *they'd* hidden from her.

Stop. These people don't even know you.

But now, everything seemed suspicious and unsafe. And she couldn't get her footing.

Eka, on the other hand, strode right up to everyone, with a big smile, as Ben started introductions.

How can she be so calm, so unaffected?

"Christelle, I want you to meet Terra and Kole." Ben smiled at two adults in the circle of mainly kids.

A woman with long dark hair, sitting cross-legged in the circle, waved at her. The dark-haired man sitting next to her nodded.

"Hi," Christelle said, then gestured to Eka. "This is my friend Eka."

Terra and Kole nodded at Eka.

"Um, yeah," Ben stammered. "Anyway, Terra and Kole are leading this year's training groups. Our young trainees are seven now and starting to learn their gifts."

"I'm seven and a half!" a red-headed boy from the circle piped up.

"Yes you are, Bryant." Kole said.

"I'm seven and a half, too!" a blonde girl shouted.

"Sara's not a half!" Bryant pouted to Terra.

"Am too!" Sara crossed her arms.

"I'm almost eight!" a curly, dark-haired girl shouted above Sara.

"Leta's not eight!" Bryant made a face at Leta then turned to Kole.

"She's not even a half yet."

"Am too!"

Soon, all three kids were shouting accomplishments, trying to outdo the others.

"Okay, everyone." Terra waved her hands high above their heads, holding back a laugh. "You are all very mature and ready to learn to work with your gifts."

At the mention of gifts, they all quieted and straightened up.

"Now, we have guests today. They're new to our community and have to learn about us and their own gifts," Terra explained. The children's eyes grew as they turned toward Christelle and Eka.

"They don't know how to use their gifts?" Bryant asked.

Christelle shook her head.

"But they're old!" He scrunched up his face.

"Hey!" Eka glared at him. "I'm not old."

"Are too!"

"Kids." Terra glanced at Eka, then at the children in the circle. "I think maybe we should share the Gaia story with our newcomers, so they can learn about Wakers."

"No!"

"Not that again."

"We want to hear about Badger."

"Not Badger. What about Poto."

The debate went round the circle until Kole and Terra raised their hands.

"We are starting with the Gaia story. Then maybe the others," Terra stated and everyone grew quiet. With pouting.

"If you listen well," Kole added.

The children grumbled for a moment more, but quieted down again. Kole gestured for Christelle and Eka to join, and the women slid into the circle.

"Old," Bryant whispered from where he sat next to Eka and she stuck her tongue out.

Christelle, elbowed Eka. "Hey, pay attention."

Terra closed her eyes for a moment and dropped her shoulders. Her deep inhale seemed to be the only sound in the garden and everyone in the circle leaned closer to her, as if drawn in with the breath. As she exhaled, light drifted out from her umber skin, tinging it blue. The periwinkle light flowed down to the ground then snaked slowly around into a spiral, circling inward until it reached the center. Abruptly, Terra's eyes shot open and her hands reached upward, sending everyone backwards as periwinkle exploded out of the center of the spiral and collected into a large, nebulous floating mass above them. Random bits of dirt, grass, leaves and flowers were pulled up into a swirling, lighted mass.

"This was a long time ago," Sara whispered loudly to Christelle from across the circle.

"That's right, Sara," Terra nodded. "This was a long time ago. Before Gaia was here. Instead of planets and stars, all around were just bits and pieces, floating in emptiness."

"What are bits and pieces?" Bryant asked.

"Ahhh," Terra smiled. "These were the things that made up Gaia and the rest of her family. Like the cells that make up your skin and hair." Periwinkle energy sparkled and pulsated in the mass, pushing the bits and pieces into tiny dancing spheres. A large ball of dried yellow grass coalesced in the center of it all, while around it smaller spheres formed. These smaller globes circled the yellow sphere like little children playing close to their parents.

"That's Gaia's orrerrerra!" Leta squealed.

Kole laughed. "Orrery, Leta."

"I said that." Leta pouted and crossed her arms.

"No you didn't!" Bryant pointed at her.

"Did too!"

"Like you could say it," Eka mumbled to Bryant.

"Kids!" Kole shook his head at Eka. "Focus. Sol's about to wake up." A golden energy wound out from Kole's taupe skin and into the yellow ball, illuminating it from within and around the sun, and the small orbs glowed with the same golden light.

"All Sol's children were born with his energy. Gaia and her sisters and brothers, growing, playing, having fun." Terra's voice broke the trance Christelle had been in from watching the mesmerizing orrery. "Gaia loved her siblings very much."

"But not her brother." Leta glared at Bryant.

"Exactly," Eka joined in.

"Yeah!" Sara chimed in.

"Eka!" Christelle elbowed her, yet again.

"Just saying." Eka shrugged and turned towards the floating solar system.

Terra sighed. "She loved *all* of them."

Next to the sun, a sphere of gray pebbles zoomed around like a Ferrari on the Autobahn. Next to it, a little farther from the sun, a slightly larger globe of pale yellow grass and light tan dust swirled. It moved slower than the gray ball, less hurried. A third ball, of blue and white petals, seemed to laugh as it spun past the yellow and tan sphere. Just past the bright blue and white ball, a red-petaled sphere trailed lazily. Larger orbs of tans and blues coalesced further from the sun but somehow, they seemed distant and disinterested.

"But after a while Gaia wanted more friends, to play different games."

The blue and white sphere seemed to sigh.

"Did that ball just make a noise?" Christelle whispered. She turned towards Eka, but she and Bryant were throwing bits of dirt at each other behind their backs. She elbowed Eka. This was getting ridiculous. "Stop it!" Christelle whisper-yelled.

"He started it."

"Can you focus just once? This is background."

Eka and Bryant glared at each other, then Eka turned back to the circle, the spheres spinning and dancing. "This is so cool."

Christelle sighed and shook her head.

"So," Terra raised her eyebrows in Eka's direction, "Gaia loved her brothers and sisters but wanted more friends and new games. She had dreams where she met some new friends and they shared all their adventures with her, even taking her to strange new places with them."

"I went on an adventure with the air people." Bryant hopped up and pointed in the sky. "We traveled across water and went to islands. It was so cool."

"There are air people?" Eka asked.

Christelle leaned closer as Bryant nodded vigorously. "On ships!"

"Bryant, sit down. We can talk about the that later."

Eka whispered to Bryant. "You've got to tell me about that."

"Yeah," Christelle added.

What do air people do? Are there water people?

Bryant hopped down, still fidgeting as Terra resumed.

"Then," Terra leaned into the circle, "Gaia heard new voices. Voices that seemed to come from inside her."

The other spheres disintegrated and fell away. The dirt, leaves, pebbles, and flowers drifted over to the blue orb, expanding it. Christelle planted her hands on the ground, as the view seemed to zip toward the surface of the orb, as if she were watching a movie that suddenly zoomed onto the planet's surface from outer space. Blue and white petals shifted to reveal green and blue petals, the lands and oceans of earth. Grass, flowers, and all the other bits and pieces swirled into scenes of continents and oceans. Then the scene shifted again, even closer, to mountains and grasslands. Soon the bits and pieces became small landscapes and she could see whales breaking through water, monkeys climbing trees and humans walking around. Red, silver, blue and green light flowed through everything.

"Do you feel queasy?" she asked Eka.

"Nope. Like the rides at the amusement parks. You know, the movie's playing and you're flying along with it. Then the movie takes a right turn and your seat moves…"

Christelle's stomach heaved and she held up her hand. "Got it."

"What did the voices say?" Sara asked while Christelle laid back, closing her eyes and breathing deep, talking her stomach down.

"They said all kinds of things because they were from monkeys and dolphins and trees and so many of the things living on Gaia. All because she dreamed them awake."

All the kids murmured 'wow' at the same time.

"And she loved the voices. She listened to them constantly. And sometimes she actually could *be* them. Could see the world from a monkey's eyes as it swung through trees. Then she could feel the breeze blowing through the leaves of a tree. And she could see through human eyes too."

Christelle popped an eye opened to see what was happening. She waited for her stomach to protest but it was quiet.

The scene in front of her shifted to a group of humans traveling through a meadow, their red clay skin bright against the green, waving grasses. One figure at the back of the loose group paused, looking around.

As the figure stood there, sea and earth swirled together into the bright form of a another woman. Gaia. The straggling clay figure looked around but seemed to be the only member from her group to notice. She reached out to Gaia and their energies spun together, the world blurring around them.

"That's Anise!" Bryant shouted.

Kole smiled at him. "Good guess. Anise is our Uon, or our spiritual leader and the spiritual center of our community." This last bit he directed to Christelle and Eka. "She can feel what Gaia's feeling and direct us that way, but only a few special Wakers can talk with Gaia."

Christelle's stomach suddenly tightened. Why was she here, listening to this crap? As if this was some wonderful tale of a benevolent spirit and her wise woman friend. Anise was no one's spiritual anything.

"Christelle?" Eka whispered.

"What!"

The orrery froze and everyone turned towards Christelle.

Her face heated up. "Sorry."

Terra nodded and the tale resumed.

"Hey it's just a story. A fairy tale," Eka whispered.

Christelle nodded, her fists clenched. Before her, the clay woman sat with a small clay boy next to her. They both watched Gaia. The woman's hand gestured in wide strokes and Gaia responded. Soon, the woman grew old and the boy grew tall, taking the woman's place and talking with Gaia. Generations passed and the humans grew up and grew old, but Gaia remained the same.

"Who here sees Gaia's energy?"

Three little hands shot up.

"I see it!" Sara shouted.

"I see it more!" Bryant shouted louder.

"No you don't. We all see it the same!" Leta shouted over Bryant.

"Okay!" Terra held up her hands, laughing. "You all see the energy, because Gaia's energy is everywhere. At first, everything had a little bit of her energy, just enough to live. But Gaia wanted to share more with all the life on earth. And she loved how her human friends told stories. Stories that created laughter and tears. She was amazed at how they loved this world as much as she did. So she taught them how to channel her energy to all the living things on earth, to be the caretakers of all life. To help it grow even stronger."

The Gaia figure guided her latest human connection to a place glowing with her light. The clay figure showed other humans the light and soon they became glowing conduits. Light flowed into them and then out into other life forms. Quickly they learned to use the energy to create beautiful homes in trees, grow food and heal. The world glowed.

"But," Kole's voice grew low, "some people weren't happy. They were too busy admiring themselves to notice the world around them or even Gaia. As they lost their connection with Gaia, they had less energy. Then, they became jealous of the people with Gaia's energy, wanted that energy. And wanted. And wanted."

Christelle huffed, then frowned at everyone's stare.

Maybe they just didn't believe in someone controlling their life.

A group of clay figures, dimmer than all the others, swarmed the tree homes and pushed out the bright figures. They hoarded stolen food and fought with each other. The energy inside them grew dimmer until it was barely perceptible and the few energy connections they had with the world around them evaporated.

"Why did they want to hurt everybody?" Sara asked.

"Because they're bullies." Leta eyed Bryant.

"I'm not a bully," Bryant huffed.

"No, you're not a bully." Kole stretched his legs and back. "Sometimes people are broken and they can't hear all the songs of beauty around them. Only the sounds in their head of anger, loneliness, jealousy."

The circle grew quiet.

"These people were mad they couldn't have all the energy they wanted. To control it and everything around them. But their desire for control took them away from the world and all the abilities that Wakers have. They didn't understand that Wakers live in an equal relationship with the world, giving and receiving. So, jealous of the Wakers but, without any gifts, they learned to make tools."

The dim people created tools to cut trees and build homes. They cleared forests and meadows to plant crops.

"They built big cities and impressive machines. But they still wanted more, because without Gaia's light and connections, they were alone and empty inside, even in their cities. All around them was an amazing world full of life but they couldn't see it. They became Asleep."

"They were sad," Leta whispered and Terra nodded.

Frustration grew inside Christelle.

Maybe they had a reason to be sad. And angry.

"And soon, the Asleep were using their tools to try and take control again," Terra sighed.

Cities with tall spires grew from the ground and spread as if they were eating everything around them. The dim figures attacked the lighted people with exploding devices they dropped from the air under mechanical wings and from underground drilling machines that opened up the earth and swallowed everything above. The lighted figures countered with natural storms and attacks from other species, who fought by their side, but neither group seemed to be winning. Clay figures lay strewn across machines. Forests smoldered and former meadows were now dusty swaths.

"Gaia was sad at all this death and decided to put an end to it. She brought a few Wakers together and gave them special gifts."

Gaia, crying at all the devastation, gathered a few lighted humans. Energy poured out of her and into them and they glowed so bright Christelle had to shield her eyes until the light dimmed. They looked like tiny knights in armor. Gaia whispered to each of them, and their connection to her grew immense.

The glowing figures approached the cities, lifted their arms. Tornadoes whipped through the buildings, ripping out sections while the earth rippled, toppling structures and destroying foundations. Water poured in from air and sea, flooding the rubble. Tiny figures ran across the waves of rubble and falling debris. When the water rushed through, they disappeared. City after city fell until there were none left. The earth finally quieted and the water drained away. The little knights came together, exhausted and horrified at what they'd done. Slowly, all their hair paled to white as if they had aged a hundred years.

"Christelle," Eka whispered.

Christelle nodded and touched her own white hair, a color that no one else seemed to have. It was just a fluke, right? It couldn't mean anything, could it?

"Gaia, sharing the sadness of what she had done with her warriors, made them a special place to live. Away from everyone else. To heal."

On the field, Gaia gathered the warriors up in her arms, and took them to the ocean. In front of her, the water bubbled and churned until a large mass of land rose up. She nurtured great plants that seemed made for an ocean forest and placed the warriors amongst the vegetation. As the land sunk, the viewers sunk as well. Christelle watched the land mass settle on the bottom of the ocean. Underwater homes were built within the plants as the warriors created a community. They developed incredible speed as they swam around, seeming to breathe underwater. Then, one of the warriors swam up, breaking the surface, somehow able to breathe in air as well. The figure went out into the world, meeting with other lighted people.

Christelle absently touched her neck, then checked if anyone saw and dropped her hand.

Of course there's no gills.

"A few of the Asleep lived through the war and started building again."

Little figures, full of light, sat around the energy pools as dim figures walked into the distance. The blue and gold energy dissipated with the scene, becoming bits and pieces again and falling to the ground. The circle's collective breath exhaled and the children started chattering, speaking over one another. Christelle barely noticed as she stood up and left.

Eka raced after her, finally catching up halfway back to the truck. "Hey, you okay?"

Christelle spun. "Kind of convenient that Gaia is so wonderful and caring and anyone who opposes her is horrible and angry and deserves to die."

Eka shrugged.

"Didn't you see that? Those people destroying all those cities? Killing everyone in it?"

Eka opened her mouth then shut it.

"Great, now you're on their side." Christelle turned away from Eka.

Eka slid in front of her. "I'm not on anyone's side. I just think it was a kids' story. You know, kinda simplified. Things are always more complicated than that."

Christelle stood, arms crossed, breathing loudly and staring at her friend. "That's worse. Getting kids to love a monster that destroys cities just because they can. If she cared she would have found a way to save everyone, not just decide some people don't deserve to live."

"Or remember?" Eka added.

"Yes! How could anyone believe in this … thing that would do that?"

"Hey." Eka laid her hand on Christelle's arm. "It's just a story. Their story."

"Yeah." She wiped a tear off her face. "But they believe it. Anise believes." Her voice fell with her tears. "And she took everything from me, in Gaia's name, then lied to me for all these years."

"What they did was bullshit. A total crap fest."

Christelle nodded.

"But maybe, with your mom out there, there could be something better. Right?"

"I guess." She wiped off her face. "Maybe."

"And you don't have to accept any of it."

"Yeah."

"And when we figure out what's going on, really going on, you can tell them to piss off."

Christelle smiled the tiniest bit. "Okay. I can do that."

"And maybe the story sucked but it was a pretty cool performance. Better than 3D IMax VR."

"That doesn't exist."

"Are you sure?" Eka grinned.

"Hey." Christelle touched her hair, remembering the little figure with white hair. "You don't think…"

"It's just a story. Besides, they probably saw your hair, thought it was cool and put it in."

"I guess."

"Christelle," Ben interrupted them.

Christelle jumped at his voice.

"Sorry." He smiled cautiously. "Are you okay?"

Christelle shrugged. "Yeah."

"Well." He seemed to search for the right words. "This is your world now too. I hope that helped you to understand more about this world."

Around her, the grasses and flowers seemed to still, leaning in as if they were waiting. Her stomach clenched and shoulders tightened. "I…I don't think you…"

"Hey," Eka ran through the meadow toward the pines. "I wonder how a treehouse would look here?"

Christelle glanced at Ben then turned to see Eka climbing a pine. "You want to live there?" Christelle yelled.

"Might be cool!"

"You should visit our home," Ben interrupted again. "It's in one of those oaks you saw that first day. We even have a room for you."

Christelle frowned in confusion.

"Room? In a treehouse? I don't understand."

"Yeah." Ben's body stiffened and his voice was low.

"But, what about our home? The place we all live in?"

"Um." Ben tapped his thigh. "Most of that was for you. I mean a small part of it we keep in case any Asleep visit, but most of it we made for your time here. We already took everything but the essential house down."

"What! But what about my room!"

Eka, who had come back from the pines, placed her hand on Christelle's arm but she pulled it away.

"*That's* my home."

Ben looked down at Christelle then pulled her shaking body into his arms.

"I'm so sorry Christelle. We didn't even think that you might want to stay there."

Christelle pushed away from Ben and slid to the ground.

"How about this." He sat next to her. "You can keep staying there for as long as you want."

Christelle nodded.

The house was just another lie.

Ben put his arm around Christelle's shoulders. "Maybe you need a little more time for all this? We can finish the tour another day."

Christelle shook her head and looked at Eka.

Eka half smiled back and nodded at her.

"No, this is all…great." She sniffed. "But yeah, I think I need time."

Ben hugged her again. "Of course. We love you, Christelle. And I know this is a lot. Whatever you need to help you get used to this, we're just glad to have you home."

Christelle shook herself off. "I'm happy to be home too. Um, I was wondering if you could tell me about the Wakers that were killed?"

Ben froze.

Christelle glanced at Eka who shrugged.

"Uncle Ben?"

"I think we should head back." He got up and headed down the path but Christelle ran after him and jumped in front of him.

"Please. There's too much secrecy. You all keep saying you're sorry, but you're still hiding things. If you want me to trust you, you have to tell me everything that's going on."

He stood still for what seemed like forever and Christelle gave up on an answer. Just as she was about to leave, Ben nodded.

"Okay." He started to pace. "It's true, there's been some deaths in the community. The bodies were…"

"Ash?" Eka asked.

Ben's eyes went wide as he nodded at her.

"How'd you know that Eka?" Christelle frowned.

Eka's voice came as a whisper. "Like my parents."

Christelle's breath caught and she reached for Eka, who seemed ready to bolt. "I'm sorry."

Eka seemed to not hear. "What's doing this? Is it the same thing that attacked my parents?"

Ben zoomed in on Eka. "We don't know. But it started after you showed up."

"Uncle Ben, what are you saying?"

Ben continued to lock eyes with Eka. "I'm saying that more than once Wakers have been killed near her. And they were unnatural deaths."

Christelle stepped between them. "Eka would never do something to hurt others. Especially her family."

Ben sneered. "You can't know that. Her energy is corrupted. Just look at…"

Christelle turned as he trailed off to find Eka running. Without hesitating, she took off after Eka, zipping through the pines and out to the truck. But Eka was nowhere.

A hand on her shoulder startled her and she whipped around to find Ben there with her.

"How could you say that!"

"Christelle, we're trying to protect you, this community, maybe even all Wakers. The danger is big and it's here again. You don't know anything about what happened to her family. No one does because she was the only survivor."

Christelle shook her head. "Yeah, well as it turns out, I don't know anything about you. Or Aunt Anise. Or even myself. You keep saying all this is to protect me, but it seems like it's all just lies for your own purposes. And by the way, these deaths started when I showed up too."

Christelle took off down the road, not looking back as Ben called her name, running until she finally caught up to Eka.

"Hey." She slowed down to match Eka's march down the road.

"Hey." Eka's voice seemed blunt and angry.

"I'm sorry."

"No worries." Eka stared ahead as she stomped on. "I was thinking of taking a job with 'Folly or Farce'."

Christelle grabbed Eka's shoulder and spun her around. "You can't leave! What about your family? Finding out about our past?"

Eka looked down at her hands then back up at Christelle and sighed. "I may have been a Waker once but I don't seem to be one now. Not exactly." She turned her hands over; the gray energy inside her still sludgy. "I don't seem to have normal energy, whatever that is, and no signs of any magic. And what about all these dark visions? Maybe something happened to me when my family…that night." Eka continued to stare at her hands. "Maybe it's best for everyone if I don't know what happened. That I don't have magic. Who knows what it'd be."

Christelle regarded the gray energy moving slowly inside Eka. "Your energy is different. So what? We don't know everything about this world. We don't know what having our gifts and memories suppressed did to us. And," she looked back down the road, her fists tightening, "it's not like they're helping."

She turned back to Eka. "Please. You're the first real friend I've had. And I need a friend right now. I can't do this alone." She blinked away tears. "And I would be alone."

Eka stared at Christelle for a moment then took a deep breath. "Okay." She started back toward the truck, Christelle joining her. "I guess we can cross your uncle off the list of 'potentially helpful'."

Christelle nodded and rolled her eyes. "I suppose people dying could make you paranoid. But Anise…"

Why did she feel like such an outsider with the family?

"Why are they still so secretive with you?" Eka asked.

"Yeah."

Eka punched her shoulder. "There's gotta be others that are a little less, let's say uptight, about our status here. Maybe we could still crack the secrets in this community, figure out what happened. Maybe even learn more magical stuff."

Christelle's adrenaline kicked up and she hopped a few paces. "Yeah. We don't need them for the magic. Energy. Whatever."

"Kinda like the term magic." Eka grinned.

"Me too. I've always wanted to have magical abilities." Christelle giggled, finally relaxing a bit. "Hey, maybe we should try Grams again."

"Hmmm," Eka responded. "She is a wild card. And evasive. But at least she's fun. Sure, why not."

"Awesome!" Christelle smiled at Eka. "I promise we'll figure this out.

"Okay, Pollyanna," Eka laughed.

Bander's Place

"Come on, ladies, keep up." Shirley motioned to Eka and Christelle as she sprinted ahead.

"I can't believe it only took a day to get Grams to show us around," Christelle whispered.

Eka nodded as she followed Shirley, fascinated by the woman's shamrock-green straw sun hat, adorned with daisy-yellow ribbons. The hat bobbed atop Shirley's head as she led the way to a little shack on the water.

Eka managed to catch up to Shirley. "That's quite a hat."

"Bander's Place is *the* Waker hot spot here. Always like to be stylish when I go out."

"I can see that," Eka grinned.

Reddish-orange light from the setting sun silhouetted figures sitting along the dock. At the edge of the dock a shack leaned so much off the planks it seemed to defy gravity. A few bits of curling green paint held on to the otherwise bare wooden slats of the walls, and holes in the wall exposed wallpaper from inside the building, while the wood was definitely losing a battle with the elements. A few of the boards were split and broken, some laying on the ground, apparently forgotten. Shirley walked up to a screen door that dangled from a single, last hinge that a slight breeze threatened to pull off.

Eka leaned toward Christelle, "Five bucks says that screen falls off."

Christelle scrunched her face up. "Grams, are you sure the building is safe?"

"What?" Shirley seemed confused for a moment, then grinned. "Oh, that. You girls are just looking at it wrong. What with the 'being new' thing and all. Look again, just with Waker eyes."

"What are Waker eyes, Grams?" Christelle turned to Eka. "Do you have any idea what that means?"

Eka shook her head.

Before either on of them could question her further, Shirley seemed to walk through the screen as if it wasn't really there.

Eka blinked and rubbed her eyes. "Holy crap!" She stepped up to the screen and punched jumping back as it gave up the ghost and fell. "Seems real enough." Chatter erupted from around her, dock-sitters focusing on the ruckus. Which she ignored. Pointedly.

"Really? Punching it?" Christelle shook her head and squatted next to the screen.

Eka took the bigger picture route and stepped back, examining the shack from every angle. It didn't seem like anything but an old building desperately in need of repair.

Waker eyes, huh?

"Maybe we're supposed to focus on the energy?" she mumbled.

Christelle glanced up. "Energy." She stood and they both stared at the building. "Okay."

Eka had seen big displays of energy since the night of the storm, but most of the time she only caught faint glimmers of it around her. Could she do something Wakery? See the energy at will?

She glanced at the gray slowly moving under her skin and took a deep breath. Couldn't hurt to try. Cocking her head left, she squinted at the building. Eka focused on the feeling of that first time, when she'd seen the world light up. How her senses seemed to come alive as they'd never done before. At least in her current memory. A hint of decaying seaweed abruptly invaded her olfactory sense and a hint of salt exploded on her tongue, like an open shaker of salt just dumped in her mouth.

"Ugh." In front of her, the tilt of the shack remained, but a slight shimmer went through it like a ripple. She blinked and the wall and screen faded, exposing people walking around on top of mangroves, as if they were moving across carpet, while others sat in branches shaped as chairs. At the edge closest to them, a number of branches grew up and over, creating a shaded canopy. Eka stared as a woman, seated on a mangrove chair, raised her hand behind her back, coaxing a funnel of water up from the adjacent river and behind her companion. The funnel lazily circled above her companion a number of times before dumping on the unsuspecting man, causing the perpetrator to burst into laughter.

Shirley, suddenly appearing a few feet from them, clapped once to get their attention. "Girls, pull yourselves together and stop staring."

Eka blinked and the hint of the forlorn building shimmered briefly into focus before she caught herself, calming her breath and focusing again. The building faded, and the mangroves and people were visible.

"Eka, did…you see it change?"

Eka nodded. "You?"

"Yeah," Christelle whispered. "Grams, how? What is this? What happened?"

"Just a bit of Waker trickery. Scramblin what people see, what they sense. Keeps any Asleep that might wander off the path, from stumblin' on us. Seeing things they shouldn't. Remember Jon? He's one of the Wakers that does that here."

The unpleasant guy, from the day at the oak tree, popped in Eka's mind. "You mean cranky pants?"

Shirley laughed. "Cranky pants! Ha! That's perfect." She continued laughing until Christelle coughed.

"Cranky pants." Shirley shook her head. "Anyway, he's our main lighter, light being his strongest gift. Can coax it to do anything, including hiding us. And that's no mean feat. Light can be some tricky stuff, can't always trust it. In fact, we've lost a few lighters over the years." She leaned in closer to Eka and Christelle. "Wakers that deal with light have a tendency to be a bit off."

Eka squinted at Shirley.

Seems she would know.

Shirley turned. "Anyway, lighters like Jon are important. I mean, light scrambles a bit of the information for him so non-Wakers see what he wants them too. And he's really upped his game lately. This used to look like a wall of bushes."

Christlle's brow furrowed, "He manipulates light?"

"Manipulate? Pay attention kiddo. No Waker manipulates anything. Doesn't work that way. Everything around ya has a will, its own life. Ya have to ask it. And, like I said, light is trickier than most things. But Jon does have a way of convincing it."

"What about the voices? I didn't hear anyone talking," Christelle asked.

"And how'd I feel that screen door?" Eka added.

"Oh, we have Wakers for that too."

Eka and Christelle exchanged a look as Shirley turned and effortlessly climbed up the mangroves onto the leafy platform.

"I think Grams was right before; my head is gonna explode." Christelle stood staring after Shirley.

Eka smiled and elbowed Christelle. "If you can't explain 'em, join 'em!" Then she leapt off the dock and up on the mangrove branches. Her feet sank into the dense foliage, a soft, airy surface. "Hey Christelle, check this out." She bounce-stepped across the living platform, leaping higher with each step. "Woot woot!"

Laughter bubbled up inside Eka with each bounce and Christelle giggled at her moon-walk impression.

"Kids." Shirley pulled Eka over as she bounced by, then turned to a table comprised of living mangroves.

Eka bounced onto a mangrove chair, next to the table while Christelle hesitantly walked across the platform, like a new-born deer trying to walk for the first time.

"You can make it! Just jump!"

Christelle shook her head hard, tumbling and slipping part-way into the branches. Christelle had seemed more coordinated than that; maybe learning about this world and magic was throwing her off her game. Eka shrugged as Wakers sitting near Christelle ran over and hauled her out, helping her to the table. Mumbling a thank you, she dropped her red face into her arms.

Shirley patted her back. "Well, kiddo. Never seen someone fall through before."

"Thanks, Grams."

A tiny spot of heat flared against Eka's chest, where her pendant rested. She glanced down and touched the warm metal, the pendant vibrating against her fingers as tiny rainbow lights outlined the bird. She pulled her hand away and it briefly fluttered it's wings. She squinted, looking at it closely, but the metal had already cooled and the lights had dissipated into the air around her.

What the…?

That was the second time it'd seemed to come alive. She stared at the pendant, waiting, but nothing else happened. It hung there like a normal necklace, just a chain with a colorful little metal bird. She glanced up, but all around her, the conversation continued, uninterrupted.

"Huh," She muttered. "Did either of you notice my necklace?"

Christelle nodded. "It's very pretty."

Shirley cocked her head, examining the necklace. "Why? Don't like it?"

"No, just…wondered."

"Interestin'." Shirley took in the necklace a moment more, then sighed and turned to the table behind them, catching up on gossip.

"Is something wrong with your necklace?" Christelle whispered.

Eka examined it again. "No." She lowered her voice, ignoring the necklace's show. One mystery at a time. "So," she nodded at Shirley, "what are you going to ask her?"

"Now?" Christelle whispered.

"Yeah. This was your idea, what're you waiting for?"

"I just…what should I ask? I mean, should I ask her about our memories? Or maybe the conversation she had with Anise. Or the danger we were supposed to be in."

"What are you two going on about?" Shirley asked, facing them with raised eyebrows.

"Grams, I uh, was wondering…" Christelle stared at her hands.

Eka rolled her eyes. "Shirley," she leaned against the short chair back, "we were hoping that you might enlighten…" Eka lost her balance and fell backward off the mangrove chair, wedging herself into some branches in the floor.

"Enlighten you about your balance?" Shirley chuckled.

Christelle stepped slowly over and pulled Eka up as she struggled out of the floor.

"Hey, Jon." Shirley waved the man over, as Eka and Christelle crawled back on their seats.

"You remember my granddaughter, Christelle and her friend Eka?"

Jon harrumphed as Wallace joined them. "Good morning."

Shirley purposefully ignored him too.

"I've heard plenty of what they've been up to." Jon shook his head. "Messing with those plants in the meadow was just plain rude."

"Well," Shirley's grin deepened, "Christelle seems to be full of gifts. She might even be special."

Jon rolled his eyes. "Everyone thinks their grandchildren are special."

Shirley narrowed her eyes at Jon then turned to Christelle and grinned. "She was just going to give us a demonstration of her gift with plants."

Christelle's eyes widened and, trying to respond, just replied, "mmphra."

"You can do this!" Shirley slapped Christelle on the back. "Just focus."

Wallace's eyes grew wide and he exchanged a look with Jon, then they quickly walked away from the table. Eka and Christelle watched them leave.

"Grams, maybe this isn't the best place," Christelle said.

She waved dismissively. "Don't worry about them. Do you want to learn about your heritage?"

"Yeah, but I don't think I'm ready for…"

"Of course you want to know. So the best way to learn is to dive right in. Get your feet wet. Questions are so abstract, but doin' will getcha where you're goin'!"

"Okaaay."

This should be fun.

Eka grinned and leaned back, but not too far. She could almost hear Christelle's heartbeat race as she brought her hand to hover over a branch of their mangrove table. Her fingertips brushed the leaves gently and a ripple passed through their waxiness. Christelle's face seemed to strain as she laid her hand fully on the branch. Moments dragged by as lavender light poured out of Christelle's hand and flowed down the mangrove, the leaves surrounding her hand fluttering briefly. Then the mangrove erupted in growing branches that engulfed the platform and snaked out of the floor, tables, and chairs across Bander's Place. They twisted up legs and hooked on clothes, lifting Wakers in the air as they grew upwards. Some individuals slipped out of the manic foliage and into the river while others dangled higher and higher above the mayhem. A branch entangled with the back of Eka's shirt and shot up. She struggled to unwrap it but, after a few tries, gave up and hung, twisting, above the mangroves.

Amid the chaos, Shirley's laughter rang out from under a static tangle of branches.

Then, the chaos slowed. From Eka's vantage point, a large bear of a man appeared from the corner of the platform, trailing his hand along the foliage. Everywhere he touched, branches seemed to halt their spread and ease into stillness. He whispered to the mangroves near him and the new growth shriveled up and fell off the trees or twisted into new tables and chairs. He continued across the mayhem, restoring the jungle to a manicured, living floor. As he neared her, Eka reached up to grab a branch behind her and prepared to drop. Instead, it withered slowly, gently placing her on the floor. She lay there, watching him finish the clean-up. This place was definitely more exciting than her campground.

When he was done, he walked over to Shirley's hiding place and reduced it to a pile of twigs, his glare almost palpable.

"Shirley, why are you exciting everyone?" His accent sounded vaguely Eastern European and he looked as though he would be more at home in some mountains wearing snow gear than in Florida with its beaches and humidity.

Shirley climbed to her feet and brushed herself off. "Bander, my granddaughter, Christelle, and her friend, Eka, needed an introduction. You understand."

"Ack. Always stirring trouble." He shook his head and walked back to the edge of the platform, where he had entered from.

All around Eka, the former patrons were recovering, some standing up in the river, some returning from shore, and others giving up and walking away from Bander's. A few crawled over to the chairs Bander had created, eyeing Christelle as they kept their distance. Christelle finally dragged herself up, her shaky hands grabbing hold of a chair for support.

"You okay?" Eka asked.

Christelle shook her head. "I…I was completely out of control." She fell into the seat, her head in her hands.

Shirley sauntered over to them. "Christelle, my girl, you're quite the plant wonder!"

Christelle's glare rivaled Bander's. "I could have hurt someone!"

"Ahh pssht. You're fine, they're fine."

Christelle's glare seemed to emanate enough heat to dry out everyone's clothes. But, as usual, Shirley didn't notice. She waved at the stragglers in the river.

"Grams, that was horrible. You don't even care about your own people! How can I trust you to care about me?"

Shirley stopped smiling and lowered herself next to Christelle. "Christelle, luv. No one was gonna get hurt, I promise."

"Maybe." She breathed deeply for a few minutes then shook her head. "But why should I trust your promises?" She took another loud breath. "Or anything any of you say?"

Shirley sat very still for a long while. Eka started to wonder if she was going to dodge the question like she usually did.

"I'm sorry, Christelle. I wish I could have changed things. I thought the choice to hide you the way they did was wrong." Shirley glanced at Eka. "Wrong for both of you. But, I was in the minority."

"But you could have told me. Not kept me in the dark, letting the lies go on."

"This was a while ago, but the fear still has a grip on a lot of Wakers. Back then," Shirley whistled low and long, "very few Wakers were thinking straight. And Anise had the worries of everyone on her shoulders. And it wasn't just this place. All the Waker communities around the world was lookin' at what we would do. Everyone was on edge." Shirley gazed out on the river. "My poor girl."

"Grams! Don't feel sorry for Anise. She decided to do all this then make up a story about a stupid spirit of Earth being responsible."

Shirley turned back to them and locked eyes with Christelle. "I may not agree with your *aunt*, and she is still your aunt, but she tried to do the right thing. Don't be so quick to judge. You've never had a community full of hysterical people expecting you to protect them. Or have the child you love like your own almost die from some monster. A monster that is still out there."

Christelle stared at the table, pushing some leaves around. "I guess."

"And, while I'm sure Anise thought Gaia wanted to bury you so deep no one could find you, I suspect it was more of what Anise's heart told her."

Christelle rolled her eyes. "You really believe all that Gaia stuff?"

Shirley grinned. "Doesn't matter what I think. But don't be so hasty to close your heart to possibilities. Anyways, you were both brought here to

Wake up. And I gave ya both clues."

"What?" Christelle asked.

"Hello, the rune."

Eka rolled her eyes this time. "How's that a clue?"

"Initiation. Secrecy. Come on, it was so obvious." Shirley crossed her arms.

"Of course, so obvious. I should have seen right away there was a world full of magic that had been hidden from me because my memories were stolen. It was all on the rune," Christelle frowned.

"Well, I made sure you overheard Anise and me talking. I hope you appreciate that."

Christelle sighed. "Grams, I'm trying to recover my life, not play 'Clue'."

Eka glanced down at a shimmer within the table. Shirley and Christelle's conversation faded into the background chatter of the other patrons and she leaned in closer, eye to eye with a branch that seemed to sparkle.

Closer up, she noticed brilliant pinpoints of sparkling aqua that drifted amongst the browns and greens of the foliage. While leaves and twigs pressed against her face, there was a faint feeling of itchiness in the back of her mind as the tiny lights held her attention. The little sparkles moved toward her face, then, inches from her, they coalesced into a misty form. Eka blinked. A tendril, made of light and blue and air, lifted gently toward her face and brushed her nose. She jerked back and the lighted tendril reacted similarly, pulling deeper into the branches. A sense of calm washed over her as the hint of a musty fragrance tickled her nostrils and peaked her curiosity.

She wiggled her hand into the branches, toward the tendril. The light slowly twisted up and curled around Eka's fingers, then a sense of sun penetrated her body, overwhelming her. Simultaneously, a sense of wet muck surrounded her. She wiggled her fingers through slimy mud to feel it swiftly dried by the sunlight flowing deep into her skin.

"Eka?"

She blinked and the tendril-light was gone. She pulled her face away from the table and gazed around, trying to orient herself. Shirley and Christelle stared at her.

Christelle gently pulled something off Eka's chin, then held up a leaf. "Are you okay?"

"Uh, sure. Just distracted."

"Strange way to show it, burying your face in the table." Shirley cocked her head, the hint of a smile threatening.

Eka looked down at the branches, but there was only the background energy now. "I thought I saw…some kind of misty something. Like a rope. It just kind of reached up and…" she shrugged.

"Really? Like the energy in that oak tree?" Christelle said.

"No, it was different. Like a bright blue rope. And I felt weird sensations," Eka mumbled to herself as the heat of the sun and wet feel of muck lingered.

"Well, I'll be." Shirley drummed her fingers against the mangroves. She picked up one of Eka's hands and scrutinized it, front and back. Then she did the same with the other one. "Didn't expect this," she said to no one in particular.

Christelle leaned over the table to check out Eka's hands. "What didn't you expect?"

"I think you saw a spirit. Mighty unusual." She dropped Eka's hand. "Pretty rare, especially for someone so young, who hasn't even found her bent yet."

"She saw a spirit? Like our souls?" Christelle asked.

"And what's a bent?" Eka interrupted Christelle.

"I keep forgetting how little you both know. Like children." She pinched Christelle's cheek.

"Hey!" Christelle leaned out of Shirley's reach and crossed her arms.

"Well, a soul is a completely different thing than a spirit. And a bent is the gift someone is a natural at. Like Bander and his plants."

"Don't use me in your crazy stories!" Bander shouted at them.

"Just saying what a great man you are." Shirley smiled at Bander with the Cheshire Cat grin Eka had started to recognize. She couldn't blame him for wanting to distance himself from Shirley's schemes. Although they were pretty entertaining schemes.

"Anyway." She refocused on Eka and Christelle "He's learned many gifts, but his bent is plants. That's the one that'll always work best for him. This is how it is with Wakers, although a few are more unusual. Like Cranky pants' gift." Shirley slapped her knee laughing and looked over at where Jon had been. "Oh, guess he left."

"Kinda swam away," Christelle blushed.

Shirley wiped a tear away as she chuckled. "As I told ya, he's a lighter which is an important gift for our community. Most lighters are good with electricity too, which helps some of us live amongst the Asleep. Especially these days with all their gadgets and digital connections."

Eka took her phone out of her pocket and examined it. "Are you saying you can hack things?"

"Oh no. I don't have that gift. And, while most gifts can be learned by all of us, there are some that are different, like electricity. Rare for someone not born with the bent to learn it." Shirley cocked her head and tapped her lips with her index finger. "Not really sure why? Maybe the loose connection to Gaia those forces have. Huh." She shook her head as if shaking out thoughts. "Anyway, we don't hack things. More like work with the electricity, or wind, or whatever, to get what we need. We offer extra Gaia energy and that's usually enough to get help."

"Now that would be a useful gift." Eka tried to connect with the tiny amount of electricity running through her phone but it ignored her.

Shirley kept on going past Eka's distraction. "Seeing a spirit is a strange gift." She seemed to examine Eka for another moment. "As uncommon as my gift." Shirley puffed up her chest. "Reading the future."

"I knew it! You really can see the future!" Christelle rejoined the conversation as she scooted to the edge of her chair and closer to the group.

"More like I can see strong possibilities in things. Like the two of you coming back and becoming friends. Seemed, when I saw that, it was important. So Sema and I helped you too along."

Eka glanced at Christelle who returned a quick look. An almost shocked look. Were they set up from the beginning? By Shirley and Sema?

"At least that's what I saw. Not everything is always clear. And maybe once or twice I was off."

"Once or twice? Try many, many times," Bander added from his corner.

Shirley glared at him. "This talk is private."

"Then go somewhere private to share your incorrect predictions."

"Huh!" Shirley turned sideways on her chair, back to Bander. "Not everyone appreciates this gift."

"Not a real gift!"

Shirley held up her hand behind her. "Stop or I'll tell everyone about the reading I gave you the other day. About your mangroves and a certain inner tube."

Bander froze, closing his mouth before he replied. He turned back to the group at the bar he was tending, without another comment.

Christelle nudged Eka under the table, eyebrows raised.

Eka coughed. "Um, yeah. So, I saw a spirit. What do I do with that?"

Shirley squinted at Eka. "Don't know. Never knew someone with that gift. More like a rumor. But I'm excited to see what you come up with." The Cheshire Cat grin returned.

"Wow, that's weird and awesome! You have a gift."

Eka pulled her eyes off Shirley's suspicious grin, not sure what the woman was up to now. "Yeah, guess I do. I can see things others can't. Yeah, magic." Eka sighed.

"They're gifts," Shirley stated.

"Right you are." Eka gave Shirley a thumbs up. Shirley dropped her grin and narrowed her eyes at Eka who quickly turned to Christelle.

"Whatever you do, don't say 'magic'," Eka whispered to Christelle, loudly.

"There's so many questions." Christelle ignored Eka's comment. "I got the wind to pick up Eka and plants to grow and the water to dance on my hands. Are these my bents? All three?"

"Three main bents is definitely a lot for a Waker, but we'll have to see. Some of your relatives had quite a few, though. Maybe you're following their lead."

"My relatives? Like my mom?" Christelle's body seemed tense as she leaned toward Shirley. "What was she like? Was she a Waker? Was she from here? Where did she go?"

Shirley took a hold of Christelle's hand. "Luv, I think that's a better conversation when your dad is around." Before Christelle could open her mouth in response, Shirley sat straight and held up her hand. "I'm exhausted and need refreshments. Why don't you two take some time to let everything soak in? Wouldn't want you to overload with information and blow a circuit. Have a drink. Mingle. You never know what could happen."

Shirley got up and walked over to the bar where Bander stood. He immediately slid to the far end.

Christelle turned in her seat and watched her for a moment before turning back. "I still have so many questions."

"Yeah. But that's more information than we've gotten from anyone else." Eka looked around. "And maybe she's got a point. There's a whole room full of people that know more than us."

"You think they'd talk to me after what I did?" Christelle hunched her shoulders and seemed to shrink into her chair.

"Well, we can't get anything if we don't try. Drink and mingle?"

"Sure," Christelle sighed.

They walked over to the bar and slid next to Shirley.

"Bander, this is my granddaughter, Christelle, and a family friend, Eka."

Bander, the big bear of a man, actually rolled his eyes. "Your mind is slipping. You introduced us already." He gave a brief nod to the two as he ignored Shirley.

Of course, Shirley went right on through his avoidance. "Their gifts are starting to show. I'm so proud of them."

"Never too late." A woman down the bar grinned at Christelle. "Just take Wallace; he was a late bloomer."

The man next to her sighed. "Too bad about his parents. Never got to see him become a Waker."

"Who's Wallace?" Christelle looked between the couple at the bar and Shirley.

"I'll catch you up later." Eka whispered as to Christelle as the bar became quiet.

"Okay, okay. This is sad business. And private." Bander eyed a frowning Shirley, who nodded. "Let's have a drink to happier things."

Eka watched the two and wondered just how many secrets Shirley had.

Bander grabbed a bottle of Cabernet, pouring everyone a glass. "To happy times."

The whole bar joined the cheer then he lowered the bottle to a branch and the bottle disappeared.

"Hey, where'd that bottle go?" Eka leaned over the bar and looked down.

"They're new," Shirley interjected.

Shirley seemed unfazed by Bander's narrow-eyed response. "Yes. We all know who they are and that they're new," he huffed as he turned to Eka. "We keep drink in water for cooling."

"Yep, we've got Wakers that can work with temperature to keep our drinks cool. Cooperation, ladies. That's how we roll." Shirley rolled her hips around while Bander rolled his eyes. Again.

Eka turned from the bar, watching the Wakers around them. All these people were so relaxed and at home. They chatted as if they were old friends or family. Probably some of both. She sighed and touched the shell on her wrist.

"Bridget!" Shirley yelled, turning her wandering attention to a woman seated out on the mangroves. Eka recognized her as the woman who had doused her friend with river water when they'd first gotten to Bander's. "My granddaughter has done some nice work with water."

The woman's yellow hair bobbed around her shoulders as she turned around. "If she's as good with water as she is with plants then we are a lucky bunch." She looked at Christelle with a warm smile. "We'd love if you'd join us." She waved Christelle over then turned back to her table.

The group started talking again and Shirley's attention went to the end of the bar and a heated debate on fire versus plant gifts.

Christelle nudged Eka and whispered, "So, who is Wallace?"

"He was with Jon earlier. I met them both at the tree. Right after you left."

Christelle's blush was quicker than normal. "I was angry."

Eka nodded. "Yeah, bad moment. Anyway, he seemed to know Sema. And, if I remember right, he's got the gift of electricity. Pretty lucky, if you ask me."

"If he didn't always have his gifts, maybe he's like us."

"I don't know. We can try and ask Shirley later," Eka whispered back. "She doesn't like him but maybe she'll give us an answer."

Christelle's face dropped. "Great. If we can hold her attention to ask a question. Grams has the attention span of a gnat."

Eka giggled. "Maybe we could get a squeaky toy to keep her attention."

Christelle giggled too, her shoulders relaxing then Eka nudged Christelle and pointed to Bridget.

"You should check out some other Wakers. Maybe they're more forthcoming than the ones we know," she winked.

"What about you?"

"I'll be fine. I'll just check out the place."

Eka's second nudge was all Christelle needed to walk over to the group. Within minutes, Bridget was showing Christelle the funnel she'd created earlier. Eka looked around at the other Wakers, people who actively practiced magic. Her only real connection to them was a family she barely remembered. And her only real connection to the magic was her ability to watch it happen and see spirits.

And the price to have all this? Embrace a world that had swallowed her family and left her alone. She pushed off the bar and exited Bander's, taking off down the dock, absently making a left at the end, and wandering along the river's edge. No new memories had surfaced since the canoe trip. She wished, unsettling darkness or not, that she could recapture more times with her parents and Ke. Preferably some happy times.

Or maybe she should realize that wishing they were here was just a fantasy and forget the whole thing. They were never coming back.

Stop wishing the past was different. I can't change it.

She stood on the edge of an emotional cliff, her rediscovered life a big leap from the well worn ground of the old one. She couldn't decide which way to go. Yet.

"Ahhhh! Why is this so hard!" she shouted, startling some birds in a nearby tree.

Did anyone hear her? She really didn't need Christelle and Shirley running to check on her. Surveying her surroundings, she noticed Bander's was just a tiny dot behind her.

Frustrated, she plopped down, trying to soak up the calm and quiet of her little spot by the river.

Was I better off not knowing?

Lying back, she absently watched energy flow all around her.

The sun had set and the moon, waiting for the chance, shone bright in the twilight sky, lunar reflections rippling across the river. A few distant frogs called across the water expectantly and were quickly rewarded. Eka breathed in the humid air and relaxed into the soft grass. Behind her, something shuffled in the bushes and she craned her neck around. From behind the bushes a heron took to flight, releasing a deep, guttural call. It sailed over the water, interrupting the moon's reflection. She lay back again, watching it as she drifted off to the sound of frogs.

Suddenly, Ea jerked awake and sat up, groggy. She looked down at a spot of heat on her chest, trying to focus. A little bird made of rainbow lights hovered above her warm pendant.

"What's happening?" she whispered, disoriented, in the silence. A shuffle came from the bushes again. She turned, but this time, no heron took off.

Hello Eka.

A vaguely familiar voice jolted her as the words rang in her head, sending a shiver through her body.

"Hello?"

She pushed herself up and crept over to the bushes. Her body wanted to run but something about this seemed familiar. Something important. But what? When she neared the bush, a cold invisible hand seemed to reach out and grab her. Her breath caught and she stumbled then hit the ground as multicolored lights exploded out of her pendant like a spotlight. The cold embrace abruptly dissipated, then the world faded.

"Eka! Eka wake up."

She felt a slap against her cheek and sat bolt upright, shivering.

"Wha…wha…happened?"

"We don't know, Kiddo." Shirley was staring at her. "Can you remember anything?"

"I don't know. I heard…heard something there," she pointed towards the bushes, "and then…then there was darkness."

Shirley walked over to the bush and touched it. The leaf she tried pulling off blew away in a million flakes of gray. "Poor thing."

"What is it, Grams?" Christelle's voice stayed low.

Shirley looked at them. "Don't know, but it ain't good."

Eka stared at the ash floating away and a chill crept through her cold body.

It's like the island.

Christelle knelt down next to Eka. "We were so worried. You were gone, then," Christelle paused, frowning, "something awful and cold just…just went through us. Everyone freaked and no one knew where you were, so we started looking."

"Yep. And we found you here. Enough chit chat; let's get you somewhere warm."

"Shirley!" Bander came stomping up to them just as they pulled Eka up. He eyed her, then the bush, and came to an abrupt halt, staring.

"Bander, what in the mangroves did ya come crashin' in here for?" Shirley seemed to get taller, or at least a ton more intimidating, snapping him out of his silence.

"Three more Wakers were found. Like that." His big hands had the slightest tremor as he pointed to the bush, never taking his eyes off Eka. "Anise was right," he mumbled, "she should never have come back."

Eka looked at the bush.

There's no way he thinks I did that.

Christelle jumped in front of her, staring him down. Or up, as he towered over them all. "Take that back!"

Shirley stepped between them, somehow still more formidable than the bear of a man. "Bander, pull yourself together. This one here was passed out when we found her, almost as cold as the arctic. That bush, or those Wakers, ain't got nothin' ta do with her." Shirley reached down and helped Eka up. "Now, get back to the bar and calm those people down."

Eka finally noticed the panicked voices coming from the bar, even from this distance. Bander stared for a second more, then backed up and disappeared through the brush toward the bar.

"Grams, they can't think Eka did anything, right?" Christelle held Eka up on the other side as they made their way back to what she hoped was her vardo.

Shirley suddenly seemed small and tired. "Can't worry about that now. Let's get her to her trailer."

As Shirley cut off any further protests from Christelle, Eka couldn't help hear Shirley's unspoken words. Get her to her trailer where she's safer.

Where the Nalo Are

Eka paced around her vardo. Her fingers twisted the bracelet around her wrist, absently tapping the shell as it passed. "This is going to be alright."

Visions of a bush disintegrating, an ash island, and her family engulfed in darkness rushed back through her mind. Then there was that cold voice in her head that knew her name. And the dead Wakers.

This is not going to be okay.

"Stop!" She shook her head violently. "I'm just tired." She stepped faster, a movement just short of a run, and the camper seemed to shrink to two steps across.

People died; were left like that bush.

That bush. A shiver went through her. It was real, all of it.

Christelle and Shirley saw the bush last night. They felt that cold. It wasn't just me. And that voice; someone said my name. Crap!

She paused mid-step. Could there really be someone after her and Christelle? Someone who killed her family? Some psychopath Waker? A chill went through her.

The door slammed open and she jumped, all her thoughts briefly scattered.

"Sorry," Christelle crept in. "Just wanted to see how you are."

A vestige of a shiver went through Eka again, then she sighed and sunk into a chair. "I'm okay."

Christelle sat opposite her at the petite table, frowning. "I'm starting to freak out. Those people died." Christelle's voice was just a whisper now. "Do you think whatever attacked us is back? Killed those…"

"I…I don't know." Eka's thumb pressed the shell against her wrist and she stared at the table. "But maybe Anise is right about me."

"What are you talking about?"

Eka's eyes met Christelle's. "I heard my name." The cold of the voice crept back through her and goosebumps spread across her back. "I found that bush, then something…cold grabbed me. And said my name. Whoever it was knew me." Her quiet voice barely reached her own ears.

Christelle stared at her, not uttering a word. Silence began to smoother Eka, so she hopped up and put on a smile. "Hey, does it feel stuffy in here? I feel a night out coming on."

"Eka, please. This is serious." Christelle reached for Eka, but she sidestepped to the sink. "I don't believe Anise is right about you. Maybe there's something out there after us. Maybe it knows your name. But that doesn't mean your hurt anyone."

Why am I the only one hearing it? Why hasn't it said your name?

Eka frowned briefly, then plastered on a smile again. "Hey, I was probably just hallucinating that voice after getting cold. Maybe the bush isn't related to the deaths." She shuddered, visions of ash people slamming her thoughts.

No!

Words, any words, tumbled out of her to counter the thoughts. "Maybe it was just a newbie Waker learning how to use their gifts."

Christelle rubbed the back of her hand, her eyebrows pinched together. "I don't think that's how it works. Grams…"

Eka's skin started crawling, itching at all the energy building up in her. She really needed to move; to shut down her brain. "Come on. There's plenty of time to figure out everything. Besides, if we're freaked out, we can't think straight, right?"

"I guess."

"Then let's go have some fun. Relax. We'll be able to think better then." She batted her eyelashes and pouted. "I know you want to."

Christelle took a deep breath. "Fine, but I think we should be careful."

"We'll be super careful, go where there's other people. Now, let's go check out the hot-spots in Manatee Isles." Eka slung her arm around

Christelle's shoulder. "Just two Waker newbies painting the town…"she held up Christelle's arm next to hers, "lavender and gray."

Christelle shook her head but a corner of her mouth crept up. "Okay. Fine."

Eka sprinted out of the small space toward her truck, threw open the driver's side door and dove onto the front seat of the cab.

"Hey!" Christelle shouted from behind the truck.

Eka turned and leaned out the door to find the vardo still hooked up to her truck. "Ugh. I guess we'll have to unhook."

She climbed back out of the cab and came to a stop in front of Christelle, who stood staring at the campsite.

"Why is everything packed up and the vardo ready to go? Were you…leaving?"

Damn.

Eka looked down, spinning her bracelet. "I…"

Christelle frowned and crossed her arms. "Without a goodbye."

"The truth?"

Christelle nodded.

"Probably."

Christelle inhaled and turned away, walking out of the campground. Eka sped after her and grabbed her shoulders, but Christelle pushed her away.

"Hey, I started to leave but I didn't."

Christelle stopped walking and crossed her arms again.

Eka's heart raced and she stood for a long moment staring at her friend.

"Whatever." Christelle started back out of the campground.

"I'm sorry. I just freaked out. I don't know what's going on and I'm…" Eka said from behind her.

Christelle turned back. "Scared?"

Eka shrugged. "Those people just died. Were turned to ash." She shuddered and sucked in air. "I'm the only one getting these visions, and yesterday…it was directed at me. Whatever is doing this knows me." She looked at the weird energy flowing through her. Her voice became a whisper. "What if it's connected to me? What if that's why I'm not like you? Don't have gifts?"

Christelle's frown dropped and she walked back to Eka. "You are not like whatever that thing is." She shook Eka lightly. "Bad things may have happened to us, but it's not who we are."

"Thanks for believing, but we don't know anything. I mean, we don't know what really happened." Eka inhaled deeply. "I might be damaged. Dangerous."

Christelle stared straight into Eka's eyes as she took her hand. "If whatever danger's here because of us…"

"Me," Eka interjected.

"Both our families were attacked." Christelle glared briefly. "So, if that's true, we might still be in danger from it. We need to figure out what's really going on so we can stop it."

Christelle took Eka's hand and gave it a squeeze. "Okay?"

"Owww! How strong are you?"

"Sorry." A slight smile flickered across Christelle's face. "But I need you to snap out of the self-doubt."

"Hey! Look who's talking," Eka grinned.

"Then I should recognize that quirk. Doesn't look good on you." Christelle headed back towards the truck. "And no more trying to sneak off."

Eka walked up next to her and leaned against the truck. "Deal."

The road turned into town a few hundred feet to the right and Eka parked in a grassy lot just outside of an abandoned building. A few other cars were scattered around the grass, apparently the local community parking lot. Without a pause, Eka jumped out and headed along a grassy path toward the tiny downtown. Christelle caught up just as they passed the first building in town, a small trailer home on the right.

"Hey." Christelle nudged Eka with her shoulder. "Why are you in such a hurry?"

"Feeling better, huh?" Eka nudged her back.

"Maybe. But don't Shirley the question."

Eka stopped and spun toward Christelle. "Nice. I think I'm gonna hang on to that one. Good job." She chuckled then sauntered down the path, Christelle keeping up this time. Before the inquiry could continue, she intercepted the conversation. "Hey, I have a date this week."

"A date?" Christelle frowned, taking the distraction. "When did you set up a date?"

"A day ago. Thought Devlon might also be open to answering some questions. He seemed awfully guilty when I ran into him by the treehouse." She winked at Christelle. "Besides, he's not bad on the eyes."

"Uh, okay. I guess he could have some information."

Suddenly, they were on the main avenue of the little town and thoughts of her date dissipated. Eka could read more of the signs from this spot; a particular neon one on her left seemed to shout BOB'S as it blinked on and off. Under it, smaller neon signs promised pool and cold beers.

"Perfect."

She grabbed the door handle to the little bar, on the corner of a small, two-story building, and pulled open the wooden door which was covered in a thick coat of black paint pretending to hide layers of unidentifiable stains. In spite of the paint, the neon signs hanging above the door illuminated layers of gunk. Trying not to wonder about the stains, she glanced inside and smiled at the sound of Elvis coming from the jukebox.

"You're kidding, right?" Christelle asked from behind.

Eka turned to find her a few feet away on the sidewalk.

"What'd you think we were gonna find here? The population is like 40. And remember, new adventures." Eka attempted a sinister grin. "Who knows what things lurk behind this opening."

"Not helping."

"It'll be fine. If it looks bad, we'll turn around and leave."

Christelle threw up her hands. "Fine, but I better not catch anything."

"Maybe a sense of fun?" Eka mumbled and pushed open the door. Her eyes struggled in the darkness, taking a few moments to see in the gloom.

"What do you see?"

Eka turned to Christelle, standing directly behind her. "Nothing ventured." She wiggled her eyebrows and pulled Christelle inside, the door shutting behind them.

"Yeah. Or curiosity killed the cat," Christelle mumbled back.

When her eyes adjusted, Eka scanned around. A couple of pool tables sat behind a small island bar while a few tables and booths lined the walls. Two men played pool in the back and a small group sat at a table along the right wall. Besides those patrons and the bartender, the place was empty.

"I think we're fine." Eka walked up to the bar and ordered two beers, then turned and leaned her elbows back on the bar. Christelle, on the other hand, leaned rigidly against the bar, as if she were a plank of wood, her eyes darting around like two rabbits caught in the open.

"Relax. Nothing's going to go wrong. We'll just…"

Her necklace warmed and fluttered as raised voices came from a long table against the wall.

"Hey, isn't that the grumpy lighter guy, Jon?" Christelle pointed to a man standing at the end of a table full of people, his hands on the shoulders of a seated woman.

Eka nodded toward the man next to them. "Yeah and I think that's that other guy, uh, what was his name?" She tapped her lips for a moment, then she snapped her fingers. "Wallace."

The group looked over at her finger snap and Eka smiled, raising her beer. The seated woman turned revealing herself to be Janice, Devlon's friend. Eka's grin widened and she waved at Janice, receiving a very clear gesture in return.

"Whoa," Christelle whistled. "Not a fan?"

"A friend of Devlon's." Eka took a drag of her beer.

"Ohhhh."

"Apparently I'm coveting one of her two favorite things."

"What's the other?"

Eka took another drink. "Coffee. Particularly his coffee." She wiggled her eyebrows.

Christelle blushed but she did seem more relaxed.

Jon's scowl killed their vibe briefly, then he bent down as Janice whispered to him.

"He really is a downer." Christelle shook her head.

Eka nodded. "He doesn't seem to like anyone but her. Go figure."

After a moment, he gestured toward the door and she stood and headed out. As Jon followed, he glanced back at Wallace. "You leave her alone." The statement carried across the bar, the few patrons glued to the exchange. Wallace just smiled and waved as Jon navigated Janice out. As she exited, Janice gave Eka one more look.

"Wow, she really doesn't like you," Christelle commented.

Eka opened her arms wide. "Just don't understand. What's not to like?"

"Besides stealing her boyfriend?"

Eka raised an eyebrow. "I think it's more of her hobby, or obsession. Wonder if she secretly takes pictures of him."

"Devlon wallpaper?"

Eka grinned wide. "You, my friend, are on a roll."

A movement at Wallace's table caught her eye and she glanced over to find him waving her toward the group. She nudged Christelle and pointed her beer at the table, but Christelle took a sip of her own beer and looked at the dartboard.

"You know, not really feeling like being with a crowd. Maybe I'll try darts. New adventures, right?"

"Never played before, huh? Then I think we should start with a small bet."

"Bet?" Christelle's face dropped. "I don't really have any money."

Eka nudged her. "You grab us a board and try a few throws. I'm going to see what Wallace wants. Maybe he knows something about what happened to our families."

Christelle shivered. "Or those Wakers they found yesterday."

"Yeah." Eka stared at her beer, the two of them quiet for a moment. The ashy bush flashed through her mind and she suddenly wasn't sure she was ready for this.

"Hey," Christelle nudged her. "We don't have to do any of this tonight."

Was Christelle reading her mind? Eka shook her head. "No. Better to jump in. It's not going to get easier and we need to know if we're in danger."

"Yeah," Christelle nodded and pushed off the bar. "See you in a few." She stepped warily around the bar and pool tables and headed to the dartboard. Eka watched her for a few moments while she tried throwing some darts. Luckily the walls around the dartboards were littered with holes so Christelle's aim didn't cause any damage to them. Or the floor. Or ceiling? The two men playing pool dropped their cues and hurried to the other side of the bar.

Eka grimaced and quickly turned away, pushing out thoughts of Christelle and the darts.

Okay, question time.

She turned and sauntered over to Wallace's table. All six people with him stopped talking and fixed their eyes on her.

"Hey, people." Eka's grin, and very friendly wave, was met with blank stares.

At the far end of the table, Wallace waved her into a seat near him. "Please, join us."

One friendly face was enough and Eka slid next to him. She immediately hitched her head at the door. "So, do people always leave your table so angry?"

Wallace shook his head. "Just a disagreement. Nothing to worry about."

Maybe he won't be so willing to open up.

"Glad you joined us. I was hoping to catch up with you, introduce you to our little community."

"Your community?" Eka leaned closer to Wallace and lowered her voice. "I thought most of *the community* stayed away from," she looked around then back to him, "town."

"Ah." He leaned in closer. "We are a little different. We…" He straightened up a little and nodded his head at the others sitting at their table. "They are still waiting for their gifts. They're like you."

Eka sat back and scrutinized the men and women sitting with her as they returned to their conversations. Their energy seemed muted, almost nothing compared to the few other Wakers she'd met. They seemed more like the ordinary multitudes of people who resided in all the towns and cities she had ever passed through. Yet this small group lived in this secret world of magic, like she did now, where all they could do was watch, never dance.

Maybe I am like them. Maybe I'm different from other Wakers because of normal reasons not … because of that thing.

"So what happened that they don't have gifts?" she whispered to Wallace.

"You don't have to whisper. None of the Asleep that hang out here pay attention to us. And our little group, the Nalo, is fine with anything you need to know."

"Nalo?" The word hit her with a sense of familiarity.

"It's a haunting little word I picked up from some Wakers in Hawaii. Embodies the sense of something lost or vanished. Fits us, don't you think?"

"You were in Hawaii?" Eka touched the shell on her wrist. Why would he have been there?

"There are Waker communities all over. Traveling helped me forget about being an outsider and I made some helpful friends." His eyes gleamed and his grayish-blue energy seemed to boil inside him. "Now, since I have my gifts, so many wonderful possibilities have opened up." The head of the man next to Wallace dropped and Wallace's enthusiasm followed. He sighed and patted the man on the back. "But I've also met so many Nalo that have been ignored or forgotten, like us. None of us deserve that, so I've made it my goal to search for ways to unlock their gifts."

Smiles grew out of the now attentive group and hope seemed to bubble up as they all looked towards Wallace. They hung on his every word, straightening with each hint of salvation. Around her the muted energy of the Nalo and Asleep pulsed weakly. The brightest energy outside of Christelle was the shimmering teal of a tiny lizard that ran across the table.

If her energy was normal, but she never found a way to work the magic, would she be able to live in this world? Could she just hang out, like they did, hoping and waiting for just a taste of what the Wakers didn't think twice about? The lizard looked at her and she absently touched its head. The teal lights tentatively wrapped around her finger then quickly retreated as it contacted the gray inside her. The lizard darted to the edge of the table. No, she wouldn't sit around waiting for a miracle. She was either a full-fledged member or she was out. But she still needed answers about her past so she was stuck for now.

A glass broke at the bar, snapping Eka out of her musings of the lizard and magic and unfulfilled yearnings. "So, do you know how you got your magic up and running?"

Wallace sat pressed back against the booth, staring at the lizard sitting next to him on the table.

"Wallace?"

The lizard hopped across the bench and disappeared around the back. Wallace sat still for a moment longer, then scanned the seat and relaxed.

"Are you okay?"

He plastered a smile on his face, but there were a few drops of sweat on his forehead. "Sorry, just a bad lizard experience."

"Too many Godzilla movies?"

"Just a silly kid thing." His shoulders sagged away from his ears.

"Locked in a box with lizards for days?"

He glared briefly then waved the questions off. "What were you asking about my gifts?"

What could possibly have happened to him? Mutant lizards? Was that a magic thing? She so wanted to know, but his face said not happening, so she let it go. For now.

"Did you figure out how you got your powers back?"

A shadow passed across his face. "I'm not sure. My gifts seemed to start up when my parents died. Maybe it was shock."

She caught her breath. "Are they the ones that…?" She wasn't sure how to finish the question.

He sighed. "They died a few months back. They were…ash, like those others yesterday." His face paled and he seemed to zone out.

Okay, not the person to ask about this.

"Wallace, I'm sorry to bring this up just, no one wants to talk about it."

He shook his head. "No. I understand being left in the dark. Left behind. You didn't know. That's why I wanted to talk to you. We understand the frustration of not belonging. Of being the outsider and alone."

Eka blinked.

I have people. Maybe I don't belong in this world but I have Sema and Win; My career.

She waved him off. "No. You've got it wrong. I've got people. Family. Just haven't found a place to settle yet. Lots of the world to check out."

Wallace leaned back. "Maybe I'm wrong. Maybe you don't mind that your life and gifts were taken away by the Gaians and now they don't want you here."

Eka frowned. "Gaians? As in Wakers who follow Gaia, 'The source of everything'."

Wallace laughed and slapped his hand on the table. "Gaians are those daft enough to blindly follow." He leaned closer. "Maybe there is some benevolent spirit running everything, but seems she should be better at it." The shadow of a scowl passed over his face. "Not play favorites."

He didn't seem to believe in Gaia like the Wakers she'd met. What did he believe in? This world was getting more and more complicated.

"…different."

She turned to Wallace. "Huh?"

Wallace grinned. "Now that powers are up and running, things can be different. For me, for them. Maybe even for you. You don't have to be left behind. We can help you get back what you lost."

Eka scanned the group at the table; their sagging shoulders and downcast eyes didn't inspire hope. But Wallace had gotten his powers back on his own. According to the others, this was impossible without Gaia's help, but here he was. Maybe he could help her get answers and any magic would be a bonus.

A beer appeared in front of her and she looked up at Christelle.

"Ready for the challenge? I think I've got this dart thing down."

Eka reached down and pulled a dart out of the toe of Christelle's shoe. "Uh-huh. Maybe you need some instructions."

Christelle cringed and took the dart. "Yeah."

Eka stood up and grabbed the beer, tipping it towards Wallace. "Thanks. Definitely something to think about."

"Of course," he nodded. "If you decide you're interested, let me know."

She turned to Christelle. "Alright, how much you putting up?"

Christelle's eyes went wide.

"Betting? but I thought you were giving me some lessons first?"

She placed her arm around Christelle. "Yeah. We're betting on how the training goes. I mean, that's what makes it interesting. Having something at stake. Otherwise, it doesn't really matter."

As they walked away, she noticed Wallace nodding as he mumbled, "So true."

Dinner with Devlon

Eka strolled along the walkway of River Road, where a few shops tempted pedestrians to enter with displays of candles, clothing, and trinkets. Her fingers brushed the windows as she passed Jack-o-lanterns that took center stage in storefront displays, rich with orange, black, purple, and green decorations. She smiled at the festive trappings, remembering all the pumpkins she'd carved and all the costumes she'd made with Sema and Win. Trick-or-treating with them, in neighborhoods lit by thousands of tiny orange and purple lights, had been a magic world she had loved.

The elevated walkway ended at the last store and she hopped off the edge and onto a winding sidewalk, small trees and bushes growing in a dense line along the river to the left. Despite the thick foliage, hints of water glistened through the leaves, reflecting light from street lamps.

A cobblestone drive appeared on her left through a break in the trees. Just on the other side of it, a tall lighted sign announced The Lost Table. Peering down to the end of the winding cobbled path, she discovered a building that jutted out over the water. Images of trees, river, and a lush garden reflected off the floor-to-ceiling windows that encircled the round building, glass doors propped open at the front. Through the wide open floor plan and open back doors, the sparsely lit river sparkled just past the deck.

Well, Devlon had promised her a dining experience she would remember and this had all the potential for an incredible meal. She just hoped information was a part of the evening.

She sashayed inside, her pale blue skirt swishing mid-thigh, which might have been a slight error in judgment as her white, short-sleeved sweater reminded her that Florida still had a fall season, even if it was spotty.

The restaurant was one big room, tables and chairs circling the oval bar in the middle. Just a few tables and bar stools were occupied; otherwise the place was empty. Eka spotted Devlon at the bar, sipping a beer and chatting with the bartender. Unaware of her, she slipped behind him as he listened to a story about the bartender's kids, wife, and home repairs. As she bent close to his neck, the bartender spotted Eka and stopped mid-sentence.

"Mind if I interrupt?" she whispered in Devlon's ear. Under her breath, goose-bumps trailed down his neck.

He swiveled slowly, his mouth stopping inches from hers. "You came."

She stared into his brown eyes for a long moment. "Worried?"

"No."

She raised an eyebrow.

His smile crept up. "Maybe."

"Eka, this is Bill." He twisted back to the bartender, who was suddenly at the far end of the bar. Bill waved at them then focused on drying glasses.

Devlon turned back and shrugged, glancing toward the deck. "I have a table waiting, if you're ready."

She nodded and they made their way out onto the empty patio. Stained wooden slats and tiny railing lights gave the deck a tropical feel. Out on the water, the reflections of the railing lights and the reds, oranges, and yellows of the setting sun mixed together to create a moving watercolor abstract. Beneath the deck, rhythmic splashes of water slapped against the deck posts, creating a beat for the chirping crickets and throaty calls of a few frogs.

"This is a beautiful location. It's like we have our own little hideaway."

"Well, the restaurant is not usually open on Mondays." He slid out her seat. "But the owners, Jim and Cheryl, are good friends."

"Must be really good friends."

A waitress sauntered up to Devlon's chair, grinning at them as she passed them menus. "Hey Dev."

"Hi, Cheryl. This is Eka."

Cheryl stuck out her hand and Eka shook it, recognizing the muted energy of an Asleep, so obvious now, with all the energy flowing around her. Kinda weird thing to notice about people. "Hi."

"I see Dev already has a beer. Would you like something to drink?"

"Um, do you have Cabernet?"

Cheryl nodded.

Devlon leaned over the table. "Would you like to try an amazing wine?"

"Of course."

"If you don't mind, Cheryl," Devlon interrupted, "would you bring out a sample of the house Cab?"

"Sure." She patted him on the back then walked toward a door on the far side of the main room.

After she left, Eka laughed. "Dev, huh?"

Devlon blushed. "I've known them since I moved here. They're like family."

"Like?"

His infectious smile dropped. "Well, they're not part of the community. But they're good people."

Finally, someone willing to share.

"So." She narrowed her eyes. "About your community of Wakers. Seems like there's a lot of secrets. And lies."

He grimaced and dropped his gaze as he tapped his index finger on the table. After a few minutes of nothing but tapping, she sighed and pushed her chair back to get up. "This has been fun, but I've got things to do."

"Wait." The tapping stopped and he met her eyes. "I don't know what to say but sorry."

She examined him as she played with her bracelet. Was he going to open up? Keep hiding things? She didn't know him at all and he *was* one of them.

"Hey, it's your world. No biggie. I just thought you'd like to set the record straight. But you were right, this is an awesome restaurant."

She reached for her purse.

"Eka, I'm really sorry." He leaned closer, his smell of sun and sea distracting her. "Give me a chance to explain, please."

His warm hand touched hers and she could see his biceps twitch under his thin, pale T-shirt. A tingling started in her stomach.

Stop it, body!

She eased back into her chair and retrieved her hand. "Okay, fine."

His shoulders and neck seemed to relax and he gave her a crooked little grin. "But let me eat something first. I haven't eaten all day and I think I'm going to need my strength."

"Deal." She raised an eyebrow. "But if you back out after we eat, I'm going to have to call in Janice to take over for me. I'm sure she'd love to listen to all your non-informative stories."

He raised his hands. "I promise not to back out on the threat of Janice."

The wine arrived and Cheryl helped them pick out the freshest foods of the season. Eka breathed in the salt air from the brackish river water and the earthiness of the surrounding greenery, letting Devlon steer the conversation to the more mundane topics of life on Manatee Isles. As she ate under the night sky, she listened to his stories while magical energy drifted within the sounds, sights, and smells of their little area on the river and settled within her skin, helping to dissipate her irritation. When they finished the meal she almost wished she could just continue enjoying the magic, but she knew this chance for information could slip away at any moment.

"So, what was growing up Waker like?"

"No warm-up questions, huh?"

"A deal's a deal."

He sat back and took a deep breath. "I know this is new for you. This was new for me once." His brows came together briefly, followed by a slight frown.

"You weren't born into this life?"

"No." His voice was soft. Almost humble. "I was born with latent gifts. Born into an Asleep family."

"How is that possible?" Eka spun her bracelet.

Devlon tapped the table again. He seemed to struggle for the right words. "All humans have a bit of potential to connect to the world. To see the energy in and around them. A few, Wakers, are completely aware of the connections and can access the energy of all the life around them. Most, though, are like the people you grew up around. All the people out there in cities and towns, the Asleep, with their lost and broken connections to the world. Sometimes, someone with a working connection, is born into an

Asleep family. They can see everything we see, but their gifts are inactive. They can't interact with the energy they see. They're caught between worlds and have no one to tell them what's happening."

Eka looked around at this new world buzzing around her, so amazing and yet just out of reach for her. She looked back at Devlon. All that time she and Christelle had searched for answers and had been in the dark, they still had each other to share the confusion and excitement. He had been alone.

"Wow."

He took a deep breath and closed his eyes but didn't continue.

She rested her chin on her palm and waited a few moments while he seemed lost in thought. Finally, she spoke up and broke the silence. "I'm sorry you went through that alone. Being Latent must suck."

He opened his eyes and nodded. "It does. Usually there's no one around to even tell you you're not crazy. I don't know what happens to those that stay like that, but my gifts eventually kicked in."

"Does that happen a lot?" Maybe she was like a Latent now.

He shrugged. "Not often, but sometimes. Wakers are always on the lookout for any Latent born out in the Asleep world, to try to get them help. Sometimes it works out great, like Anise."

"Wait, what?" Eka frowned. "Anise? She wasn't born into this?"

"No. Her parents were both Asleep and young. Not a great combination, especially to raise a Latent child. She was lucky there was a Waker community near them in Texas. Those Wakers were able to bring Anise out of the situation. Shirley and Bu adopted her and raised her with their son Jake."

Eka sat quietly. He seemed eager to talk now and she didn't want to accidentally jar him out of it.

He played with his glass, watching the wine swish around. "Many Latents aren't so lucky. I could see things I couldn't explain and my family thought I was crazy. So did I." His frown morphed to a scowl as he gripped the glass stem. "It's hell not to know."

"Hey."

He seemed to notice her again and reluctantly continued. "Anyways, when I was ten, I almost drowned and my gifts just started working. It really freaked everyone out. They thought I was possessed or something, and they tried sending me off to a school for troubled kids in Sydney. I decided I'd be better off alone so I slipped out the night before I was supposed to go."

"But you're here now and part of this community." She crossed her arms. "And joining the others in hiding things from us when you knew what it was like to stumble around lost."

She saw the grimace return briefly.

"Eka, I…you've got to understand. After I ran off, I wandered around. I worked odd jobs and tried to keep to myself. Hide what I was seeing and what I could do. I was just a kid and I had no one." He stared over the river, lost in thought again. After a few minutes he turned back. "I thought if I left Australia, found a new place, I could leave everything behind. Become someone new without the strange sensations around me or crazy abilities I didn't want. So I worked a ship to California. But it was all the same until…" The hint of a smile crossed his face. "Until some Wakers found me. They saved my life."

What would she have done if Sema and Win had thrown her away? After she lost her family, with nowhere to go?

"I'm sorry." She reached across the table and touched his hand. His body sagged and the hint of a smile turned to a full grin.

"Thanks. And I hope you understand. Wakers embraced me and showed me everything I'd been missing. They are my family."

He interlaced his fingers with hers and squeezed. "I know you haven't had the best welcome, but this is a good community. I could help you settle in, learn about this world."

A cloying warmth spread through her. Despite being outside, the air seemed claustrophobic. She recovered her hand and fanned her sweater in the breeze.

"Are you okay?"

Eka nodded. "Yeah, just kinda warm. Hey." She quickly found another topic. "How did the police not find you? I mean, you were so young. I would guess kids in Australia can't just leave home and wander around or board ships without anyone noticing."

Devlon frowned and opened his mouth but stopped. He sat back, eyeing her. "Um, back then, not many people cared. Especially if they wanted you gone."

Eka released her breath, the breeze finally cooling her down. "Australia must be really different. Have you ever contacted any of your family?"

Devlon shook his head. "There's no one left that remembers me."

"Holy crap, everyone died? What happened?"

Devlon seemed to fight a smile.

He thinks that's funny?

His smile dropped as he watched her. "They died of old age. I left home over a hundred years ago."

"A hundred years? What?"

"You didn't know?" He shrugged. "We live a bit longer than your average person."

Eka lowered her face to her palms and let the information flow over her.

"Eka?" Devlon leaned across the table. "Too much?"

She looked up with a goofy grin and whisper-shouted, "That's amazing!"

He laughed. "You adjust pretty quick."

"I mean, this hasn't been all wine and roses, but holy crap." She leaned forward and whispered. "Like, a really long life. That explains why Sema and Win and Shirley and all of them look so young. Can you image the possibilities?"

He opened his mouth but she continued.

"Of course you do. I mean, you're living it." Her laughter bounced around the restaurant.

"Hey," Devlon interrupted.

"What?"

"There's great benefits to being a Waker, but there are boundaries and responsibilities too." He sighed. "Sometimes they're hard."

She furrowed her brow. "Like what?"

He inhaled a deep slow breath and as he exhaled, he leaned back and gazed up. After a few long moments, her hand started tapping along with her foot. She stopped fidgeting and reached over to tap him. "Hello? You wander off a lot. You were talking about the hard parts of being a Waker."

He looked back down and refocused on her.

"Yeah. You'll realize that there are very few Wakers at any time. While we live a long time, most of us can only ever have one child."

"Okay. One or no kids. Cool."

Devlon's brow furrowed. "Not everyone thinks it's cool."

She shrugged. "Can't you just do what Asleep do? Get medical help?"

He shook his head. "This is hard to put into words. All this energy, all these gifts, they're part of a bigger picture. There is a connection to everything. But Gaia has safe-guards in place to keep everything in balance."

"Uh-huh. Blah blah blah, Gaia."

He narrowed his eyes at her. "Gaia is the source of all this energy. We just help spread it around, like a conduit."

Eka leaned back herself and raised an eyebrow. "How do you know Gaia's a real thing? Have you ever seen her? Has she ever talked to you?"

Devlon stared at Eka, mouth slightly open. "No. But, I mean, it's not like Gaia just waltzes in and hangs with us. She usually has a member of the group that senses her, like Anise."

Concentrating on not rolling her eyes, she took a deep breath

Who cares what he believes; you're not setting up house with him.

"Whatever. Sounds like Anise has you all wrapped around her little finger." The last bit slipped out and made her smile.

His face flushed red. "She is an amazing leader. She would never take advantage of us or lie."

Eka plastered him with a stare. "Really? Well, that's not my experience. But if you're into leaders that erase people's lives at will, then more power to you."

Devlon held up his hands. "I wasn't here for that. I honestly don't know what happened, but I'm really sorry it did."

Her breathing slowed. "No worries." After a moment, she leaned in. "You can make it all up to me with one question."

He cocked his head, frowning. "Okay?"

Would he answer? She could only ask. "What happened to those Wakers that died?"

He gave her a really big sigh; not what she expected at all. Then he shook his head. "I don't know. I heard the rumors their bodies were changed to…ash." His whole body winced and she wished, very briefly, she hadn't asked. "Look," he leaned toward her, "I know everyone's on edge, and I can't pretend to know what's happening with those bodies. But I don't…"

Cheryl suddenly walked up. "Dev, I hate to bring this to an end, but our babysitter needs to go home so we need to close up."

They looked around, realizing how late it was.

"Cheryl, sorry to keep you."

She smiled and rested a hand on his shoulder. "You're always welcome to close us down. And tonight is on us."

"What, no. I can't let you do that." He pulled his wallet out but she waved it away.

"Our treat, although we still expect you to help with the house Saturday."

"Deal."

He stood and hugged her. Eka hopped up to thank Cheryl before following Devlon out of the restaurant. As they came out the front of the building, Devlon stopped. "Eka, I know there's other rumors. About you." She opened her mouth but he plowed on. "I don't believe you had anything to do with what happened to those Wakers."

She studied him. "You don't even know me."

"It's a vibe, and I'm good with those." He smiled and, before she could counter his vibe argument, detoured the conversation. "How did you get here?"

Eka frowned. "Walked."

"Well, I have a much better way home." He stuck out his hand. "Trust me?"

"Really?"

He didn't move, just waited. Well, vibes were kinda her thing.

And he is cute.

She shrugged and took his hand.

What the hell.

Before he could get to the big reveal of his way home, she heard someone call out. "Devlon!"

They turned as Janice emerged from the shadows.

Devlon squinted briefly at her. "Janice?"

Eka could swear Janice was trying to kill her with a stare.

"I can't believe I caught you!" Janice shuffled up to where they stood then tried to wiggle between them and managed to knock Devlon's hand out of Eka's.

"Um." Devlon stepped back. "Janice, we were just leaving."

"Do you have to go?" Janice stepped closer to him. "I was just hanging out and saw you. What a wonderful surprise. We could go downtown for a while."

Devlon reached around Janice and reconnected with Eka's hand, pulling her past Janice and down toward the water. "Gotta go."

They rushed to some stairs, leading to a dock with a sailboat tied to a clip; they were down the stairs and on the sailboat before Janice could reply. Devlon untied and pushed off in a blur, opening a sail that unfurled and billowed out in a strangely abrupt wind. She watched magenta energy move from him then mix with some silver energy in the air, coalescing into a swirl in the sail.

"Well, at least she wasn't hiding in the bushes." Devlon laughed half-heatedly.

Eka craned her head behind her. On the retreating dock, Janice's figure grew smaller and smaller. "Is she a Waker?"

Devlon looked toward her disappearing figure. "She is a Waker. In a way."

"Latent?"

"Not exactly Latent. There are a few people born Wakers but for some reason never really figure out how to connect with the world. I mean, they see the energy and others working with it; they even have the potential for working gifts. But they can't seem to channel energy properly. Eventually their ability dims, like a muscle that's never used. Their lives are short, like Asleep and Latents, and they never learn to dance with the world."

Nalo.

"Do you want to dance with the world, Eka?"

"What?"

Devlon spun around and pulled Eka close to him.

"Oh." She blinked as he danced her around the bow then leaned his face close to hers as they moved and their eyes locked.

"Using our gifts is not a matter of making things happen, forcing them," he whispered into her ear. "It's not about controlling, but more of a dance. Sometimes you have to let part of yourself go, to work with others. To feel their moves while they feel yours."

His body pressed against hers and together their hips rolled as they glided around the bow. Light-headed from his impossible scent of sun and salty air, and the warmth of him against her, she let herself follow his body around the deck.

His mouth moved closer to hers and she focused in on his inviting lips. His wine-infused breath enveloped her and she inhaled and closed her eyes. Softness brushed her lips just as her heel hit something hard and she tumbled backward, Devlon stumbling after. She flailed, her arms coming out of his grip and grabbing at anything to stop her backward fall. But her hands came up empty and she hit the railing and flipped over it.

"Eka!"

Suspended briefly in the dark water, a dim green glow erupted around her hands as she pushed toward the moonlit surface. Breaking the surface, she spun toward the boat in a phosphorescent glow. Forgetting her fall, she slapped the water and giggled as small, glowing ripples spread out.

Is he doing this? It's so beautiful.

Before she could stir the water more, a funnel of magenta and silver lit the water around her. The bright, colorful bubbles spun under her and floated her up and out of the water on a swirl of air, then dropped her lightly on the boat.

Devlon rushed over with a towel. "Are you alright? I'm so sorry!"

She looked at his worried face then flicked water at him. "That was amazing! Did you see the glow?"

"The glow?"

She dropped to the deck and swished the water. "The water is glowing. Did you do that?"

He furrowed his brows for a moment then grinned and dropped next to her, shaking his head. "No, that's bioluminescence. There's these little creatures that put off that glow when they're disturbed."

"They're cool little creatures."

He shook his head again, still smiling. "You're kinda crazy."

"Yeah."

The wake of the boat glowed a dim bluish-green as they putted down the river. Around them small lights from the buildings on shore mixed with starlight, reflecting on the water.

She melted into a cushion on the deck, wearing his dry sweats and T-shirt, lost in the quiet around her. Her life was pretty cool. Maybe not perfect, maybe a bit solitary, but fun. So why was she chasing answers that wouldn't change what happened to her family? Might bring answers she didn't want?

A shiver went through her.

"Penny for your thoughts." Devlon brought her back to the present.

She'd never questioned anything this much before.

Snap out of it before you lose your mind.

She shook off the endless questions and focused on the river again. The boat meandered through luminescent water as it stirred up the little lighted creatures. After a few, long, mesmerizing moments, she turned away from the view and grinned at Devlon.

"I thought Wakers didn't use Asleep stuff." She patted the deck. "Like boats."

"Well, I did grow up in the Asleep world." He ran his hand along the wooden surface. "Some things just stick with you. Guess that's why I'm at Jim and Cheryl's so much. And have a business the Asleep use."

She put her hand on his, ready for more mundane talk. "So, you're from Australia? What happened to the accent?"

"I lost it a while back. Kinda picked up the local dialect."

She wiggle her eyebrows. "Always thought an Australian accent was sexy."

"I'll keep that in mind." He smiled at her then stood to slow the boat, dropping the sail and setting the anchor. The river was wider here and they had anchored in its middle, the farthest from the lights from both shores. Above, the sky seemed alive with stars. Devlon walked around to the back, returning with large pillows and a few blankets.

She moved to the front and laid back on the blanket he'd spread across the bow. "Looks like a favorite spot of yours."

He nodded. "It's the best star viewing area around."

He joined her and they lay in a comfortable silence as the boat rocked gently back and forth. Eka let her head slowly roll onto Devlon's shoulder and she rested her hand on his abs as he put his arm around her.

Okay, despite his taste in hero worship, I can't argue with his taste in venues.

What is Family?

Christelle dug her fingers into the grass under her. She inhaled the grassy smell and let the familiar tickle of energy flow from the grass into her hands then roll through the rest of her. At some point over the last few months, and she couldn't remember exactly when, this connection to the life around her had morphed from disconcerting to natural. Part of who she was.

"Christelle?"

She looked up at Anise.

Why did Eka get to go on a date with a cute guy last night for her questions and I get to talk to Anise?

"Christelle!" Anise called again.

She sighed.

Because she's my *aunt.*

Christelle met Anise's eyes then looked away. Her aunt's expression and voice seemed to be full of sorrow and pleading. But Christelle couldn't find her way through her anger yet to understand if she was just painting emotions over reality again. She'd read Anise wrong before and she was still shattered.

Christelle sighed again and reluctantly released the warm and comforting grass and stood up. A light breeze rippled across the grass and ruffled the edges of some rose petals. The wispy wind spiraled up her arm, its silver energy a twinkling, lacy pattern against her skin; a comforting tingle that replaced the warmness of the grass.

Standing under a giant oak treehouse, Anise smiled tightly at Christelle and smoothed her dress down. Christelle knew that movement; Anise had made it a million times before. In fact, the first time Christelle had visited Hapton's Farm, well the first time she remembered visiting it, she had fallen out of a tree and Anise had run to pick her up. But Christelle had called for her mom and Anise had stopped, then smoothed her dress repeatedly, as if it helped her figure something out. Then she'd scooped up Christelle and hugged her tight until the crying stopped. Anise was rarely unsure, but that little movement gave away her vulnerability. Christelle's heart ached as a shock of love punctured her anger. Love for her aunt who had helped raised her when her mom died.

But she didn't die. She went away and they all agreed she should disappear. And they lied to me about her death. Even her mom lied, she'd never come back or tried to make contact. Not once.

And just like that, the anger flooded through Christelle and her body tensed as she walked over to Anise.

"I thought, well, since you're so proficient in working with plants," Anise smoothed her dress again, "I could help you in that area. Working with plant life is my strongest gift." As she spoke, Anise cradled some beautiful bluish-green and gold roses growing at the base of the oak. Christelle leaned toward the unusual plant to see deep green energy flowing off Anise's hand and into the stems, thick with green leaves and thorns. Bright bluish-green energy sparkled and danced with Anise's energy, lighting up the roses at the end of each branch. As her aunt's energy soaked into the stalks, a slight tremor traveled across the surface.

Christelle waited for something, anything really, to happen but the moments ticked by in stillness. She lightly brushed her fingers across the still, quiet vine. "I don't think anything … " Leaves shot out from all over the plant.

Christelle rocked back and sucked in her breath. "Wow!"

Anise finally laughed then leaned over and gave Christelle a quick hug. "You like it, huh?"

Christelle nearly nodded her head off. "How did you get just the leaves to sprout? Without it growing crazy?"

"Ahhh. You have to be very clear with your intentions, in their language. It's what we call Connecting."

"I can't even get other people to understand what I want, how am I supposed to get a plant to guess what I need?"

"Just try Connecting." Anise placed Christelle's hand on a rose. "Create a clear picture of what you want and send it."

Christelle took a deep breath and gently nudged some energy across to the rose. She tried to control the energy, hoping that less energy would be less potent. After a few moments of trying without results, a lethargy swept through her. She dropped to the ground, resting her head on her hands. The bush swayed in the wind, small and unchanged. She sighed and closed her eyes.

Nothing.

Vibrations suddenly shook her and her eyes flew open as branches shot out of the rose bushes, speeding across the ground as giant leaves and thorns sprung out of the branches. Fixated on the process, she gasped when hands went around her waist and jerked her back, pulling her on top of Anise as a branch came to a stop at their feet. Christelle lay there a moment, not sure she wanted to see, but of course, finally peeked. And gaped up at a vine that rested high above the crown of an oak, like a beanstalk climbing to the land of giants.

"I need to breathe." Anise huffed.

"Oh, sorry!" Chritelle rolled off, then slumped back, exhausted. "I'll never get the control."

Anise sat up and brushed leaves off her dress. "Sweetheart, you can't just try to control it. You have to talk with the plant. Create a relationship. That's why we call it Connecting."

"But I was connecting. I felt the plant. Gave it energy."

"Let me show you."

She wrapped her hand around Christelle's then guided their hands onto the giant bush. Soon, deep green energy flowed from Anise's hand and curled around Christelle's pale lavender energy where their hands intertwined. A shimmering and colorful spiral spun out of their hands and into the twisted forest of the rose bush.

Christelle could sense Anise's heartbeat. The quick beat slowed to an echo of her own, then love, overwhelming and warm, enveloped her. Within this blanket of warmth was the taste of strength and protection and sacrifice. Anise's essence. The crashing wave of love receded into the background and Christelle could sense an earthiness and warmth that seemed to spread out within the bluish-green energy. In that moment, she was Anise and the bush and Christelle, all jumbled together.

She allowed the sensations to travel through her with no agenda, letting Anise guided her. She became the green essence as it lightly spun up through the branches. Instead of dumping an overload of energy into the bush, Christelle followed Anise as their combined essence paused then spiraled around a small spot on a branch. Somehow Christelle could feel a question in the movement, asking if an offering of energy was wanted. The bluish-green shimmer glowed brighter at the spot and acceptance of the gift washed over Christelle. The small spiral sunk into the branch and then a tiny leaf, illuminated with deep green, lavender, and bluish-green energy, shot out of the branch and unfurled. More bits of green performed the same spiral dance.

Suddenly, Christelle was unfurling from the connection. She flowed along with Anise's essence as she unwound herself from the rose bush and a hard border knitted itself between them and the bush. They were now two. Grief overwhelmed her as a brief moment of intense loss shot through her. Then Anise's energy wove itself around her and drained away the sadness. Her aunt's love and protection shielded her, as it had for so many years, before it retreated and Christelle was once again just herself. And then there were three.

Christelle blinked. As the sensations faded, her brain took over, trying to understand what had been a purely visceral encounter. "I felt it but it was so different than before! Like I was there but I wasn't just me? Like we were all one thing. And we offered and we accepted and…"

Anise smiled and nodded. "It's hard to explain in words. We just stick with Connection. It's spiritual in nature."

Christelle stared at the roses. "I thought it was just energy. But Grams mentioned spirits. Is this like our souls? Connecting?"

Anise shook her head. "No. Souls are a tricky topic. But as a Waker you'll learn how to Connect, at different levels, to other spirits. Spirits are all around us; a few Wakers can even see them."

Christelle touched the rose again, watching as the energies mixed. "Grams said the same thing, that most Wakers can't see spirits. Just the energy." She was feeling so comfortable with Anise, she decided not to mention Eka's ability to see spirits at Bander's. Why stir up trouble.

Anise nodded. "And you felt how it was an offer, not a demand?"

Christelle nodded back. "But I was everyone for a moment. Like I was offering the energy to myself."

Anise laughed. A sound Christelle hadn't heard in a long time. And she didn't remember any sense of joy or laughter when their energy had mixed, just strength and responsibility and love.

"…afraid." Anise inhaled deeply but when she exhaled her shoulders stayed hitched. "Wallace's parents set off enough of a panic, but now, there are more." She clenched her fists. "I don't even know what is attacking, or how to protect anyone."

Christelle refocused on Anise, who was actually communicating with her. She stepped closer to Anise. "Are you okay?"

Anise stared at the ground for a moment then shook her head and looked Christelle in the eyes. "I can feel the panic, even if no one is saying anything. When Wallace's parents died, we tried to keep the way they died quiet," Anise held up her hand when Christelle started to protest, "just until we knew what was happening. But now, with these new deaths, found so out in the open, there's no hiding that whatever was here before must be back. We've even started training with ancient fighting techniques that haven't been used for a long time. Every Waker community has joined, afraid they're next. We don't even know if we can fight it, but we need something to hold on to." Her voice dropped to a whisper, almost haunted. "They were found drained; nothing left but ash."

Christelle lightly touched Anise's shoulder and Anise blinked at her niece. "How can a Waker do something like that? Take someone's energy and leave just that, like the bush at Banders?"

Anise's face seemed suddenly old, or maybe Christelle could feel the wariness emanating from her energy, like the weight of the world wearing down her shoulders. "This isn't a Waker. We've confronted Wakers trying to do this before. This is something else. Not human. And we might be dealing with something our abilities can't stop. We'll need Wakers with greater abilities. We'll need Ysians."

"Ysians?"

Anise focused on the roses beside her instead of the question. She ran her hand along the edges of the petals and they seemed to wrap themselves gently around her fingers in response. She sighed, her shoulders relaxing, finally speaking. "Long before my time, there was a threat. One that could have been catastrophic for life everywhere. That was the last time our abilities weren't enough. When the Ysians were created." She turned back to Christelle. "And now, there's a new threat, maybe something greater, and you need to know because you are from that line."

Christelle sat, unmoving. This was like that story about those super charged Wakers who had destroyed cities for Gaia. "This is crazy. You think I'm going to be some kind of killing energy conduit? First, I don't even know how to control my own energy and second, this is not *my* community. I was thrown out of it. And third, I'm not destroying cities or even killing anyone, like those people in that Gaia story."

Christelle's breathing was the only sound for a few minutes. Anise gently placed her hand on Christelle's arm. "I'm trying to tell you what I know. Give you answers."

Calm down. This is what you asked for.

Christelle took a few controlled breaths and her heart rate slowed. "Sorry."

Christelle hadn't realized Anise's hand was still on her arm. Her body would still automatically calm down when Anise comforted her, despite everything.

"Do you know you used to dance with the energy? Actually float in midair with all kinds of energy flowing around you?" Anise asked.

"Really?"

"Uh-huh. I remember you were barely walking, but everything around you responded to your essence. It was like you were conducting a symphony with the world."

The image of her parents with her in the field resurfaced, her mother's warm hand in hers as the flowers grew. She quickly wiped away a tear.

"Why did my mother leave?"

Anise frowned and sighed deeply. "Isamea was afraid for you. She had to find out what the danger was, how to stop it."

"But why her? Why hasn't she come back?"

Anise took both Christelle's hands in hers. "When your parents showed up with you, they didn't understand what had attacked them or why. Whatever it was, none of us were safe, including you." Anise touched Christelle's hair. " Your mother is Ysian and you have her hair, like all of them." She seemed to be lost in her own thoughts until Christelle tapped her hand.

A wisp of a smile flitted across her face. "And it's her nature to protect her family, her community. Since there were no answers in the Waker communities, she disappeared into the world of the Asleep, trying to find clues. Your father was left to protect you. He moved you around while your mother searched." Anise met Christelle's eyes. "I think if she had found any real answers she'd have come back."

"But why did all of you let me believe she was dead?"

"Christelle. I'm so sorry for that. Your parents thought it would keep you from looking for her. They couldn't tell you about what really happened and thought you'd put yourself in danger searching for her."

"So she left to protect me?" Christelle whispered the question to no one.

Would she have done the same to save someone she loved? Just left, giving up a future and all her dreams and love for her family, for their safety? Maybe there were reasons but her heart still lay in pieces.

"I guess I get it." She wiped her blurry eyes. "I just wished I'd known her."

Anise squeezed Christelle's shoulder. "I know. But she loved you more than anything. More than herself."

Maybe her mother had a reason to leave, but it still left her to deal with a childhood without her. All the times she wished to talk to her, times her dad refused to talk about what happened. All the times she had been utterly alone.

"How about a break for lunch?" Anise stood and Christelle absently nodded.

Anise stood up and brushed her dress off as Christelle got up. "When Jake brought you here, when you were first born, you were so quiet. Watching the world, like you were studying it. I took you on so many walks, showed you so much of our world." She squeezed Christelle's hand. "You're part of this family Christelle. We love you so much."

All of the secrets had torn Christelle up inside, but maybe answers could help her heal. Help the family heal. She returned the hand squeeze.

Anise brushed her hand along the edges of the blues and greens of the rose petals, then reached in the pocket of her dress and handed Christelle a palm full of seeds. "Maybe they can help you practice."

Christelle looked down at the seeds then up at the full-grown roses.

"They're beautiful. Thank you." She hesitated, then pulled her aunt into a hug.

Anise stood unmoving for a moment, then wrapped her arms around Christelle. "We never meant to hurt you."

A wet drop fell on Christelle's shoulder and she heard a sniff.

"Thank you, Aunt Anise," Christelle answered.

Anise pushed her back a little and looked her in the eyes. "Then you're here for good?"

Christelle looked at the ground and shoved her hands, and the seeds, into her pockets. "Sure."

Would she really stay? Could she believe in them enough, again, to trust them? Feel safe? Her heart really wanted to but she just didn't know.

Anise's fingertips tightened slightly on Christelle's shoulders, then her hands dropped. "Ben is making us a lunch. Shall we?"

Ben had a spread set out when they entered the kitchen. Christelle's stomach rumbled as the smell of gourd soup and a spicy bean dish filled her nostrils

"Ben," Anise smiled. "Christelle is coming along so quickly."

"That's great. And we have your room ready whenever you want."

The room they'd made for her in their treehouse sat empty across from the kitchen. She hadn't been able to bring herself to go in it. Memories of her visits to Hapton's Place as a child centered around the building she thought was their home. All the scary nights Anise or Ben or Gramps or Grams had sat with her in her real room back at the house. And she had left so many little things there over the years. Anise and Ben had always laughed at her forgetfulness, but it wasn't forgetfulness when she had left the hairbrush from her mom on the bedside table. Or the stuffed giraffe her dad had won for her on the bed. The giraffe that had come from the only carnival he'd taken her to. How could she ever forget those mementos? She had put them in that room, in her room. The only place that seemed like a home. Now she looked around at this house in a tree, what they referred to as their 'real' home. Back at the farm, the glass dome was gone. It was only ever there, she learned, so they felt comfortable when she visited. Now she slept alone in the house, her family living in trees. She forced a smile for her aunt and uncle, knowing they loved her and that she loved them. But the weave of that love seemed less solid, less dependable. And she couldn't make sense of it right now.

"So," Christelle pushed her food around with her fork, "We met some Wakers in town. Well, I'm not sure they were Wakers. They didn't seem to have their gifts yet."

Ben and Anise exchanged frowns.

"Christelle," he shook her head, "they are…troubled."

Christelle stilled her hands and looked directly into Anise's eyes. "But they will get their gifts, right?"

Anise sighed deeply. "We don't know. They are off balance with this world. Like the Connection I showed you with the bush. Did you feel how it was a conversation, an understanding of an exchange?

Christelle nodded.

"They don't seem to understand that part. We've all tried to help but, so far, nothing."

Christelle's hands tightened around her fork. "But Wallace got his gifts back and he was like them, like Eka. I mean, you're a community. A family. You don't give up on each other, right?"

Ben cleared his throat. "Yes. But for now, you should stick with Wakers who have working gifts. Learn more about your own. Wallace might be an exception but they are not like us."

"And neither is Eka," Anise stated, flatly.

Christelle's hand didn't move. "Why?"

"Christelle, honey," Anise sighed. "You're just starting your journey, and your gifts are more special than most. You are important. Some individuals are…disruptive to that."

"You mean inconvenient." Christelle's breathing sped up. "Are you gonna make all these disruptive people disappear too? Was I disruptive, inconvenient? Maybe I'm useful right now but if that changes, are you going to throw me away again?"

She stood up and dropped her fork on the plate.

"Why do you get to decide who is important and who's not? They matter, Eka matters, I matter. Not because of any stupid gifts."

She turned and fled before the tears started.

"They don't care about anyone but their little group. I can't do this anymore!" Christelle argued to no one as she stumbled around the bases of the tree houses. "Why should I care about any of these people! I don't know them!" she shouted, wind picking up through the treetops. An image of Anise holding her when she had stubbed her toe, soothing her pain and hurt, shot through her mind and she crumpled to the ground, sobbing.

"Hey, kiddo."

Christelle looked up at Shirley kneeling beside her.

"You okay?" Shirley brushed a few tears off her chin.

Christelle shook her head, smearing dirt into her wet cheek. Shirley sighed and sat down next to her. "What's happened?"

She shook her head again, examining her hands.

Grams won't listen. She's one of them, keeping secrets and lying.

"I really don't want to talk."

Shirley lifted Christelle's chin so they were eye to eye. "I know there's a lot going on, but you can't work it out all by yourself. You need help, and you and I are family."

"A family that lies," Christelle blurted out. Her hand covered her mouth as her teary eyes widened.

Shirley narrowed her gaze, then sighed, and finally nodded. "You're right. We all lied. Can't say we were all in agreement but," her shoulders sagged, "we all participated."

Shirley picked up a pebble and skipped it across a clearing. "We all make choices, kiddo. Mistakes sometimes. And we have to live with any consequences."

"That's not enough. I would never hurt someone like that."

Shirley's gaze shifted back towards Anise's house. After a few moments, Christelle began fidgeting. Should she leave? *Maybe this is really what my family does, avoid the truth.*

"I was right about there." Shirley suddenly pointed to the middle of the treeline. "I was clearing out some debris from a storm, bending down. That's why I didn't see them right away." She frowned at the spot, furrowing her brow. "But I did catch the burst of colorful light. A strange light; seemed alive. Couldn't figure out where it came from. Then, behind me there was…" her face contorted and Christelle instinctively put her hand on Shirley's arm. Shirley tried a smile but it fell flat and Christelle frowned.

"Grams?"

Shirley nodded and continued. "I think I stared for a minute or two before I even knew what I was looking at." She grimaced briefly and took a deep breath, her voice a whisper. "Jake was so pale and gray. And I didn't…" Her breath caught as she wiped her eyes. "I didn't see any energy, any movement. I thought he was…" She blinked and rubbed her face again.

"Dad was what?" Christelle whispered.

"Almost dead."

She could feel Shirley's pain and she fought between wanting to know and not wanting to picture her dad dead. "You don't have to keep going."

"No, you need to know. I think I didn't even realize Isamae was under him. She crawled out with you. And Jake wasn't dead, but Anise almost died saving him. Took nearly all her energy." Tears fell down Shirley's cheek before she caught them. "That's when I saw Eka. Standing blank-faced, by a tree."

"Eka? Here?"

With us?

Shirley nodded. "When Jake and Isamae could talk about what happened, we all tried to make sense of it. But, their memories were fragmented. Probably shock and the strangeness of it all." She patted Christelle's hand. "You were too young. Eka was a little older but hadn't spoken to anyone. When he came to, Jake remembered seeing the gray, ashy bodies. Apparently your mom had family that was in the house when it was attacked." Shirley took a moment to breathe before she continued. "Jake blanked out after that, from loss of energy. Isamae saw the most. She said some shadowy haze was pulling Jake's energy. She tried to stop it, but I think she was in shock from seeing her family dead like that. Then she saw colorful lights and all of you were suddenly here."

"What do you mean, we were suddenly here?"

Shirley stood and walked over to a tree, scaling up to a nook and motioning to Christelle.

"Grams?"

"Just come up."

"Really? Right now?" Christelle stood and walked to the tree, staring up. Grams and Eka took fidgeting to another level. She took a deep, calming breath and pulled herself up the trunk, scraping her hands and knees. She squeezed her arm past Shirley, trying to get her body into the nook.

"Scoot over, Grams, there's no room."

Shirley scooted an inch. "There's plenty of room, girl. Just sit."

Christelle squeezed and twisted until she was squished between one branch of the trunk and Shirley. Who seemed to have plenty of space.

"I hope this relates to this story."

Shirley grinned. "Nope, I just like it here."

Christelle turned her head on scrunched shoulders, huffing and looking at Shirley. "Are you kidding?"

"Anyway. If you look over there," Shirley pointed to an area of the clearing by the dense treeline, "That's where I was. And right there," she pointed to a tiny spot behind it, "That's where the you showed up with your parents and Eka." She twisted to the right, pointing off into the distance. "And about 4400 miles that way is France. You were in France, then a blink of an eye later, you were here. Somehow moved instantaneously."

Christelle's head spun and she struggled to grab a single thought. "But…is that a Waker thing?"

Shirley shook her head. "Nope. That's just one of the mysteries about that day. I'll say this, if that jump hadn't happened, I might not be talkin' to you."

Christelle stared at the spot where they had appeared. "Teleported."

Shirley slapped Christelle's knee. "Exactly!"

"Ow, Grams!" Christelle rubbed her knee with the hand not stuck between her side and the tree. "What about Eka?"

Shirley turned to her left and pointed, then drew an arc to her right side. "About 4700 miles from Hawaii to France. Seems Eka teleported to France first." Shirley smiled wider and ribbed Christelle, who tried to rub her side. "Nice word, by the way. And Eka did it twice, first from Hawaii to France. Then from France to here. Isamae barely remembers her during the fight. When Eka showed up here with you three, she was in shock, poor thing. Mute for a while and refused to eat."

"Grams, I don't know what, how…" Christelle was unable to describe the jumbled information.

Shirley nodded. "We were all confused. And some of us are still stuck on that day, maybe because it made no sense. But it really shook up the Waker world. And, on top of that weirdness, something dangerous was out there, with strange gifts or powers or who knows, and our gifts seemed to have no effect against it. So there's still a bunch of scared Wakers hanging on all that."

Christelle frowned, breathing deeply and imagining some hazy form attacking her parents, almost killing them.

Christelle saw what a crappy situation it was, but she still hurt. "I know you all were afraid; I just wish I'd been part of it and not kept in the dark. Had known my mom."

"Oh, kiddo." Shirley lifted her arm, pushing Christelle deeper into the bark, then laid her arm across Christelle's shoulders. "I know. You shoulda had a different childhood. Your grandpa and I didn't agree with Anise's decision but we were outnumbered."

Christelle pushed her arms out gaining more room in the nook. "Outnumbered?"

"Most of the Wakers here trust Anise's opinion." Shirley looked off, seeming to lose herself in a memory. "You know, she used to be so relaxed, easy-going even."

Christelle raised an eyebrow. "Anise?"

Shirley smiled without the hint of mischief. "Well maybe not easy-going. But Anise definitely could enjoy a good laugh." Shirley sighed, smile suddenly gone. "Something happened to her that night. Maybe her responsibility for the community was too much after the shock of seeing Isamae, Jake," Shirley patted Christelle's leg, "and you in that state. Then having Jake almost die and learning how dangerous the thing that attacked them was. And it was a thing, your parents were sure of that. The energy coming off it wasn't human or even part of Gaia."

Christelle rolled her eyes.

"I know," Shirley interrupted her own story, "that you think Gaia is just a myth, but I saw her once."

Christelle stiffened. Was there really a spirit of this planet? "But if that's true, then she did this to me."

Shirley inhaled deeply then let the breath run out of her. "It's more complicated than that. Seemed Anise needed something concrete to hold on to after the shock of seeing you four. She locked on to the idea that you were in danger and needed to be hidden. And Eka, who showed up as the sole survivor of the same type of attack in her home, but with a strange energy, was linked to that danger in her mind."

Christelle shot up straight, nearly pushing Shirley out of the tree. "I don't believe it! Eka's a good person!"

Shirley wiggled herself back into dominance in the nook. "I agree. But so many of the Wakers out there are like Anise, scared and needing something to tie that fear to. But there are a few that are worse. Anise may have had suspicions that Eka was involved somehow but nothing compared to Eka's family. The way they treated that girl."

The stories of Eka and her grandparents had seemed happy to Christelle, not stressful. "I thought Eka's grandparents loved her, raised her?"

Shirley sneered at something internal, distasteful. "I'm talking about her grandparents from Hawaii. Her grandmother Haipo strode in, all haughty and demanding. She wouldn't even look at Eka. The grandfather tried, I'll give him that, but Haipo stopped him cold and that was that." The sneer flitted over Shirley's face again. "It was that woman's idea to suppress your connection by burying your memories. She would have permanently broken the connection if she could have. And Anise, in her shock and fear, thought you'd be safer if you were hidden in the Asleep world. Hidden from anything searching for you. Anise said Gaia wanted this too, but truth be told, I'm not sure Gaia was even part of all this. Some of us argued against hiding you like that, your parents arguing the strongest." Shirley's fist clenched. "But there were so many in the Waker communities shaken up. They thought all of you would bring an unknown danger to our world and wanted all four of you gone. So, the fear won." Shirley shook her head and her fists released. "With your connection to Gaia suppressed, almost like the Asleep, your gifts didn't work anymore and any memories associated with those gifts or our world got cloudy. If you remembered anything, we'd pretend it was your imagination." Shirley sighed.

Christelle wiggled back in besides Shirley. Her shoulders sagged and she distractedly played with a fallen leaf, then brushed away a tear. "No wonder Dad never really seemed happy to settle anywhere. We were basically outcasts, living ghost lives."

Shirley tried wrapping her arms around Christelle in their tight space. They jostled for a bit, Shirley trying to hug Christelle, but gave up after her arm wedged between Christelle and the tree bark. Christelle rolled her eyes and lifted her hip, then pulled out Shirley's arm.

"I guess all of you were outcasts, with all the Waker communities wanting you gone. They even wanted to suppress your parents' memories as well, get rid of any connection to whatever that thing was." Shirley sat up taller. "But we'd had enough, your grandpa and I. So we helped you and your parents slip away into the Awake world before that happened. And Eka, thank Gaia, had Sema and Win. They took her and disappeared, themselves." Shirley slouched again and shook her head. "But then, when Isamea set off on her own mission, I think your dad had a hard time. With her gone, his community shutting him out, and hiding who he was every day, he kinda lost himself. But he has always loved you. And your mom loves you so much."

Christelle's breath caught. "Where is she?"

"Awww, kiddo. No one else believed it was a good idea to try and find whatever attacked you, except for your parents. And your mom was the best one to track it." Shirley squirmed out her arm to pat Christelle's knee but elbowed her in the face. She seemed to ignore Christelle's red nose as she kept going. "It broke her heart to leave you, but she refused to expose you to the danger. And she believed if that thing knew a Waker was searching for it, she'd never find it. So she hid herself in so deep in the Asleep world that none of us could sense her and she's been searching ever since. Not like she'd have had a great welcome to come back to."

Christelle stared at Shirley as she rubbed her nose. "How do you know she's not ..."

Shirley cocked her head, nodding. "That, kiddo, would be obvious. It's part of our Connection." The twinkle that usually lit up her eyes, disappeared. "That's how we knew about Eka's parents and the recent deaths. We all felt them. Something you'll eventually sense as well."

All of this rolled over her like a tsunami of information. Her parents.

The sacrifices. Christelle gently sobbed into her grandmother's shoulder. "I miss them so much."

Shirley nodded. "I know. Not right that this world is so new to you. Or Eka. If Haipo had her way, she would have dumped that child with some Asleep family. Or worse." Shirley spat. "But I never doubted Eka was one of us and an important clue to what happened, what will happen. Sema and Win went to Hawaii as quick as possible and took her away from Haipo, raised her the best they could. When the deaths started again and Anise told us Gaia wanted you awake, Sema, Win, and I knew Eka had to be here too. To wake up with you." Her gaze drifted for a moment. "And seems we had some colorful help with that task. Again."

"Help?"

Shirley shrugged and waved it off. "Probably fanciful thinking. Anyway, I've got a feeling you both are part of what's coming. That hair of yours is a mark of great things."

Christelle touched her hair. "My hair? Like those people in that story? The Ysians?"

"That's right."

Didn't the Wakers with the white hair destroy all those cities?

"I'm not killing anyone."

Shirley frowned back. "No one said anything about killing someone. Many of our greatest have been marked with that hair, without hurtin' anyone." She nudged Christelle. "Your mom was a pretty incredible Ysian."

Christelle took a deep breath, then tried to squeeze Shirley in a hug. She finally gave up and hopped off the tree.

"Thanks, Grams, for sharing the truth with me. And for believing in Eka. I think she needs to know everything too."

Shirley nodded. "If she has questions, I'll do my best."

"I understand everyone's afraid. I'm not sure I even want to think about what happened to us that night." She shuddered again, then crossed her arms over her chest. "Eka's a good person, Grams. And I'm going to make sure everyone learns that."

Shirley hopped down next to her. "You go, girl."

"Really, Grams?"

"What, I'm hip?" Shirley did a quick dance, or jig, probably something from the hills of Ireland in the 1800s.

"Real hip," Christelle giggled, trying to cover it with a cough, Shirley shrugging. And still dancing. "See you soon." Christelle darted off to find Eka, her steps lighter than they'd been in ages.

Spirits, Spirits Everywhere

E ka lay in bed staring at the vardo's ceiling. She grabbed her phone out of the nook where it lay charging. Four a.m. Dropping the phone back, she pulled a pillow over her face. For two nights the information Christelle had gotten from Anise, Ben and Shirley replayed in her mind.

I teleported across the world? Some crazy thing attacked my family and Christelle's family? Who were across the globe from each other. So this thing teleported too? Was it here now, killing again?

She threw off the pillow and rolled over. 4:02 am.

"Stop it, Eka."

Slowly sliding head first down the side of the bed, until the top of her head rested on the floor, she absently scanned under the bed. A few discarded socks lay in the dark recesses and to her right lay the running shoes, left there after the last time she went running.

When was *the last time?*

The rest of her body slid off the bed until the shoes were up against her head.

Ugh.

She blinked at the phone as it hung upside down, off the charging cord. 4:10 am mocked her from the screen.

"That's it!" She grabbed the shoes and crawled up to the bed, then swung the phone back to the nook, scrounging for shorts and a T-shirt.

"I just need to get out of here."

She threw on the running clothes and shoes, then stepped out of the vardo to her perfect camping spot, hidden by tall pines and nestled between the Banana River and the private road through Hapton's Place. Dense pines thinned as Eka found the road, stretching out under early-morning stars. Stars hinted that morning was a ways away while the pre-dawn morning tickled her senses; the rhythm of cicada calls echoed through the trees and a light wind swept across her face and down the road, a silent challenge to her slow pace. She pushed herself, racing the breeze, laughing as the wind fell behind and the moon hovered low on the horizon, a distant spectator to the competition.

Lost in the sensations of her run, she almost tripped when a rainbow shimmer buzzed around her head then darted into the shadows of an oak hammock. Suddenly, she sensed her body tugged toward the shimmer, like someone pulling on her arm. She stumbled to a stop, glancing down at her stomach where the pulling sensation was strongest. From her mid-section, a faint line of colorful lights connected to her gray energy then stretched across to the hammock and disappeared within the dark contours of the oaks. A multicolored glow flitted around in those oaks, illuminating tiny bits of trees and brush and pulling the lighted trail around like a rope. She dipped her fingers into the colorful connection and a vibration went through her.

What the hell?

The flitting glow, at the end of the lighted rope, dissolved into a swirl of color and spiraled into the undergrowth of the trees, then the entire rope-like trail of lights dissipated. A sense of emptiness flared up in Eka as it dissolved. She quickly crossed the road, stopping at the edge of the expansive hammock. From within the dense trees she heard frogs calling to one another and the rustling of animals starting their day, but nothing that seemed out of place. Pushing aside some branches, she peered in for any sign of the lights. Out of darkness, a swirl of colorful light flashed in front of her, now the shape of the bird from her pendant. She glanced at her necklace, but it still looked normal. Yet somehow it was now more like a hunk of metal and stones, no longer vibrating with an energy she hadn't even noticed until it was gone.

The little, lighted bird flitted in front of her face and zoomed around her head.

"Hey!"

She swatted at it, but her hand went right through the lights, then the bird darted into the brush. Without even a pause, she took off after it. At first her feet caught on roots and branches as she followed the slowly moving light. Somehow, even without the lights that connected them tugging at her, she could feel the presence of the glowing bird. Step by step the presence became her focus and they sped up, her and the bird. Goosebumps spread across her arms from leaves brushing her skin as they flew through the woods. All around her, energy in the form of iridescent light, grew stronger, emanating from every branch, blade of grass, and palm frond. With each step, her breathing deepened, as if a thick blanket had been removed from her nose and mouth. In the back of her mind, she knew her speed was impossible, but at that moment nothing mattered but following the shimmering bird, and the sense of freedom washing over her. A part of her had been suppressed, buried so deep she had missed it completely. Now it was returning and she was coming back to life, as if she'd burst out into the sun after years in the dark.

"Woot, woot!"

Despite her speed, the bird stayed ahead, its light blurring against the forest's lighted energy. Then, the bird swerved right and, without thought or hesitation, she slid along the same path. The forest was now just a tunnel of color all around her; winds singing past her ears as she zig-zagged through the foliage in pursuit of the little specter.

How could I have lost all this?

The light ahead abruptly changed, a pinpoint of illumination appearing ahead and moving toward her like a train. She reined in her speed, but momentum, which often wins, carried her past the last trees and into a glowing grass clearing where she slid and tumbled for several feet Rolling to a stop, legs and arms sprawled out, anchoring her solidly to the ground as she stared up at slowly spinning stars. Her stomach lurched.

"Ugh." She wrapped arms around her middle and closed her eyes until the queasiness faded. Luckily, this only took a few minutes and the nausea was defeated. She could finally open her eyes.

The clearing she'd rolled into glowed with pale green illumination and her russet-colored skin reflected the green. Bright fluttering, at the edge of the clearing, caught her attention and the little rainbow bird flew from the trees and across to land on Eka's shoulder.

"You are pretty fast, crazy bird."

Reaching up, her fingers grazed the lights of its beak and the surface rippled while her stomach fluttered.

Did I just feel that?

She stared into the bird's glowing eyes. "We're connected?"

It fluttered.

"So, a yes."

Its lighted head shook, as if it was shaking water off, then it lifted off her shoulder, circled her head, and dove into her pendant with a rainbow splash, illuminating the pendant briefly before it dimmed to nothing. Eka gingerly touched it, prepared for some kind of strange feeling inside her. But nothing happened.

For a long while she sat alone and in quiet, a field of glowing green grasses surrounding her.

"Okay. That was pretty fun. Uh, thanks." She tapped the pendant a couple of times.

Then, from out of the treeline that circled the clearing, thousands of tiny lights, like the ones in the glowing bird, swarmed out and danced around her, circling tighter and tighter.

"Are these fairies?" she whispered, then shouted. "Are fairies a Waker thing?"

After a few spins around her head, the lights ended the slow spiral at a point right above her. Although the point remained the same size, the thousands of colored lights all disappeared into it until it was a single, tiny, hovering white light, drifting down to a spot a few feet from her. For a few moments, the light lay there, doing nothing. Eka rolled over and low-crawled toward it, her hand hovering just above it.

"Should I touch it?" She hoped the pendant would give her a clue, but it was silent. Normal, really. "Okay, I'm doing…"

Before her words were out, the white light exploded into a large round spotlight on the ground and expanded upward. Eka flew back on her butt, while still fixed on the light show and only faintly aware of dew soaking through her thin running clothes. The spotlight morphed, reshaping itself into something, maybe a form of some sort? Shielding her eyes, she squinted up as the brightness dimmed to reveal a swirling, rainbow-lighted shape.

"Is that a…woman?"

A woman did indeed look down at Eka.

Hello, Eka.

It was a familiar voice, like glass clinking in the wind. Eka tried to focus on the face, but the lights swirled around and blurred all the features. Only the eyes were unchanging. The swirling, rainbow eyes.

"Do I know you?" Eka muttered, confused.

Somehow, her mind caught a rainbow smile.

Yes.

"Whoa."

Eka kept trying to bring the woman into focus, but her eyes slid off the features, as the zipping lights creating the form, pulled her attention this way and that.

"Who…who are you?" Eka whispered. The woman seemed so foreign as she stood next to Eka, composed of nothing but lights, yet still familiar.

The form seemed to blink in and out before resuming a human shape.

I am Irida.

"Irida? Are you a Waker?"

The form laughed that tinkling glass laugh.

No, not a Waker.

"Wait, are you a spirit? I'm supposed to be able to see those."

Of a sort. I have been near, but I am weak. You could only hear me in dreams.

"That was you in the kayak?"

Yes. I need to explain, so I am here in this form. But it is difficult. I must use so much energy to keep this form, and the energy here is…difficult to use.

Irida blinked out and in.

Eka, I am like your Gaia, a celestial spirit. I think that's the correct word, celestial.

There was a pause and Eka pointed straight up, as Irida glided around her. "You mean like in space?"

Irida nodded.

There are many such spirits. Another, Lintu, is here but we don't belong. He must be stopped.

Eka could almost hear anger in the tinkling glass voice.

"Are you talking about that thing in the bush, in my vision?"

Yes. I have chased him for a long time and stopped him so many times before. The last time we fought you were so young, you and your friend, your families. So much unnecessary suffering in that moment, which is always his way. But I lost so much and have not recovered.

A chill went through Eka. "You were there when my family … "

I had to help you when you were a child and, because of that, you are no longer just a child of Gaia. Your are part of me as well.

A few lights floated off Irida and settled onto Eka. They sank beneath Eka's skin and, for a moment, her gray energy undulated and shifted to bright rainbow lights, swirling around a stream of violet. The sensation of freedom and flying returned before she sank back into separateness. Her energy was gray again.

You need to see. To understand.

A few more lights floated into her and then, the clearing was gone; she was falling into an open field, stars just pin-pricks in a billowing cloth above her. The full moon sat low in the sky, dimly illuminating a field. A colorful, familiar glow undulated in the distance and she ran toward it, a slight tug reeling her in. Around her, the landscape jumped and morphed, like a bad slide show of someone's vacation, a sense of disorientation lapping at her awareness. Ignoring the unsettling landscape, she focused on the glow in the distance until she reached it, running into a glowing lump on the ground.

Near her feet, a figure lay prone and naked, cocooned in pulsating light. Rainbow lights interwove with violet lights, all wrapping around the body. The lights almost seemed to be jostling for dominance. Eka leaned closer to the form, to come face to face with herself. She fell next to her cocooned body, lying still in the grass and wrapped in the swirling lights. Just then a bright, hairline fissure formed along the top of the cocoon, cracking it open and exposing the form. Like the opening of a dam, the two separate sources of lights flowed through the crack, waterfalling into the form. As the last drop of light fell into the body, her other self stirred, and the colorful woman's narration was back.

You are not made yet, but soon.

Eka blinked at her other self and was once again in the clearing with Irida. At that moment, her mind decided it was done. Just done.

I did not mean for this confusion in you, but I couldn't let Lintu repeat his actions. Maybe I could not save her from him, but I can save others.

Irida's form blinked several times and disappeared for a long moment.

Eka, still confused, whipped her head around. "Hey! You can't leave! What does all this mean? What happened that night? To my family?"

Irida blinked and Eka could sense sadness in her as if Eka was feeling it, then Irida leaned in close and she blurred even more.

That is a long story and I am almost depleted. I believe that is the correct word, depleted. There is danger, coming faster than I imagined. You have to be ready for it.

Irida stared into the sky, hints of purple and red predicting sunrise as fewer stars shone down. After a long moment, Irida looked back at Eka.

The sky is so beautiful. I forget the beauty of all of it.

The form blinked again then turned to Eka and sighed again.

You will finish becoming soon. You are needed here and there is less time.

Blink.

He will try to use you but you must protect yourself.

The form blinked again, this time leaving only the glowing forest lights in her wake.

"Wait!" Eka stepped into an empty space. "What about my past? What is this dangerous spirit thing from outer space?"

The singing of cicadas was the only reply.

"Cryptic doesn't help!" she yelled. "Why am I shouting at an empty field?"

Morning rays shone into the clearing as a colorful flutter buzzed around Eka's head. The bird, dim against the sun, flew around her again, then to the edge of the clearing. Fog seeped into her brain and she stumbled up to squint at the bird. It seemed to be pulling her toward it.

"Guess you're my escort out of this trip. Or flashback. I don't remember them being this real?"

She shook her head, the pulsing energy from the life all around her cutting through her fogginess. She trudged after her colorful little guide as all the information from Irida swirled through her head, trying to process it all. But nothing concrete would stick, just a mushy confusion turning her mind inside out and back.

Irida was there when my family was attacked? She's from outer space and I was attacked by a dangerous thing from outer space that she's been fighting? I'm part Gaia, part Irida? What does that even mean? Am I a Waker?

"Great job on the communication," she mumbled. "Had time to ask about word choice, but not tell me what happened that night." She huffed. "I think you meant fortune-cookie-saying, not telling-me-something."

Just before her frustration exploded, the little bird did a spin around her head and dove into her pendant, lighting it up like a varicolored spotlight before fading with a brief fluttering of wings.

"Am I crazy?" She gaped at it then stopped, mind engulfed in the encounter with whatever Irida was. Then, a sensation bubbled just below her frustration; a taste of release, escape.

Why hadn't she noticed that feeling of release before this morning? Was it because she was doing this becoming thing and her cocoon was opening? Was she changing somehow? Could the answers she'd been searching for be related to her changing?

She jumped at her stomach growling. "Snap out of it. You desperately need breakfast." She laughed, her tension dissipating as she headed to Christelle's.

Eka burst into Christelle's room. "You won't believe what happened this morning!"

Christelle looked up from her bed, rubbing her eyes. "What time is it?"

"Six. Anyway, I went for a run."

Christelle narrowed her eyes. "I hate your early morning nature."

"I couldn't sleep and running always helps. Besides, it's beautiful outside."

Christelle pulled herself up to a sitting position and yawned. "Well, good for you, morning person."

"Thanks." Eka bounced onto the swinging bed, rocking it back and forth. "Anyway, I saw that rainbow bird from the forest."

"What bird?"

"Oh yeah, you only saw the lights. When we were in the woods and found the hedge to this freaky new world, there were those lights. It was actually a lighted bird that led me to the hedge."

"Eka." Christelle put her hands on Eka's expressive hands and stilled them. "What are you talking about?"

"Don't really know. But the lights looked like a bird and my gut said follow."

"Wow." Christelle stared.

"I know, right?"

Eka's disjointed explanation elicited deeper and deeper frowns from Christelle until she lowered her head to her palms. "Head. Exploding."

"I know it's a little confusing."

Christelle peeked at Eka through her fingers and narrowed her eyes. "A little?"

Eka jumped up and started pacing. "I followed a glowing bird into the woods and there was a glowing spirit woman calling herself Irida. Clear?"

Christelle shook her head in her palms. Eka sat back down beside her and put her arm across Christelle's shoulders.

"Are you alright?"

"Grams was right again. I need to take all of this slow. I feel like a rubber band about to snap."

Eka sighed. "You and me both. But now I have some answers. Confusing answers with loads more questions. But still, at least the questions aren't as vague. Like 'what's going on?' questions. But specific questions."

Christelle's head snapped up. "Really? You think there are questions in that rambling story?"

Eka nodded. "Look. A couple of months ago, magic would have been a crazy idea. Now, I don't know. Magic is possible and I guess planets have spirits and there are other universes."

Christelle rested her head on her chin. "I guess."

Eka shook her head. "I don't know where the limits of all this are, but I think my idea of possibilities just blew wide-open. And maybe the questions I have are Alice-in-Wonderland-type questions, but I think that's the territory we're in. I guess what I'm saying is, maybe we haven't been asking the right questions to know what really happened to us and now we can."

Christelle frowned and fell back, covering her head. "Or maybe you're just hallucinating because thinking about everything I've learned makes me feel like I'm hallucinating."

"Could be," Eka shrugged and hopped off the bed. "But this Irida told me I was changing. Somehow I'm part her and part Gaia."

Christelle uncovered her head. "What does that mean?"

"That's a good question. Seems she did something to me, changed me the night I was attacked, and that's why my energy is weird. And she said this change is finishing soon. That I need to be here to help somehow, but there's danger."

Christelle's eyes grew wide. "You think that thing that attacked us is the danger she mentioned?"

"Maybe. She called it Lintu." Excitement bubbled up in Eka. "But you know what all this means, right?"

"What?"

"That we're close to finding out what happened. To getting all the answers."

To figuring out what I am and what happened to Mom, Dad, and Ke.

"Maybe," Christelle whispered. "If we survive."

The Unexpected Gift

Eka sat outside her vardo and focused on her hands, willing light, any freaking color of light, out of the grayness of her mucky energy. Once in a while, a pop of violet in the gray reminded her that she was once a Waker. Ever since the encounter in the forest a few weeks ago, she resided in some sort of liminal space, waiting to become…what?

A squeeze on her shoulder brought her back to the present and she relaxed into Devlon's massage. "Just what I needed."

"So, what's stressing you out?"

"What stress?"

He dug into her neck.

"Ow."

"My point is, your neck is like a wall."

She sighed and reclined her chair back, staring up at soft white clouds as they drifted by. Eka and Christelle had kept Shirley's info dump, and Irida's visit, to themselves. The Wakers already thought Eka was bad news; learning that part of her energy might not be from Gaia could be just the fuel to turn distrust into an out-of-control fear fire. And while Devlon seemed to care for her, all his actions and words let her know his first loyalty was to Wakers and this local group in particular.

But he's fun. And sexy. And giving a great massage.

She smiled up at him. "Just trying to get something to happen with my energy."

Didn't think that cocoon meant I'd wait weeks.

"Look." Devlon pulled her face to his. "You'll find what you need. Here."

She ran her fingers gently across his cheek as he leaned over her. "You're biased."

She wiggled eyebrows and he leaned in further, his lips finding hers, losing awareness until he pulled her up and into him. Sinking into his warmth, their connection, she barely noticed his magenta light flowing across her, reaching for her, until it faded as it hit her gray dimness and receded. She jerked back, falling out of their embrace and back on the chair.

"What? Did I do something wrong?" Devlon's brows furrowed.

"No, you're fine. I just can't be a Waker charity case. Half-formed and confused." She stared at her dull energy again.

Maybe Irida was wrong.

"Maybe I don't belong here," she said to no one.

"You'd leave?" He dropped into another chair.

Eka refocused on Devlon. "I don't know. I mean, it's been a while since Iri…since I thought I might be getting somewhere," she held up her gray hands, "with all this energy stuff." She thought Irida would have come back with more answers. She was starting to think she'd dreamed it all. Not only was she giftless, there hadn't been any kind of attack despite Irida's warnings.

Guess I should be happy about that.

Devlon rose, pacing around the campsite, Eka leaning ever closer as she watched. He probably needed to walk it off, whatever it was. He was really cute when he walked, pacing around, muscles twitching.

"Eka." He spun toward her, cutting through her mental tangent. "Let me help you with your energy and gifts. I've been an outsider, remember. I know what that's like."

She flashed back to Irida, the cocoon and her chase of the little I'iwi bird. Would he be able to understand any of that?But then, ow could he help her if she wouldn't tell him. "I…don't know."

A gust blew up with a flick of his hand, picking Eka off the ground as magenta energy flowed across her, tickling her skin. The light floatiness pushed worry from every nook of her psyche, laughter erupting out of the stress. "Two more weeks," He suggested, as she floated gently into his arms. "That's all I'm asking. If you haven't made a breakthrough by then, I'll help you pack."

Still giggling, his plea turned frown-ward and he set her down, crossing his arms.

"That was supposed to be romantic."

"No," She struggled to calm down and breathe. And talk. "No, sorry. It's just amazing and wonderful and incredible." She'd finally relaxed, thanks to him. "All these things that you guys can do. I…" She caressed his face, his arms wrapping around her. "That was wonderful."

"I have a lot of surprises," Devlon whispered, frown no where in sight.

"Well, I do like the way you negotiate."

He leaned over, drawing her into another lingering kiss. "Spend the day with me and I promise to seal the deal."

She nodded and they made their way, by air, to the oak homes that would always symbolize the Waker world for Eka. Up in a short, unadorned oak, she could make out something buried in the sprawling canopy, a platform of tightly twisted branches, edged with twigs dripping with Spanish moss.

"I'd like to show you to my lair." He wiggled his eyebrows and tried an evil laugh.

"Nice," she laughed while quietly rising up toward the platform, Devlon floating next to her.

How amazing was this world? Would she be able to do all these things when she was 'formed'? Could he really help her?

Wouldn't bet on that.

He set them down on the living platform and she tested the surface by jumping around the house. "More sturdy than I thought," she grinned, then jumped up and caught an overhead branch, swung up and walked around the large overhanging branches for a few moments. Bits of the surrounding trees peeked through the dense leaves. Kind of a housing development, if all the houses were in trees.

"Hey, don't break the house."

She waved him off and hopped down. "I've seen the repair team. You'll be fine."

While the platform was camouflaged by canopy, she could still see across to Hapton's farm and even to the river, where the glow of the setting sun skipped across the surface, a thousand jewels floating in the water.

"This is beautiful. I can't believe you didn't mention you lived here."

"We all have our secrets," Devlon winked.

Yes we do.

Eka frowned down at her hands and all the secrets that seemed to be the problem right now.

Devlon frowned back and intertwined his fingers with hers as she looked up at him. "Hey, I was just kidding; I wouldn't keep a secret from you."

Eka shook her head. "No worries. Life would be dull if we didn't have our private lives."

His stared at her face, brows furrowing briefly as he squeezed their fingers together slightly. "I haven't brought anyone here before. This is the place I come to get away from work. Kinda why there's no stairs."

But we just met.

A tickle of anxiety flitted through her before she shook it off.

"So, this place is really amazing." She pulled out of his hand as she spun around for a second look. In the middle of the platform, thick vines twisted down from the canopy and around a bed-like pallet, suspending it as it swayed in a strong breeze. On the far side of the swinging bed, a blanket lay spread out on the platform, covered with a picnic. Scattered throughout the food dishes were candles floating in bowls of water.

"Uh, thanks." Devlon pointed at the blanket. "I thought you might be hungry."

She slid over to the blanket. "This looks wonderful. Perfect."

A small quirk of a smile appeared on his face and he wandered to her side. "I'm glad you like it."

"I do have to wonder if you're tired of my vardo?"

"Never." He stared directly into her eyes and placed his palm against her cheek. "As long as you're in it."

Her breath caught. Why did he have to be so sexy?

"I just wanted to show you my other place." He turned and grabbed a bottle of Cabernet. As he poured, she jumped on the bed then patted the space beside her.

"Priorities, my friend."

The wine dropped from his hand as he leapt for the bed and melted into her.

Later, as they swayed under the night, Eka relaxed. She gazed at the deep blue sky overhead, twinkling with a million stars. She forgot about secrets and energy and magic for that brief moment and let the slight wind that brushed across her face lull her to sleep.

A pre-dawn breeze blew across Eka's calves as she sat on the edge of the platform, wrapped in a sheet discarded on the floor earlier. Her bare legs dangled off the side while soft leaves tickled the bottoms of her feet and an old bottle of soap bubbles, lost under the bed, sat open next to her.

Soapy bubbles drifted off the wand, her breath filling dozens of shiny spheres, so like blowing bubbles out the car window with Sema and Win. Bubbles rolled in the breeze, spinning as if caught in an invisible and very lazy vortex, their shimmer mesmerizing. She reached under one and it bounced once on her palm then landed lightly, wiggling. The colors glimmered and a flash of glistening red brought back another memory, of a sweet and minty treat from shortly after Sema and Win had taken her in.

She'd been tired from riding in the car and Win decided they needed to stretch, so they'd detoured into a nearby town. Within minutes Eka had homed in on a confectionery, the front window displaying hundreds of bright bursts of sweet colors that left her salivating. She'd only had to implore Sema once to take her in before they were deep in a candy wonderland; sweet smells tempted her from all directions until she caught sight of a giant peppermint stick. The red and white strands twined lazily together and shimmered with promises of sugary bliss. And it really was the sweetest taste she'd ever had.

The bubble vibrated on her palm, bringing her back to the moment. She lifted the bubble to her mouth, which still watered at the lingering memory of the red and white delight that had melted on her tongue and down her throat. As she tried to blow the bubble off her hand, the bubble's top elongated and the glistening colors twisted and stretched, morphing from a sphere to a tube. She inhaled to blow the bubble again then stopped, as the transformation finally registered in her mind. The bubble had lost some of its transparency and felt heavier in her hand. The wide range of colors shimmered as the soapy surface morphed into red and white. The two colors of the now solid rod twisted around one another as a blast of sugary sweetness hit her nose.

She stared at the thing in her hand, the thing that looked exactly like her memory of a peppermint stick. She momentarily forgot the stick as her mind played the memory again, trying to process…anything. At that moment, the candy fell out of her hand and collided with the edge of the platform, popping into a million bits of soapy color that dripped to the ground.

"How…? Did that really…? What…?"

She tried another one, focusing on the candy shape, watching as each time a bubble briefly transformed into a solid peppermint stick.

"Eka?"

She jerked; it seemed she jumped every time Devlon said her name.

Devlon bent down, lifting her hair away from her neck and brushing his lips across her skin, sending shivers rippling down her back as memories of last night momentarily distracted her.

"Hey, you found my stash of stress bubbles. I wondered where they went."

He borrowed the wand and blew a few rounds, Eka watching carefully for anything unusual to happen.

"Are these special bubbles?"

"What do you mean?"

"Do they, you know, do funky stuff? Waker stuff?"

He looked closely at her. "I'm not really sure what Waker bubbles would do. They're soap."

She examined the bottle, then blew out a shower of bubbles. Her palm opened and a few of the iridescent creations landed without bursting. She focused on them, then briefly closed her eyes and imagined the candy form. The bubbles shimmied slightly as if in a breeze, then sat still on her hand.

"You okay?"

She frowned at the bubbles, which sat doing nothing, then turned to Devlon. "They changed before. Into candy."

He frowned. "Candy?" He glanced at the bubbles and back at her. "Maybe you're tired." He wiggled his brows. "We did have a late night."

"I'm fine." She kissed his cheek then relaxed into the sensations within her memory. Hints of sugary sweetness rolled around her tongue and electrified her olfactory senses. Bright red and white twists danced through her mind. A warmth started in her chest then rolled through her whole body. Then, one of the bubbles shook on her hand and began to stretch and twist. Devlon's breathing quieted as the bubble became a solid red and white twist and she dropped the stick in her left hand, confirming its solidness. Before she could second guess herself, she tasted it. A familiar sweet aroma filled her nose and sugar flowed across her tongue. She nudged Devlon with the stick and he let her lift it to his lips for a taste.

"It's real!" He looked at her and his expression grew wider. "Your eyes."

"What?" she asked, distracted.

At that moment, the candy melted into a runny mess, dripping down her hand. And the sweetness on her tongue turned to soap. Eka and Devlon both spat over the side while desperately trying to wipe soap off their tongues, she felt a wave of pressure roiling over her as the tree rattled. Her stomach lurched and without warning she heaved more than soap over the side of the platform, Devlon grabbing her before she fell.

"Maybe you should lie down," he recommended.

She nodded, suddenly weak, and crawled back into the bed as he found some water for them both before joining her.

"My gifts," she mumbled. "Something finally happened." Her triumph was laced with the lingering taste of soap as she drifted off to sleep.

She woke up, rejuvenated and excited. Devlon sat next to her in bed, the sheets hanging low on his hips. A sense of contentment and giddiness raced through her and she instinctively ran her fingers along his stomach, just above the sheet. He shuddered as her finger traveled along his abs and he quickly moved her hand away.

"Eka…"

She looked up from the warm crook of his arm and smiled while running her fingertips along the inside of his leg. He closed his eyes and breathed deeply, then jerked himself out of her reach and stood up. The sheet fell off and Eka rolled on her stomach to watch the rounded muscles of his glutes move with his pacing.

"Eka, we need to talk about yesterday. About the bubbles."

She rolled on her back and looked at the sky through the leaves of the branches.

"You are too distracting."

A soft shuffling came from behind her and she glanced over as he put on a pair of boxers, then sat next to her. "I'm worried."

The energy inside her, that had been sluggish, now seemed to rush around with unlimited potential.

Maybe I'm coming out of that cocoon.

She sat up and put her hand on his knee. "I'm sure it's fine. And I feel like I'm finally getting somewhere in all of this. Like maybe I'm finally starting my own magic journey." She grinned and squeezed his hands between hers. "Come on, this is exciting."

His face seemed sad as he squeezed her hands back. "You will get your gifts. And I'll be really happy for you. I mean, I want you to feel at home as a Waker. Home here with us. But I've never heard of that kind of gift."

Her throat and shoulders tightened. "And?"

"It doesn't feel natural. I mean, you changed one thing into something else. How is that possible? Wakers don't have that ability."

Was he that afraid of the unknown? Like Anise and Ben? Sure there were dangers, but...

But he doesn't trust me enough. Why would he, we barely know each other.

She breathed deeply, focusing on slowing her heart rate.

I don't really know him.

"Eka?"

She opened her eyes and forced a smile. "I get it. You're worried."

She jumped out of bed and put on shorts and a T-shirt. "I am totally into talking about this, but I need some coffee first." She looked side-ways at him and grinned. "Mind getting some?"

He seemed uncertain but pulled her into a hug. "Of course."

Against his chest his smell, now of the sun and warm breezes and the sea, flooded her with memories of the last few hours. When he finally left to get coffee, his scent lingered and a small weight of sadness sank in her chest.

Had this been a mistake? Was it time to go?

The rustling of leaves drew her attention up into the branches, wind dancing through the sun-dappled tree top. Inhaling scents of the earthy oak and fall air, the weight dissipated.

She looked at the edge of the platform where he had floated off toward the ground and she smiled. "What's that saying? Always believe someone when they show you who they are. And I think he just showed me his boundaries."

We all have them. Just a shame ours don't overlap; he's a good guy.

"And really sexy." She sighed then started tying bedsheets together.

Trees rushed by as she power-walked toward Christelle's house. Devlon would be pissed when he got back, but she needed some space from him. He wasn't going to help her handle her magic so she wasn't sure what to do about him.

"I'll cross that bridge later."

Then the image of him pacing naked around the bed popped in her head.

Doesn't mean there isn't any fun left.

Right now she needed to find Christelle; she had magic to share. As she sped up the path to the house, she stumbled on a tree root and nearly tumbled to the ground.

"Where did that root come from?" She scrambled up and bumped directly into Janice.

"Janice!" Eka backed up from the woman, preparing for a tirade.

"Eka, hi." Janice barely noticed her, bending down to collect various sheets of paper that had fallen from a book she was carrying.

Eka stared at the weirdly pleasant Janice, then picked up a few sheets. She paused as she tried to read the strange marks on them. The lines and curves looked somewhat like words but with half of each letter erased.

"Give me that!" Janice snatched the papers from Eka and shoved them into the book, which had similar writing on the cover.

Eka held up her hands and backed up another step. "Whoa. Just trying to help."

Janice's frown dropped and slowly became a smile. "Um, oh, of course. Thanks." She looked around before abruptly continuing up the path, side stepping roots until finally disappearing around a tree.

She's so strange.

Eka shrugged and took off to the house. When she got to the building, she stood out front for a moment, disoriented at the structure. Anise and Ben really had dismantled most of the building. No dome, just an old stucco two-bedroom cottage that looked as though it was from the 1950s.

"They're fast." Even the grounds looked undisturbed. "They'd really be handy for show break-downs."

Humming drifted out from inside the cottage.

She shook off the weirdness of the place and made her way to Anise's old bedroom, apparently a studio now. Inside, Christelle danced to whatever was playing on her headphones, conducting with her paintbrush. Eka tiptoed behind her to the right and tapped her left shoulder. Of course, Christelle looked left. So, Eka hopped left and tapped her right shoulder. Christelle spun, inches from Eka's face, and stumbled back into her easel and wet canvas, grabbing Eka as she fell; all three went down in a tangled heap.

Eka climbed up on her feet, unusually clean for one of her misadventures. "Busy painting, huh?"

Christelle, face and body smeared with wet gouache, slowly rolled over and wiped paint out of her eye. She narrowed her eyes and pushed herself up, throwing off her smock and grabbing towels, apparently to smear globs of paint all over it. "I've been working on that painting for ages." They looked at the runny canvas. "Now, I guess it's trash."

"Sorry." Eka really was sorry, which was another unusual event.

Eka started to pick up the painting but Christelle grabbed it from her.

"I got it." Christelle leaned it against the wall and faced Eka, arms crossed. "Okay, what's so important you needed to destroy my art?"

"Yes." Shirley, suddenly noticeable in a lounger in the corner of the room, sat up. "What's so important?"

Eka hesitated. Should she tell Shirley about her strange magic? Would she freak out? Shirley had been open with Christelle when no one else had. Had even disagreed with Anise. Maybe she could help.

Eka hopped over and put her arm around Shirley and the woman's latest Clash Couture.

"Glad you're here, Shirley. I think I found my magic!"

"Eka, that's awesome!' Christelle's smile erupted out of a deep scowl.

Shirley wiggled her eyebrows. "So, which gift?"

Eka winked at them. "Something amazing! I was sitting this morning blowing bubbles…"

"Bubbles?"

"Yeah, bubbles." She pulled the bottle of soap out of her pocket and handed it to Christelle.

"So, I was blowing bubbles and thinking of candy."

"What kind of candy?"

"Oh, you know those peppermint sticks that twist?"

"I love those!"

Shirley hopped up. "I'm on the edge of my seat. What happened?"

"Well," Eka paused, because she knew Shirley couldn't handle it. And she was right.

"You're gonna kill me. Just get on with it!" Shirley rolled her arm.

"A bubble turned into that peppermint stick."

"No way! Awesome!" Christelle jumped up and down.

Shirley eyed Eka. "So, it's an air gift? You shaped the bubble into something?"

"No. The bubble *became* a piece of candy. I even tasted it. So did Devlon."

Christelle's eyebrows wiggled. "Devlon, huh?"

Eka crinkled her eyes in a smile. "A lady never tells."

"So," Shirley interjected. "What you're saying is you changed one thing into another."

Eka nodded.

"Can't say I've heard of that gift."

Eka tensed. "Devlon said something like that, but I know he can't be right. It happened. We both saw it."

Shirley knitted her brow. "We have a lot of gifts, but changing the nature of something, well…"

The three of them stood without speaking until Christelle broke the awkwardness by handing Eka the bubbles.

"Show us."

Eka looked at the bottle.

It did happen, I was there.

Christelle nodded and gave a small smile. Eka drew in a deep breath and pulled the wand out of the bottle. She blew softly and a dozen small, shimmering spheres floated out into the room. She held her palm under a descending sphere and it landed without a whisper before she lifted it to her face. As she reached into her childhood memory, the sweet sensations flooded back. Warmth spread through her and the sphere extended, twisting and pulling, into a red and white stick. It began to loose transparency and flexibility, eventually coming to rest as a peppermint stick. Eka heard an intake of breath at the same moment that Christelle whooped.

"I knew you could do it!"

Sporting an unreadable expression, Shirley slowly reached over to Eka's palm and touched the peppermint stick.

"Interesting." Shirley pulled her gaze from the candy, finally staring at Eka. "Your eyes are a bit off."

Ignoring this, Eka started jumping up and down and Christelle joined her. "It's real!"

Then, without warning, Christelle grabbed the candy. Eka guessed what she was about to do and tried to stop the tragedy, but she was a second too late.

Christelle popped it into her mouth. "It's sweet!"

At that moment, a slight tremor moved through the room. Eka's stomach roiled and Christelle's smile dropped.

"Ugh! Helpth." Christelle grabbed a towel and wiped her mouth violently.

"Sorry," Eka grimaced. "Forgot to mention it seems temporary."

Shirley looked at Eka then at Christelle, patting her on the back and pointing to the sink. "Water might help with that, kiddo." Then she zipped off, Shirley style.

Eka watched her leave, confusion and exhaustion overwhelming her. Did she misjudge Shirley? Would this lead to more fear in the community?

"'O gro'."

She turned from Shirley's exit to find Christelle still frantically rubbing her tongue. Eka dragged Christelle to the bathroom sink before dropping to a bench.

"Thanghs," Christelle managed, rinsing until the last bit of soapy water turned clear then slumping next to Eka.

"Where'd Grams go?"

Eka shrugged. "Don't know. She seemed less than excited, like I did something crazy. You'd have thought I materialized an elephant out of thin air by the way some people are acting."

Christelle giggled. "That would be pretty cool, though."

"Right!"

"You know," Christelle's head cocked, "your eyes changed. Just like at the preserve."

"That's what Devlon said. I wonder why?"

"Lots of strange things going on," Christelle sighed. "All this is still so weird. So out of my context. But what you did was really amazing. Do you think you'll be able to do more?"

Eka's stomach fluttered and a jolt of excitement ran through her. "I kinda hope so, but it's just nice to have something. And something so," she grinned, "awesome!"

Something she could possibly use to protect herself.

Maybe.

Christelle smiled back and lightly pushed Eka's shoulder. "Maybe Anise will cut you some slack."

Eka shrugged. She wasn't telling anyone else for a while and she hoped Shirley wouldn't either.

"Well, it's a cool gift," Christelle said. "Just don't kill yourself or change something important."

Eka raised her hand up with three closed fingers. "Scout's honor."

Christelle rolled her eyes. "Like you were ever a scout."

"What?" Eka threw her arm across her forehead. "How could you doubt me? Wait." She hopped up. "Before you answer that and devastate my world, how about lunch?"

"Sure, but I've got to clean up."

"Then let's get this done before I change your art into lunch."

Christelle stuck out her tongue. "I'm not going for that trick twice. Don't want to end up with a mouthful of paint."

Adrien Tells It All

Christelle hid behind a tree searching for a signal, any signal. Her body tensed against the tree and she struggled to focus.

I can't believe I went along with this.

Her temporary teammate Bryan's hand flashed lights briefly, from three trees away. This was the sign that their target, Adrien, was on the move.

She really had no desire to learn to fight, but it seemed the only way to get a moment with Adrien, the Ysian with the same white hair as her. If only he had been available before this session, she'd have asked this outsider questions about their world, the danger, her mother. But he was only here for two days, to teach some kind of old Ysian fighting techniques to all the Wakers at Hapton's. So here she was, waiting for any moment to corner him and trying not to be part of some army Anise might be building.

She placed one hand on the trunk of the tree and another on the ground, then sent a tendril of energy through the network of the trunks, searching for Adrien's energy signal.

If only Eka's gifts were more reliable, she could be the one here. She wouldn't be bothered by doing this; probably treat it like a game.

Suddenly a yell erupted off to her left and she jumped.

Focus, Christelle, focus.

She peaked around the tree. A hundred feet to the left, another teammate, Sessie, burst out of the underbrush. She zig-zagged through trees, heading for the clearing. Orange energy spilled from her and into the ground behind her. Wherever it landed, vegetation shot up like a protective wall. But as quickly as it grew, thick sharpened vines snaked through holes in the foliage and sped after her.

Christelle's grip tightened on the tree trunk as the vines narrowed the gap to a few inches from Sessie. A tendril caught the tip of Sessie's flying blonde hair, wind whipped out from Bryan's direction, pushing Sessie out of the way of the vines and tumbling toward Christelle. Adrien, pulsing with light blue energy, pushed through the undergrowth Sessie had just grown, while directing half the vines to follow her. He redirected the other half over to the tree Bryan sat in.

Christelle placed both her hands on the ground. Her energy was now an extension of her and, as some of it flowed out of her body and deep into the earth, the sensation of warm earthiness wrapped around her. Under her feet, a light vibration started and moved toward the others. A wave of earth grew quickly from Christelle's request, rolling under Sessie then passing her as it gained momentum. Dirt and rocks grew into a wave, cresting high above Adrien then rolling over him. Lost in the tumbling earth, his vines missed Sessie and Bryan while another wind, bright with Bryan's light red energy, swept down from the tree Bryan sat in and along the ground, scooping up Adrien and suspending him in the air. Sessie stumbled up and ran over, her orange energy sending vines twisting around Adrien, like a spider catching prey. Soon he was suspended in a net of woven vegetation.

"Yes!" Bryan yelled from high up in the tree, the wind still flattening Adrien into the net. Christelle joined Sessie below them.

"Bryan." Sessie gestured to him. "Should we bring him down?"

Bryan looked at the squirming vegetation, rattling it with a gust.

"You ready to call it?"

Christelle looked up. A drop of water fell in her eye and she brushed it away. She looked up through the trees at the clear sky.

Weird.

Adrien's net wiggled again.

They really had a man suspended in the tree tops with magic! Maybe fighting wasn't her thing, but she couldn't ignore the adrenaline running through her.

Another drop hit her face. "Did you guys feel raindrops?"

"He's not giving up. I say let him squirm!" Bryan yelled from above, ignoring her question.

The drops of water she had smeared on her cheek reformed into a drop. "What the...?"

She rubbed at the water again as another drop hit her, sticking to the first and forming a larger drop. She looked back up as drops fell faster onto her face.

"Guys, something weird's happening."

Sessie followed Christelle's gaze upward as drops pelted them both.

"Bryan!" Christelle shouted. But before she could tell if he heard her, a huge sphere of water engulfed her head, cutting off her air. Scratching and pulling at the bubble of liquid, her hands only plunged into the water without budging it. Her lungs burning, she desperately searched for something to help, but everything was blurry and her fear-locked brain stopped processing anything except her need for air.

The moment before she inhaled, the sphere of water dropped away in a sheet of rain and she fell to the ground, alternating between sucking in air and coughing; the others' gasps making it through her own struggle. As she finally stopped coughing, she noticed two boots standing next to her. Adrien's boots.

He pulled her up onto shaking legs. Leaning against him, Christelle's brain slowly took in the world again. Bryan leaned against a tree nearby while Sessie slumped next to him, both breathing shakily.

Christelle stared at Adrien. "You…almost…killed…" She finished with a gesture at the three of them, still gasping.

He shook his head. "The water wouldn't have gone in your lungs."

"Felt…it." She pointed at her chest.

"This was only practice," he shrugged. "Take a break to recover."

Christelle and her teammates stared at each other, lost for air and words, then stumbled out of the woods and into a clearing while Adrien stayed behind. Christelle spotted Eka lounging on a large sheet in the center of the open space. Tired and still coughing, she trudged over to her. Was that a lunch spread out next to her?

"Eka?"

Eka grabbed some sandwiches and passed them to Bryan and Sessie who had followed Christelle. They took the food and plopped down at the edge of the sheet, keeping their distance.

"You're welcome." Eka waved at them.

Christelle fell next to her and took a sandwich. "This is great but I didn't expect you."

"Not much going on at the campsite and there's no rigging work so I thought I'd go where the action was. You three were pretty good."

"Until Adrien tried to drown us."

Sessie and Bryan grumbled in agreement.

"I'm sure you were fine. They wouldn't drown their star pupil," Eka winked.

Christelle frowned, her sandwich halfway to her mouth. "You know I'm not into this," she hissed. "I'm not joining Anise's army or whatever this is. I'm here because he," she pointed toward the tree line where Adrien was approaching, "might know something about what's happening and actually tell us."

Adrien strode up and rested next to Christelle, digging into the lunch.

"Please," Christelle rolled her eyes, "Help yourself."

"Thank you." Adrien clapped her shoulder. "After the break, I want to do an open ground practice. Then we can review all the drills."

Bryan interrupted, pointing a finger at Adrien. "I'm not doing anything else. You tried to drown us."

"No," Adrien held up his hands and shook his head, "the water was not meant to kill you."

Christelle could only narrow her eyes at him.

Adrien looked around the group. "This is not a thought experiment or an argument of strategy. This is a time to try anything and everything that works. Use what you have. There's a lot worse than me out there and you have to be ready. The water wouldn't have killed you but you panicked, didn't think through possible escapes, counterattacks. You were easily distracted by a false win. If this had been real, you all would've been dead."

Bryan grumbled something inaudible then he and Sessie turned away and seemed to ignore the rest of them. Christelle still frowned at Adrien. Was the danger the same one she and Eka had faced as kids, or was something new killing Wakers and threatening them both? And, whatever *it* was, how could she fight this danger and the insane fear that had chased her and her family out of a community that was supposed to be family, to protect her.

Christelle crossed her arms. "I think all this is a bit much. I mean, it's awful that some people died, but everyone's acting liking like it's the apocalypse. People die."

Adrien's face relaxed and he leaned back, breaking into a smile. "You are so much like your mother."

"My mother?" Christelle's anger faded and her arms dropped. "You knew her?"

Adrien paused in mid-bite and put his sandwich down. Christelle held her breath. He seemed to examine her, size her up. "Yes, I knew Isamae." He went back to eating. Apparently that was all he had to say about her mother.

"Thanks." Christelle sagged back to the blanket and shoved a roll in her mouth.

Eka elbowed Christelle and nodded towards Adrien as he pulled off a corner of his sandwich to stare at the contents. Christelle glared at Eka then shook her head and mouthed 'no'. Eka kicked her.

"Owww." Christelle rubbed her ankle.

Adrien looked up. "Something wrong?"

"No." Christelle glared briefly at Eka. "I think I twisted my ankle."

Eka rolled her eyes. "So, tell us about her. Was she friendly? Strict? Sexy?"

"Hey!" Christelle spewed bread everywhere, bits flying into Adrien's hair. "Oh, sorry." Her face now burning.

He'll never answer that ridiculous question.

"Your mother was one of the most skilled, composed, dedicated fighters in our community. She is a legend," Adrien shared as he picked crumbs out of his hair.

Christelle blinked at his words, a picture of her mother forming in her head.

"And you look a lot like her."

I look like my mother?

A smile crept across her face. A face that she might see on her mother someday.

"Okay, but the big question is," Eka jumped in, "do you know where she is now?"

Would he answer? Maybe he couldn't say or he didn't think they deserved to know. Why would she ask that so soon, he just started opening up?

The picnic fell silent, Adrien brushing off the last bits of roll from his shoulders. Eka shrugged and mouthed 'sorry', but Christelle wanted to cry.

"I saw her last about a year ago. In Estonia."

Christelle leaned in, suddenly glad Eka asked.

"She was on the hunt for something." He laid his hand on Christelle's shoulder. "She made me promise not to say anything, but I think she'd want you to know, considering everything."

She's still out there. He actually saw her!

He sighed and lowered his voice to just the three of them. "I think what happened to your family was the wrong decision. So do all the Ysians."

Christelle blinked back tears. "Thank you." There were others who agreed with Shirley? Who might actually help?

He looked pointedly at Christelle. "Whatever killed before is back and your mother believed, when I saw her, that she was close to finding it. Before the helplessness and fear sets in again, we're trying to train all Wakers with ancient techniques from Ys." He glanced briefly at Christelle's hair. "Which is the community you should have been raised in. Our community has always been ready for a moment like this. And has always feared it."

"My community?" She touched her hair and her eyes grew wide. "You mean the one from that story about Gaia. Destroying cities?"

Adrien grew quiet again and no one seemed to know what to say.

I'm not a killer, no matter what this guy says. Is my mother?

"Well, that was an awesome answer." Eka broke the silence. "So not even a tiny guess where Isamae might be now?"

Adrien eyed Eka then shook his head. "No. I haven't been home in a while, but maybe there's news there. And since the danger has escalated, I think she might come out of hiding soon, to share what she's learned." He turned to Christelle. "And maybe, with enough skills, you could join her."

Christelle froze. Join her mother? Meet her? A chance to find out who she really was.

"Christelle?" Eka shook her.

"You really think I could meet her?"

Adrien's smile was easy and open. A first all day. "Yes. Maybe you could visit your home. Learn about your family, the people who developed all these techniques you're learning."

Christelle's throat tightened. She couldn't care less about the home of ancient killers but she really did want to find her mother. And Adrien was offering her the first real chance to make that happen. Christelle jerked out of her thoughts as Eka's shook her again.

"Space cadet."

Christelle smiled at Adrien. "I think we should practice some more."

He returned the smile. "You have natural abilities and a great number of gifts, again like Isamae. But you have to be focused. I took out your whole group easily. Never let your guard down."

"*My* group?"

Lead? A group of fighters?

A pit formed in her stomach and she looked at her two team members. "We didn't decide on that, did we?"

The others, apparently listening, shook their heads.

"We've been here longer. I don't know why you think she's in charge," Bryan grumbled. Sessie nodded her agreement.

Adrien shrugged and stood up. "This is up to you three. But I know when I see a leader."

Don't let this opportunity go. You need him.

Christelle turned to Bryan and Sessie. "I know I'm new and I just got my gifts. I need all the practice I can get. But let's try it his way. If I totally blow it, you can always remind him how wrong he was."

Bryan unfolded his arms. "Fine." He turned towards Adrien. "But not so close this time. We almost drowned."

Adrien nodded. "Fine." He indicated the clearing. "This time, open ground combat. And you all need to focus. Think of the small things, not such large, isolated gestures. If you each contribute something to a bigger whole, then the impact will be much stronger. There were a few good moves before but you need to work as a team, not individuals."

He got up and strode out to the field, Bryan and Sessie following.

"Good job on the pep talk." Eka nudged Christelle as she stood to follow the group.

"I don't care about fighting. Being the leader of those two. But Adrien's the only one that's seen my mom and he's actually talking about her." She rolled her eyes. "When did I get to be such a user?"

"Keeping a group positive and working as a team seems like leadership to me. Even if your motivation is learning about your mom."

"Maybe." Christelle followed the three figures out into the field. Maybe she did motivate the group. Just because she wanted something else didn't mean she couldn't do well here. And she didn't have to end up fighting just because she was training with Adrien.

Just think of it as a game, not a fight.

Adrien, well ahead of Bryan and Sessie, turned abruptly. Before he could make any move, Christelle released energy into the earth, seeking seeds between her teammates and Adrien. In a split second, her energy found the seeds and a small grass hedge shot up in protection.

Bryan frowned. "Hey, give us a second Christelle!"

Christelle wiggled her eyebrows as she ran past him.

"Impressive!" Adrien yelled from behind the living wall. "Battle doesn't have a starting time. You can find yourself with very little cover and fewer apparent resources in an open space."

He walked from behind the hedge and out to the edge of the treeline, then turned to face them. Christelle glanced back at Bryan and Sessie when a flash caught her eye. Adrien sent spheres of water hurtling across the field toward them and her lungs reflexively sought air. Behind her, Sessie yelled, then turned and ran into the woods while Bryan froze, eyes wide.

"Christelle!" Eka yelled.

Her name snapped her back. She shook her head and squeezed her fist, calling the wind with a tendril of lavender that rose into the air like a kite's tail and mixed with silver air energy. A gust, shimmering with lavender and silver, caught the spheres of water and rammed them into the trees above Adrien, but he shook off the sudden rain shower and moved back toward them. Christelle turned and rammed Bryan, shaking him out of his stupor, then slammed her hands on the ground, drilling lavender into it. The solid, stable earth around her rumbled and the grass undulated in waves throughout the field while Bryan intensified the gust Christelle had started, turning it into a mini-tornado heading for Adrien. Suddenly, from directly behind them, bushes shot up out of the field, branches wrapping around Christelle and Bryan, quickly pinning their arms and legs to their sides. Christelle's shock waves sputtered out and Bryan's tornado dissipated as they were pulled into the dense foliage. Christelle struggled to send her energy to the foliage, but it was already saturated with pale blue light and seemed uninterested in her. Then Adrien was there again, keeping them bound tightly with branches, wearing that stupid smug smile. Christelle tried kicking out her one free leg, but the branchs tightened, squeezing her like a python. Next to her Bryan was gasping for air.

"You must concede," Adrien stated flatly. "Or this lesson is not over."

Bryan tried to say something, but nothing coherent came out.

"That could be a yes. Christelle?"

She opened her mouth, then noticed some soapy bubbles floating over Adrien's head, falling slightly behind him. She traced the trail of bubbles back to Eka, who blew out some more and winked. He glanced back to where she watched the bubbles land, but he didn't seem to notice them.

"Do you concede?" Adrien snapped his fingers. Christelle opened her mouth, trying to watch Eka without watching her.

Meanwhile, Eka held up three fingers and counted down. On the last count, Christelle looked at the bubbles above Adrien. The bubbles collapsed to small points and fell, hitting his head and exploding like firecrackers.

Adrien grabbed his ears, falling at the explosions and, apparently, breaking his concentration and connection to the bushes which quickly released Christelle and Bryan. Christelle ran over to Adrien, now rolling on the ground, and slapped her hands next to him, lavender engulfing the earth around him. A ground wave rolled out from under her hands and over Adrien, creating an Adrien-in-a-dirt-blanket. Only his head stuck out of the roll of dirt and grass. He was caught, his hand pressed tightly against his head and his energy trapped inside.

"Okay," He nodded. "You have won."

Bryan walked over, jaw hanging open at their victory. "That was awesome!"

Christelle jumped up and down.

After a celebration dance, which was thankfully not captured on any camera, she finally released Adrien with a last gloat. He stood and dusted off his clothes.

"Well done," he grinned and glanced back to Eka. "I have to say I haven't seen that particular technique before."

Christelle and Bryan continued dancing around as she gave Eka a thumbs up and, for the first time, allowed herself to really think about meeting her mom.

What is Up With Her?

igh-pitched scraping jerked Eka out of her first nap back at the campground after working away and her dreams of abs and flying and magic dissipated.

"What the hell?"

Shielding her eyes as she lounged, Eka scanned her little campground and sighed. Across the fire pit, Anise dragged a chair toward her. The woman's stiff smile and rigid face left Eka so not ready to deal with this situation. Really, when had Anise ever signaled a good time?

Eka closed her eyes again. "Lost?"

The chair creaked and feet shuffled. When Eka finally opened her eyes again, maybe a little curious, she jumped. Anise's face was inches from hers.

"Geees. Can you not be so sneaky," she sat up and mumbled. "And weird."

"I need to talk with you."

At least she backed up.

Eka sighed. "I'm super tired, Anise. I just got back from a two-week gig in Orlando. Could we do this some other time?"

Anise shook her head. Her tight, neat hair was frantically attempting to escape her headband while her dress sagged, barely holding on to her body, ready to just let it all go. Everything about Anise screamed she was fraying at the edges as she reached into a satchel and pulled out a bottle of bubbles. "I'd like to see."

Eka dropped her frown, completely unready for this request. "What's this about?"

Anise's rigid demeanor dropped. "Please."

Is she really asking this? Does she want to know? Understand?

Probably not. But it's my magic and she'll have to deal with it.

Eka shrugged, picked up the bottle and opened it. As she blew the bubbles, Eka's thoughts turned to maple trees in a New England fall as the shimmering spheres languidly fell past her. One by one, they exploded in a slow, dreamlike manner, as if the universe's clock was now on vacation, running on island time. The colorful fall leaves dancing through her mind suddenly manifested in front of her as the spheres opened and the edges began to lose their transparency. Yellows and browns spread through the filmy substance as jagged edges formed. The change sped up as the shapes flattened, then stopped in mid-air. For a brief moment, Eka's body seemed to pull out of itself, like a rubber band stretched tight, before returning to normal. She stuck her hand under the suspended leaves as they unfroze, catching one as two others reached the ground. She smiled at the tiny veins running through the surface and the delicate edges forming the shape of a maple leaf.

"A real leaf!" Her whisper carried across the camp. But a glance at Anise stopped her enthusiasm and killed her smile. The woman had a look she could only interpret as terror.

"Are you okay?"

Anise sucked in a breath she must have been holding for the entire demonstration and sunk into her chair. "No." Her chest heaved and she zoned out for a long, uncomfortable while.

Eka fidgeted for an eternity; at least that's what her body told her. "Hello. Are you still here?"

Anise just sat there.

"Well, this is awkward," Eka mumbled.

She may have been waiting for it, but Eka still jumped at Anise's voice.

"It has a strange, familiar signature. I thought maybe I was wrong. But the," her hands shook, "smell of your energy is overwhelming when you do that." She spat out the last word and pointed at the leaves. And, as her focus came back, pinpointed on Eka, her words flowed fast. "There was a similar strangeness on the bodies found a few weeks ago, on the bodies left behind when Christelle and her family were attacked and when your family was attacked." She narrowed her eyes at Eka. "And on the recent deaths."

Eka dropped the bottle of bubbles, slimy soap running over the dirt. She grabbed her bracelet and twisted it rapidly until the shell slid under her thumb. Somehow, the night her family died had changed her; Irida had changed her. Into what she still wasn't sure, but not a killer.

Beats pounded rapidly against her chest. Could her magic be dangerous? Could it have hurt her family? Other Wakers?

Anise's face, a mask of contempt, sat across the fire pit in obvious judgment.

Nothing in that *face will ever believe I was good. Or even try to believe. More likely, throw me under a bus.*

"And two more Wakers are dead in another community." Anise's hands clenched. "This danger is spreading and I'll do what I have to do stop it."

"Your shoe's untied."

Anise frowned and looked down at her sandals.

An almost hysterical giggle escaped Eka.

"What is wrong with you? People are dying and you make stupid jokes?"

Eka took a deep breath and set the bubble bottle upright. "Just because you're some Gaia high priestess doesn't mean you know everything. I didn't kill anyone."

Anise stood up, her stance aggressive. "I'm not naive; I know you didn't kill those people. But somehow you're connected. With your tainted energy…"

"You don't know what you're talking about." Eka stood up and headed toward the vardo. If the danger was spreading to other places maybe there'd be answers in other Waker communities, away from all this suspicion.

"These are my people." Anise's voice became low. "Every single Waker in this community is my responsibility. The deaths here…are my fault. I wasn't careful enough. But I won't let that happen again."

Eka turned back. "I'm sorry those people died, but I had nothing to do with it. My energy might be different, but it's not connected to whatever killed them. My own family was attacked, just like Christelle and those other people."

Anise stiffened and squeezed her hands into fists. "You stay away from Christelle from now on. She's my family and I'll do whatever I have to do to protect her."

Eka studied Anise. She knew she was never going to be her best friend, but this hate coming off her was palpable. Maybe Wallace was right about Wakers and where she fit in.

"Ladies." Shirley unexpectedly stepped into the campsite, smiling suspiciously. "Anise, dear. Ben needs you back at the farm."

Anise didn't so much as blink, so Shirley walked over and stepped in front of her. "Said some tourists wandered up the drive and are super curious about a tour of the farm."

Anise stood still for a few more breaths then turned.

"You coming, Mom?" she asked without a backwards glance.

Shirley waved her off. "No, you go ahead. I feel like a walk."

When Anise finally disappeared, Shirley hopped over to Eka and put her hand on her shoulder. "Walk with me."

Shirley's absurdly bright and multi-patterned outfit untied Eka's stomach a bit and she let her shoulders drop as a wave of exhaustion rippled through her adrenaline buzz. "I'm kinda tired."

Shirley guided Eka toward a path, leading away from the secluded campsite. "You know, your grandmother told me about you and your brother, when you were little."

Eka's body tightened again, adrenaline ready to rush back as she grabbed her bracelet.

"Said you two were quite a pair. Getting into trouble. And always watching each other's backs."

"Yeah."

Shirley walked on for a while, holding her arms out and moving her hand in a wave whenever the wind made a pass. Eka swore she heard a giggle from the woman.

"So," Shirley continued abruptly. "Christelle never had that."

Eka stopped, dropping her hand from her wrist.

"She looks up to you, you know," Shirley continued.

"And Anise thinks I'm a dangerous influence."

Shirley turned back, sighing. "Maybe, but Anise worries more than she should. Christelle is a smart girl. But…" Shirley frowned, then started back down the path.

Eka watched Shirley's retreating figure. "You're not going to finish that?"

Shirley waved her over and Eka rolled her eyes.

Do I really care? This whole thing has been a pain in the ass. Maybe Wallace would be more understanding.

Up ahead, Shirley seemed to do a little jig.

She sighed and caught up to the brightly dressed woman, meandering along. Each step of silence grated on Eka's nerves until she couldn't hold back.

"Come on. Stop being so enigmatic," Eka blurted out. When had she gotten so irritable? That so wasn't her bag.

Shirley stopped and whirled around on Eka, who stumbled and slid to a stop. "Have you ever played with clay?"

Eka stared at Shirley. "Played with clay?"

"Just follow along."

"Fine."

Shirley's hands moved as though she were molding clay. "With clay you can make houses, horses, cars. Anything you want."

"Yeah, you can make a model of anything."

Shirley's molding movements stopped. "No, not a model. Okay, let's start over." Shirley scrunched her face and tapped her lips. Suddenly, her face lit up. "You know how wood can be whittled into anything? A house, a horse, a car?"

"Yesss. Like clay?" Eka fought to hold in a grin as Shirley paced, her hands and arms waving around like a juggler losing control.

"For pepper's sake. No, not like clay. What I'm telling you is that all things like to be what they are, no matter how much we try to make 'um otherwise."

"What's clay or wood got to do with that?" Eka leaned against an oak tree, arms across her chest, one leg over the other.

"By an analogy. Thought that might help introduce the concept of the set nature of things."

"An analogy?"

"Yes, a comparison between two things..."

Eka put her hand on the oak. "How about 'trees are flexible in the wind, but too much pressure against their nature can destroy them'."

Shirley stared at Eka, then waved her hand. "Okay, okay. I'm no philosopher but I see you get the message."

Eka frowned. "Shirley, what's all this got to do with Christelle having siblings or Anise accusing me of being involved in the murders of Wakers?"

Shirley stopped walking and slowly shook her head. "I do love my daughter but she can sure jump to a conclusion or two. Listen." She slid over to Eka. "Just 'cause some Wakers are more attuned to the spirit of our world doesn't mean they can't be confused by their own emotions. The gift you have is strange; different. That can scare some Wakers, especially in this unsettling time. But gifts are about how you use them."

Eka stared at Shirley, a crazy-dressing, fortune-telling, eccentric member of this new world. Yet she seemed to be the most grounded and sane.

"Shirley, it's great that you're trying to…" Eka cocked her head and looked off to the side, grasping for the right words. "I guess cheer me up? But I feel like I'm always on a carousel with you, going around and around. One minute, seems like you know more than you're letting on and wanna tell me something, then boom, you take a left turn and ditch the conversation. And I'm back at the start, not sure I went anywhere."

Shirley sighed. "Wish I knew more than I do." She frowned. "Or maybe less." She sat on a nearby tree stump, pulling her legs up cross-legged. Eka stayed leaning against the tree, ready to move whenever Shirley sprinted off.

"Here's the thing about my gift. Not many Wakers understand the nature of it. Some even doubt it's a real gift. Can't blame them. It's strange even to me and I live it every day."

Eka glanced at the woman's clothes again. "Well, you don't really advertise serious."

Shirley laughed and slapped her knee. "That's true. I guess I went with the 'kinda out there' persona. Works for me. Anyways, I've always caught glimpses of possible futures, little bits of images, smells, even emotions." She looked straight into Eka's eyes. "And I've learned the hard way about assuming connections. Too many have been hurt by my jumping to conclusions about things." She seemed to smile at a distant thought. "I guess in that way, we're a bit alike."

"Alike?"

"Not many teachers for my gift. It's a rare one. So most of my lessons were learned the hard way."

Eka remembered stumbling into her gifts. How so much was chance.

"I get it. But is there a point to all this?"

"You're as impatient as the rest," Shirley huffed. "My point is that I've been having glimpses of future stuff, ever since the night you showed up here as a child."

"What kind of glimpses?"

"Well, when you all showed up it was in a burst of colorful light, with traces of darkness on you. There's speculation that a Waker has gone rogue or some non-Wakers have stumbled onto something they shouldn't have."

"But you don't think so."

Shirley shrugged. "Maybe that's happening, but I believe it's something else. My gifts aren't tied to Gaia the way most of the others are. My energy has a bit of a foreign element. Never really understood it." Shirley looked at her own arms, smiling at the silver and gold energy running through them. "That night, I felt another foreignness coming from the colorful lights that flashed with your arrival. And the foreignness also seemed to be in that hint of darkness still hangin' over the four of you." She got up and walked over to Eka, taking her hand. "The glimpses I've been getting since then are of a lighted form and a shadow form, hope and fear. And you and Christelle are always in the middle. Like the center of a scale."

She squeezed Eka's hand hard. "I'm taking a chance telling you this, without context or understanding. I think you're a good person and, perhaps, important in all this. But you have to be careful. These are strange forces. We don't know anything about them yet except that most of the Wakers that have had direct contact with that shadow thing haven't fared well."

"And the colorful lights? What about those?"

Shirley shrugged. "Don't know. But, whatever they were, they seemed to be the thing that brought you all over here from France before that shadow got to ya. That's a plus in my book." Shirley raised her eyebrows. "Any thoughts you have on those lights?"

Shirley had been more open than anyone so far, but Eka still wasn't ready to share her weird encounter with Irida. Maybe Shirley wouldn't be so understanding if she thought Eka was part of another spirit; something unearthly.

Eka sighed, the last of the adrenaline flowing out of her. "No. But if I think of something…"

"Uh, huh." Shirley narrowed her gaze briefly then grinned. "Whenever you think of something, I'll be here. Till then, take care."

Eka genuinely smiled at the enigma of Shirley. "I hear what you're saying and I'll be careful. And respectful."

"Good. Now Bu and I are having a special dinner with the family next week. Like it if you'd be there."

Eka squinted at Shirley. "You were just at the campsite, with Anise, right?"

Shirley waved her off.

"Don't let Anise put you off. Her heart's in the right place. So see you then."

Eka watched the woman head out and shook her head. That should be a fun dinner.

Dinner of the Damned Irritating

Late afternoon sun dappled the ground as Christelle pounded on the vardo's door. "Eka, I know you're in there. I'm not going away."

She tried the door again but it was still locked.

"Come on Eka!"

Stubborn silence answered so she jumped off the steps and around the side, testing each window until she found one loose. Why did her windows have to be so high? Christelle's hands barely grasped the open window edge. She huffed and pulled down on the sticky pane, her arms starting to burn. The last tug yanked it open and the window squealed across the rail.

She stared at the opening her fingertips barely touched. "How am I supposed to get up there?" More planning would have helped, but here she was.

Nothing around the camp looked promising as a ladder, so she stepped a few feet back and ran, jumping to lift herself into the opening. And missing, over and over. On the last try, she slammed her hand into the side of the window and scraped it down the frame.

"Owww!" she yelled, shaking her hand out.

"There's a door over here."

Christelle looked up to see Eka's head disappearing around the end of the vardo and she followed, still holding her hand and stepping through the door as Eka crawled into bed and pulled the covers over her head.

Is she serious?

Christelle sighed and stepped over a few bags of chips, past a table with empty wine bottles and empty cartons of ice cream, and plopped next to Eka on the bed.

"What are you doing sleeping? You're the morning person."

"I'm busy," Eka mumbled from under the blanket.

Christelle pulled the blanket down and looked Eka over. "You've been moping in here for days. What's going on?"

Eka rolled over, her hair stuck against her face. "I'm just sleepy."

"Oh!" Christelle pushed Eka's head away. Far away. "What died in your mouth?"

"Your bedside manner sucks," Eka grumped, pulling the blanket back over her head.

"Uh, huh." Christelle grabbed the blanket and threw it on the floor and laid next to Eka. She reached over to the table and grabbed a bag of open chips then dangled them over Eka's head. "Hungry?"

Eka eyed them for a moment. "Damn you and your evil insights." She grabbed the bag.

Christelle snatched a handful of chips, before they were all gone. "So really, what truck hit you? You're definitely not the moping type."

Eka shrugged. "Everyone has the right to sulk."

Christelle shook her head and stared at Eka.

"Fine." Eka lifted herself up on her elbow. "This whole situation sucks."

Christelle frowned. "What?"

Eka fell back and stared at the ceiling as she held up one finger. "My magic lets me transform bubbles into useless stuff like leaves." She held up two fingers. "No one seems to have any real answers to explain what happened the night we were attacked as kids." She held up a third finger. "This Waker community feels like it's ready to grab pitchforks and torches and storm something." She turned to meet Christelle's eyes. "Probably my camper." She held up four fingers. "The only job near here is two days' drive and what with the first three fingers, I'm not sure I'd come back."

Christelle slapped her fingers down. "No one is attacking you with pitchforks and you only just discovered that you have magic." She smiled briefly before sighing. "Magic no one else seems to have, true, so you're stuck figuring it out on your own. But you don't need a job right now because you told me the last one set you up for a while, so you have time to figure it out."

Eka sat up. "I've been trying for days to expand this magic beyond candy and leaves. Nothing is happening."

"You are the most impatient person I know." Christelle huffed and crossed her arms.

"Have you met Shirley?"

"Fine. You're tied."

Eka's mouth opened, looking to reply, then shut. She shrugged. "Fair enough."

Christelle stared at Eka, running a finger along patterns in the ceiling. "This is like watching gravity win over the Road Runner. I'm getting you out of here." Christelle stood and pulled Eka's dead weight toward the edge of the bed. "And you need a shower."

"You're not my keeper."

Christelle pulled her friend's arm up and over, burying Eka's nose in her own armpit. And she quickly rolled away and took a gulp of air. "Okay. Fine. I'll get a shower."

Christelle looked around. "And I'll clean this place up before it's condemned."

Eka climbed into her barrel shower and pulled the curtain. "Hey, don't knock my shabby chic."

"As long as you show up for the dinner I promise to reconsider this disaster zone."

"That's the worst offer I've ever gotten," Eka mumbled and Christelle ignored it as she cleaned.

Where Are You, Janice

Eka sat on a picnic table by the river at Salty's Bait and Beer, the sun starting to sink. Staring out over the water, she peeled off small bits of flaking wood from the table then took a swig of her beer. Out in the river, a few kayaks glided across the surface and sent small waves rippling out. A cool breeze blew across her skin and she sank into her shirt while the tranquil moment sunk into her bones.

If only she could hold on to all this calm.

She took another sip as she examined her hand, multitudes of color popping and shimmering and flowing within her. The violet, which she now remembered from her childhood, was somehow just a tiny bit brighter, and different, than the rest. She glanced down as her pendant warmed and fluttered.

Am I finally done becoming? Is that what you're saying?

"Whatever that means," she mumbled and flashed back to the cocoon of light Irida had shown her.

Her energy had more color than other Wakers. A lot of color. And she could finally access some magic. A flutter went through her at the memory of morphing one thing into another.

How many things could she change?

"But," she sighed, "It never lasts."

And what was with that shock wave thing that seemed to happen when her magic faded? And was there a limit to the things she could change? She'd tried asking Sema but her grandparents seemed as clueless as everyone else.

A candy wrapper blew by the table. It reminded her of the red and gold confetti she'd thrown, as a kid, at some random town's holiday parade. Grateful for a distraction, she focused on the piece of paper tumbling past her, imagining the confetti, along with a noise maker Sema had given her during the parade. The wrapper shivered as she narrowed her gaze on it. Patches of rainbow light bubbled up from her skin, then a tiny stream of it shot out of her and into the wrapper. The paper shook and a shimmer wove across its surface, then it burst into confetti that wafted to the ground as a faint sound of noise makers drifted across the table.

Eka slapped the table. "Now, how is that not cool?"

"Eka?"

She spun to the right to find Wallace loading a backpack and thermos onto a jon boat.

"Oh, hey, Wallace."

"Did you do that confetti thing?"

She shrugged. "Yeah. My unusual gift."

"Well," he threw a hat in the boat, "that's a pretty cool gift. But you might want to practice somewhere less…" He looked around Salty's. "Full of Asleep."

She grinned. "Probably. But it would definitely put some excitement in their lives."

"True. So what are you doing out here?"

"Enjoying the quiet. You?"

"Same." He started to sit down in the boat.

"Hey, you might want to clean off that seat." She pointed at the dirty boat bench.

Wallace hopped up and pulled a dark green towel out of his backpack, wiping off the grayish smear from the seat. "Had a campfire last night and forgot to clean up the boat," he rambled as he finished wiping it off. When he finally sat down, he gazed out at the water. "Guess I'm feeling more comfortable out on the river these days. Just me and an island getaway."

"Sounds like a nice escape."

Wallace cocked his head at her. "Waker life not suiting you?"

Eka shrugged. "Just wish some people were less opinionated."

Or that they weren't going to be at Shirley's dinner.

Wallace turned toward the motor and checked the gas and oil.

"I did hear there was some thoughts about your gift going around," Wallace said as he primed the engine.

A small quirk of a smile snuck out of her frustration. "Yeah. I'm told it's 'not a Waker gift'."

Wallace studied her a moment then sat down again. "Some of us have a bigger view of the world than others. Who's to say what a Waker gift is. Besides, I think transforming something is astounding."

Eka sat up straight. "Exactly."

"You know, you could be a great inspiration to everyone on our side of the fence. I mean, you got your gift working and our group needs to believe they can too." Within Wallace, gray-blue energy spun and churned.

Maybe she just needed to accept she didn't fit as a Waker anymore and should explore other facets of this new world. As always, Wallace was way easier to deal with than the other Wakers she'd met.

"I also heard you were looking for information about your past."

Eka froze. "Why?"

Wallace held up his hands. "Didn't mean anything by it. Just, Nalo may not have Waker gifts but we are a tight community. I've been chatting online with someone from the Hawaii community. He might be able to find out something."

Could there actually be someone with another perspective on that night? Maybe more details?

Another flutter of excitement went through her. "I think I'll take you up on that. Thanks."

"I'll let you know if he has anything and when we're all meeting again. I think you could be a real inspiration for our group. Remember what I said, we could help with what you've lost." Wallace started the engine then tipped his hat and headed out. He puttered out of the no-wake zone and into the channel, picking up speed and disappearing down the river.

She slammed the rest of her beer and headed out to dinner. "I think things are looking up all around."

"Come on Eka, move."

Eka stopped and looked down the path, spinning her bracelet.

Christelle shoved her and she stumbled forward.

"Why are you so nervous?" Christelle asked.

Eka slid sideways and Christelle tumbled a few steps forward. "I'm not nervous."

Christelle recovered her footing and rolled her eyes.

"What?" Eka asked. "But I'm not really hungry."

"Look, it'll be fine, it's just a casual dinner." Christelle smiled. "You've had dinner hundreds of times. You know how to do it. Just pick up the fork and…"

"Fine, fine." Eka scowled and started down the path. "No need to snark."

"And Aunt Anise promised to be on her best behavior."

Eka rolled her eyes. "Alright. But all unprovoked food fights are on you."

"Awesome! So…" Christelle wiggled her eyebrows, "I hear Devlon's coming."

Eka grinned back. "Yeah, he got over my disappearing act."

"How is he handling your magic?"

She sighed. "He's still trying to understand the changing things magic. But I'm guessing Anise isn't even trying."

Christelle's face dropped. "Probably not."

They stopped outside Shirley's place. "Okay, treehouse of infinite danger, here we come."

Eka dropped her fork on her plate and leaned back in her chair. Having lost the draw to clean up after dinner, Devlon and Christelle were collecting mostly full dishes from the outdoor table and taking them up into the tree. A slight breeze blew over the table which sat at the base of the tree.

"Anise, thanks for the great meal! You'll have to thank Ben when he gets back." Bu rubbed his stomach.

Anise nodded. She had been quiet all afternoon and her strained smile seemed to amplify her reticence to talk.

Shirley hopped up to help Devlon and Christelle with coffee while Eka sat with the hushed Bu and sulking Anise. After what seemed like a never-ending silence, the three returned with the drinks and Eka relaxed.

"Nice to have someone there when I get back with the coffee." Devlon winked at Eka as he handed her a cup.

"Oh?" Eka asked, innocently.

He smiled. "Seems I'm on my own with coffee these days." His eyes met hers and her face flushed.

Maybe he hasn't forgotten the disappearing act.

"What about your admirer Janice? I'm sure she'd love coffee with you." Eka nudged him.

He nudged her back. "I haven't seen her in a while. Kinda strange; I haven't noticed her at the Bakery she works at."

Shirley nodded. "Haven't seen her there either and I've been downtown a few times the past two weeks. Huh."

"I saw her a few weeks back," Eka added. "I ran into her at the farm house. She was acting friendly, which was weird."

Shirley and Bu nodded.

Devlon frowned. "She can be friendly."

Eka shrugged. "Oh, and she had some book that was falling apart. Dropped pages everywhere."

"Didn't know she was much of a reader," Shirley frowned.

"She must know some other language because it wasn't English."

Bu stretched and stood up. "How about we take this into the house before those clouds arrive?"

Even though the night sky was moonless, the dark clouds rolling toward them were clear as they blanked out stars. A distant wall of rain, and the faint sound of thunder, gave ample warning to head inside. They grabbed their stuff and headed up into the tree, just as Shirley brought out a key lime pie.

Christelle sat straight up. "My favorite!"

Eka, tired of sitting and too full for pie, left the group and wandered around the large open room. Branches intertwined below her feet, creating a rough and slightly uneven floor. These same branches grew upward as they enclosed the room in a living wall, intertwining with the branches overhead. All around her the room seemed to breathe, the green energy within the tree pulsing like a heartbeat. She traced a limb all the way to one of the window-like openings within the wall, formed by two other branches. She leaned out and let the wind sweep her hair back, while above, dark clouds rolled past. Humid air settled around her as tiny drops of shimmering blue water fell past her, distorted reflections of her and the treehouse moving across their surfaces.

She leaned over and caught some drops of water falling from the leaves above. Eka stretched out past the leaves and stuck her hand out into the rainfall. Raindrops drummed on her hand and she was lost in the rich sensations, until the jerky wind changed directions and whipped rain in her face. Her hand slipped and she almost fell before jumping back in. Over at the table, Shirley and Bu, backs to her, were telling some story as the others stared at their food. Apparently not a great story, but no one seemed to notice her almost fall.

Should I be happy about that?

She shrugged, then walked back along the wall of the room, trying to dry her face and tie up her hair. Along the wall, branches curved out into small shelves lined with books, which Eka proceeded to pull out and explore.

"Be careful with those books." Anise broke her silence.

"Really, she notices *that*?" Eka mumbled to herself.

She pulled another book down and read the title.

Tarot Through the Ages

"Is this yours, Shirley?" Eka held up the book.

"Yep."

"Do you need help with your magic?"

Shirley brushed away the comment. "I'm fine with my gift. Just sometimes I do readings for the town folks and they like it to look traditional."

Eka re-shelved the book then walked her fingers down a few titles. Sticking out from behind the rest, a book was wedged in a nook. It had a vaguely familiar, yet foreign script. She pulled it out and flipped through it. The strange letters clicked in her mind; she recognized the script from Janice's book. Eka walked back to the group and laid the book on the table.

"Hey, what language is this? It looks familiar."

Before anyone could answer, Anise grabbed it and glared at Eka.

"Where did you get this?"

Eka raised her eyebrows at Anise's irritability. "Behind the rest of the books."

"Wait." Anise suddenly frowned. "What do you mean, familiar?"

Eka frowned back and crossed her arms. Anise's tension seemed to fill the room. "The book Janice was carrying the other day. This looks like that language."

Shirley leaned over Anise's shoulder. "Looks like lighter script."

Anise dropped the book and sagged into the chair.

"Anise?" Shirley put her hand on Anise's shoulders.

Eka could feel something big was about to be revealed, so she sat down between Devlon and Christelle as they all waited.

Anise's voice was like a whisper; Eka had to lean in to hear.

"I mean, I just asked her…" Anise looked at them. "Janice. I just asked her to get something from the house when we were moving back over here. I thought I had the Book of Celei and all the copies of it."

Christelle frowned and glanced at Eka. Eka shrugged.

"Like pulling teeth," Eka whispered and Christelle elbowed her.

"Why would Janice want a book you have?" Devlon asked and Anise pulled it close.

"I don't know why Janice would want it. But there are others who do." She stared at Christelle. "When your parents showed up here with you they brought that book, the Book of Celei, with them. And I think that's the reason your family was attacked."

"That book?" Christelle straightened, pointing at the one Anise held.

Anise shook her head. "No, this is a lighter dictionary of sorts. I thought it would help me read the Book of Celei, understand it, but it didn't. I must have left this here during the move. It's been a while since I worked on the book. So much going on."

"I can't believe you had that book." Shirley sagged into a chair. "Anise, tell them about it."

Anise inhaled for a moment and looked at Christelle. Christelle stared back.

"It was so long ago. No one is alive who remembers," Anise started. "There was a Waker, Celei, who was lost from our community as a child. By the time he found his way back, he was a bit unbalanced. Not that he let on."

Shirley and Bu grimaced.

"Grams?"

Shirley shook her head. "Go on Anise."

"The worst part," Anise continued, "was that his particular gift was persuasion. Normally, this has little effect on us, only on non-Wakers. But somehow Celei figured out how to work it on Wakers. By the time Gaia, or any Waker, was aware that he was causing all this destruction, his abilities had grown out of control."

"What did he do?" Devlon asked.

Anise looked directly at Eka. "I think maybe we should continue later. When it's just family."

Really? Now she's pulling this?

"Fine." Eka stood to leave.

"No!" Christelle nearly shouted. "You don't get to set any rules."

Anise opened her mouth but Shirley nodded her agreement.

"I love you, sweetheart, but there's been too many secrets already."

Bu spoke up. "You need to share."

Anise turned to Christelle. "I'm sorry."

"Whatever."

Anise wiped her cheek and continued. "This Waker, Celei, he did many horrible things to get the thing he wanted, to steal Waker energy. The energy that keeps all spirits healthy and us tethered to this world. He thought this would make him powerful, in charge, admired. And, before we had discovered who was stealing energy, he had destroyed hundreds of Wakers. And, with that much energy and coercive power, all life on Gaia was in danger." Anise's voice faded and the room grew quiet.

"So, how does the book tie in?" Devlon once again broke the silence.

"The book," Anise replied, "is a record of the methods Celei used to steal energy. And our methods to stop him. Since everyone involved has long since passed, this book allows us to keep the information hidden but accessible. Just in case. Now Janice seems to have a copy of it."

"She must have been coerced," Devlon interjected. "Maybe someone knew where the book was, forced her."

Anise shrugged.

"Well, it's in lighter script so Janice'd need someone who could read it," Shirley piped up. "Hopefully she, or whoever, hasn't figured that out.

But we'll need to find her."

"Why did my family have that book?" Christelle interjected.

Anise reached across but Christelle leaned back, away from her. "I wanted to tell you but..."

"Tell me now."

Christelle sounded so calm yet Eka watched her energy roil within her.

Anise sighed. "Your Ysian family has been in charge of the book since it was written. Very few knew about it. Jon and I are the only ones who knew it was here. I can't imagine how anyone else found out about it, unless..." Anise looked directly at Christelle. "No."

"What?"

"I was worried that who ever had attacked you as a child would be looking for you now, tracking where your family might have gone with the book. That's why I didn't want you to do things like set up a website. Anything traceable to you, your mom, or dad."

"What are you saying?" Christelle glared. "That I brought them here?"

Anise tried to pat Christelle's hand, but Christelle jerked it away. "It's not your fault."

"Of course it's not. If you had been honest, I could've made a better decision. This is your fault!" Christelle's face was red and lavender energy surged through the room.

Eka coughed and Christelle leaned back, energy still moving.

"But why do you have this dictionary?" Devlon asked, ignoring the building drama.

"I was making a few copies of the Book of Celei for other communities and needed help, so Jon gave me the dictionary and started helping with copies," Anise admitted. "Right now there are similar things happening to what's described in the book. Bodies drained of their energy, nothing but ash left. So much of this information has been forgotten by most and it might help us strike back and protect ourselves. The fighting techniques Adrien is teaching are good, but we need more to stop the attacks." She glanced at Eka.

"Really?" Eka sighed.

"Anise, can we focus?" Devlon interjected. "We need to know what's going on. Why Janice is involved."

Eka frowned. "Actually, I saw Jon with Janice the other night."

Anise shook her head. "Jon wouldn't do something like that."

"Well, I can't imagine what Janice wants with it either," Devlon weighed in.

"We'll have to check any lighters who have passed through lately." Anise seemed to go into planning mode.

"We'll check on the lighters," Bu nodded. "Devlon, I'll need help."

Bu and Devlon left. Anise turned to Christelle, who glared at her with crossed arms, then Shirley. But Shirley just shook her head and Anise paused, clutching the book. She stared at Christelle for another moment then her shoulders sagged and she left.

"Why don't you take Christelle home, Eka?" Shirley said. "I'll clean up here."

Eka nodded. "Christelle, feel like a walk?"

Christelle stood up, lavender still roiling around her. They silently walked back toward Eka's truck and climbed in the cab. When the passenger's door slammed shut, Christelle bent over and shook as sobs escaped her.

"I'm so tired." Christelle's voice sounded hoarse and so much smaller than Eka had ever heard. "When will she be honest? Stop hiding things?"

"Yeah." Should she say something else? Probably. "Why don't you stay at my place tonight?"

Christelle nodded, sinking into the bucket seat as Eka drove back to the vardo.

I'll Trade You Three Clues for an Answer

A couple of women walked toward Eka on the sidewalk. She tried to hide her face in her hoodie, but stumbled when Christelle bumped her from behind. The women quickly swerved away from them, Eka almost crouching in the shadows at this point. Christelle, on the other hand, waved at the women as they passed. "Hi."

They disappeared and Eka spun around and raised her eyebrows. "What?"

Eka placed her hands on Christelle's shoulders. "We are on a stealth mission. Trying to keep a low profile."

Christelle nodded and paced around Eka, rubbing her palms on her hips. "I know. It's just, I've never," she lowered her voice, "broke into somewhere before."

Eka looked around, spotting a bench, and dragged Christelle toward it. Why had she brought her on this potentially jail-worthy adventure? After yesterday's dinner, it seemed like a great idea for the two of them to take on this challenge together. Now she wasn't so sure.

Christelle stepped off the sidewalk, catching her toe on the grass, and smacked into the ground. Eka tried to cover Christelle's mouth before she yelped but was a moment too late.

"Take a breath."

Christelle yanked away from Eka, trying to pull out a stick from her shoe as she stood. "It freakin hurts!" Her whisper-yell died in her second trip, sending her stumbling to a bench before collapsing.

Eka stared down at the mess of a woman and pulled a piece of grass from Christelle's hair. What could her friend possibly contribute here, other than getting them busted? Eka sighed, shaking her head and dropping on the bench. "Are you sure you're up for this?"

Christelle wiggled up, crossed her legs under her, and checked for any debris. "Of course."

Uh, huh. She might sound sure, but she was doing everything but make eye contact with Eka.

"Hey." Eka elbowed Christelle. "You don't have to pretend you're cool with this. We might find nothing and end up arrested."

Christelle sighed. "I have to start figuring things out for myself, stop relying on my family's decisions. Somehow I'm involved with all this whether I wanted it or not. We both are. So we need better answers."

Eka stared at her hands. Did she believe Shirley and Irida? That she and Christelle were in the middle of some light and dark thing? And was part of her energy really from some off-world spirit that was chasing a dangerous other-universe thing? "Does it all feel a bit scifi? Or like we slipped into some fantasy world?"

"A little bit."

Eka raised an eyebrow.

"Okay, a lot," Christelle agreed. "But we still need to stop letting others set the agenda. I mean, if whatever is killing Wakers now was what attacked my family and yours, we should know. And if they found us because of me, I should know."

"Hey, this isn't your fault. Anise was grasping at straws when she mentioned your website."

Christelle's mouth set in a thin line and she crossed her arms. "Maybe, but I'm not waiting for others to throw us crumbs. If this Book of Celei is a link to whatever is going on, and Janice stole a copy, she might be involved and we need to check her place out."

Eka eyed her. "Since when did you start taking charge?"

A small smile cracked Christelle's face. "Too much?"

Eka smiled back. "No. More like wow."

Eka was actually glad Christelle had come, despite her lack of skills. But her friend's nervousness wasn't going to help her get into the apartment unnoticed.

Eka tapped her lips a few times. "Okay, how about this? You stay here and keep watch."

"What!" Christelle glared again, ready to jump in with some argument.

"Look," Eka jumped in first. "I'll need to know if someone is headed my way so I can get out of the apartment, or hide." She looked up at the building. "And this is a perfect spot to see the entrance but far enough away that no one suspects you. I have my phone and you can text if you see anything."

"You sure?"

Eka nodded then looked back up at the building.

"You know," Christelle stared at the plain structure. "This place feels really sad."

Eka glanced around, taking it all in. The plain doors, the shades of beige barely defining structural pieces, the few straggling trees.

"You're right. Tried to avoided places like this. Always felt so…"

"Lifeless."

"Yeah." This was where Janice went home every night. "Maybe Janice liked it."

Christelle frowned. "You really think anyone would like this dead space?"

Eka shrugged. "She was kind of a bystander in the Wakers' world. She saw the stuff everyone saw but wasn't really part of it." Eka squinted, her voice lowering. "Maybe this was easier."

"Huh."

They stared at the empty places, where very little energy flowed. Eka sighed and finally stood up. "Better get started."

Christelle nodded. "Got your back." Her big thumbs up and obvious wink caused Eka to spin away from Christelle and chocked back a laugh.

Eka walked over to the exterior staircase and up to the third floor to Janice's corner apartment, right at the top of the stairs. The lightbulb at this end of the open walkway was out, shadowing Janice's and relaxing Eka a bit. Eka glanced through the railing at Christelle, getting a repeat of the thumbs up then even more exaggerated arm pumps. Eka smiled back, hiding a grimace and hoping there weren't any cameras she hadn't noticed. With a final sigh she turned to the door to check the lock mechanism and found it was a very simple crack. She smiled to herself then nearly jumped off the landing when her phone buzzed. Pulling herself off the ground she stared at the message.

All clear, 😊
Christelle

Eka turned to look down at a smiling Christelle and texted back.

Thanks
Maybe wait until someone is coming before you
text me.

Christelle nodded and gave her another thumbs up on reading the message. Eka checked the landing for people, then pulled out a small velvet roll from her backpack and unfurled the soft package. She ran her hands over the small metal pieces inside. Sliding her fingertips over the door again confirmed it was a simple big box store lock, the type so many developers used. She silently inserted slender metal tools into it and quickly popped the locking mechanism.

Eka stepped in and closed the door. Stumbling as she felt around for the light, she remembered how dark places could be without all the background energy glowing.

Giving up on the switch, she groped around in her bag. She finally wrapped her fingers around a long thin metal tube and pulled out a penlight, clicking it on. The light's tight beam sliced through the darkness of a studio apartment, dust particles and pollen floating within the tiny beam of light, creating a ghost-like filter of the room. She took a few steps forward and peered into a closet on the left; the light muted as it passed over the gray and black wardrobe that hung in the closet. Hints of shirts and pants disappeared in the blackness and a lone pair of black sneakers occupied the dusty floor.

How long had Janice been gone? And did she have any other color in her wardrobe?

A door next to the closet sat open and Eka peered inside at a tiny, cramped bathroom. Musty dampness hit her nose, wrinkling it in response. How could Janice stand this?

An aging vanity and sink sat against thinly painted drywall. Next to the vanity, a toilet balanced on a cracked pedestal. Above the toilet, a dusty and unused green towel hung, the only bit of color in an otherwise dull canvas. A dusty tub, because everything was dusty here, took up the wall off Eka's right. Not usually claustrophobic, the lack of windows and disuse made the small space seem to press in and she backed out quickly.

Back in the main room, she passed a twin bed with a tiny window just above it. The simple bedsheets were placed in almost military style on the bed, with neat corners and no wrinkles.

A small lopsided nightstand carried the weight of dozens of paperbacks and, judging by the sea of books on the floor, the little table had not been up to the task. Eka knelt next to the stand, looking through title after title, all romances. As the stack shrunk, a beautifully lilted picture frame of two people in an embrace emerged from behind. She pulled the frame closer, realizing the faces were familiar.

"Devlon and Janice. Huh." She stared. "Seems he forgot to mention something."

She flashed the light around the walls, noticing more pictures showing the two involved in lots of outdoor adventures, always holding hands or embracing. She studied the first photo again, then picked it out of the frame and shoved it in her pocket. As she leaned over the books to replace the frame, she bumped the stand and the little table, unable to handle this knock, finally succumbed to gravity. It landed on the books it had once held, the rest of the romances sliding off its top. As it thumped onto the books, a small drawer slid open and a photo album tumbled out.

"Can't even imagine what's in here," Eka whispered to herself as she glanced at the wall of pictures.

She plopped on the floor and flipped open the album on her lap, expecting more photos of Janice and Devlon. Instead of pictures, she found page after page of empty slips. Until the middle. A blobby image was taped to the paper but she had to hold the flashlight closer to really understand what she was looking at.

A sonogram.

"Did Janice have a kid?"

The sonogram, worn and faded, held the outline of a child. Eka's beam slid to the facing page. A certificate was taped carefully to the paper declaring that Lillian had lived for two hours before succumbing to immense, physical symptoms. Janice's name was on the mother's line but no father's name appeared.

Eka stared at the pages and her heart tightened. Another piece of paper was taped under the certificate. Her beam flashed over it.

We can help you get her back if you bring the book.

Before her mind processed any of it, she heard a noise at the front door. She flung the album back in the drawer and scanned for a hiding spot. Two steps later, just as the front door opened, she dove into the bathroom and locked herself in.

Then remembered there wasn't a way out.

No windows. Damnit!

A vaguely familiar male voice mumbled from the room and she pushed her ear against the door to listen. 'Not a servant' was all she heard before her phone vibrated, echoing in the small tiled space.

Someone coming :O

Christelle

She backed up to the wall as footsteps stopped outside the bathroom and a weak light appeared under the door. Eka watched as the light began to creep along the floor, bluish-gray energy flowing through it.

A Waker?

She looked around, searching for any way to get out. All she needed was a window.

The light crept closer as she backed up to the wall. Why weren't there any windows? If only she were magic…

I've changed a bubble into candy; maybe a window wouldn't be much different?

Even she didn't believe it.

But the light crept closer along the floor, jerking toward her as if it were fighting against the movement, and at that point, she didn't care anymore if she believed or not. Spinning to the outer wall, she placed her hand on it.

You can do this.

She inhaled deeply and pictured a window, focusing her entire being on the image. The door rattled and her heart rate jacked up.

Focus Eka.

She took another breath and focused on details; the cross bracing of the window, decorative purple shutters. A ripple flowed across the wall and then a pinhole opened. Eka's breath caught as the hole expanded, forming an open window. With shutters.

"Hey, is someone in there?"

The faint light was almost at her feet when the window settled. She hopped up on the seal as light brushed her shoe.

"I knew it." The man outside shook the door harder.

She crawled onto the window and looked at the ground, three stories down.

Whoo whoo!

The door rattled violently.

Picturing the wall, instead of the window, she dropped to the tiny ledge and shoved her fingers into indentations in the stucco as the window disappeared. Behind her came a muffled 'what the hell?'.

She was out of the bathroom, but…below her was a three-story drop. And the roof was about ten feet above her. Neither one inviting. And whoever was in the apartment might come out looking for her.

A rainbow of colors flashed from her pendant and gave her a brief sensations of feathers and flying.

"Irida? Is that you?" she whispered.

A second colorful flash and a set of wings formed in her mind.

"Bird? What do I do with a bird?"

Images flashed rapidly through her head. When they stopped she was left with a movie of her body shifting into a bird.

"You want me to what?" she whispered again, unable to grasp the message as her fingers grew numb and her feet slipped.

Bird. Change.

"What? I can't…" she whisper-screamed until she slipped more.

Fine. I'll just change into a bird. Nothing crazy about that.

Breathing deeply, she started to focus on a bird flitting through the skies, untethered to any structure.

Her left hand slipped again.

Focus!

She thought of the bird again and an itch on her right shoulder flared up. Reflexively her left hand went to scratch it and touched some feathers.

No.

A single feather floated toward the ground, and when she looked back to her shoulder another feather stuck out of her shirt. She looked between the ground and her shoulder, her fingers slipping again and missing the ledge with her free hand.

I can do this.

She concentrated on the feather laying below her and the bird started to form in her mind as itchy sensations erupted all over her body and the pressure on her hands eased up.

Suddenly, chattering grabbed her attention and her head jerked around to a squirrel sitting in a tree adjacent to the building, fussing at her. At that moment, everything squirrel filled her mind. Then, an instant later, the tree seemed to shoot up before her. She frowned and looked down. Instead of feathers, her arms and legs were now covered in fuzzy gray fur and ended in paws that sprawled across the wall of the building.

Not a bird!

The thought floated away and she pushed off the wall, easily catching the now giant tree. Eka-squirrel landed next to the original squirrel, who screamed and scampered off.

"Hey!"

At least that was her thought, but what came out was distinctly not human. Human words drifted off, replaced with a need to find a nest. Or food. She scampered across the tree in the direction of the other squirrel, wind blowing across her fur and the scent of nuts filling the air.

"Eka?"

She paused at the familiar sound and looked down at a pale human. The human jumped and threw its arms up and down. Eka-squirrel twisted away and ran across to another tree then up a branch, colliding with a large pair of eyes and flashing claws.

Monster!

She back-flipped and ran chattering to a further tree, speeding over branch after branch, eluding the pursuing monster, claws swiping so close, a tip grazing her from behind.

Suddenly, the trees violently shook under and around her. Her gray, furry limbs stretched and shed fur as the branch beneath her seemed to shrink. Her claws retracted and Eka, just Eka, tipped off the tiny branch, hit the ground and rolled up. Off in the distance, a building rattled and a far-off voice called a familiar name. Her name. She blinked, face to face with a cat that suddenly seemed small.

"You monster! Get!" She waved frantically at the cat.

The cat howled and shot off.

"What happened?" Her skin, so smooth, seemed familiar and alien. The air smelled bland and she felt heavy and clumsy. After a few minutes, her mind gave up and she dropped in exhaustion, drifting off to sleep.

A warmth along her skin slowly turned into a broiling sensation and Eka opened her eyes to the early-morning sun. She tried to focus on where exactly she was, but everything around her seemed so bright she gave up and just lay on the scratchy ground.

What happened?

The apartment, the window, and the squirrel floated back into her mind.

"I was a squirrel!"

She managed to sit up, patting herself and searching for any lingering hint of squirrel. Fur? A tail? Nothing. Where was she and where was Christelle?

Her eyes adjusted to the light around her and she noticed a strand of unfamiliar trees ahead of her. Beyond them, she could hear water.

Pushing up from a bed of leaves, pain shot through her ankle and she fell back.

"Eka! You're awake!" Christelle trudged out from the trees and sunk next to Eka.

Eka stared at her. "What happened?"

"I don't really know. I felt energy, like your bubble stuff, from the building and I saw you change." Her voice lowered on the last part. "You were a squirrel." They stared silently at each other for a moment, 'cause what was there to say to that.

Finally, a shiver went across Eka's skin. "You have anything I could put on?"

"Oh!" Christelle held up Eka's bag and pulled out last night's clothes. As Eka dressed, Christelle babbled on. "I looked for you all night, then I found you here and…" Her voice caught. "I…I didn't know what happened. What to do."

Eka smiled at Christelle's practicality. "Thanks. I promise I'm fine. But I think I need a bath."

Her previous night's search through Janice's apartment resurfaced in her memories. "And you won't believe what I found." She winked, then dressed, and touched the folded-up picture in her pants. That would come in handy later.

Looking around the detritus, Eka found a long, smooth stick, leaning on it and Christelle as she hop-walked through the brush. Stumbling along, she struggled to recall events, but with Christelle adding her bits, they managed to piece together a picture of the whole adventure.

"You actually changed into a squirrel!"

Eka nodded but didn't quite believe it.

How did I even do that? Was that Irida?

Questions floated through her head but no answers appeared. They made it to the truck and Eka managed to drive the stick shift the short distance to the vardo, hobbling inside and beelining it to the barrel shower. As the warm water streamed down her, her mind cleared and her body relaxed.

"I can't believe you were a squirrel!" Christelle shouted.

"Uh-huh," Eka answered.

"A squirrel! Chased by a cat! I'm so glad it didn't get you before you changed back."

"Yeah." Eka said as she finished in the shower and crawled into bed.

"I wonder what else you could be. Oh, a giraffe! That'd be cool."

She drifted off to Christelle's musings.

Hunger jolted Eka out of her sleep, vague memories of scampering through trees and flashes of fur and claws, taunting her. She rolled over to find Christelle asleep in a chair next to her, her pack on the floor, and the events of last night and this morning sprang back to her mind. Apartment, squirrel, and all. She reached down and gingerly touched her ankle to find the pain was gone.

How?

The ankle had no swelling, no discoloration. She swung her legs over the side and slowly stood up.

"Woot woot! And Anise said no good could come of my gifts. Ha!"

"Where were you last night?" Devlon stood in the door, his posture a sour note. "We were supposed to meet."

Christelle stirred from her chair, stretching. Then stopped mid-stretch when she noticed Devlon. She quietly stood, making her way to the door. "I think I need a walk."

"Devlon." Eka's body tensed remembering the picture in her pocket, the photo album, and his defensiveness of Janice.

"What?"

She pulled the photo she'd removed from the frame out of her shorts and handed it to him. "Did you date Janice?"

He took the photo and unfolded it. "What's this?"

"Exactly. What is it?"

"Eka, I don't know where you got this but it's not a photo of me."

"Really?" She crossed her arms.

"Yes. I've never had a photo taken by Gary's Gallery."

"What?" She looked at the studio mark on the photo.

"And," Devlon pointed at the figures, "the heads don't match the bodies."

Eka took the photo back and looked. In the full sunlight she noticed that the heads had indeed been added to the bodies.

"So," Eka stared off, "she changed them. The penlight was really crappy in that apartment. I can't believe I didn't notice that."

"What apartment?" Devlon stepped up to Eka and turned her towards him. She blinked at him, smiled and tapped his nose with her finger, then started striding around the trailer, tapping the photo on her other hand.

"Your girlfriend has a lot of these photos all over her apartment."

"Wait. What girlfriend? What apartment?"

"Janice."

"You were at Janice's apartment? Where's she been?"

"She wasn't home and, by the dust, I'd say she's been gone for a few days at least."

"You broke in?" Devlon's voice went higher.

Eka shrugged. "She took a copy of that book and disappeared. Thought I might find something. And I did." She sighed at the memory of the sonogram and the note. "Not sure, but the book seems to have been an exchange for something to do with her baby who died. Or didn't die. It's confusing."

Devlon stepped in front of Eka. "You're not making any sense. What baby?"

"Thought it might be yours." She nodded at the photo. "Well, with all the cozy pictures of your time together."

"What!"

"Guess not."

"Eka, those aren't real." He looked solemnly at her and she winked back.

"Whatever," He huffed.

"Hey." She pulled him to her then looked up. "If you'd had a relationship with Janice, I wouldn't care." He started to speak and she held up her hand. "I'd just hate to find out you wouldn't admit it."

He stared at her and let a corner of his mouth raise. "I would never deny I dated someone. We just never dated. She's not my type."

"Really?" she whispered, "What is your type?"

"I uh…" he mumbled.

She pressed against him. "Yes?"

"Um, someone who is more in tuned with their gifts. With our world."

A real Waker.

She dropped her hands and took a step back. "Oh. Well probably for the best." Eka looked away from him, needing to be away from him. Or for him to leave, as it was her vardo.

"Eka, you okay? Did I say something?"

"No, I um…I'm just sad she lost a baby. She kept the sonogram and the death certificate in an album. And now she has the book. Probably setting up some kind of exchange for it, if it hasn't happened already."

Devlon stood and took a turn at pacing the small space. "None of this is making sense."

Eka held up the doctored photo. "I don't really get it either. The note and the baby and the other guy who broke in."

He stopped pacing. "Someone else broke in?"

Eka nodded. "Must be a lighter by the way he used light to try and find me while I hid in the bathroom."

"You had to hide from him?" Devlon's voice pitched up again as he rubbed his forehead. "Eka, I think we need to tell the others about this."

She patted his shoulder. "I agree." She opened the door. "Tell me how that goes."

He frowned as he stepped toward the door. "I think you should be the one to explain the details."

She fake-yawned, stretching her arms. "I wish I could but I need to get some sleep after that long night of breaking in. But I think you'll do great."

She held out the picture but he shook his head.

"Hey, maybe Christelle wants to go." She poked her head out the door, smiling at Devlon. "Christelle, want to go with Devlon to tell Anise and the others about last night?"

"No!"

"Guess you're on your own. Have fun and I believe in you." She pushed him out onto the steps and gave him two thumbs up before shutting the door.

Now they just needed to figure out where Janice was, who wanted the book, where the exchange would take place if it hadn't yet, how to stop it…

"Piece of cake." She sighed and called Christelle back in.

The Darkest Cove

Eka walked out of the vardo and past a snoozing Christelle, who'd stayed to make sure Eka was okay. But between Christelle's snoring and her racing mind, Eka had gotten little sleep. Images of squirrels and secret books kept her awake and now she dragged her exhausted body out into the early morning.

A lonely little dirt path caught tree-filtered sunlight, casting mesmerizing patterns in front of her. Crickets and frogs sang in the distance, somehow keeping rhythm with the changing patterns of light on the ground.

I changed into a squirrel. A squirrel.

"How is that even possible." She looked at her energy again. Brilliant rainbow colors danced within her. "What is happening to me?"

A flash of colorful lights stopped her on the path.

"Irida?" she whispered.

Flashes went off in the bushes to the left and she rushed in. Sabal palm fronds tore across her arms and legs but she barely noticed in the search for the lights. After a few painful minutes of trudging through dense brush, she pushed her way into a small, shaded clearing and found nothing. She searched the open area and under bushes and small trees lining the open spot, but the illumination was gone.

Finally crawling out of a bush, she sat back on her heels. "Irida? If you're here, just flash or something."

Her voice echoed briefly then died, replaced by the faint song of cicadas. Suddenly so very tired, she lay back and stared up, past the branches of the trees next to her, at the pale blue morning sky. She scratched at a tickle on her neck. Two more tickling sensations irritated her skin under her necklace and she glanced at her pendant as she scratched under the chain. The metal bird fluttered its wings and an I'iwi bird of shimmering, colorful light burst out of the pendant and flew in a circle above her. Color spun faster and faster, creating a dark circle just above her head that spread, blotting out her view of the sky. Despite the ominous circle, Eka stared, mesmerized by the colors as the circle descended and enveloped her as if she had passed through a dark mirror.

At first, everything seemed fuzzy, slightly out of focus, until she blinked and rubbed her eyes. She was still in the clearing. But the area seemed dim and surreal, like that starry night painting. At least that's what her foggy brain told her. Then the trees around her began to desiccate and turn to ash. Like the island she'd seen on the river. Her mushy brain noticed a faint chill go through her body.

As the last tree turned gray, a dark hole appeared at the edge of the clearing. This time she clearly felt her body go rigid with cold, the same coldness from outside Bander's. The hole grew from a small pinpoint to door sized, while just in front lay three objects. Objects that hadn't been there a moment before. She squinted, trying to shake her brain into gear and get a grip, but, before her brain could jostle awake, she found herself hovering just above the three objects.

I'm floating? Is this a dream?

She tried to look around but her gaze was fixed on the objects, now bright in the dim surroundings. The first one resembled the book Janice had taken and Eka's ghostly hand moved over it, almost of its own volition. When her fingers touched the surface of the book, light rolled over the cover and illuminated the missing parts of the script. With each new letter of light, pain shot into her senses, scraping her breath out. She recoiled from the book, floating without will, passing the middle object, to hover over to the last item. The pain subsided as she came into the light of two orbs of swirling colors. The spheres orbited one another as they floated above a pendant that resembled her own. With a blink of light the orbs stopped moving and became eyes. Eyes like Irida's. They opened and closed a few times then shifted to swirling, colorful lights that spiraled down into the pendant. Then she was moving again, to the middle object. A small circular piece of vine lay intertwined around a single shell and at the sight of it her breath stopped. She reached out to the shell. When her hand made contact, four heartbeats pulsed against the shell. Her family.

Her own heartbeat drummed rapidly.

Calm down. This is a dream and I'll wake up.

After all, she had been tired and probably just fell asleep in the clearing and was running through all the stuff she'd seen.

Okay then wake up.

A movement from the dark hole caught her attention. She hovered closer and another chill went through her. Before she could move, a hand reached out of the hole and grabbed the bracelet.

No!

She instinctively grabbed for it but the dark hand wrapped around her wrist, stopping her.

Eka.

The voice slithered through her mind as the misty hand pulled at her wrist and dragged her hovering form toward the black pit. She tried jerking her arm free, but her ghostly form seemed weak.

Just ignore the creepy voice.

I've been wanting to talk with you.

Creepy salesperson voice. Can't talk right now.

That's really all her mind could handle.

Irida shouldn't leave you open like this. I'll have to thank her.

Okay, wake up Eka. Wake up!

Don't be so hasty to leave. You're looking for answers to what happened to your family. I can help.

What?

The pendant laying under her erupted in brilliant light, overwhelming Eka's senses. A warmth spread through her, dissipating the burning chill. She reached for the bracelet she knew had been next to the pendant but the strange clearing began to fade. The dark opening receded along with the bright lights, the objects and the dead trees. Her ghost form flew back, slamming into her prone body.

As she lay there, her breath echoed through the clearing. Her wrist throbbed, her body vibrated and ached, but when she managed to touch her other wrist to find her bracelet still there, relief washed over her. And despite the pain and cold, her wrist had no marks. Tears streaked across her cheek as she touched the quiet shell tied in the vines. No heartbeats now.

"Bastard!" The word echoed through the woods as longing, frustration, and heartache welled up inside her. She jerked up and punched the ground. "Ow."

She shook out her hand and let the tears flow until there was nothing left and she finally gave in to a dreamless sleep.

"Eka."

A hand shook her and she blinked. Christelle stared down at her, shaking her awake.

"What?" Eka sat up.

"What happened to you?" Christelle asked as she dropped her hands.

Eka blanked for a moment, the words unscrambling at a turtle's pace. A dark hand, a book, eyes and a bracelet with multiple heartbeats.

Eka touched the still pendant. "I had a vision."

"Huh?"

"A vision." Eka focused on Christelle. "All the clues. The book, the pendant from Irida with hovering eyes, the bracelet. They were all in it. And coldness, like the cold coming off that bush that turned to ash. Ash like those trees on the…I know where to go!"

"You lost me."

"Irida sent a vision."

At least I hope it was Irida.

Eka held up a hand as Christelle opened her mouth to speak. "We've learned about secret magical communities, hidden memories, and magical humans. Just accept this new thing."

Christelle raised her hands in surrender and nodded. "Okay."

Eka explained her vision, as best she could, and Christelle's mouth fell more open with each word. At the end all Christelle could handle was to plop down next to Eka. "Wow."

"Yeah."

"You think Grams was right? Light and Shadow."

An image of Irida and Lintu fighting, with Eka and Christelle in the middle, swept over Eka and she shivered.

"What?" Christelle frowned.

Eka shook her head. "Crazy images of celestial fighting."

There was a moment of silence then Christelle nodded. "Oh."

Eka stood up, took a deep breath, then pulled her thoughts back to the vision as she brushed debris off her clothes and out of her hair. "Yeah. Anyway, there were ashy trees in the vision. Like the bush outside Bander's and that island I was at. I think the island might hold some clues."

"You know," Christelle stood and pulled a few lingering sticks out of Eka's hair, "this new wilderness look, not really working for you."

Eka put her hand on her hip and hitched it up then cradled her head with the other hand, smiling.

"No." Christelle shook her head.

Eka shrugged and started walking back out through the foliage, Christelle following.

"So, where's this island?"

"You'll see," Eka said as she plowed through some palms.

Christelle huffed behind her. "Don't be so secretive, Anise."

Eka stopped and turned. "Now that's just rude." She frowned at her friend. "So unlike you."

"I'm not rude. I've never complained about your snoring."

Eka opened her mouth in shock. "I'm not the one that snores."

"I think there were a couple of trees uprooting themselves and running," Christelle grinned.

Eka laughed, the lingering heaviness dissipating.

"So, about this island," Christelle reminded her.

Christelle plopped down in her chair. "We may have learned a lot, but I still feel like we're light years away from really understanding all this."

"Maybe it's like one of those murder mysteries, where it all makes sense after you get the answer."

Christelle grimaced. "Great. So we go out to the island and try to wing it, hoping that some creepy, murdery voice isn't there? Or crossing our fingers it's not a trap?"

Eka shrugged. "Maybe."

Across from her, Christelle stood and paced around the fire pit. "Sounds fun. Maybe we could follow that up by skydiving without a parachute onto a mattress."

Eka sighed. She had never wanted to see that island again. It had felt nothing but dangerous, now, though, it seemed linked to that book and her past. She shivered at the memory of that voice and the coldness from her vision. And it had said something about her family, if only she could remember. But she couldn't trust Lintu. And how could she drag Christelle into something that dangerous?

"I've got to go out there if there's even a chance that I could get some answers about what happened to my family. To me." She looked up at Christelle. "But maybe I should go alone."

Christelle stopped and stared at her.

"Do we have to go through this every time? This is an 'all in' thing." She crossed her arms. "Wherever the clues lead, we do this together."

Eka sighed again. "Anise could be right. I might not be a great influence on you and this might be a really bad idea."

Christelle grabbed Eka and shook her.

"Hey." Eka stepped back, holding her head as it whipped around.

"Get some sense. I love Anise but she doesn't know what I need or she'd have told me everything a long time ago. Regardless of the attack on my family." She frowned. "So, we both go. Period."

Eka smiled and nodded. "Okay. Two musketeers."

"Two sounds so sad."

"Thelma and Louise!"

They looked at each other and shook their heads.

"Maybe not for this trip. Definitely more a Xena and Gabrielle sort of adventure."

"Right. So, know where we can get a boat?"

Christelle smiled. "I think I know a guy."

Eka followed Chriselle to a dock where Bu and another man stood, next to a flats boat. The small, shallow water craft danced on the surface as the men addressed each other, hands flying around in frantic gestures.

"What'd you think is going on?"

Christelle shrugged. "I don't know."

They paused for a moment waiting for a break in the conversation.

"Gramps?" Christelle called out.

The men stopped and turned, Bu frowning a moment before a giant smile spread across his face. "Christelle!"

Christelle's shoulders relaxed and she walked down the dock, allowing Bu to wrap her in a bear hug.

He finally pushed her back a step and looked her up and down. "How are you?"

Christelle avoided his gaze, looking at the boat.

He sighed and turned to Eka.

"Hello, Eka."

"Hey Bu, how's things?"

"Good, good."

Silence hung around them until the other man spoke up.

"So, ya gonna introduce us?"

"Billy, this is my granddaughter Christelle and…" He paused and Christelle turned to her grandfather.

"The newest member of our community, Eka."

Christelle smiled and stepped closer to him, touching his arm briefly.

"Glad to meet ya." Billy nodded curtly before turning back to the water and yelling. "Sam, I know you're out there!"

Eka looked down the dock and back at Christelle who mouthed 'Who's Sam?'

Eka shrugged.

"Gramps." Christelle's voice was barely audible over the breeze. "Who's Sam?"

At that moment, a rounded tail rose up and hurled a bucket-sized amount of water at Billy and, before he could step away, drenched him. He stood there in silence for a few seconds as water dripped off him, his face slowly contorting into an angry scowl, his eyes narrowing to mere slits. When his mouth pressed briefly into a thin line, he held his fist up and shouted. "Your days are numbered, Sam!"

The water broke as a manatee flipper stood straight up into the air. Christelle's eyes widened at the shape of the flipper.

"I think Billy got that message," Eka laughed.

Billy grabbed a giant slingshot hooked to the dock. From a bucket, Billy took out a head of iceberg lettuce and placed it into the stretched rubber. He looked over the water then stretched back the rubber farther.

"Did you see that slingshot?" Eka asked Christelle before hoping over to Billy's side. "What'cha doin' with the lettuce?"

"Not now, I'm busy." Billy adjusted the slingshot then let the lettuce fly. Suddenly a flipper was back in the air, swinging toward the lettuce. The manatee lobbed the flying greens back, in a direct path with Billy's head, sending him sprawling backward on the dock. Eka nudged him with her foot but go nothing.

"I think he's okay."

Bu sighed and shook his head. "They do this all the time."

Christelle frowned. "Is he a Waker?"

"He's one of us but he doesn't have his gifts."

"Do you think he's happy?" Christelle asked. "I mean, we met some Wakers at Bob's without gifts and they seemed sad and maybe angry."

Bu looked out at the water. "There have always been a few of us that can't seem to be happy, gifts or not. Billy ain't one of them." He shook his head as if clearing thoughts and looked back at Eka and Chriselle. "I'm not trying to tell you what to do here, but I'm asking you to keep a distance from that group at Bob's. They usually find trouble wherever they go and blame others for that trouble."

Christelle nodded toward Billy's prone figure. "Well, Billy seems not so happy himself."

He laughed. "Billy's harmless; just a bit ornery. That guy would give you his last bit of food and the shirt off his back. He just likes people to think he's grumpy."

Christelle's shoulders relaxed and she squeezed Bu's hand. "Thanks for sharing Gramps."

He nodded. "We should have talked to you before. I didn't like hiding things, but I went along. So, I'm sorry for what I didn't do."

She grabbed him in a hug, squeezing until he coughed. "Love you Gramps."

He chuckled and hugged her back. "Love you too."

"So." Eka turned from Christelle and Bu to Billy, who was now sitting. "What's up with the lettuce?"

Billy shook his head. "Sam and his kind are destroying this river. Have been since they moved into the area."

A flipper hurled water at the dock, where it splashed onto everyone. Billy scowled. "That's right, you invasive pest. Stop killing the river grasses!"

He grabbed a head of lettuce and grinned then lowered his voice and leaned up toward Eka. "They hate lettuce."

Christelle glanced at Bu and he shrugged.

"So we told him a story that wasn't exactly true," Bu whispered to Christelle. "But trust me, the fight was far worse before. This way he stays out of trouble and they're happy." He pointed out toward the manatees.

As Billy struggled up, Eka grabbed the slingshot, rammed a lettuce in it and aimed.

"Sam, Billy's up!"

She released the lettuce and watched as the light green ball streaked out into the river.

"Woot woot!"

She quickly reloaded and loosed a second round before Billy grabbed the lettuce hurler from her.

"This is between Sam and me."

"Of course." Eka bowed and stepped away from the veggie launcher. Lowering her voice, she leaned toward Billy. "I could've sworn Sam was laughing when you fell."

Billy focused on the river while rubbing his head. "That's it Sam!"

He rained down a barrage of green on the water. When his assault was over, he surveyed the field of floating lettuce; not a manatee in sight. With a smile he walked back up the dock and, as he disappeared, a number of manatees surfaced, munching on the boon. Eka erupted in laughter, before nudging Christelle and nodding at the boat.

"Hey, Gramps, could we borrow the flats boat?"

"Sure. What'cha plannin'?"

Eka interjected. "We just thought a sunset ride would be a nice break from all the drama."

Bu narrowed his eyes as he looked between them, then shook off whatever thoughts were bothering him and walked to the boat. "Alright then."

He stepped on the deck of the boat and went to the dash. "Now you two pay attention. This here boat runs beautifully but needs a little TLC to get goin'."

Bu showed them how to jiggle the key to get the motor started and how to bang on the steering to get it moving. Eka looked at Christelle with raised eyebrows.

"You sure love this boat, Bu."

"Not many of us Wakers have machines, but this here boat and I, we've been through a lot." He patted the hull. "She's a survivor. Like us."

Eka and Christelle climbed aboard as he stepped off. And, after Christelle went through the starting routine, and the engine hummed to life, Bu gave a nod of approval. She put the boat in gear and pulled away from the dock and out into the channel.

"Thanks, Gramps." She waved at him. "See you soon and love ya."

"Love you too and take care."

They waved until Bu was a small, indistinct figure waving back from the little dock. As they putted down the river, and away from the known, images of a dark, dead island invaded Eka's thoughts of the vision and what they might be walking into.

What Were We Thinking?

Christelle gazed at the shimmering water. Pelicans glided just above the surface while a lone osprey hovered over potential prey. "Wonder what we'll find," she mumbled, more to herself than anything around her, but glanced back at Eka anyway.

Behind her Eka trailed her hand through the water. "Don't know. Maybe nothing." Eka glanced up at Christelle. "But I feel like there's a reason I had that vision today. I really feel it was hinting about the island."

"Does it feel like we're being led around? Like all of this is someone's plan we're following?"

Eka swirled her hand in the river a moment then nodded. "Yeah. Feels like Gaia, Irida and this Lintu are kinda pulling our strings." Eka burst out in a brief laugh. "Now that's something I never dreamed I'd say. The spirit of a planet and other outer space things are playing chess and I'm one of the pieces. Wow."

"I hadn't thought of it like that. That's definitely 'wow'." She'd been so concentrated on her family she hadn't really thought of the bigger players. Did she believe in these 'people'? She believed Eka and Eka had met Irida, so…maybe. If they were real, what were the connections between everyone? What were their motivations? Where did she and Eka fit in?

"Do you have any guesses at what's going on?"

Eka cocked her head to the side and shrugged. "If what Shirley told us is true, then we seem to be involved in some major power struggle between planetary spirits. But I have no idea about the why. Of course, it's Shirley, so who knows."

"I can't believe Anise is still hiding things. How am I supposed to protect myself from planets and spirits from outer space if I don't even know what's going on?"

"Did you just hear what you said?" Eka giggled. "'Spirits from outer space'."

Christelle grinned. "You're right. That's so MST3K movie stuff."

"I love that show!"

Christelle and Eka drifted through memories of silly shows and for a moment all Christelle's worries were forgotten.

"I suppose it's too out there even for Wakers." Christelle slumped.

"Yeah. Maybe Anise and the others just couldn't wrap their heads around this universe-sized problem, so they hid and looked for an easier answer to explain the destruction. To keep you safe."

"Well, great job. Here I am, headed to a spooky island, based on a creepy vision."

Eka nodded slightly and stared back at her hand as it made trails in the water. Christelle turned back to the front.

Was this a good idea? Maybe not, but there weren't really any other options, not if she still wanted to know what the danger really was.

As the sun set, a large, full moon rose to illuminate the river, it's light quickly replacing the sunlight as a guide. They puttered languidly along, night sounds floating over the gentle purr of the engine like an owl calling out from the shore and receiving a lonely reply. The avian exchange eventually faded into the rhythm of the lapping waves.

Christelle looked toward the trees and the fading sounds of owls. "What do you think they're saying?"

"Who?" Eka smiled.

Christelle's face soured. "Very funny."

"It was." Eka grinned louder. "Thanks."

Christelle's more quiet grin just peeked out. "Whatever."

They continued on in the quiet fall night, gentle waves and distant shore sounds surrounding them. Suddenly, Eka jerked upright, knocking a towel off the bench. Christelle could see the goosebumps running across her arms.

"You okay?"

Eka shook her head and caught Christelle's gaze. "I don't know, something feels close. I think we've got to be extra careful on this one."

Christelle nodded and went back to steering, a shiver finding it's way up her spine. Was this really the only option? Maybe they had missed a clue that would lead somewhere else.

Then they came to a Y in the waterway.

Christelle looked left. The moon cast its partial image across this branch of the river, the reflection rippling down the length of it.

Then she faced right, a path of shadows.

Please be left.

"Can you remember which way we should go?"

Eka scanned both ways then pointed right. "This way."

Christelle steered to the right and the boat lazily swung around. After a few moments moving through increasing darkness, Eka led them into another smaller channel off to the left, the boat lights and moonlight barely able to find the path through the crowded islands and deep shadows. They jerked to a stop as the boat beached itself on a sandbar. Without disrupting the pressing shadows and silence, Eka grabbed the pole and pushed while Christelle worked the engine to aid her movements.

"Come on," she whispered to herself as she timed their movements with the pole, but even that whisper seemed to echo through the darkness. Inky water swirled around them as the boat rocked back and forth. Would they have to get in the water to push?

Her body shuddered and silently willed the boat to go.

Please move.

"Christelle, maybe you can use magic stuff to move us." Eka's voice seemed to come from a megaphone in the deep silence.

Christelle snapped out of her creep-out. Why hadn't she thought of that? All of this was so new it probably wasn't instinctual yet.

And this place is freaking me out.

She slowly slid her hand in the water and let her energy flow.

Get us out of here, please!

The thought was more desperate than she'd wanted and the blue energy responded, raising the water and throwing them off the sandbar. Eka and the pole were hurled off the back as Christelle stumbled to the back of the boat.

"Whoa!" Eka shouted as she came up for air. "Can't see anything in here."

Christelle leaned over the back and grabbed the pole from Eka as she climbed onto the boat. "Sorry."

"Your magic is getting better." Eka gave her a thumbs up before squeezing water out of her clothes and hair; the little shake out spraying Christelle.

Barely noticing the water as she absently brushed it off, Christelle still couldn't raise her voice above a whisper. "I was just a little freaked out."

Eka looked around them. "Yeah. Kinda foreboding."

"That's a word." Christelle grinned for the first time in this warm, humid, dark, very silent area.

Moving on down the river passage, lined with mangroves, their way narrowed even further as they navigated mainly with their small front lights through a myriad of islands. Islands that seemed to lean toward her; vegetation reaching out from the shores and over the narrowing path, blocking out the sky even more. Maybe this was a beautiful natural area, but all Christelle wanted was to get out.

This is a stupid idea!

Just as she was about to turn around, and probably scream out loud, they rounded another island and an empty coldness rolled over her from a gray mass ahead.

"There." Eka pointed.

A shadowed island squatted in the middle of the surrounding islands, which seemed to bend and twist away from it. The water calmed to glass around the shore while moonlight faded around it, leaving the island an almost hole in the landscape. Christelle sat unmoving, queasy dread roiling in her stomach as her mind tried to shape the island into something resembling normal.

This is crazy! That thing is wrong!

She took a deep breath and steadied her hands.

Okay, okay. You chose to be here. Follow this through or go home and quit.

She put the boat in gear and turned them toward the island. The boat moved sluggishly, as if reluctant to reach their goal.

They finally made shore despite the boat's resistance, and the hull slid up onto the sand. Christelle stared, frozen, as the sand floated up into the air, like dust motes, and the boat slid back off the disappearing shore and into the water. A piece of the floating sand landed on Christelle's arm, a cold gray whisper she rubbed off quickly, leaving just a light streak across her skin. Ash.

Something resembling trees stood ahead on the fragile shore, but their shadowed shapes were distorted within the tiny amount of moonlight. She squinted at the silhouette tops, then stumbled back a step at the flatness across them. A small breeze touched the crowns, or where the crowns should have been, and swirls kicked up, like fall leaves in gusty wind. But these weren't leaves. The edges of those crowns smoothed as bits of them blew away, creating a shorter shadow, as if someone were erasing bits from the tops. The reality fought with her expectations of complete trees and her mind slipped away from the disintegrating shadows. Just past those silhouettes, blackness enfolded the interior, a seeming fortress against the moonlight.

Christelle turned and met Eka's eyes. "I…I don't feel any energy."

Eka turned back to the isolated landscape. "I think it's all dead." Without a moment to consider what that meant, Eka lowered herself out of the boat. Taking the cue, and before her fears turned her back, Christelle turned off the boat and stepped through the shallow water and onto the ashy sand, sinking a few inches. She stood for a moment to let her eyes adjust to the lack of boat lights. Just a small bit of moonlight.

Everything is dead. Nothing left to hurt you.

Eka waded forward through the still water while Christelle shivered as ash floated into the air.

The ash won't hurt you. And please be true.

Christelle took a long, deep breath and started after Eka. Her own footsteps were only a muffled thump that stirred up the ashy sand. A branch, lying on the beach, crumbled to greasy powder when she tried to pick it up. Ahead of her, Eka's dark outline seemed to be swallowed by the distorted tree silhouettes. Christelle gulped and trudged into the shadows after her.

The trees were the same ashen, flaky gray as the sand. She paused in front of one of the lifeless trunks and ran her hand down the bark. It crumbled away from her touch, shooting intense cold through her fingertips. She jerked her hand back and hurried after Eka, skirting the ghostly remnants around her.

"Eka." Her voice barely made it to her own ears. "Maybe we should get help."

Ahead of her, Eka turned back. "It's fine if you want to stay with the boat."

Alone?

Still shivering, she shook her head and sped past Eka. "I'm fine," she whispered.

An ashen landscape surrounded them. As they wiggled through a dense strand of ash trees, Christelle contorted to keep from touching them.

What had happened here?

Then, through the darkness ahead, she caught sight of a flickering glow. She turned to announce what she had seen but Eka put a finger to her lips and slowed to a snail's pace. Christelle mimicked Eka as she crouched, trying to avoid skin contact with anything while creeping closer to the glow. A clearing opened ahead. A woman sat in the center of it, barely visible in the moonlight.

Janice.

Christelle leaned over to Eka and whispered. "She's here. Your vision was right."

Eka stared, mesmerized.

A movement on the far side of Janice caught Christelle's attention and she squinted as a figure emerged. Her eyes and mouth opened wide as Wallace walked up to Janice. Eka nudged her and she turned and shook her head, not sure what to say.

"Wallace, how much longer? We've been waiting forever," Janice sighed.

"I don't know. But he said tonight, so we wait."

Janice frowned. "What do you think's in the book? I mean, everyone seems to want it."

Wallace sat next to Janice. "I'm not sure, but it's our key out of limbo. I'm not going back to that giftless life and neither should any of the others. And soon all of those *Wakers*," his voice charged with disgust at the one word, "will learn to listen. They'll have no choice and neither will all the stupid life around us. Nothing will be able to ignore us any longer."

Janice frowned. "But you won't hurt anyone, right?"

He shook his head and focused on her. After a moment he sighed then put his arm around Janice. "I just want us to have a place. The place we deserve." He gave her shoulder a squeeze. "And what about your happiness? You deserve to be with your daughter."

Janice wiped at her face. "I still don't see how this is possible. How could she be alive?"

Wallace stepped around to face Janice. "I don't know, but if he can't keep his promise, we'll leave. But, he did get my gifts working somewhat." Wallace seemed to loose focus on Janice and muse to himself. "I mean, whoever heard of a gift working even if there is no connection. Just pure force. Sure it takes a lot of energy but I can *make* things happen. Think of the possibilities."

"Wallace?" Janice frowned at him.

He shook his head and refocused on her again. "So, with that kind of power, maybe he does know something about Lillian."

Christelle sat on the ground and pulled Eka down next to her. "I can't believe Wallace is involved," she whispered.

Eka only nodded, staring at the two figures.

"Are you okay?"

Eka shook her head, then put her forehead in her palms. "I can't believe I was so stupid to trust Wallace."

Christelle frowned. "You didn't know he'd do this." She looked at the two figures and wondered exactly what *this* was.

"No." Eka shook her head again. "I just thought he had an answer to what was going on with me. Now look." She pointed at the two. "He's helped someone steal deadly information for who knows what reason. And his magic is bullshit."

Christelle looked back to the campfire. Wallace held Janice, comforting her. "It looks like he still cares. Maybe we could talk to them." She started to stand but Eka pulled her back.

"I think we should wait to see who shows up. We can't know what they'll do. Besides, others from the community may be involved. Let's just find out and let Shirley and Bu know."

Christelle studied Eka. Her body sagged and her face seemed to contort in pain. She'd never seen her like this.

"Fine," Eka mumbled.

Christelle looked back at the campfire and Janice and Wallace. Questions swirled around in her head. Why would Janice, or Wallace, do something like this? I mean, the community took care of them, didn't hide things from them. And who could possibly help Janice with her baby? She really hoped it wasn't Lintu.

My head hurts.

They watched for a while. Christelle started to doze and leaned back, then her hands slipped into cold, slimy ash and she started. Of course, just when she was finally tired.

How am I tired here?

She sat up and swiped at the cold, ghostly, floating reminders of the death all around her, then pulled her knees up and rested her head on her arms. And strangely, dozed off, again. Dark shadows, killer books, and a sea of familiar, but somehow unfamiliar, faces swirled through her head until she woke to Eka shaking her.

She scanned around her, groggy and confused. "Where…"

Eka's hand shot out and covered her mouth. She frowned and Eka pointed at two figures, past the bushes they crouched in.

Wallace was standing, staring into the dark brush. She suddenly remembered where she was and peeled Eka's hand off her face then mouthed 'what's happening?'. Eka shook her head and mouthed 'Just started' back to her. Squinting at the dim scene, to a spot past Wallace, the shadows seemed to deepen and a cold wave rolled across her. She hugged her body closer and glanced at Eka's pale face.

"Eka?" Christelle whispered. Eka continued to stare, not responding.

"Wallace?" Janice stood, spinning in half-circles, searching, as a shadowy haze flowed out of the ashy treeline and spread over the open area.

"Just stay where you are, Janice. It'll be okay," Wallace answered, voice barely audible.

The haze swirled slowly around the two then spiraled over to a single spot near them, swirling up into a column devoid of any moonlight. The column shuddered as hazy branches twisted and turned from the center, contorting into arms, legs, a torso, and a head. The somehow featureless, yet humanoid, form grew more solid. But, when Christelle tried to focus on it, it seemed as if it wasn't there at all; her eyes blurred and slid away from it.

Wallace stepped in front of Janice. "We have what you want."

Good.

The voice came from inside Christelle's head, grating inside her and churning up her energy.

"First, you need to keep your end," Janice squeaked out.

Wallace glared at Janice, then turned back to the form. "We, uh, we were promised an exchange."

Yes.

Dark haze flowed out of the figure and around Wallace, who didn't seem to be able to move. The haze wrapped around some of Wallace's blue-green grayish energy and pulled it out, like a thread from a seam, then flowed back into the shadowy form, while Wallace slumped next to Janice.

"Eka…"

Before the rest of the whisper left her mouth, the torso of the figure seemed to rip open and the scene wavered, as though reality stumbled, and Christelle bent over, her stomach roiling. A flat square flew out of the dark split and Janice stumbled over to it as it floated to the ground. She kneeled down beside it, holding her stomach.

"It can't be." One hand covered her mouth and she hesitantly reached out with the other one, touching the square. Wallace, awake but wobbly, crawled to her side, watching the there-but-not-there figure the whole time. He glanced down and his eyebrows shot up.

"Janice, is that your daughter?"

Janice nodded. "I feel her." She turned to Wallace. "Do you feel it too?"

Wallace placed his hand on Janice's shoulder. "Sure."

She turned back as the square flew from her hand and hovered, spinning like a diamond in front of her. It shimmered then jerkily expanded in all directions, like silly putty stretched by invisible hands, until it was the size of a door. But it was an image and it moved. In it, a young woman in a dress stood inside it, smiling and waving at Janice.

Janice scooted on her knees until she could touch the image. From within, the woman placed her fingers against Janice's.

"She's really here. I can actually feel her fingers." Janice didn't seem to be speaking to anyone but herself at this point.

Wallace frowned. "I know this is what you wanted," he wheezed, "but be careful."

She nodded as her fingers intertwined with her daughter's. Wallace looked back at the shadowy figure.

"What did you do to me?"

His question died in a silenced that stretched on and on.

"No answers? Fine. But you promised my people their gifts. And I know you can do that without stealing…anything from me. If I got the book, translated it, you said you'd show me how to keep our gifts."

Yes. The book first and I will show you.

Wallace reached into Janice's bag, now discarded on the ground, and pulled out a book. Behind him, Janice moved closer to the image of her daughter, a smile spreading across her face. Then, Janice actually stepped into the picture and her form shimmered briefly before the young woman embraced her.

"What's in this book anyway?" Wallace asked shakily, glancing between Janice and the misty figure.

Did you not look?

Wallace nodded toward Janice. "Too busy keeping her hidden and not letting those Wakers," he spat the word again, "find her or the book."

You will know soon but this form is difficult to occupy. Now, the book.

Behind Wallace, the picture shimmered again and Janice frowned, looking around. She tried to walk out, but seemed to slam into a wall. She was trapped. Wrapping her arms around her daughter and shouting at Wallace, her voice barely made it out of the image. Unfortunately, Wallace was flipping through the book and didn't notice, even when the image began to collapse into itself, shrinking. Janice's eyes widened as everything inside the image shrunk but her and her daughter.

"She needs help." Christelle's whisper was loud now, but Eka didn't notice. She was almost in a trance, mesmerized by the scene playing out.

Okay, she's gonna be useless.

Christelle's heart raced. Wallace wasn't even looking at Janice, just staring at that stupid book.

Janice curled into a ball around her daughter, as her artificial world grew smaller and pain contorted her face. Both women were crying. A surge of anger bubbled up in Christelle; she swallowed and stood up.

"Wallace! Janice needs help!"

Wallace spun to glance at Christelle then to Janice. He stared at the shrinking image, Janice pressed on all sides, nothing else visible.

"Janice?" He turned back to the figure. "What are you doing? Stop!" He ran to the image and clawed at it, but the contracting continued until it was no bigger than a postage stamp, a faint scream echoing through the area before fading. He stumbled away from it, squeezing his eyes shut briefly. Then his body went rigid and his face contorted. "You killed her!"

I cannot control the permanence of these things, they anomalies. But I kept the deal. The book.

"No!" Wallace slung the bag over his body and shoved the book into it. He glared up at the form. "You killed her!"

Dark haze slithered out from the bottom of the form toward Wallace. "No!" Christelle shouted.

The haze stopped and the form turned toward Christelle. She sucked in her breath as Wallace side-stepped, disappearing unnoticed into the treeline.

You are too weak to stop me, child.

"I'm not a child!" Christelle raised her hand, closed her eyes and reached out to the energy around her. Nothing happened.

There's no life here for your powers to work with.

The form shimmered and a force slammed into Christelle, reaching deep into her. Clawing and ripping, it ran through her, pulling her energy out of her and toward it.

You are stronger than I thought. Thank you.

She fell to the ground and was sure she was screaming, her essence starting to fray into tattered shreds. Her hearing grew muffled and she couldn't breathe as her chest and stomach seemed to be pulled out of her body. Even her legs, always reliable, weren't available to crawl away. Her heart thumped a beat as a painful, oily voice stretched and dragged over her until she was curled up into a ball. Was she still screaming or could she still hear Janice? Her heart beat again and hazy laughter ripped through her, tearing apart her soul.

Then a hand, maybe Eka's, reached down beside her in a slow-motion arc. It grabbed at the ashy ground, gray bits flying all around. Then ash became rain. As the rain grew thick and shiny, the tearing and pulling stopped and the voice finally faded.

Her lungs strained for air as every movement sent shock waves through her. The faint remnant of her energy still there, blew in tattered strips within the vast emptiness inside her. She dragged herself up on all fours, ghostly pain ripping through her at every move, and squinted up at a shiny clear dome in front of her. Dark haze flowed around outside it and there was Eka, kneeling beside her. Eka shook Christelle, yelling something she couldn't hear, or understand, and pointing at the ground. A long gray board lay next to her. When she looked back up Eka was pushing her on it. Christelle, every movement a disconnected motion, rolled onto the board and it rose up, hovering, as Eka pulled it out of the camp area and into the ashen trees.

"Christelle." Eka's voice seemed far away but she could finally understand it.

Christelle rolled her head and looked back. The shiny dome seemed to hover over them as they moved. Nauseating sounds came from within trees behind them. Was there a monster there? She seemed to remember one.

Her head rolled back as real time caught up. Eka was pulling her on the hovering board through the forest, knocking out ash-chunks of trees as she ran and the sounds of a monster seemed to fade behind them. They broke through to the beach and she saw the boat off to the left as Eka sped up. They were almost to the boat when a shimmer went over them. A wave of energy hit and the board under her crumbled to ash and dropped her on the beach with a muted thud as the dome disappeared. Eka dropped to her knees and a guttural yell exploded inside the forest.

Fear erupted in every cell as Christelle pulled herself up on jelly legs. Eka grabbed her arm and dragged her, stumbling, to the boat and shoved her over the side then hopped in after. Eka's body, or Eka, Christelle's mind couldn't decide, ran to the controls, banging and jiggling until the the engine turned over. Once the engine had caught, she gunned it away from shore. Christelle flew back, rolling without control, then slammed to a stop; the boat was stuck.

Was there a sandbar when they came here? Maybe? Her mind grasped at memories of how they had gotten here.

Turning slowly back to the beach, Christelle watched as the whole treeline disintegrated and a dark form flowed out, heading toward them.

"Move, damnit!" Eka's muffled yell flowed over and past her while the boat thrummed under her, jerking backward and forward. As the boat rolled, the sounds and sights began to make sense. Her memories came back just as the form ripped and expanded. It was somehow pulling her remaining energy out of her again. Breath racing, she held herself up with shaking hands. Up front, Eka revved the engine again and the boat slammed into reverse. The little boat flew backward in an arc, passing within feet of the figure.

"Eka!"

Eka glanced at her, eyes widening briefly then slamming closed as her face contorted in concentration. A shimmering, transparent wall rose up around the boat and Eka collapsed to the deck. The clawing and pulling inside Christelle suddenly stopped. She sucked in a breath and focused on the island. On shore, a shimmering dome surrounded the figure. Saving all the analyzing and understanding for later, Christelle tumbled forward with a surge of adrenaline, to take control of the boat. She slammed the controls into gear and the boat gunned and jerked forward, nearly missing another island. They flew through the narrow waterway, barely avoiding obstacles, until they broke through to the main channel.

After driving for an eternity at full speed, Christelle finally slowed the boat and sat back on the cushion, disoriented at the emptiness inside her. She turned toward Eka, who was sitting next to her, holding a small, blank square.

"Is that...?"

Eka stared at the image. "That thing killed her. In a picture it had created."

Christelle heard a rumbling and turned back toward the island. Small waves rushed toward them and, as the waves hit the hull, a rumbling wave of energy rocked the boat. Christelle guessed that the forgotten, transparent wall collapsed.

After they steadied themselves, Eka brought her knees up and dropped her head in her arms. "My magic," she murmured.

"What?" Christelle looked over at her.

Eka didn't respond and Christelle was too tired to ask again as she lay back against the seat. With the little energy she had left, she headed the boat in the direction of Bu's dock. A hollow cavern was now all she felt inside except for the fluttering from the tattered remains of her essence.

Am I the Sum or the Parts?

"What were you thinking!"

Anise looked directly at Christelle, then turned to Eka. "And you, taking her."

"Anise." Ben placed his hands on her shoulders. "Calm down, it's not helping."

She shook him off, trembling. "There are Wakers being murdered, Ben. And she just wandered right into the center of it."

"Okay." He soothed her and she collapsed into his arms crying.

Eka looked over at Shirley, but she just shook her head. Next to her, Bu stood with his arms crossed. Eka's body still shook, even after eighteen hours of sleep. She glanced at Christelle's tear stained-face and guessed she'd slept less.

"We didn't know this would happen. We thought it was Janice and Wallace, maybe other…people." Christelle looked past Eka to Shirley, pleading.

"Why would they make a deal with that thing!" Bu went rigid, fists banging on the table.

"Yes," Anise addressed the gathering, "someone who had been accepted into our community, who suddenly got their gifts." She held up the paper with the strange energy signature, a piece of paper that used to be a picture. "And is connected to gifts that no Waker should have." She turned to Eka. "Sound like anyone here?"

Christelle shook her head and whispered. "Eka is not like Wallace. She saved my life!"

"After putting your life in danger!" Anise yelled. Ben pulled her back slightly and shook his head.

How did *I protect us?*

Eka looked at her hands, turning them over and over.

How did I change that ash into a dome around that creature? How did it hold at all? How did it stop Lintu's attack? Was *that Lintu?*

Eka looked at the group, the pounding in her skull competing with the ache of every muscle in her body and the emotional grating of Anise's words. "I've told you guys everything I know. I'm exhausted."

Devlon sat quietly nearby.

"Eka." Christelle looked at her, but all Eka saw was the ghost of her friend.

Eka gave a small nod, then stood and hurried out the door before the conversation resumed. Devlon followed, shadowing her but not trying to stop her. At her truck she spun and faced him.

"What?"

"I…Are you okay?"

She stared at him. A flash of Janice inside a shrinking picture, a dead island made of ash, and Christelle passed out in pain all swirled in her head. Adrenaline surged through her.

"No! No, I'm not okay! Janice is dead and some *thing* killed her!" Something with an energy that felt familiar. "And Christelle…"

She slumped back against the truck, dropping her head in her palms.

Devlon stood silently away from her. She slowed her breath and let the adrenaline wane. "There's not even a body to bury."

"What?"

"Janice," she leaned back and rubbed her face, "there's no body to bury."

Devlon's tense shoulders relaxed. "There's never a body in the Waker community."

Her breath halted and she stared at him. "You destroy bodies?"

"No," he shook his head. "It's, well our bodies just, kinda return to the earth, in about a day."

"Oh," she rolled her eyes. "Waker stuff. Lucky you."

She looked up at the stars. The same stars that had witnessed everything she had, just a day ago. What did they think of it? Of her? She dropped her head down. "What if that's what my gift really is? Like that picture."

He stood, unmoving. She stared at him. "Go ahead and finish for me. Abnormal, wrong, dangerous, evil?" She pushed off the truck and bumped him.

He stumbled back as she swung her door open. "No," he shook his head, "that's not what I'm saying."

She hopped in the cab and slammed the door, sticking her head out the window. "You're not saying anything. I'll tell you what, why don't you get back to me when all of you have figured out what's happened and how to deal with me?"

She slammed the keys into the ignition, her hands shaking as she shifted into gear. Peeling out, she watched Devlon fade away in the rear-view mirror.

What happened out on that island? That thing had taken energy from Wallace and changed reality. And she had felt it happening. A familiar tingle. The inside-out feeling.

My magic can't be like that. Can it?

She pulled into her campsite and stomped inside, then collapsed into bed. With every minute of every hour, the scenes on the island dug deeper into her essence, seeming more and more like her own, unexplained magic. The words 'weird' and 'wrong' kept popping up in her mind. And what was that thing? Lintu? Was it from the same place as Irida? Where part of her energy came from? When it arrived on the island, she'd frozen at the familiar feel of its energy. So like her own. If Christelle hadn't screamed, what would she have done? Just sat there and let it kill Christelle? She pushed her face into the pillow, trying to shut out the thoughts.

"Just sleep!"

But instead, she tossed for hours more. When muted light illuminated the shutters of her camper, her head still pounded and her mind still swirled with the events on the island. Finally, she pulled herself up and shouted to the vardo.

"Screw this!"

Eka jumped out of bed and rushed outside. She grabbed her stuff from around the campsite and shoved it in the camper then hooked the vardo to the truck. Inside the cab, images of Christelle flashed through her mind and her adrenaline subsided, replaced with sadness. Even the thought of leaving Devlon held regret. She had to say something, so she gripped the steering wheel with shaking hands then took a deep breath and relaxed her death-hold and leaned over to the glove box. Behind the three pairs of gas station sunglasses, travel tissues, a tattered U.S. map and lip gloss, she found a crumpled-up napkin and a pen missing its cap. Carefully spreading out the napkin on the seat beside her, she started composing.

~~Dear Devlon,~~
~~Devlon~~
~~Hey~~
~~I'm out~~

"Damnit!" She looked down and shook out her hand.

Look,
I'm sorry. Really. I guess all this was too much-
whatever. But I had fun and you were great.
Have a great life,
Eka

She folded the napkin and wrote his name on the back. Then stared at it before starting the truck.

This is the right thing to do. I can't put her…anyone in danger. What if the energy in me turns out like that…thing.

She flashed to the picture shrinking with Janice.

This is definitely the right thing to do.

The drive over to Christelle's house was a blur. When she finally realized where she was, she had to slam on the breaks, skidding to a stop in the front drive.

"Calm down. Don't spaz out."

A few deep breaths later, which really did nothing but bring her close to hyperventilating, she grabbed the note and ran to Christelle's window.

She banged on the glass until she noticed Christelle standing with her hands over her ears just on the other side. Eka gasped at her paleness as Christelle opened the window and looked out.

"Eka?"

Christelle's voice seemed faint and fragile. Eka sucked in her tears then looked down to her note. "Um. Hey."

"Hey."

Eka inhaled deeply and placed the note on the sill, avoiding Christelle's eyes. "Listen, could you give this to Devlon? I'm not sure where he is but…"

Christelle's gaze wandered out to the truck and vardo. "You're leaving?"

Eka looked up and nodded, spinning her bracelet.

"You're way better off without me." She turned, looking at the distant oaks. "I almost got you killed. Anise is right."

"Eka." Christelle reached out. "This wasn't you. Please, you can't go."

Eka looked up at Christelle's pale, empty gaze. She wanted to give Christelle a hug and grow more crazy plants and discover more magic. But magic had got them here. And magic like hers almost killed Christelle. She pulled her hand away and stepped back.

"You need their help. Your family. I can't…"

She turned and ran back to the truck. She spun the tires as she pulled out, nearly flipping the vardo in the same spot she'd crashed the night she'd arrived.

Focus, damn it!

Blaring music to keep out the thoughts, she drove until her head fell forward, hours later. When she jerked awake, the truck was slowly driving over the shoulder and off the road. Rolling to a stop, she found a nearby RV park that had spaces, according to her phone (always a risky proposition with camping sites), and she snagged a secluded spot in the woods.

Hey, sometimes the phone isn't messing around.

She grabbed a sandwich and some wine from the RV shop then ate and showered before passing out in exhaustion.

Darkness surrounded her as she tried to run toward the closing door.

Coldness spread up her legs and slammed her movement to a crawl. A light tinkling sound tickled her ears.

Eka. You are not like It. You are needed. You must go back.

Two rainbow eyes opened in front of her and the cold in her body receded. She reached toward the swirling lights and blinked then morphed to brown. The tinkling took on a deeper, earthy tone. A familiar tone.

"Eka."

She blinked awake to brown eyes smiling down at her. A brown hand reached out to her cheek and caressed her face. Eka jerked awake and grabbed the hand. "Sema?"

The woman lowered herself to sit next to Eka and smoothed back Eka's hair. "Hello, little bird."

Eka leaned into her grandmother. All her tension jumped ship, her body finally relaxing as Sema ran her hand along her hair, like she did when Eka was a child. As the tension let go, sadness poured through Eka releasing a damn of tears. She clutched her grandmother's hand and pressed her face against Sema's palm. Sema sat quietly, running her other hand through Eka's hair until Eka's shaking and sobbing stopped. After a long while, Eka finally rolled over, hiccuping as Sema ran a warm damp towel across her face and cupped her cheek.

"You all good now?"

Eka nodded and Sema brushed a few straggling tears away.

"Okay then. I think we need some waves."

Eka smiled.

"Well? Get your bum up, we're going."

"Okay." Eka sat up and looked out a window. "Is there a beach around here?"

"No, but I know a perfect spot close by." She held up the keys. "I'm driving."

Eka narrowed her gaze at Sema. "I don't remember you driving much."

"I know," she smiled. "I feel like a kid every time I'm behind the wheel."

Eka barely had time to blink before Sema hopped out of the vardo. Eka threw on her jacket and ran after her, just managing to seatbelt herself in before Sema started the truck and spun out the tires. Sema laughed, plowing out of the campground and barely missing the curb. When they finally found the highway and the road straightened, Sema's driving calmed down and Eka let herself drift off into a quiet sleep, no dreams or voices disturbing her.

She shook awake as they pulled into a small RV park, Sema attempting to hit every bump and curb in their vicinity.

"Sema." Eka stared out the window, more rested and relaxed. "Think you missed that curb back there."

"Just saving it till tomorrow."

Eka finally laughed. A heaviness she hadn't known was weighing on her had lifted. She leaned over and hugged her grandmother.

Sema hugged her back, taking both hands off the wheel and letting the truck head for the fence.

"Sema!"

"Okay, okay." Sema turned the truck back onto the road. "Feel like eating?" Her eyebrows wiggled. "I brought my favorite finger food."

Eka forgot the driving as her stomach soured. She pictured her fridge and what she could pull together quickly. "Oh, no worries. I've got something that's quick."

Sema frowned. "Okay, if you're sure?"

Eka nodded vigorously. The drive was surprisingly short and, as soon as they got to their camp, she ran into the vardo to throw together an impromptu meal. Meanwhile, Sema pulled out camping gear and soon they had a fire and dinner under a blanket of stars.

Staring into the flames, Eka tried to imagine all of the magic and darkness as part of a different life, focusing on her childhood. She was little again and traveling with Sema and Win. Her only worry was not getting caught as she snuck out.

"Sema."

"Yes?"

"How did you find me in that campsite?"

Sema smiled and patted her hand. "I have a very good Eka radar." She took her granddaughter's hand and placed it on the ground. "Close your eyes."

Eka looked at her hand against the earth. "Why?"

Sema smiled. "Just trust me."

Eka shrugged and closed her eyes.

"Now relax your mind and think of me."

Eka pictured Sema sitting next to her, an image of what she had seen just a second ago. A warm feeling expanded in the image and Eka felt the location of her grandmother in her chest. Her breath caught as she felt her grandmother stand and move around; images of her grandmother's activities soon played in her head like a movie. Eka remembered all the times she thought she'd found a way to elude her grandparents only to find them waiting for her at curfew in the weirdest spots. She opened her eyes, already looking at the spot where Sema stood.

"You always could find me."

Sema nodded and laughed.

"But, how? Can everyone do this? I mean Wakers."

Sema sat back next to Eka. "Communication happens through the heart. By choice. And anyone can choose to be connected like that." She sighed. "I always wanted to tell you these things. Show you our world. And I'm so sorry I couldn't." She shook her head. "What happened to you was wrong. You are a beautiful person, kind and caring, always fitting in everywhere you went. You should have grown up in our world." She shifted her gaze to the fire and stirred the waning flame. "But your energy was different after…the accident. And not everyone is comfortable with different."

Eka leaned forward. "Different how?"

Sema shook her head and kept poking the fire. "I don't know. Your energy; it just feels foreign."

An image of the island, the creature with the familiar energy, and Janice dying flew into her mind.

"Was I the reason they died?" Eka blurted out. "Mom, Dad, Ke?"

Her grandmother spun toward Eka, looking directly in her eyes and grabbed her hand. "No. Whatever happened, you were a victim as much as your family. And this strange energy? Well, it may be a part of you, but it doesn't define you. No one's energy does. I know who you are." She tapped Eka's chest. "Your heart is beautiful."

Sema ran her hand down Eka's cheek.

Eka sat rigidly, listening as she squeezed the end of an armrest.

"There's something wrong." Eka turned toward the fire. "Maybe you *should* be afraid of me."

Sema hit the fire hard, bringing Eka's attention back from her thoughts.

"You have never done anything that I'm not proud of. When Ses…" she looked up, "when we lost her, I thought…felt…"

She turned her head away, wiping at her face. It was Eka's turn to comfort Sema, so she squeezed her grandmother's hand. Sema coughed then turned back. "You are the joy of our lives and we were fortunate that you came to live with us. Being a Waker doesn't mean you're perfect. There are plenty that are judgmental, short-sighted, and down right mean." She leaned forward and nudged Eka. "Especially your other grandparents." She winked. "I think they have sticks up their asses, but don't quote me on that."

Eka burst into laughter, joined by her grandmother.

Sema finally stood and doused the last of the fire as the sky lightened. "I need some sleep. I've got to kick your butt in surfing tomorrow."

"Yeah, we'll see."

Eka woke a second time to Sema's prompting. "Wake up, little bird. Time for some waves."

She rubbed her eyes and looked at her phone. Five pm. "Okay, okay."

She dragged herself up, stumbling around for coffee. The first sip slowly ran down her throat, energizing her whole body. Like that first morning of magic, with Christelle. A pang hit her in the heart,

Stop it.

She set the cup down and threw on her swimsuit. When she finally walked outside, two boards were leaning up against the vardo and Sema was stretching.

How does she always find boards? Can she make them out of other stuff, like me?

Eka's eyes popped before she reality-checked herself. That was not a Waker gift.

"Hey, space case. Ready for some amazing surfing?"

Eka shook her head clear and grinned. "So ready."

Sema gulped the rest of her coffee then grabbed her board and headed down a sandy path toward the ocean, Eka right behind. Along the way, fireflies illuminated the early-evening path in front of Sema, all the way down to a glassy ocean.

"Uh." Eka stared at the wave-less ocean. "Hope you got some tricks. That's pretty calm."

Her grandmother's eyes twinkled and Sema walked a few feet out into the water, lay down on her board and paddled out. Eka joined, waiting for something as they floated in the still water.

"You ready?"

"Sure."

Sema focused on the water. Red energy bubbled around her then shot out into the distance. A moment later, the water lit up with a bubbling blue, twining with the red energy, and began to roll in, wave after wave building to a perfect ride. Eka's mouth fell open as her board rocked from the waves that targeted just them, while all around them the water sat mostly flat. Next to her, Sema grabbed a wave and rode toward shore.

Laughter, easy and needed, bubbled up in Eka and she turned to face the waves. Paddling out, she took a deep inhale of the salty water, waiting for the familiar tug on her legs. At just the right amount of pull, she turned the board and paddled fast, hopping up. An eruption of flutters swept through her at the slow, rising motion of the board on the glowing wave. Any lingering tension drifted away as she lost herself in the surf, riding waves that just kept going, embracing wind running across her skin and blowing her hair straight back. She closed her eyes and let her body sink into the board, responding to every movement. When she opened her eyes, she was riding into a barrel as the water arched over her in a glowing swirl. Her fingers found the edge, where water met air, and trailed the spinning surface of the watery tube. Her spirit lifted, pushing her through the barrel, out the end, and close to shore. Floating further out, Sema gave her a thumbs up while Eka yelled in victory.

She hadn't even known she needed this. This was why she loved her grandparents.

They rode until late in the night, eventually coming in and stretching out on the beach.

Eka looked out at the calm ocean. So far from the turmoil back at Manatee Isles. Turmoil she'd left. People she'd left.

"I ran away," she whispered.

"I know."

"I've never looked back before." Eka looked at her bracelet, fiddling with the shell.

"And now?"

"Now I feel like I let her down." She breathed deeply. "I just couldn't…that thing was like me. What if I hurt someone?"

Sema sighed. "Shirley told me what she could. You got in over your head, got scared. But you are not like that thing."

Eka rolled her bracelet around. "How do you know that? The energy is from the same place. And it did magic stuff like me. Non-Waker magic."

Sema squeezed her hand. "Do you know we found two energy signatures at your house after the attack?"

Eka spun around. "Really?"

Sema nodded. "Haipo refused to see it, but Win and I, we searched the entire place. They were faint, but there. Two energies that seemed connected, but different." She frowned, seeming to zone out. "I always thought they were like two sides of a coin." She shook her head and refocused on Eka. "Only one of those energies gave me the shivers. Whatever happened, we think something saved you. Saved Christelle and her family. Shirley agrees but unfortunately we are in the minority. So you need to stop thinking you're evil or wrong. You may be connected to those energies, but I'd place odds on which one."

Could she be okay? Not corrupted or dangerous? So what Irida had told her must have been true; she had saved Eka that night.

She looked at her energy, colorful and alive. Like Irida, not that shadow, not Lintu. "I did have a strange encounter with something. A lighted woman. All colorful."

Sema narrowed her eyes. "When did this happen?"

"Right before my magic started working. It was really cryptic, but I got the impression something was changing in me." Eka touched her pendant, trying to remember the vision. "I think she was part of the vision too. Said the shadow thing had a name. Lintu."

Sema leaned back, eyeing her. "Well, would have been nice to know this before."

Eka sighed. "Sorry. I should have said something, but with all the confusion and half-truths…"

Sema sagged and held up her hand. "You're right. We've all kept things. And now, events seem to be happening faster than we thought. Eka, I don't know what your gift means, but whatever it is, you will take care of it and use it well. Right now, all us traveling Wakers are being asked to join the communities, for safety and to figure out what's going on. I'm heading back to meet with your grandfather, then we're going to the islands. I was hoping you'd come with us."

Go with Sema and Win. But if she really did have a gift that wasn't corrupted, she should go back. Help. But what if she had already burnt that bridge?

"You're not coming, are you?"

Eka shook her head. "I think I have to go back. I think a friend needs me. Maybe I can meet up with you later."

Sema nodded. "Okay. I'm not leaving till tomorrow night, so maybe we'll catch one more set of waves."

Eka leaned over and hugged Sema. "Thanks. I really needed this."

They rode again in the early morning darkness, carrying on well into the early morning. Sema finally rode to shore, signaling the end of surfing. When she grabbed her small pack from the vardo, Eka knew she was leaving. They headed to an open space, finally stopping at a random spot where Sema spun and hugged Eka fiercely.

"When you're ready, you know how to reach me."

Eka nodded, wiping away a tear. "So, you got a ride?"

Sema smiled and placed her hand on the ground. After a short wait, the ground rumbled slightly then erupted, dirt spewing up and into piles around them. The dirt settled, but the rumbling continued, louder and louder, until a sphere, made of rock, rolled out of a newly formed hole. One side of the sphere spun open like a shutter and Sema stepped inside.

"My ride is here."

"But…are you serious?" Eka stared. "That's awesome!"

Her grandmother winked. "See you soon, little bird."

The door on the rock sphere closed, then the whole thing sunk into the ground and the dirt filled in as the hole disappeared.

"Holy hell."

Eka wandered back to camp, amazed again at this new world. She hopped in her truck and, once on the highway, she took a deep breath and called Christelle. No one answered so she left a message as she headed back toward Manatee Isles.

Forgiving is the Greatest Quest

Christelle laid on her bed, staring at the ceiling, scratching hard at her stomach trying to get at the tattered shreds of what was left of her energy. Scratch marks turned to welts as she clawed at her skin, a deep, internal itching pulsing inside her. If she could only tear it all out, make it stop.

A light knock sounded on the door of her room. She dropped her hand from her stomach, the thoughts paused. Anise came in, hesitantly sitting on the edge of the bed. She reached out and touched Christelle's shoulder. "Christelle, honey,…I need to try to heal you."

"Don't touch me." Christelle flinched away from Anise.

"If only that woman hadn't come. Awakened with you."

Christelle sat up and glared at Anise. "Are you still trying to blame everything on Eka! You're the one who stole my life, then acted like you're a saint! I could have trained with my mom, maybe been ready for this. But you took away my chance!"

"Christelle, you don't know that."

"Neither do you."

Anise pulled back, wrapping her arms around herself. "We were trying to protect you."

"Great job!" Christelle pushed off the bed and turned to Anise. "If I'd lived in this world, known everything that'd happened, maybe I would've known what to look out for. But no. You can't even admit your mistakes.

You just keep making them over and over! I'm done with all of it!" She ran out of her room then the back of the house, blindly stumbling through some open fields and into woods.

She remembered the note Eka had left a few days before and fell to the ground, empty and lost. Footsteps came from behind and she spun, ready to run. But instead of Anise, Shirley stood over her.

"Grams?" Her voice hoarse, even too herself.

Her grandmother sighed then bent down and wrapped her arm around Christelle's shoulders, helping her up. Christelle looked around and realized she'd ran all the way to Shirley's tree-house.

"Come on, let's get you upstairs." They made their way into the treehouse, Christelle too exhausted to protest.

Shirley settled her on a bed structure made of trees, leaves, and vines, then sat on the floor next to her. Christelle tried to focus on the life around her, the magical world she'd grown to love and find comfort in, but the once bright energy flowing through all things around her now came to her piecemeal, as though through a prism, dull and fractured. Her own lavender energy sputtered through her.

"Christelle, you need help."

Christelle stared at the ceiling, pushing the itching away. "I asked for help." She turned to Shirley. "And they hid things from me again. A book connected to my family."

Shirley sighed. "All the secrets here have really put us in a jam."

Christelle rolled over to Shirley. "She left."

"I know." Shirley patted her hand. "I'm sorry."

"Yeah, you're the only one. Doesn't matter now."

"Oh I don't know. Things kinda work themselves out sometimes." Shirley pulled out her bag of runes and laid some of them on the floor. Christelle watched absently as Shirley's hands spread them out and moved them around, pulling out a few and placing them in a formation. As she flipped the last stone, Christelle thought she saw the hint of patterns moving around. She blinked at the runes, but the patterns were gone.

"Grams, do you always see things with your gift?"

Shirley shook her head. "Nah. I get glimpses sometimes, but they're never clear as to their meaning."

"Sounds like a frustrating gift."

Shirley smiled. "I've thrown so many of these in frustration, I can actually hit a target with my eyes closed and still get a good spread."

Christelle smiled briefly at the image of Shirley ranting and throwing runes.

"I used to get miffed at all these other Wakers with their natural abilities with water and air and you-name-it. But I found out it didn't help much. I've gained some other gifts through practice but they've never gotten as strong as seeing the future. Foresight is what I got and it's part of me. I can be bitter or I can revamp my outlook and claim my life as mine. Nurture myself as needs be." She looked up at Christelle. "Life don't care if you adapt, it just keeps on."

Christelle frowned. "Wait, are you telling me I should just accept what's happened?"

Shirley looked back at the stones. "I'm not telling you anything. It's your life, your choice. Just sharing my experience with you."

Christelle rolled on her back, scratching her skin. How could she reclaim this brokenness, with that thing's signature all over the pieces. All over and in her. She curled up, sobbing into her pillow. Shirley placed her hand on Christelle's back, tears falling on Christelle's shoulder.

"My beautiful girl. I'm so sorry."

"Why did this happen!" She scratched herself. "I can't get that darkness out!"

Shirley grabbed her hands as they drew blood. "Stop, Christelle!"

She rolled over and stared again at the ceiling. "I'm contaminated. I feel it."

They sat in the room, a breeze blowing through the openings. Shirley slid back down to her runic spread. She rested her elbow on her knee and her head in her palm, pushing stones around with her other hand.

"Sweetheart, I don't know how to help you and I can't see any answers right now. I wish I knew what exactly happened out there, but seems like you and Eka are connected to this puzzle and trying to keep you out of it is the more dangerous route."

Shirley stood up and walked over to a book shelf then pulled a volume down and handed it to Christelle. "This is a copy of that book."

Shirley knelt next to Christelle and held her hands.

"I know that thing, Lintu, tore at your energy. Tried to kill you like it killed the others. Anise thinks our gifts can heal you, but I'm not so sure."

The tattered rips inside Christelle flapped more quickly, the lingering fingerprint of that thing all over them. She shook violently and Shirley held her until the shaking had passed. When Christelle looked up, Shirley's eyes glistened. "Maybe there's some answers in here."

Christelle tried to cry again but only a small sadness blew inside. Shirley grabbed her and pulled her back into a hug and Christelle sank into Shirley's arms, lost at the emptiness inside her.

Christelle woke to Shirley playing with runes next to her.

"Hey kiddo."

Christelle stretched before dark memories invaded her mind. She shivered and quickly scanned the room.

Shirley laid her hand on Christelle's arm. "You're safe here, kiddo."

Christelle nodded, still glancing around.

"I have some errands to run." Shirley packed up the runes and stood. "You gonna be okay if I leave?"

Christelle scanned around her again. The quietness seemed harmless as bright moonlight flowed across the room.

I can stay alone. I'm fine.

Christelle nodded and Shirley patted her on the leg. At the top of the stairs, she turned back. "Christelle, I know you should've known about all of this a long time ago. For my part, I'll always be sorry."

"Thanks, Grams."

Shirley nodded and gave Christelle a tiny smile before disappearing down the stairs.

Christelle lay in the still room staring at the branches above her. A small breeze moved over her and through the limbs. Leaves fluttered and a lizard scurried across the bark. Crickets sang outside the window. Everything seemed so normal. Yet, her mind drifted away from the room and onto an island. A dark haze wrapped around her then plunged inside her stomach and ripped her apart.

"No!" she sat up and scratched at her stomach. When blood smeared across her skin, she stopped and shook her head. "I've got to do something."

She swung her legs off the bed and her foot landed on the book Grams had given her. It was a copy of the book Janice had taken. She pulled it up on the bed and laid it on her crossed legs, her fingers tingling against the wood as she traced each letter of the strange writing on the front. An incomprehensible language.

Maybe Grams was right and there were answers for her here. After all, that thing, Lintu, wanted it. There must be a reason.

She'd never tried working with light in the short time she'd awoken into the Waker world. Could she manage it? Could she do anything at all anymore? She laid the book aside and crawled out of bed. Inhaling, she wobbled over to one of the vines on the wall then gently laid her fingers on the fuzzy surface.

Come on. I can do this.

She closed her eyes and reached out to it. Her sputtering energy skittered and bounced along the edges inside her like a pinball slamming into raw wounds. When she finally opened her eyes, the plant hadn't changed and there wasn't even a sign of her energy lingering on it. She inhaled again as she tried to ease the pain inside.

"Dammit! How am I supposed to read that stupid book when I don't even work!"

She grabbed the book and threw it across the room. It hit the wall and fell to the floor. Anger and frustration mixed with pain and her fear of losing her world a second time.

"Why is this happening!"

Exhausted, she slid against the bed to the floor. The storm inside her sputtered in the quiet of the room and she brushed at a small tickle on her foot. What was she thinking. She'd never get light to work for her. The tickle was back and she rubbed vigorously against her sole.

Why am I broken? Why did Eka leave?

She slumped to the floor and stared at nothing, absently rubbing her foot. Her foot that was starting to heat up.

"What the hell?"

She stopped rubbing it as the warmth spread across her foot, moving up her legs and across her body. Bright swirls of red, silver, green, and blue followed the heat.

Relaxation overwhelmed her and she watched, detached, as the bright colors covered her entire body then sunk into her skin. The ticklish sensation grew, pushing and pulling inside as it filled the empty cavern of her spirit with new energy that weaved into her broken bits. Sensations of earth, wind, sea, and fire overwhelmed her. She became swirls of sand, blowing through a desert, molten rock flowing against a melting surface, drops of water forming from a cloud. Tastes, sounds, images, textures, and smells encompassed her change in the swirl of a kaleidoscope. Then, she shook violently as colors burst from her and disappeared through the openings in the treehouse. Finally, her body lay still as her mind and emotions quieted with the dissipation of the intense sensations, replaced with something else. Something that caught her breath. The empty, torn feelings were gone and her energy was whole. But different; a new tapestry flowed within her. Her body pulsed with this new energy. One that contained all the colors that had washed over her earlier.

Hello Christelle.

Christelle looked around as a swirling red, silver, green, and blue haze coalesced into the form of a woman. Green skin glowed with changing hues as if made of growing moss. Her curly silver hair moved in an invisible breeze and the solid, deep blue eyes rolled as if waves were breaking inside them. Red lit up the ends of her hair, her eyebrows and nails, almost dancing with flames. She wore short pants and a flowing top reflecting all the colors of her form. Christelle blink at the familiar yet strange woman

"Anise?"

A rumble shook the room, turning into a laugh that floated through the air. The figure in front of her was laughing.

Laughing?

She rubbed her eyes.

No. I'm Gaia, sweet girl. My spirit rarely takes a human form and Anise seemed to be someone you love, so I picked her.

Gaia wiggled her feet and smiled.

Feels wonderful! But if this form bothers you, I can change.

"Uh, no. That's fine."

I'm just not talking to Anise right now.

I know. She loves you.

"Are you reading my mind?" Christelle tried not to think of anything and failed miserably.

Well, I'm not really speaking, if you haven't noticed.

Christelle realized the voice was entirely in her head, as if her own brain was whispering. She suddenly felt incredibly naked.

Oh, don't worry too much. Your feelings have been familiar for a long time. And I'm sorry you've had so much trouble recently. So much pain.

Christelle's breath caught as the memories of the shadow ripping her energy out crashed over her.

Gaia frowned and reached out, her hand dissolving into a hazy stream that swirled around Christelle. A warm, comforting blanket seemed to wrap around her for a moment, then the haze unwound and flowed back into Gaia. Christelle rubbed her arms and legs then touched her face.

"It's all gone. The emptiness." She looked up at Gaia. "But how?"

Gaia leaned forward.

I healed you.

"You what?"

Your energy got an upgrade.

Gaia winked at Christelle whose mouth hung open. The spirit smiled and looked around the room. She took a step then dissolved, colors flowing from beside Christelle to the bookshelf and reassembling into the woman. She touched a book then giggled and ran her hand along the whole library before turning back.

I forgot the sensations of being so concentrated.

She shivered and hugged herself.

"Hello?" Christelle spoke to hear her own voice. "I think I'm losing it."

Oh, no. You're perfectly sane. And special. Your line is always born more in tune than most Wakers. You were meant to be one of the spiritual leaders for your people. To train with your mother and become her successor.

"My mother?"

Yes. And I was hopeful that you both could help with some troubling times that are ahead. But, this knew danger revealed itself and became a priority. This shadow thing has sidelined many things.

"Sidelined?" Christelle's shoulders tensed and her hands balled into fists. "Sidelined what? Something like in that story. Where cities full of people were killed for you!"

Gaia looked at Christelle, shimmering.

That…was a long time ago. I can't explain why but sometimes there are no right answers. Sometimes hearts are so shut that they'll will burn the world before opening.

"But how could you kill them?"

Christelle, they were my children. I loved them. And I tried to reach them. I had to chose to save some or let all of life die.

"There had to be another way. Just like taking our memories."
Gaia's form seemed to sigh.

I am so sorry your memories were hidden from you. I wish that hadn't happened but the decision was made before I could reach them.

"Wait. What do you mean?"
Gaia kind of dissolved then solidified, sitting on the ground, brows furrowed. She placed her hand over her chin and closed here eyes, seeming to think about something.

Emotions are a funny thing, I've learned. Humans are so overwhelmed by them sometimes. Even those who I'm strongly connected to, who help guide the Waker communities. This includes Anise. That night, when you were attacked, Anise lost herself and let her emotions cloud all judgment. And she stopped hearing me. But you should remember, she was muddled out of love, not malice.

Christelle deflated, exhaustion hitting her. "I keep hearing that, but that one decision took so much away." Christelle narrowed her eyes at Gaia. "Why didn't you show up like this? Tell Anise?"

This isn't easy, let me tell you. For any spirit trying to take on another form. The level of concentration and energy is immense. Besides, Anise and the others that I guide, they can only feel me, when they are open to me. I had to change the very nature of who you are for this type of connection. I wouldn't do that to someone lightly.

Christelle hugged herself. "What do you mean you changed my nature? I liked me."

Gaia's laugh rumbled through the room again.

You're still Christelle. You just aren't really a Waker anymore. You were too torn up from that thing to heal your energy. And all this mess makes me think I need a direct connection for whatever struggle we're in for. And you, beautiful girl, were already born to communicate with me. You just needed help, so now you're a bit of an energy source. Like me.

Gaia's whole form lit up, brightening her smile in an uncomfortable way.

"Okay, okay. I appreciate the help, really." Christelle fidgeted. "But I'm not sure I'm comfortable with being a source of anything."

Gaia stood up and took a few steps before dissolving and reappearing by the kitchen.

I think I'm remembering this walking thing.

Gaia giggled briefly.

A planet, that looked like a cosplaying Anise, was giggling in Gram's treehouse. Sure, why not.

Gaia's smile dropped and she sighed.

I know this is a lot to take in. You haven't had much time to adjust to being a Waker. But your world is in danger, a danger I didn't recognize earlier. And I might need help with it.

I can't even help myself. How can I help the world?

Gaia dissolved and reappeared next to Christelle. The warm blanket feeling was back and she couldn't help but sink into it.

You have a lot of people who love you, who'll be there for you. You might be a source of energy, but this'll be a team effort. And trust your gut with Eka. You two are in the same boat with a broken paddle, as you humans say. Now, I'm exhausted so I'll say goodbye. But I'll be around. Take care.

Gaia smiled and dissolved, the colors floating out of the tree-house.

"What did she mean, Eka and I are in the same boat?" Christelle yawned, suddenly exhausted. "With a broken paddle?" Her thoughts drifted away as she sunk into a deep, peaceful sleep for the first time in days.

Can You See What I'm Saying?

Eka knocked on the door to Christelle's room at the Hapton's. No answer. Shuffling came from inside and Eka pushed open the door to find Christelle by her bed stuffing a satchel with objects. She looked up at Eka then back down at her bag, violently shoving a jacket in.

"I thought you left."

Eka stared at the woman then threw up her hands. "Surprise," she announced weakly.

Christelle raised her head, then shook it. "Screw you." She stood and grabbed her bag, heading toward the door.

When had Christelle started cursing?

Eka jumped in her path. "I'm sorry."

Christelle, inches from her face, glared. "Whatever."

She stepped around but Eka spun and grabbed her arm. Christelle's face flared and she shoved Eka back. "Don't touch me!"

Eka stumbled back then recovered her footing and stepped closer again. "I shouldn't have left. I was wrong."

"You…" Christelle took another step toward the door. "You left me here, broken." She spun into Eka's face. "I needed a friend and you left!"

"I couldn't think." Eka looked away from Christelle.

Christelle leaned back from Eka and yelled into the room, then punched the wall.

Eka jumped at this new Christelle's anger.

"What about me!" Christelle shouted at her. "That thing ripped me apart and you left me like that!"

Eka nodded and then sunk onto the bed. "You're right."

She grabbed a throw pillow, pulling at a thread that had wiggled free over time. When she looked up, Christelle stood in the doorway, breathing rapidly as her hand turned red.

"I couldn't handle it." Eka pulled a long thread out, the seam disappearing. "I saw that thing. Its energy was…was like mine. I mean, it changed a stupid piece of paper into a picture that killed Janice." Eka's voice caught and she took a few deep breaths. "It was too close. My magic does the same type of thing. I thought maybe that's what my magic was becoming. Dangerous. Evil."

Silence settled over the room. Eka stared at the pillow, pulling at the thread. After a few moments, Christelle coughed and Eka glanced up. Christelle dropped her hand from the door frame.

"I never blamed you for any of that. But you left me with them."

Eka nodded. "I did. And I'm sorry. I wasn't thinking, just scared."

Christelle sighed and walked over to a window. Her body moved warily across the room as if ready to bolt. How had they gotten here? It had been them against it all before. Eka yanked on the thread of another pillow, the strand pulling out and releasing a patch of cloth, exposing the stuffing. Her eyes widened and she pushed the pillow behind her.

"How can I ever trust you again?" Christelle asked as she stared out the window. "That you won't just take off in the worst situations?"

"Christelle." Eka walked over to the window next to her. "I would have stayed with you on that island. Even if I didn't have this magic. Even if I couldn't have stopped that thing."

Christelle's breathing stilled.

"You are the best friend I've ever had. Well, really the only one. I was afraid. Afraid I was the reason you almost died, that this magic might turn bad someday and be used against…"

"I…he…." Christelle hiccuped, "barely left anything inside."

Eka sucked in her breath.

"I couldn't feel anything. Like I wasn't there." Christelle finally looked at her and Eka pulled her into a hug. Christelle twitched back briefly, then sagged, her body shaking as they sank to the floor and Eka held her as she cried it out.

Okay. Now what?

Memories of calmness as Sema ran her hand over Eka's hair ran through

her mind. Eka hesitantly ran her hand down Christelle's hair and her friend's body relaxed further. Eka continued as the moonlight moved slowly across the room and they both drifted off as well.

Jostling against her legs woke Eka. She blinked and stretched as she took in her surroundings. *Where am I?*

She saw the hanging bed and remembered yesterday. At some point Christelle had rolled over and lay next to her on the floor. She scanned the room and realized she hadn't really noticed much about it before. Probably because there wasn't much to notice. No posters, no colorful walls, not even a cheesy, worn-out blanket kept because it had warded against all the childhood nightmares.

"Is she really attached to this room?" Eka mumbled.

Christelle shifted next to her and yawned. "What?"

"It's so empty in here. You really think of this as home?"

Next to her Christelle looked around the room and shrugged. "I thought so. I mean all my time at Hapton's was here. Memories."

Eka frowned. "Really? I mean, it's fine for a room. Pretty solid. But nothing screams Christelle."

Christelle grabbed the bag she'd packed, pulling it open. "All my personal stuff is in here now. I kinda shoved it all in here yesterday." She pulled out a brush. "This was the brush my mom used on me when I was a baby."

She pulled out a frame.

"This is when we went to Disney."

"Wait." Eka sat up. "Are you saying Anise and Ben went to Disney?"

"Nope. Grams and Gramps took me."

"Holy crap. What was that like?"

Christelle giggled, the first Eka had heard since she'd gotten back.

"Let's just say that the Splash Mountain incident makes a whole lot more sense now that I know about Wakers. I always assumed water was supposed to create tunnels around the ride cars." She smiled at the picture. "We had to slip out of the park early."

Eka laughed at the picture of Christelle's family about to get on the water ride, imagining the after photo.

"And this is the bag I came from France with. It was my parents' travel bag. Before me."

Christelle held up the satchel of worn patches of cloth, stitched together and covered with travel patches from spots all over the world. A vagabond's traveling bag.

Eka raised her eyebrow. "Were you leaving Hapton's?"

Christelle plopped on the bed, nodding. "I still have a lot of questions. And you know I can't get much more here."

"Yeah. Just never thought you'd have the guts to leave."

A pillow slammed into Eka's face and she held up her hands. "I see I'm wrong."

"So, I thought I'd try to find other Wakers. Other communities. Try to learn what's going on from people who aren't so invested in hiding things from me."

Eka sighed. "Ya know, I always liked mysteries in my stories. But as an actual character in the story, mysteries really sucks."

"Pretty much."

"Hey," Eka grinned. "I have a ride. We could figure this out together." She raised both eyebrows and cocked her head. "We are a pretty good team."

Christelle shrugged. "Maybe."

Take this slow.

Eka crawled over to the bed and picked up a book. "Hey, what's this?"

"That's a copy of the book everyone seems to want. I've been reading it. Trying to figure out what's so special about the information."

"And?"

"Well." Christelle raised her eyes. "There's some crazy stuff about how to steal energy but also how to stop someone from stealing it. I'm not sure

I get everything, but I think I understand one of the blocking methods. Could be useful against Lintu or whatever that thing is." Christelle shivered and pulled her knees up.

"Are you okay?"

Christelle nodded. "Yeah. Anyway, the book mentioned a possible weapon, but I don't really understand how to actually make it."

"What's it do?"

"It works like an electrical overload. He tries to pull," she sucked in a breath and swallowed, "energy in, and he gets a surge. An overload."

Eka crawled back next to Christelle. "You don't have to talk about this right now."

Christelle shook her head but wrapped her arms around her knees. "No. I want to."

"Okay. Um, where does it come from?"

"Where does what come from?"

"The extra energy; where do you get it?"

"Oh. That's the part I don't know yet. Anyways, I'll keep studying it."

Eka raised an eyebrow again. "We can figure it out together."

"Maybe. Testing this stuff might be a team effort. In case something goes wrong."

Eka sighed and turned the book over absently, looking at the language. Half letters that made no sense. "Who helped you translate this?"

A half smile crossed Christelle's face. "I got an upgrade."

"A what?"

"And I met Gaia."

Eka stared at Christelle. "*The* Gaia? Spirit of this planet?"

Christelle nodded.

"I've only been gone a few days. How the hell did that happen?"

"She kind of…" She shuddered.

"Maybe you can tell me later," Eka whispered.

"No, I'm fine. Fine." Christelle squeezed her legs tighter. "She changed out my energy. Said I wasn't really a Waker anymore. That I have her energy now."

Eka narrowed her eyes at Christelle. Now that she was truly looking, she could make out how the energy was different. Red lights pulsed and twisted around silver energy. Blues and greens and lavender intertwined in a shimmering brilliance. She really had been distracted to miss those colors.

"Holy crap! I see it. Your energy!" Eka reached out and touched Christelle's arm. A deep, strong, multi-hued energy pulsated under her skin. "Wow. Are you like a mini-Gaia now?"

Christelle shrugged. "She said something about being a source for her in the future. In case there's danger. And that I'm one of a few that can see her."

"I thought Anise could?"

"Nope. I guess Anise can feel her or something. But..." Christelle lowered her voice. "She talked to me. She was a spirit and she flowed around the room and talked and laughed. It was kind of weird."

"And kind of amazing!" Eka's hands waved around with her excitement. "What did she look like?"

"It was crazy. She was green with silver and red hair and crazy blue eyes."

"That is so cool!"

"And looked like Anise." Christelle frowned, then quickly added, "Just to be familiar."

"Not as cool." Eka shook her head.

"Yeah. Anyways, I think my being some sort of source thing is important but I don't know what it means yet. One more thing to figure out. And Gaia took off before she really explained everything. Said it was hard keeping a human form."

"Irida said the same thing. Huh."

Wonder if anything else has that trouble.

"So that's where I'm at. And why I'm leaving." Christelle's statement snapped Eka out of her thoughts.

"I'm in. But is there a plan other than leave here? Do you know where you're headed?"

Christelle looked down. "No. Just thought I'd start looking for my mom."

"Okay, I get that. But maybe we could start with some kind of destination. Get a few clues to help us."

"Why do you want this?" Christelle blurted out. "With me, I mean. I'm glad you came back and let me know why you took off, but now you're trying to make plans with me like you never left."

Eka sighed. "You are an amazing person Christelle. You are loyal and always there for people. Things I don't really do well. But I want to; I want to be that kind of friend to you. I know I really messed up, but I'm here to try again. Whatever your plan is, I'm here to support it and make it happen. Just try me."

"Wow." Christelle raised her eyebrows. "You're being so open."

"And you're being exceptionally strong."

"Hey! I'm strong."

"I know." Eka smiled and nudged Christelle with her elbow. "Can you take a chance on me?"

"Fine." Christelle elbowed Eka hard. "But only because I like ABBA."

"Ow!" Eka held her side.

Christelle smiled. "Now I feel like I'm moving past it."

"Great." Eka rubbed her ribs. "So this plan of yours."

"Yeah. That's all I got right now."

"Hmmm." Eka walked over to the window, thinking back on that horrific night on the island. Images whirled through her mind of a shadow creature creating a picture that killed Janice then Wallace running away with the book.

Wait.

Wallace running with that book.

She spun around. "I think I have something. That night on the island, when everything went south, remember Wallace took off with the book?"

Christelle frowned. "Right. We all took off. That thing probably killed him and has the book."

Eka sighed. "I know he was wrong, and misguided, and put us all at risk. But what if he got away? Maybe he knows something more about that creature. Lintu." She didn't have evidence, but she felt that the shadowy creature was the Lintu that Irida had mentioned.

Christelle glared. "Why would he tell us? He was helping that thing. Screw him."

"You're right," Eka nodded. "But he was devastated about Janice. And he tried to keep the book after that, instead of handing it over. Maybe he regrets the deal, I mean, after what happened to her."

Christelle sat staring at her and Eka waited for a few tense moments. But when Christelle didn't move, she sighed and slouched back against the wall. "Look, I'm not saying he's a good guy. But he's our only connection to Lintu," the name sounding more and more natural, " and if we're looking for answers about it he might be the best place to start."

Working with someone else is hard. I mean I never have to convince myself to do things. I just do them. What is taking her so long!

"Okay."

Eka shot up. "Okay?"

Christelle nodded. "Okay."

"Awesome. Now we just have to find him."

"But let's figure this out somewhere else." Christelle looked around the room. "This doesn't feel like home anymore."

"We can go back to the campsite. It's pretty secluded."

"Great," Christelle said as she stood up. She walked around the room and grabbed a few remaining items then shoved them in her satchel. "Oh, and Gaia said that you and I are in the same boat with a broken paddle."

Eka frowned. "What? Is that a saying?"

Christelle shrugged. "How am I supposed to know what a planet's spirit means?"

"Come on, you're mini-me Gaia now. Can't you channel her?"

Christelle threw her pack over her shoulder, rolling her eyes. "Yeah, that's how all this works. Easy answers."

"Exactly." Eka followed Christelle out the door. "I'd say at this point we're working the odds. There's got to be at least one easy answer. So why not this? Right?"

"No. If we're getting something easily, I want to know what happened to us."

"Oh, please. Now you're just being ridiculous." Eka threw up her arms as they headed into the truck. "Like the universe is gonna let that be the throw-away question. You had to search three days to figure out what Wakers use for toilet paper, and you want the end of the quest to just jump in your lap?"

"Shut up." But Christelle giggled at the statement.

Eka smiled as they climbed into her truck then headed back toward the campsite.

"And what's with this 'Lintu'? You really think that's the shadow monster?"

"I'm beginning to think so."

How Do You Stop Madness?

Christelle looked down past the blanket of shifting wind that was carrying them to the edge of Manatee Isles.

Eka squeezed her shoulder. "Wow, you really have upgraded."

"Just practice. I can't access much of this new energy yet. I mean, it's like it's still settling in."

"I get that."

Christelle pointed at an old building sitting in an abandoned field. "Hey, I think that's it."

Eka gestured toward the head of a trail leading to the building. "Maybe we should walk from here. Keep it low-key going in."

Christelle nodded and set them lightly down on the trail, the wind dissipating around them. Her magic was red hot now.

She scanned the path. Moonlight illuminated the narrow path hemmed in by tall wildflowers and bushes. The foliage appeared to be encroaching into the space, the dirt and crushed shell barely visible. In the distance a few pointed rooftops competed with oaks for visibility.

Faded orange letters painted on a pale blue wooden sign leaned up against a barbed-wire fence post. Christelle walked closer to make out the words.

Tommy's Oranges
Best Citrus in Florida
See Wild Florida and Take a Taste of Florida Home.

"You sure this is it?"

Christelle shook her head. "No, but ever since the Gaia encounter I get flashes of other people. Like where they are or where they've been. And it feels like he's been here a lot."

"Sema said she used to track me from a distance. Wonder if it's the same thing." Eka looked down the road then back at Christelle. "Look, I don't know what's gonna happen. I mean, I can't imagine Wallace getting violent, but, well I didn't expect him to hook up with some misty evil thing either." Eka breathed in deeply. "So, as much as I hate saying this, and don't freak out, but I think we should let the others know. Just in case."

Christelle stared down the road. This plan seemed so thought out last night. Maybe they should have taken more than twenty-four hours to figure out their next step. What if she didn't come back. Like her mom. Her chest tightened and she wished she had hugged Grams before she left. And kissed Gramps. And, despite everything, had some of Uncle Ben's key lime pie or even sat with Aunt Anise in the garden. And called her dad. She hadn't returned his call in weeks.

No. No matter how angry she was, they didn't deserve not to know.

Christelle nodded and took her phone out, pulling up her dad's number.

> Dad,
> I'm sorry I didn't call back. I have to do this thing
> and if anything happens, just know I love you and
> everyone.
> Love,
> Christelle

She added a location marker and showed Eka.
"What'd you think?"

"To the point."

"Yeah. I think I'm going to delay it. Don't want them showing up in ten minutes. How much time should we give?"

Eka looked up the road and back to Christelle. "Couple of hours?"

Christelle agreed and added a second delayed text.

> If I haven't texted back in 30 minutes, we went to
> get Wallace. ♥

"I think that tells the story," Eka said, voice low.

Eka texted Sema and Win a quick location of her truck and vardo if she wasn't back the next day, then they turned their phones off and headed down the road.

Christelle walked along the narrow trail, pushing flowers and leaves away from her while trying to keep an eye on the dimly lit path. She hoped nothing slithered across in front of her. And nothing did. Instead, a sharp poke shot up the bottom of her foot and she hopped around on the other foot.

"Ow!"

Eka's hand shot over her mouth. "You don't sound like wildlife."

"I 'ot it."

"What?" Eka whispered.

Christelle balanced on one foot and peeled Eka's hand off her mouth. "I got it. No shouting," she whispered back, then pulled a piece of shell from her foot. Her walking slowed as every few steps she had to tap dirt and shells out of her sandals.

"Maybe I should have worn sneakers."

"Maybe?"

All around her, crickets and frogs called from the fields, trying to hide the crunch of their steps.

Maybe off-trail's better.

She turned into the wildflowers and pushed through the stalks and bushes while keeping an eye on the building ahead. While she managed to avoid shells in her shoes, twigs ended up stuck between her toes. And the brush was way louder than the dirt-covered shell. When she finally made it back to the path, Eka's silhouette was way ahead of her. Stepping on the crushed shell as lightly as possible, she hurried to catch up.

"Hey," Christelle whispered. "Why'd you go ahead?"

"We're both headed there." Eka pointed at the building that grew larger with each step. "Knew you'd make it. So how was the safari trek?"

"Pokey." Christelle pulled another tiny twig from her shoe and held it up.

"Yeah."

Christelle pushed aside some tall grass overhanging the path and her hands began glowing.

"What the…?" She stumbled back and held her hands up in front of her face.

"Whoa." Eka touched her radiating hands. "That's amazing. Like a human flashlight."

Their area glowed bright white and Eka pointed at the old metal building, now visible through the few trees.

"As cool as your flashlight hands are, maybe turn them down?"

Christelle nodded and concentrated, imagining dialing down a dimmer switch. The light faded then went out completely.

"Ugh. I just started to learn about my old gifts and now I have to start over with brand new ones." She looked up, sighing. "I really wish these things came with a handbook."

"Right." Eka pretended to flip through a book. "Like, need a cup of tea? Oh look, page seven. Dispensing tea from my fingers."

Christelle giggled then covered her mouth with her hands, which started glowing again. She quickly stuffed them in her pockets and looked around. "Let's go before my hands give us away. Besides, if we don't pick it up, the others are going to beat us there."

They came up on a bit of lawn and turned off the path to cut across it then stopped behind an oak to check out the structure. A few lights shown through grimy windows. Christelle realized this was an old citrus packing plant. The name of the company, Tommy's Citrus, was still partially visible through the vines on the side of the building. Strewn across the wilderness of a yard, in front of the brick building, were hints of busier days. A large and sturdy office desk with missing legs lay on its side and a few bicycles, missing tires and seats, lay covered in grass and flowers.

"How should we do this?" Eka broke into her thoughts.

Christelle shook her head. "I'm not sure. I just got a hint of him, not the layout of the building."

"Okay, fine." Eka looked around then pointed to an old ladder attached to the building. "How about we go up there and peek in. Get an idea."

Christelle examined the ladder. It seemed to hang from the side of the building by just a few bolts, the bottom creaking in the light breeze. "That thing?"

Eka lifted her hands and eyebrows. "You have a better idea? You know if it gets wonky, you can float us up."

She looked around but nothing else seemed feasible. "Fine. But don't blame me if my gifts get all wonky and give us away."

They tip-toed over to the metal ladder and Eka grabbed it then pulled down. The railing pivoted with a groan and they quickly scrambled into the weeds. After a few minutes of laying silently, no one had come out and the ladder seemed to still be attached to the wall.

"You ready?" Eka asked.

Christelle inhaled deeply and nodded.

Eka grabbed the rails again and hopped up on the first rung. Christelle watched her move from one step to the next, holding her breath each time the metal creaked. When Eka finally reached the top and stepped onto a ledge under a window, she motioned Christelle up. Christelle sucked in a breath, looked around, and stepped up on the first rung. The ladder seemed to swing to her right and she gripped the rails, closing her eyes until it stopped.

"One, two, three. Everything is okay."

She opened her eyes to Eka motioning vigorously above her and slowly managed to pull each shaky foot up the rungs. At the landing, Eka yanked her over and onto her back.

"You made it!" Eka whisper-yelled and slightly punched her shoulder.

"Yeah." She weakly pumped her arms, laying flat on the landing, staring at stars.

After a few moments of grounded safety, Eka nudged her side with a foot. "Oh come on. We actually have magic. It wasn't that dangerous."

Christelle turned her head to look at Eka. "Our magic is the Lucy and Ethel kind of magic."

Eka grinned. "Yeah, it's kind of fun and unusual."

"More like a comedy of errors."

"Exactly. Now get up. We're on a mission."

Christelle rolled over on the narrow ledge and got up on all fours, bumping Eka backwards. Eka tumbled through the empty frame of a window, somehow making only a few muffled sounds as she landed inside. Christelle scrambled through the window after her and tumbled onto a dusty walkway. Of course, Eka was already up and crouching.

Christelle squatted and duck-walked over to Eka. 'Sorry,' she mouthed.

Eka waved off the sorry and pointed to the edge of the platform they stood on. Christelle nodded, taking in her surroundings as she waddled to the edge. The narrow walkway ran along the entire wall of the expansive warehouse. A number of windows opened up onto it from the outside and small ladders led up into the rafters.

At the edge, she peered over into a cavernous area below. The space was mainly empty, littered here and there with abandoned citrus equipment. A few working lanterns illuminated the middle of the area but no one seemed to be around. They crawled back against the wall.

"Do you think we got it wrong?" Eka looked at Christelle.

She shook her head. "I don't know, but I still feel him."

Eka nodded. "Okay, let's wait. Someone had to light those latterns."

Christelle closed her eyes. The feel of Wallace's energy had been overwhelming her senses since they stepped near the building. But where was he? Could she just be detecting leftover energy? His trail brought her directly here, but now she wondered if she even understood how this worked.

Minutes dragged on as the warehouse remained empty. Christelle picked at her sandals and, next to her, Eka spun her bracelet. What if the others showed up and there was nothing here? Anise would breakdown at the chance she was taking and she wasn't sure the rest of her family would have any sympathy this time. She couldn't go through that again.

Christelle jerked as a door slammed below. She glanced at Eka then they both scooted to the edge of the walkway.

Wallace walked into the area.

She tapped Eka repeatedly on the shoulder. 'He has the book,' she mouthed.

Eka nodded.

He moved to the middle of the lanterns and was joined by some of the crowd from Bob's. In the lamplight he looked a hundred years older, deep lines mapping exhaustion onto his face. Slouching and slow moving, he overturned a discarded bucket and sat down.

"Wallace." A tall, pale man with blond hair stood over him, "I know this has been hard." He placed his hand on Wallace's shoulder. "But we've been hiding here for weeks."

"Stop coddling him, Ted." A woman with gray-flecked hair strode over, then pushed the blond out of the way and glared at Wallace. "You promised that we would all get our gifts working, be free of all the Waker crap. But Janice is dead and now Wakers are searching for us and a psycho creature that could literally suck our life away, is hunting us!"

"Donna, stop." Ted glared at her.

"No." She violently shook her head. "He needs to translate that book, figure out how to boost our gifts or at least give us some defenses." She bent down close to Wallace's face. "But you can't even do that, can you. You're useless." She spat out the last words then slapped the book from his hand and stomped out of the room.

Ted sighed as the door slammed behind her. He knelt down in front of Wallace. "Hey, I know you're trying. Everyone's just on edge."

Wallace just stared at the book on the floor. After a few quiet moments Ted stood up. "I'm gonna go out for more supplies. I'm sure the others will be back soon. You okay alone for a bit?"

Wallace nodded and Ted walked out the same way Donna had. Wallace still sat, staring at the tome on the ground.

"What should we do?" Christelle whispered.

Eka shrugged.

At that moment Wallace stood and kicked the bucket, sending it skittering across the floor. Its bouncing echoed in the empty space. He stood over the book, shaking.

"Damn book! What the hell does any of this matter? I can't help anyone!" The shaking stopped and his body slumped to the ground as he covered his face with his hands. "I couldn't save Janice."

Eka started up but Christelle yanked her down. "What are you doing?" she whisper-yelled.

"I think I could talk to him."

"Are you crazy?"

Eka looked down at the small figure then at Christelle. "He cares about Janice and he seemed to like me. Maybe I can reach him."

Christelle looked between Wallace, motionless on the floor, and Eka. "Are you sure?"

"No." She shook her head. "But he's alone, so it's our best chance."

Eka stood and hopped up on the railing, dangling her legs over. "Wallace!" Her voice echoed around the empty warehouse and his head jerked up, spinning around.

"Up here."

Wallace spotted her, squinting. "Eka?"

"Yep, it's me."

"What…" He turned around, looking behind him. "What are you doing here?"

"I was actually gonna ask you that, but I think Ted summed it up. You're hiding. Because of what happened to Janice."

Wallace nodded. Even from the rafters, his eyes seemed to have lost all life. "I thought I could make it better for us. I thought I could really help us. I mean, Janice could be with her daughter." He trailed off, staring at the book.

Eka kicked the rail, jerking Wallace's attention back. "Wallace, I know what happened. I was there." She seemed to loose her concentration for a moment and Christelle motioned at her from her hiding spot. Eka blinked, then continued.

"I'm so sorry. I didn't know…I thought everything could be fixed," Wallace squeaked out.

"You mean controlled?" Eka asked.

He nodded.

"Wallace. I know you didn't mean for her to get hurt, but this thing is out there. We need to understand what it is. How to deal with it."

Wallace laughed. "You saw it. What it did. There's no dealing with it."

"That woman, Donna, she said something about boosting defenses. You must be trying if she thinks that; you must know something."

"All I know is that I was there, fishing, when that island was drained. I tried leaving but Lintu trapped me and I thought I was next." He frowned, lost in thought. "But suddenly I had my powers. I mean, no one has ever been able to help before. Or even cared. So I listened. I thought I could figure out what it did, how to work that myself. Help the others. All it wanted was this stupid book. It knew the book was hidden at Hapton's Place and promised it would give everyone their gifts. So I agreed and convinced Janice to help find it."

He started shaking then crumpled to the floor. "So I killed her. If I hadn't asked her…if I hadn't convinced her that thing could help."

He yelled and Christelle jerked, covering her mouth while Eka fell back onto the platform.

"I'm so sorry, Wallace," Eka said, pulling herself back up. "But didn't you suspect it was dangerous? That it might be killing those Wakers?"

Wallace glared at her. "Yeah, I knew it was probably killing the Wakers, but they weren't ever my people. Not really. Even my parents…" His face fell. "But Janice, she deserved better."

Eka kicked the rail again and Wallace jumped. "Look, I get it. I've been struggling with my magic." She glanced at Christelle, frowning. "Done some things I wish I hadn't."

Christelle stared back at her friend, smiled, and gave Eka a small thumbs up from the shadows of the walkway.

Eka looked back toward Wallace. "But that thing is not going to help any of us. You saw what it did. Anything you know could help us figure out how to fight it."

Wallace gazed over to where Eka had looked, then turned back. "I…I don't know much. I mean, I didn't have a sit-down or anything with that thing." His face scrunched, as if thinking hard. "There was something, when I first met it, him. I mean, I could have been imagining it but I felt like it flickered right before it disappeared."

"Flickered?"

He nodded, pacing. "I'm not sure, but the energy from him seemed to weaken. I think that's what it was anyways. Whatever he's made of." He frowned up at her. "You felt it, that weird empty sensation, like a hunger, pulling at you."

Christelle shivered at the memory of the thing's ravenous energy overwhelming her and ripping her apart. Eka seemed to shiver too and gripped the rail tighter. "Yeah. Hard to forget. So you think it weakened. Why?"

"I don't know, but maybe it used most of what it had. I was thinking maybe that's why it needs so much energy. Why it took my energy, just before it…"

Destroyed Janice.

Wallace coughed. "And, uh, I think that's why it wants the book. I don't know who wrote it but the little I've been able to read details different ways to drain energy. And to amplify that ability."

Christelle moved closer, still trying to stay in the shadows.

Eka stopped swinging her legs. "That's not good."

Christelle caught a movement from the window they'd entered.

Oh no.

"Maybe," Wallace continued as Christelle spun toward the window. "Listen, Eka. You need to be careful. That thing was interested in you."

"Me?"

Christelle caught the form of Anise just outside the window and tried to signal for her to hide.

"Yeah," Wallace nodded. "It wanted to know about you, talk with you."

"Why would it be interested in me?" Eka half whispered.

Right then, a few windows broke and doors shattered below as Anise, Ben, Devlon, and a dozen more Wakers rushed in.

Epilogue

For Every Door that Closes There's a Loud Slam

Eka spun on the railing as Wakers poured into the warehouse.

"What's going on?" Wallace yelled.

"No, he's helping us!" Eka shouted as Devlon yanked her from the rail. Then a group, led by Anise and Ben, lined up along the railing and down below.

"We know what you did, Wallace," Anise announced, looking down. "You're coming with us, as well as the book and the others. We'll deal with you back at Hapton's."

"Anise, no!" Christelle stood up and tried to grab Anise, but Ben pushed her back.

Anise glanced angrily at Christelle then focused on Eka. "This is the last time you're dragging her into any mess."

"Yeah, you always 'deal with people'," Wallace yelled up. "Like you're infallible. You're a cold bitch is what you are and I'm done with it all."

Christelle froze as a familiar tugging started in her stomach. Eka ran up to her and shook her, snapping her out of her fear.

"He's pulling energy," Eka whispered. "Like that…*thing.*"

Christelle swallowed hard. "I know." She pointed shakily at the other Wakers, who seemed oblivious. "They don't know."

"Yet," Eka replied and pulled Christelle back away from the edge of the walkway.

Wallace yelled up. "You think I didn't learn anything from this book? How to channel energy from others?"

"You mean steal," Anise spat as she descended the stairs. "You can't fight this, Wallace. You made choices and you have to live with the consequences. You were going to destroy everything."

"No, just you and your arrogant, elitist Wakers."

Time seemed to slow as Wallace raised both hands. Christelle heard her own voice shout 'no' as Anise stumbled back, shock on her face. Across the floor, Wakers stumbled and Wallace laughed.

"You Wakers aren't the only ones with power anymore." Wallace glared at Anise.

He took a few steps forward, then shimmered and stumbled. All around, Wakers seemed to recover. Christelle jerked her head toward Eka. Her rainbow light rolled in front of the Wakers like a wall, then dissipated.

"Did you do something to Wallace?" Christelle asked.

"Just tried that shield thing again." Eka smiled weakly. "Still kinda wonky."

At that moment, a Waker on the ground level started a funnel of air that headed straight at Wallace. Christelle watched as the wind came within millimeters of Wallace then died. The attacking Waker fell to the ground as his energy dimmed as green light flowed out of the him and into Wallace. Another Waker knelt by the curled up man, confusion permeating her. She dragged the immobilized Waker backward while raising a wave of earth that rolled toward Wallace.

Christelle recognized her as Bridget from Bander's place; a Waker who worked with water and, apparently, earth.

The earth-wave came close to engulfing Wallace, but he quickly turned his focus to Bridget. Before Wallace could pull energy from her, a form rose from the dirt. It looked like…an orange? It glowed with orange and brown energy that swirled around Wallace then sunk into him. He fell to the ground and the floating orange dissipated.

"Eka," Christelle whispered. "I saw something in the dirt. I think it was an…"

"Orange?"

Christelle nodded.

"Orange and brown lights?"

Nod.

"Spirit. You saw a spirit!"

"That orange was a spirit? Are you kidding me?"

Eka shrugged. "I think places have spirits and," she circled her hand around, "we are in an orange factory."

"That's just too weird. And how can I see spirits now?" Then she remembered Gaia and her multihued energy flowing into her wounds.

"Gaia," Christelle and Eka said together.

Am I really not a Waker anymore? What am I?

"No way," Eka pointed toward Wallace and the Wakers. "They're up."

Down below, Wakers were fanning out in front of Wallace. And he was up and facing them.

"Maybe he isn't very strong yet," Christelle hoped.

They watched as the Wakers came at Wallace. But every time they got close he would pull at their energy and they would fall back. And it didn't matter how many attacked. If anything came within feet of him, he stopped it by stealing energy. And type of gift the Wakers used, earth or air or metal, was drained as well. The Wakers couldn't see the spirits, but Christelle and Eka watched as they were directed at Wallace. They came in a multitude of shapes such as an orange, a cloud, and even a little pixie. Although Wallace didn't seem to notice them, he appeared to feel their energy and pull on it, causing the spirits to dissipate and emerge farther away, disabling any attack. Each time the Wakers and spirits regrouped, they seemed to have less energy. A stalemate, but a temporary one.

Christelle flashed back to the island and Eka's rescue. "Could you contain him? Like on the island?"

Eka sighed. "It'll hold for a bit, but it's unstable. Then what? He'll just wait until it's down. It might even give him a break. Let him rest."

Christelle looked at the standoff. "What is wrong with them? He was working with us." She glared at the scene below. "I don't even know how they found us. It hasn't been two hours yet, has it?"

"Probably the same way Sema always found me. Anise must've tracked you."

"Damn it!"

Eka raised her eyebrows at Christelle. "A little energy upgrade and your vocabulary goes to shit."

"Shut up." Christelle nudged her.

What could they do? Did she want to do anything? Anise didn't want her here. Just wanted her tucked away safe. But she wasn't a fragile piece of china or some kind of prize. Christelle was an adult with a life. And, right now, that adult wanted to scream.

She shoved her hands into her pockets and moved, just to not lose her mind. As she paced around, a few somethings, small and round, pressed against her right hand. She pulled out rough little spheres and examined them. Anise's forgotten seeds. How many times had they been washed and dried since Anise gave them to her? She rolled the spheres around. There was still a hint of energy in them. A potential rose bush hidden in each tiny shell. Anise had worked these roses, through many generations, to get just the color, form, and growth that she wanted. A controlled plant. And that's how she saw Christelle. Something that needed to be shaped and formed into just the right Waker. But Christelle felt more like the wild roses whose branches sprung out, messy and unformed.

Wild.

She looked down at the two sides that stood opposite one another. All the Wakers had moved to the ground level. Dozens of them spread out across from Wallace. Anise sent a vine crawling along the ground, but when the vine got within feet of Wallace, it withered and Anise stumbled. This dance repeated with other Wakers as they tried to flank Wallace. But they always failed. She knew there wasn't much time. She saw Wallace's energy building. Shadowed energy. If only Eka's shield could hold him. Or someone could disable him. But he'd probably be able to stop it, his hands pulling all that energy out of the life around them. Unless…

Christelle grabbed Eka. "Okay, I've got an idea. This is gonna sound dangerous and crazy."

Eka grinned. "Are there any other kinds?"

"Doesn't seem like it."

They both looked over the rail at the melee below.

"Guess we better hurry." Eka turned to Christelle. "Okay. Hit me."

A few minutes later, Christelle was crawling to the window. She turned back to Eka. "Remember, wait until you see me give you the signal."

"What's the signal again?"

"Are you kidding? If you can't remember that, then…"

Eka smiled shakily and gave her the thumbs up.

Christele scowled, but just for a moment, then smiled back. Who knows when they'd be able to smile at anything again. As Eka crawled up into the rafters, Christelle crept back out the window and down the swaying ladder. Her heart beat a million miles an hour; she swore the pounding would be loud enough to give her away to Wallace.

Just calm down. No one can hear your heart beating.

She brushed off the paranoid feelings and ran through the brush to the back of the building. Shadows from the nearby trees danced across the brick surface. A dark form slunk toward her and she jumped before she realized it was just a trick of moonlight and leaves.

Get a hold of yourself. They're dying in there.

A few deep inhales later, she moved along the back wall to an old window with a long broken pane. This seemed to be the only entrance on this side at ground level and she needed in now. She placed her hands on the window ledge to crawl through and a shard dug into her hand.

"Ow!"

Blood trickled down her now throbbing hand.

Great.

Christelle brushed off the blood on her shorts, then cleared off the few remaining bits of glass before scrambling through the window into a corner room littered with furniture. She stumbled over desks and filing cabinets, as she made her way to a faint light that shone dimly through a somewhat opaque window of an door. Christelle slowly pushed open the door to find a hallway that disappeared into darkness to both her right and left.

Which way?

Christelle caught sight of a sliver of light in front of her. She stepped across the hallway and realized the light was escaping from a door. Pushing it slightly open, she found herself peeking into the warehouse. And the standoff. Impossibly, her heart rate sped up as she watched the Wakers and spirits stumbling and falling, yet still fighting.

Calm down. You can do this.

She looked up, scanning for Eka. Above, on an old light hanging from the ceiling, Eka sat looking down then suddenly waved. Christelle waved back from the shadows. Luckily, everyone was too busy to notice them.

She placed the rose seeds on the ground.

"Please let this work," She whispered to herself.

The small part of her energy that was still lavender slid off her fingers and into the seeds. Lavender flashed from the seeds in tiny bursts and they…sat there.

"Come on." Her back and shoulders tensed up and she pushed more energy into the seeds.

She even imagined sprouts growing out into branches, lush bushes forming. But still nothing. No connection. Were they dead?

She plopped on the ground, lying next to her stupid idea, rolling the seeds gently with her fingers.

"Hey, little seeds, I need your help." She glanced through the door. A few Wakers lay unmoving. "I don't know if this is crazy or not, but I really need to help them." A tear fell as across the warehouse Anise stood over Ben as he fell to his knees. "Whether they were right or wrong, I love them. Please. Gaia."

Was that a tingle in her right hand?

A tiny hint of light seemed to emit from her skin. She pulled her hands closer.

They're glowing!

Her hands burst into light, followed by her body and she rolled away from the door before anyone noticed.

I'm a freakin' lighthouse!

After a moment, the light calmed down and she noticed hues of red, blue, silver and green swirling out and into the seeds. She low-crawled back to the doorway just as tiny red energy from the seeds wrapped around her colorful uliee. Then the seeds shuddered, rocked, then cracked open; green sprouts shooting out through the shells and expanding. They started covering the walls and door frame before she even realized what was happening.

Whoa.

Christelle mentally wrangle the vines, but they squirmed out of her grasp and continued spreading.

"Shit," she whispered, barely holding back a yell. "What did Anise say to do? Think."

Outside the door, more Wakers were down and not moving.

"Come on Christelle, think."

Then she remembered the connection.

Turning away from the door and singing an old nursery rhyme her dad sang when she was scared, the started breathing deeply. Her heart was the first thing to respond. Its beat gradually slowed to the beat of the song and Christelle's mind released, one thought at a time, all the worries she'd been carrying until there was just the vine in front of her. And then she let her essence sink into all the green growing from the rose seeds.

The Christelle-tendrils tunneled through the broken tile floor just inside the door then into the ground. As they hit the earth, a resistant sensation scraped against her skin. She sensed, and saw, Wallace as the tendrils burrowed closer to him, coming to a stop directly below him. As part of the underground tendrils, she sensed Wallace's dark energy dripping down around him. Her heart suddenly sped up and she/the tendrils recoiled from the empty coldness he emitted. Rubbing her clammy hands together, trying to rub the dark sensation away, she flashed to the island. To the moment her essence was shredded inside her and she froze.

No, no, no.

Suddenly a warm, multi-hued blanket of light wrapped around her, calming her racing heart.

Christelle, I am here.

"I can't do this." Christelle still lay flat against the ground but she turned away from the battle, her sense of the vines growing fainter.

You can and you're not alone. But they need you now.

She gulped and turned back to see Wakers littering the floor. Anise was the only one standing. Wallace crept closer as Anise refused to leave Ben's side. Overhead, Eka sat exposed and searching below her.

Probably looking for the signal.

"I can't abandon them; they need me."

She pulled herself up to kneeling and shook out her hands. Then she closed her eyes and reached out to the roses again. The Chrsitelle-tendrils curled up like a spring in the ground, just beneath Wallace. She swallowed as the coldness of Wallace increased, seeping through the roses and into her. Taking a deep breath, she looked up. When Eka scanned her way, she concentrated and gave the briefest pulse of light from her hand. Eka nodded and gave a thumbs up. As she stared up, Eka seemed to grow smaller, then disappear. She squinted and caught sight of a little green speck falling from the ceiling and onto Wallace.

What kind of distraction was that?

Then Wallace froze. His body stiffened and he shook violently, swatting at his back and spinning. And his energy stilled. Christelle shook the question out of her head and concentrated. The vines sprung out of the earth, wrapping around his ankles and winding up his body, neck, and head. He struggled, trying to free himself as her energy continued to flow. A faint sensation of pulling tingled in her stomach and she shoved energy into the vines. Thickening branches became dense with flowers and thorns. And screaming erupted from Wallace. She dug her fingers into the door frame, her body shaking as she dumped more energy into the bush. The thorns grew to knife size and the screaming and struggling stopped. Still she poured herself into the growing roses.

"Christelle!"

Someone was shaking her and she blinked, staring into a silent warehouse. Across the desolate building, Wakers were struggling up. Anise and Ben huddled together next to a gigantic bush exploding in bluish-green roses with gold tips. Anise gazed at them with a look that Christelle had never seen. When Anise turned away from the roses she glanced at Christelle. Christelle's heart dropped at the fear in her eyes.

"Christelle! Hey!"

She blinked again and turned back to Eka.

"I…" The room spun and she leaned against the wall, nausea erupting in her stomach. Christelle heaved a few times then vomited everything she'd ever eaten. After a few moments her stomach stopped erupting and now felt like it had been run over. She wiped the bile off her face and looked up at the rose bush. It seemed to take up half the warehouse; giant branches with roses on every inch and dagger-like thorns.

"Wallace?"

She couldn't see him.

"Maybe you should sit." Eka stepped between her and the bush.

She froze. "But he's in there."

Eka nodded and Christelle turned away from the scene. She stumbled back into the hallway, tearing across furniture to crawl back out of the window and into air.

"Breathe." She sucked in deep amounts of the air around her. "Need to breathe."

She retched again but nothing came out this time as her stomach erupted in pain. All she could do was slide down the wall on shaky legs. A few moments later, Eka stumbled out of the window and slid next to her, Christelle sitting with her arms and head resting on bent knees.

A breeze pushed the grasses around, the half moon illuminating the waves of stalks as a frog called out. Dozens of answers came back to it from across the field, almost comforting in their connection.

"Hey."

"Hey."

"Is he…Did I…" Christelle blurted out.

Eka's hand found Christelle's and squeezed.

"No. He's alive"

Christelle's breathing slowed and matched the rhythm of the frogs calling out. "I couldn't stop it."

"I know."

She lifted her head and stared at the moving grass. "And I didn't want to."

Eka squeezed her hand again.

They sat for a few more moments, staring at the night, then Eka stood and pulled Christelle with her.

"Let's get out of here."

Christelle turned as Eka's pendant fluttered bright colors.

"Your pendant."

Eka looked down and back at Christelle.

"You can see this?"

Christelle nodded.

Eka stopped and cocked her head, as if listening for something, then she turned and ran back inside. Christelle stumbled after her on weak legs. Inside, Wakers stood around an unconscious Wallace as the last of the branches shriveled up under Anise's hand and back into seeds which she picked up. Christelle could swear she heard her aunt say 'abomination'. Blood flowed from deep punctures across Wallace's body and his left leg lay at a wrong angle. Christelle turned away, noticing that Ben had the book. Christelle started toward him when Anise saw her and pulled Ben away. Somehow, Christelle's heart tore and she turned to look for Eka. Off in the corner, Eka stood as if still listening and Christelle headed over.

"Eka?"

Eka focused back on her.

"We need to get everyone out of here. Now."

"Why?"

Eka grabbed her. "Trust me?"

Christelle nodded and they turned toward the others.

"Everyone needs to get out now!" Christelle shouted.

They looked at her, shaking their heads, but no one moved and, instead, went back to their conversations.

"I heard sirens!" Eka shouted.

Everyone looked startled and started shuffling outside.

Christelle smiled. "Good call."

"Yeah, thought fire might not work, what with the water magic."

They followed behind, making sure everyone was out and moving away. When they were halfway down the path, the air stilled and a deep silence blanketed the area as if it held its breath. Christelle turned back toward the building and caught a dark flash from inside it. The building grew darker then a shadow rolled out as a coldness flowed over her. In the partial moonlight, the flat colors of the building drained away to a dull gray.

It was here; she knew it. Her body shook violently in response. Christelle seemed unable to move as the darkness rolled closer. In the distance, a breeze must have blown over the building as the top of it floated away in ash.

No, no, no.

Eka shook Christelle's shoulder and she shivered to life. Yelling erupted behind her and she spun as a misty darkness flew past and around Wallace. The mist morphed into something like a hole in existence. It wasn't there, but nothing else was there either. The Wakers floating Wallace's body down the path, jumped back and dropped him from his air transport. Wallace moaned and shifted in the dirt. He struggled to lift his head and finally looked around. He blinked at the mist, then his face contorted and he tried crawling toward anyone.

"Please…" was all he got out before he was sucked into that nothingness.

But how? Why would it take Wallace?

The recovering Wakers nearest Wallace screamed and everyone scattered.

A flash of multicolored light opened up over the darkness and the shadow and coldness, that had started to expand, pulled back. It retreated from the light that chased it into what was left of the building and everything grew deathly silent. Waiting.

Until an explosion of energy demolished the remaining building, ash flying everywhere. A second later, an energy wave hit Christelle, knocking her to the ground and littering the area with a few knocked-over Wakers, the only ones that hadn't gotten far.

Then it was silent again. As the ash fell on them, Christelle looked over at Eka. Eka's face was pale and she clutched her pendant. In front of Christelle was the field, or the remnants of an empty space; desolate ground where a building once stood. It was as if the building had never existed. Christelle sat next to Eka, the few remaining Wakers stumbling to their feet and fleeing. Even Anise and Ben had left her without a word. Her heart truly hurt at that, but the look of fear and shock she saw on Anise's face at the roses wrapped around Wallace said it all.

"They're really gone," Eka's voice stark in the quiet night.

Christelle furrowed her brows. "Who?"

Eka waved her hand toward the empty space in front of them. "The dark and the light."

"What? Gone for good?"

Eka shook her head. "I don't think so. Just, not here. I can feel Irida and she's far away. I'm not sure about Lintu."

"Okay. What do we do?"

Eka turned to Christelle. "I don't know. Wallace said Lintu was interested in me." Eka shivered.

"I think Irida has been protecting you."

"Maybe. But I don't know how Irida is involved with it. Is she stronger? Will she stick around? What if he comes for me and she's not there? I think I need to find out what he wants. If I'm going to be ready for it. And maybe the place to start is at the beginning."

Christelle nodded. "And seems like Gaia wants me to keep learning the old Waker methods of defense and learn from that freakin' book." She sighed. When had she signed up for super-Waker status? If only she could talk with her mom, maybe she had some super secret Waker information from Ys. Or a hug. "Maybe my mom could help."

If I can find her.

"Sounds like a road trip." Eka raised an eyebrow, the paleness fading back to her light brown tone.

"That's about the sum of it."

Eka smiled.

"Hey, thanks," Christelle said.

"For what?"

"For being there. The vines growing out of control. Stopping me."

"What are friends for?"

"Yeah."

They finally got up. Christelle followed Eka down to the road, not even curious how the others got home.

"You know," Eka nudged Christelle. "I was up there for a while. Starting to wonder if you had a plan."

"Yeah, well, you deserved a little payback for taking off."

"Hey, I came back!"

"Yeah." Christelle stopped and turned to Eka. "Did you really turn into a lizard?"

Eka nodded. "Yeah. Wallace freaked when he saw one, so I thought it might be just the right distraction for him." She scrunched her face up. "But not sure it was worth it."

Christelle leaned near her ear and made a buzzing sound. Eka snapped her head around then scowled. "Stop it."

Christelle laughed, relaxing for the moment as Eka quickly joined in on the laughter. There might be a lot of unknowns ahead of them, but this moment was as perfect as any and she was holding on to it.

Eka loaded Christelle's bag into the vardo's storage bin. "Is that the last one? I mean, how many bags can one person take?"

"I'm not a monk. I have stuff."

"Yeah, well this is a camper, not a luxury bus."

Christelle looked back at the house. "I know, but I can't leave anything here."

Shirley and Bu stood next to Christelle, sadness emanating from them.

"Oh, kiddo. We're gonna miss you." Shirley wrapped her arms around Christelle, hugging her tight and Bu quickly joined in.

"Thanks, Grams, Gramps." Christelle's voice muffled in the hug.

Bu and Shirley finally released her and Shirley looked her up and down. "You look so grown up."

Bu nodded and pinched her chin. "Sweetpea, wish you could stay longer. Maybe have some real Waker fun."

Christelle gazed over at the house. "I'm sorry I messed things up here."

Shirley shook Christelle's shoulders, her head whipping back and forth. "Uh, uh, uh. Okay, Grams."

"Well, you need someone to shake some sense into you. You didn't do anything. Can't say I missed being in that mess at the warehouse last night, but wish we could have helped you both."

"But Anise and Ben..."

"You let us worry about them. You just go figure out what you need to. You know your aunt has always been stubborn. And Ben will follow her anywhere."

"Wonder where that stubbornness came from?" Bu winked at Christelle.

Shirley elbowed him. "Okay peanut gallery." She reached out and cupped Christelle's cheek. "We are always here for you. No matter what."

"That's right." Bu laid his hand on Christelle's shoulder. "If you need anything."

"You too." Shirley looked at Eka, who pushed off the vardo where she had been leaning.

"Thanks."

"Now you two. Guess it's time you head out into that big Waker world, meet your fortune, find your answers." Shirley swept her arm in a large arc around her.

Bu shook his head. "This isn't a Dickens novel."

"There has to be some pomp and circumstance. I mean, they are setting off on some kind of grand adventure." She glanced between the two women. "And, if nothing else, it should be entertaining."

"Thanks, Shirley, Bu." Eka smiled and gave them both a quick hug. "We better get going."

"Good idea." Bu pulled Shirley back a few step. "Before there's a monologue."

Eka waved as she got in the cab but Christelle hesitated before joining her. "Christelle?"

Before Eka got an answer, Shirley was at the door next to Christelle hugging her again. "You two be careful and if you need anything, we have a phone." She sighed and let go of Christelle who climbed in the truck. "Wish we had something more to tell you both but seems the rest of your answers are out there." She reached up and touched Christelle's hand. "Love you, kiddo."

"Love you too, Grams."

Shirley stepped back and Christelle finally climbed in the cab. Eka pulled out into a clear day, only a few clouds in the sky as the sun sank lower on the horizon. "So, you didn't answer. You gonna be okay?"

Christelle nodded, watching the side mirror. "I feel like I'm never coming back here."

Eka glanced at Christelle. "I think the only thing I'd miss that much was my truck and vardo."

"Good thing they're mobile." Christelle turned toward the front and away from Hapton's as it disappeared behind her. "What about Devlon?"

"Just a fling," Eka shrugged.

"I thought maybe you were thinking of him."

"Nah. He wasn't really my type. A little too tribal for me."

Christelle frowned. "That's a shame. You guys seemed to connect."

Eka grinned. "Well, he did have some nice qualities. Really nice." She wiggled her eyebrows.

Christelle grinned back and rested her elbow on the window frame. "So what's the plan?"

"I talked with Sema. She and Win are hanging out in Oregon. Said they'll wait for us. 'Folly Or Farce' is heading in that direction and the manager said we had a job if we wanted it. Could tide us over until Oregon, if you want to meet up with them. Might even find some Waker communities along the way."

"Sounds great. I can dust off that static trapeze routine. Seems like a million years ago I was planning to teach and see if my art could go anywhere."

Eka nudged her. "You can still do that. I mean, I've never seen Waker art. Can you imagine if you could really capture what we're experiencing?"

"Right? All these colors, smells, everything. Hey, maybe we could put an act together. Something with a little, um, magic." Christelle batted her eyes.

"Perform?" Eka touched her bracelet. "I don't know. Not really my thing."

"Oh, come on. What happened to cannon woman?"

"Hmmm. Now *that* could be fun."

"Awesome." Christelle pulled up her legs, resting her chin on her knees. "Wonder what we are now."

"What we are?" Eka glanced at Christelle.

"Yeah. If we're not Wakers or Nalo and we're not one of the Asleep anymore, then what?"

"Huh." Eka's hands glowed with colorful energy. Christelle's arm was illuminated with lavender, red, green, silver, and blue swirling energy. No one else's energy had multiple hues. No one else seemed to see spirits all around, experience the world through those spirits.

"Well, maybe we'll find out soon." Eka rested her chin on her hands, her head moving with the steering wheel. "Real soon."

Christelle turned to Eka. "Why? You know something."

Eka took a deep breath. "Nope. But Win and Sema are headed to Hawaii. My old Waker community. Maybe we'll find some different answers to who we are, what happened to us, and what is after us."

"Yeah. Maybe they'll know something about my mom. Adrien already left, so I can't follow up, but he remembers her passing through there a while back. And any lead would be great."

Christelle laid her hand on Eka's shoulder. "But are you okay with that? I mean after what your grandmother in Hawaii did."

"I'll be fine, really. I've dealt with her before." Eka sat up, gripping the steering wheel tighter. "Of course, I know what she did now. I'm not some clueless kid."

They drove in silence for a while, the road running into the highway and the flat, dense green becoming hills.

"What'd you think happened to Wallace?" Christelle broke the quiet stillness.

Eka shivered. "I don't know. I don't even want to wonder. I'm glad they got the book back, though. That thing could have it *and* Wallace." She shivered. "Make him translate it."

Christelle clenched her hands. "If he lived."

"Yeah." Eka shook her head. "But there's something I don't get."

"What?"

"How it knew the book was here."

"Wow. Yeah. If it was my website, I've taken everything down."

"Probably for the best."

They sat in the quiet cab as the trees and hills, still green in November, rolled by in a soothing rhythm.

"Well," Eka grinned. "Nothing to do but enjoy the adventure. Shirley's orders."

Eka and Christelle will be back soon, searching for more answers to their past. If you're excited to join them on their next adventure, signup to get alerts to their whereabouts at **DreamingOfDancingBubbles.com**

Until next time, wonderful travels!